A TRIAL OF THE HEART

J.E. LARSON

1

A Trial of the Heart
Fate is a fickle master of the unknown,
and yet, fate has led me here.

I chose to take my cousin's place as the shifter champion
of the trials.
I chose to come back from death's doorstep in the
hunter's keep.
I chose to deny Gilen's claim as my mate.
I chose to travel to the Inner Kingdom with the High
Fae.
I chose to use my magic to heal instead of fighting a
fallen.
And now, I choose to follow my *heart*.

Where my heart will lead me, however—that is still
unknown.

Let the trials begin.

J.E. Larson

Trigger/content warnings: Sexually explicit scenes, language,
violence, fighting, monsters, trauma rep., torture (referred to),
forced sexual encounters (referred to).

ISBN: 979-8-9900411-4-1

DEDICATION

To my <u>rock</u> (my husband). Because I would enter the trials for you. And you would take on the world for me.

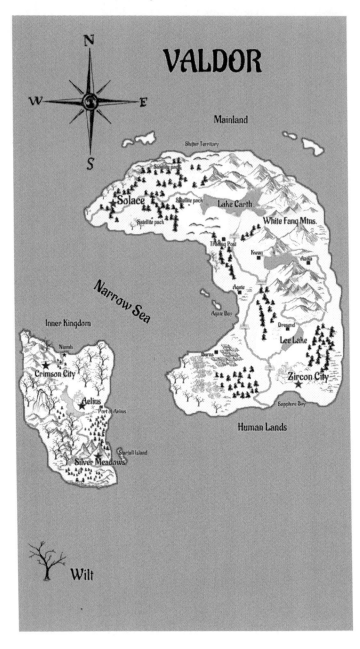

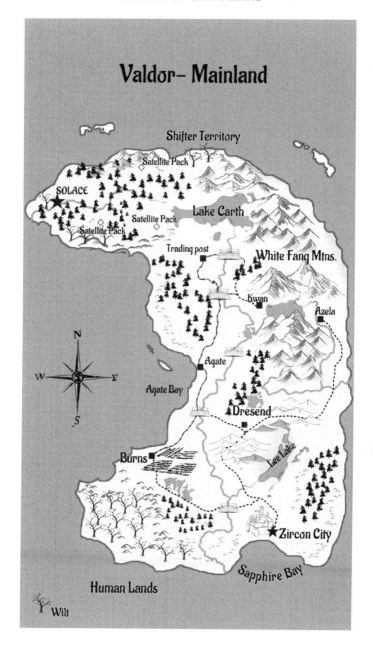

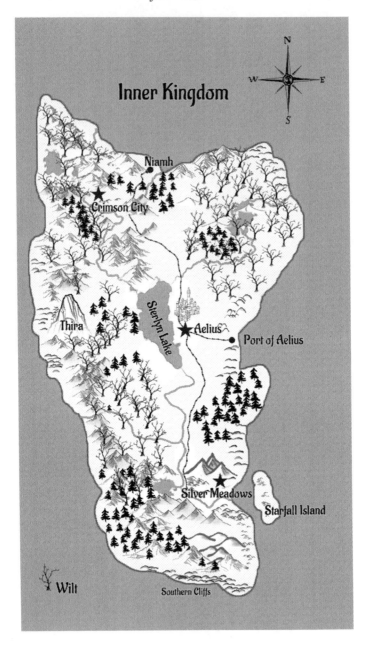

Chapter One

I didn't dream in my shifters sleep, and to be honest, I was grateful for it. There was no telling how much time had passed as I slowly regained consciousness.

The faint sound of someone steadily breathing, broke my slumbering trance. Daxton must have found some sort of sanctuary or hideaway for us after our battle with the harpies inside the wilt. I would've settled for anything as long as it was far from the decay and dark magic of that lifeless land.

I inhaled a deep breath, breaking my own trance-like sleep to further assess where I was. The air seemed thinner, indicating a significant change in the elevation. We must be high above sea level, possibly somewhere in the mountains.

Where am I?

I tried to rack my brain for more clues when one hit me smack dab in the face—it was hot. Oh, Gods, it was unbearably hot! The air had a textured thickness to it that coated my tongue and throat. I could feel my sweat-slickened skin under a light sheet made for blistering, arid climates, but it still felt like I was cooking from the inside out. I enjoyed the warmer weather of summertime in Solace, but this was something different.

I wiggled my fingers, then managed to roll over onto my side. Opening my eyes, I located the owner of the soft, steady breathing at the foot of my extravagant bed—*Daxton.*

His bottom half was seated in a plush cushioned chair with his torso folded over at my feet. His clothing was different. Judging by the lack of blood and stench from our battle in the wilt, he had bathed as well. I didn't smell his blood, meaning his healing abilities, combined with my own, had done the trick. It was odd, though, I thought. I couldn't smell him. Inhaling again, I searched for the fresh pine and mountain air scent but failed to find it.

Weird, I pondered. Then, I remembered him speaking to me on several occasions about training me to shield my own scent. However, I didn't think I needed to do that until we were in Aelius.

Oh no. *Aelius*—were we in Aelius? Was it time for the trials? I thought I had more time!

Panicked, I shot up from the bed, and Daxton woke immediately with a long knife drawn and at the ready, prepared for battle.

"Is this Aelius?" I stammered, staring at him with wide eyes. I wasn't afraid of the trials, but I was terrified of being thrown into something without proper time to prepare. "Daxton!" I yelled at him again, leaning forward onto my hands, desperate for him to answer me.

The High Prince of Silver Meadows sheathed his knife into his belt and slid onto the bed next to me. His expression was drawn and weary, but I could see a hint of ease cast in the depths of his stormy eyes. "This is Crimson City."

I immediately hung my head and sighed with relief. Dax reached out to gently place his finger on my chin, tipping my gaze up toward his and scanning over me carefully.

"Are you hungry, Spitfire?" Daxton asked, anticipating my needs even before I had a chance to voice them.

"Always." I grinned as I steadied my shaking limbs, moving to lean back against the headboard of the plush bedding. I nervously tucked my knees into my chest, curling my soft satin nightgown around me, attempting to take everything in. Dax trudged to the other side of the arid room to retrieve a tray of various fruits and slices of bread paired with meat and cheese.

"You were asleep for some time, Skylar," he said as he returned to my bedside, setting the tray of food in front of me. His tired eyes turned and stared at the open window, and I couldn't grasp how he was feeling or what type of mood he was in.

"How long?" I asked as I poked my fork into a piece of fruit.

"Four days."

"*What?*" I exclaimed, with a mouth full of food, somehow still managing not to drop a single bite. "I-I think that's the longest I've ever been in a shifter's sleep. Come to think of it. I don't know many who've ever been asleep that long." I coughed to clear my throat as he handed me a glass of water.

"They haven't," Dax muttered, keeping his blank stare fixated on anything but me.

I studied him closely, searching for hidden injuries that were often overshadowed by the bleeding wounds of battle. His eyes were heavy, and even though he was asleep when I awakened, I knew that was not the case for the previous days. He was clean and wearing fresh clothes, but he looked exhausted. Despite his valiant efforts to hide it from me, I could see it.

I pushed a plate of food over to him. "You need to eat too, Dax." It looked like he hadn't eaten in days.

"I can't possibly eat this whole tray myself and not explode."

He pursed his lips, contemplating my request. "You're sure you don't want it?"

I nodded to reassure him, and thankfully, he lifted a round sausage paired with a piece of bread off the plate and took a bite.

I definitely *could* eat everything on this plate and another, but I couldn't bring myself to devour another bite until he did, too. Dax popped another piece of sliced meat into his mouth while I returned to my tray of delectable goodness. With my stomach happily satisfied, I was able to take in the room and admire the spectacles surrounding me.

The architecture was astonishing—grander than anything we had back in Solace. The walls appeared to be uniquely hand-crafted with a delicate swirling design that adorned the columns in the corners and connected along the arched ceiling. It reminded me of wind-blown sand and the beautiful way it ebbs and flows with gusts of wild currents of air. The tan walls were draped with sheer, elegant red fabric, filling the room with a warm, airy feeling. The bed we were sitting on was in the center of the living area, with two large double doors to my left and an opening to the balcony to my right. The doorways and windows were arched, with what looked to be red sandstone decorating the archways.

Thick dark drapes covering the balcony and windows hid the rays of sunlight from outside, but I could still see streaks of the magnanimous sunrays trying to peek through. The blasted heat, however, was suffocating. Despite the light breeze from the open windows and balcony doors, they were hindered by the lavish drapery. Beads of sweat began forming along my brow, despite my lack of clothing and refreshing sips of water.

"It's morning?" I asked between bites of food.

"Midday." Dax reached for a pitcher, refilling my cup first before filling his own.

My eyes never wandered from the High Fae prince at my side. Daxton always said more with his actions than his words ever could, so for once, I patiently waited. Watching his every breath and movement.

"You never left me, did you?" I asked, even though I already knew what the answer would be. "Dax, I'm all right." I boldly reached out my hand and intertwined my fingers with his.

Daxton tensed, but he didn't pull away. I squeezed his hand tighter, trying to encourage him to turn and look at me. As his gaze met mine, I could see a mountain of worry behind those deep gray eyes. My stomach dropped, realizing that his concern was centered around me. I pulled his hand to my chest and crawled across the bed to press my brow against his.

"I'm all right," I whispered again, for once not questioning why I needed this physical contact with him.

Daxton sighed heavily, closing his eyes and leaning closer toward me. "After the first day … when you still hadn't woken up, I-I …" He coughed to clear his throat. "I refused to let Castor or anyone else carry you, and once we arrived in Crimson City, I demanded Adohan call for his best healer to assess you."

"You know it's peaceful for me in the sleep, right?" I whispered. "There's no reason to panic." I tried to ease his concern, but I couldn't undo the distress he'd already carried these past days.

Daxton scoffed and clicked his teeth at my poor attempt to humor him and lighten the mood. He adjusted himself, moving to sit closer to me on the bed, wrapping his arm around my waist and pulling me into his chest. He reached to cup my cheek in his large, calloused palm.

"The healers told me you were stable, but as the third day approached, and you still weren't awake …" He stopped and tensed, no doubt reliving the scenario in his mind. "Even the elder healers began to seek answers and question your safety."

I could feel the burden of his anxiety weighing him down. In the hushed way he spoke to me, the timid movements and creased lines of concern in his brow. I didn't know if he would ever admit his fears out loud, but I could read the signs of his distress as clear as day. He was scared, for me. To know he cared for me like this was touching, but I never wanted to cause him such pain again.

"But considering the miracle you somehow managed to achieve, well, the length of your sleep was understandable."

"The fallen!" I exclaimed, practically jumping off the bed. "Well, I mean the High Fae … Wait, she's still a High Fae, right?"

"Yes, she's still a High Fae. The female hasn't spoken a word since you healed her, but your magic *did* heal her, Skylar. There's no visible trace of the wilt's magic remaining within her."

I could hardly believe it took Dax or me this long to talk about this. I had healed the dreaded nalusa falaya and returned it—her—to her previous form. It took every drop of strength I had in me to do it, but I did. I restored what the wilt had broken and erased all evidence it was ever there to begin with. My magic, my power … it saved her.

"Wow." I leaned back and ran my fingers through my tangled mess of brown and golden hair. "I didn't really know what I was doing at the time, Dax. I was just reacting."

"You were following your instincts, which, for you, is the wisest course of action you can take."

"There's a first for everything." I huffed a laugh as I glanced around the room, looking for evidence of any others who may have visited me while I was asleep. "Where's Castor? Is he with her?"

"Yes. He's been working closely with the fallen fae to try and gain her trust, which I believe is working," Dax said. "She can understand us, and Castor's been very patient with her. He was able to convince her that we were not a threat." Daxton stroked his beard, contemplating a thought. "I doubt she would've agreed to come with us to Crimson City if I hadn't been carrying you with me, however."

"I mean, I can understand that in a way," I said sitting back on the bed. "She was a broken shell of her former self with the wilt altering her like that." I couldn't blame the female if she didn't speak a word to anyone ever again. The kind of trauma she must have endured while trapped as a fallen was unimaginable and would take time to heal. I could hear it in her voice when she tried to speak in her cursed form. Each second must have been a living agony for her.

"Castor is working to try and find ways to communicate. Signing may be an option or writing if she is unable to speak again." Daxton moved to sit next to me, leaning back against the bed frame. "Either way, she'll be safer once she's in Silver Meadows. I believe our scribes in the archives will be able to take her into their care and look after her."

I leaned against him, welcoming his strengthening presence, and basked in the warming feeling of his body close to mine. "That's a good place to start. Ironic, though."

"How so?"

"Castor loves the sound of his own voice." I chuckled. "I imagine it fills the room enough for both of them. He's the perfect one to help her."

Daxton managed a small laugh. "That he does. Cas has been tending to her while I've been focusing on you. Now that you're awake, I'll need to leave soon to check on them both." My breath stilled in my chest, realizing I didn't want Daxton to leave.

"Don't go just yet," I said as I clutched his arm, feeling his hand cover mine. "Stay with me a few minutes longer?"

"Of course," he said in a soft tone.

"Oh, I do remember there was something I wanted to ask you." I leaned forward to snag a final piece of cheese from the food tray.

"Not surprising." Daxton grinned.

"What kind of magic happens when Castor's eyes turn black?"

Dax raised his brows, tilting his head as he grinned. "You've seen him use this before, haven't you?"

"Yes, three times, actually. What is it?"

"Castor has a unique type of survival magic of the mind. That's what we describe it as anyway: a gift from our mother's heritage and the Aelius bloodline. I can be in one place magically and then another, while Cas receives visions when he or someone near him is in mortal danger. It's a premonition of death."

"Interesting. It's like a warning from death itself?" I asked, and Dax nodded. *Alright, good to know.*

"Do you think the High Fae I healed will have any residual powers or abilities?"

"That is a question Adohan and I have pondered since we arrived. I can't see why not, but it is difficult to tell. This is also why I summoned Zola as soon as we arrived in Crimson City."

"How did you manage to get a message across an entire continent?"

Dax smiled softly. "We have enchanted parchment that is able to relay messages to its counterpart—regardless of the distance. Write a message on the paper, and it disappears here and appears on its other half."

"Wow," I replied. "I don't think I'll ever get used to how effortlessly you are able to manipulate and use magic like that here."

"You will." He said it so nonchalantly, like it was a fact and nothing more. Daxton's body relaxed against mine as a tranquil breath of silence passed between us. Giving us time to relax and enjoy the beauty of the moment together.

"All right, so Zola," I murmured, trying to recall the different members of his court. "Oh, she's your spy that was …"

"Exactly. If anyone can help guide the fallen fae you healed, I believe she can."

Zola was Daxton's spymaster from his realm in Silver Meadows. Her description in my lessons with Castor was brief because she was *made* or, in other words, changed by the wilt. Infected with dark magic but somehow survived, granting her magical abilities that she didn't have before.

"Zola should be arriving shortly if she's not here already. She can travel quickly across the Inner Kingdom with her shadow-jumping abilities."

"Her what now?" I cocked an eyebrow at him, flashing him an apparently humorous look because his smile curled all the way around the side of his mouth, revealing the dimple on his right cheek.

"It's similar to my teleporting magic, actually. She can move from shadow to shadow, blending into them if needed and disappearing from sight."

"I can see why she is your lead spy."

He nodded. "That among other deadly skillsets. Castor and I trust her honesty and intuition. She was loyal to my mother and to Silver Meadows for well over five centuries. My allies are due in large part to her ability to learn and deliver secrets."

I nodded as I eagerly swallowed the rest of my water, moving to try and stand up from the bed. Dax quickly extended his hand to help me stand. Normally, I would have laughed and shooed it away, but instead, I chose to humor him. My lightweight, practically sheer nightgown flowed loosely over my torso. I imagined it was necessary to wear clothing like this in the humid desert climate. Anything more would be suffocating.

The elegant fabric flowed just past my knees with straps that crisscrossed along my back, turning into a single strap that fastened over my shoulder. It was hands down one of the finest things I had ever worn, and this was only a nightshirt. The concept of such finery, especially with clothing, was not a custom amongst the shifters, but apparently, it was for the High Fae.

Dax led me toward the balcony, reaching for a golden cord and pulling it to the side to unveil the beauty of Crimson City outside my room. Unlike the landscape where we first landed, this was a busy, bustling city full of commotion and life. Markets, homes, and a vast array of businesses lined almost every corner of the landscape spanning below.

Merchants carried various foods, fabric, or other trinkets they brought into shops for customers to buy and trade. The city was vast and seemed to stretch on for miles, with us smack dab in the center of it all. Off to the side, I noticed a wide, winding river ebbing and flowing through the center. Bridges crossed over deeper regions, while some of the calmer bends were filled with children laughing and splashing in the water to cool themselves from the blistering heat.

"What do you think?" Dax asked as he stepped behind me, discreetly brushing his palm against the small of my back.

"It-it's …" I fumbled, trying to answer. I was still a bit awestruck by the sight and sheer size of this place. "We don't have anything like this back home."

"Crimson City is a stronghold in the high desert near the Spine Range mountains, the closest realm to the main territory of the wilt." Dax directed my attention west toward the vast peaks that spanned as far as my eyes could see. Familiar shadows lurked over the land, looming with the threat of death and destruction.

"High Prince Adohan enjoys being in the center of *everything*," Daxton said, with a hint of amusement. "So naturally, he built his home at the apex of his kingdom where he can oversee his people."

"Is this how Silver Meadows is arranged?"

"No," he said, and I sighed with relief. Crimson City was thriving and beautiful, practically bursting with vivacious life and culture. But it was almost too much for me. "You'll see Silver Meadows soon enough, Spitfire. Bringing you home to my kingdom will be a day I remember for the rest of my immortal life."

When he said things like that, it made my world come to a halt. What did Dax truly want with me? He always seemed to hint toward a deeper connection or even feelings of affection, but I knew this wasn't logical.

"Because when we travel to Silver Meadows, it means you'll have successfully passed the first trial. A task none before you have accomplished."

Ah, there it is. I stepped away from Daxton in the doorway, leaning against the open window where a welcomed breeze helped cool my fevered flesh.

"Right, the trials," I said plainly, trying to ignore the sting of pain in my chest. "When will we travel to Aelius, then?"

I retreated to protect myself. I had been fooled before, imagining and believing I shared deeper feelings with someone else not too long ago. I needed something … more. I wanted someone to truly love me for me. Not because of my magic or success in the trials.

I could lust after Daxton all I wanted. No one could blame me for being attracted to him, but that just might be it. Any other feelings I thought I was having needed to be squashed *immediately*. Besides, I imagined he had a plethora of females waiting to be called on or hold his attention. Why, in all of Valdor, would he want *me*?

I gazed out the window, avoiding Dax with all my might. I could feel his perplexed stare lingering over me, calling for reasoning behind my sudden coldness, but I couldn't answer him. If I did, I would fall apart, and I wasn't sure there would be anyone to catch me this time around.

Before Dax could speak, voices boomed from outside the room. "I don't care what Daxton said, Adohan Ekon! The female is clearly awake, and I'm going in there. You males need to take a step back. I swear to the Gods above, I will stomp on your toes and break them. Don't push me, love … I'm hardly in the mood." The door handles turned, and a petite yet feisty female High Fae entered with a towering male close on her heels.

"Skylar!" the female announced with open arms, a wide welcoming grin, and a very rounded pregnant belly. She waddled, still somehow gracefully—which was amazing to me—across the room, taking my hands in hers. "Welcome to our home! It's an honor to have you here with us," she said as she hugged me tightly.

"Idris," the male behind her growled with a slight snarl in his voice.

The female, who I now understood to be Idris, snapped her attention back toward him. "Would you calm down, Adohan? There's no danger in greeting her." Adohan folded his dark-skinned muscular arms across his bare chest and scowled. "These males are so overprotective in general with their mates ... And when we're pregnant," she added, stroking her growing babe, "they're *impossible* to live with. I can't even greet a guest without him growling in protest."

So, this is Adohan and Idris Ekon, the ruling mated pair of Crimson City.

Like many High Fae I saw from my balcony, Idris and Adohan had dark skin paired with deep brown eyes. Idris was slender, with long, flowing auburn hair with small intricate braids woven in between strands that tied back against her petite oval face. Her nose was slightly flattened with full lips that held a shade of red that matched her hair. She wore an airy, flowing crimson gown with long slits on either side and cross-stitching pattern across her middle that broadcasted her growing womb. She carried herself with an air of elegance and grace, paired with a genuine smile that made me feel welcomed.

Adohan was tall, but Daxton still held a few inches over him in height. He wore a long crimson robe with cut-off sleeves and a decorative gold armband wrapped around his left bicep. His pants were white with stitched red and gold designs embedded into the seams that matched the swirling decor on the walls of the room. His dreadlocked hair was dark brown at his roots and changed from yellow to orange, then a deep red color at the tips that hung past his shoulders. His facial hair gathered in a small patch on the base of his chin and matched the dark brown coloring of his hair at the roots. On closer inspection, Adohan's eyes were a lighter shade of brown, almost a golden hazel, which gave him a regal beauty fit for a high prince of the Inner Kingdom.

"All right. You males need to get out!" Idris ordered.

Daxton looked to Adohan, who held out his palms and shrugged his shoulders. "Don't you think I've tried? I'm in no place to argue with her when she gets her mind set like this. I'm lucky she didn't have her throwing knives or her spear on her when we started this argument."

"Lucky, indeed," Idris added, narrowing her eyes toward her mate. Dax was about to protest, but Idris cut him off with a wave of her hand. "Skylar is a *lady* ... and ladies need privacy when it comes to bathing and primping. From the looks of her and what little we do know about shifters; I would imagine this nightgown might be one of the finest things ever to grace her skin." *Ouch.* Well, she wasn't wrong. I guess I'll give that to her. "*And* ... I will *not* allow that to be the sole impression of our kingdom while she is an honored guest. I'll tend to her." Her dark eyes darted to Daxton. "It's *not* your place to do so right now."

Wow. Just wow. Idris was a force to be reckoned with and didn't shy away or back down from ... well, anything, it seemed. *I like her already.*

14

"Now, out!" Idris flicked her wrists with flames twirling around her fingers, making a shooing motion at Dax as he reluctantly moved through the doorway. "She'll be *fine*, Daxton."

I placed my hand to my mouth, trying to conceal my laughter. I knew they could all hear me, and the spark of amusement in Idris's eyes only egged me on.

"We'll be in the—"

"This is *my* home, Daxton." Idris gave him a look that only a mother could master. "I know where you'll be, and I promise I'll return Skylar to your care once she is cleaned and properly dressed." She promptly closed the doors on her mate and Daxton, pivoting back to me. "Now that we have some privacy, let's get you cleaned up."

Chapter Two

The bathhouse back in Solace had *nothing*, and I mean nothing, on the glorious luxury I experienced bathing in this oversized tub. Idris filled the massive pool with bubbles and added essential oils that seeped into my aching muscles, allowing me to relax for a moment without a care in the world. I loved the feeling of being clean, and even though I was rinsed off and changed while I slept, it was nothing compared to this.

"Enjoying yourself?" Idris chuckled as she called out from behind the screen.

"Gods above." I sighed. "This is amazing." I drifted below the water to scrub my hair. When I broke through the surface, Idris was holding out a white fluffy towel for me to dry off. "*Ahhh*," I exhaled in blissful relaxation. "Can I live in here?"

Idris laughed. "No, unfortunately, that's not an option. Your fingers will prune, and you'll be reduced to nothing but mush. But I do have a surprise for you waiting in the bedroom," she said as I washed off the soap remnants. "I believe I was able to size you up just right when Daxton carried you in three days ago. And lucky for you, our seamstresses in Crimson City add their own magical touch to the garments they make. They're also wickedly fast. Case in point … your new clothes are ready."

"Thank you. That's extremely kind, but I'm not—"

"Hush," she commanded, moving around the screen. "You shifters are all the same. Granted, you're only the third one I've ever met, but the other two were just as clueless. Finery is lost on your kind, I know, I know. But … you deserve to indulge in what we can offer. It's the very least we can do, so please allow us to do it."

I blushed and sank a little further into the water. "All right, understood."

Idris beamed a bright smile that stretched from ear to ear before leaving to give me some privacy. After exiting the tub, I glanced at my reflection in the mirror, and to my surprise, I seemed well rested and not the least bit worn down. I dried my hair as best I could and wrapped the towel around my chest, tucking it firmly in place. Trying not to drip water everywhere, I quickly crossed the clean marble floor of the washroom and dashed back into the bedroom. When I emerged, I stopped in the doorway. My eyes widened with shock and awe.

Idris held her head high and her shoulders back with a prideful grin as she stood near the bedside. Lovingly stroking her pregnant belly, she lay one final garment atop the white sheets. Various dresses, casual attire, and new training clothing covered the width of the bed, and I couldn't believe how beautiful they all were.

"Oh my … Gods," I stammered. "Is this all for me?"

"Of course it is." Idris cocked her hip to the side, her brows raised and her lips pinched as she continued to caress her stomach. "No other female in this house is

17

tall enough to fit into these. And before you ask, I'm the only other one residing here, for now," she said, smiling at her growing womb. "Some outfits are for your time here, others for travel, and the warmer layered garments are for any place south of our realm. And then there's this …" Idris reached down and revealed one of the most breathtakingly beautiful deep midnight-purple gowns I had ever imagined—let alone seen.

It sparkled with silver beading that mimicked the splendor of the shimmering stars in the evening sky. The front was a deep V-cut that would stretch down to my navel with a sparkling sheer silver lining continuing over the top of my shoulders, making the gown translucent near my neck yet still covering portions of my back. The purple shade of the gown transformed from a lighter pigment to a deeper hue near the bottom that held silvery swirling stitching.

"Daxton gave the seamstress specific instructions for this gown himself," Idris said with a satisfied grin. Her small, delicate nose scrunched along the sides as her smile grew.

"Dax had this made for me?" I was surprised and touched by his attention to the details he knew I would love. I blushed, realizing he specifically chose this color because he knew it was my favorite. He had listened. He'd remembered.

Idris nodded. "I believe he intended for you to wear this at the ball in Aelius." I gave her a confused look, and she exhaled. "Forgive me. I'm sorry this is all new to you. The high queen hosts a ball the evening before the trials begin," she said, rubbing her temple. "There's some symbolic reason for this, but my mind is foggy from the pregnancy. Oh, good Gods above." Idris groaned as she sat on the corner of the bed. "As the champion … *you*, my dear, will be the main attraction of the evening."

I gulped and bit my lower lip as I moved to inspect the other items of clothing. "Well, that sounds *fun* …" I wondered if Idris would catch my sarcastic tone.

Idris's huff of a laugh in response gave me my answer. I was glad to see she had a sense of humor. From how she practically manhandled Daxton and her mate, Adohan, I concluded that she had a strong personality despite her size. In times of need, she was someone you wanted on your side.

"Daxton said as much," Idris added, looking through the various outfits laid out in front of us. "He mentioned you wouldn't be thrilled about it, which is why I imagine you haven't heard about it yet. But this gown …" She paused to run her finger over the fine decadent designs in the midnight-purple fabric. "This is one of our tailor's best works, and that is saying something. When he showed this to me, I punched Adohan and demanded why, in over three hundred years of being mated together, he hadn't commissioned a gown like this for me."

"I didn't mean to cause trouble—"

"Come on, Skylar," Idris said with a playful tone. "It's perfect timing! This baby he planted in my belly will only grow, and I need new dresses to accommodate the later months of my pregnancy."

"How far along are you?"

"Eight months if you can believe it—with only four more to go. High Fae babies take a full year to grow and mature in the womb. I'm envious of shifters and even humans with shorter gestation periods. Near the ten-month mark," she said, leaning onto the bedding, "I'm going to be ready to pop, and Adohan, unfortunately, will be taking the brunt of my frustrations. But at least this time, there is only one, and not two."

"Your twin sons Finn and Astro, right?" I asked as I slipped on my new undergarments.

"Daxton told us Castor was teaching you about the dynamics of the different courts. Great memory." She held up a long, flowing slitted skirt paired with shorts and a sheer long-sleeve top. "Yes, thank the Mother, she only blessed us with one this time. The birth of our twins nearly split me in two. The trauma I endured is why this little one took so long to join us." She smiled as she affectionately hugged her belly. "I pray the babe is female. Someone needs to help me navigate this crazy house with three males constantly running amok."

I slipped on the skirt and pulled the shirt over my head. "This is surprisingly comfortable," I said. I could get used to dressing up if it felt like this.

"The fabric is lightweight and will protect your fair skin from the intense sun rays. No offense," Idris teased in a humorous laugh, "but your light complexion would burn to a crisp in only one afternoon."

"It definitely would," I said. "Thanks for thinking of that. I've been sunburned a few times during the hot summer months back home, and I would prefer not to have that happen again."

It wasn't one of the fondest memories from my childhood. The blisters alone kept me up all night for days, and nothing I could do would cool my boiling skin.

"Now for your hair." Idris motioned for me to sit at a nearby vanity as she moved around, assessing the state of my tangled mop of brown and gold. "Would you let me braid it?"

"Sure," I said, and she immediately got to work.

Idris quickly took strands near one side of my face and braided them tightly against my head, flowing toward the back where multiple strands ended together. The other side flowed freely down past my shoulders, isolating different pieces and mixing them into the style on the opposing side.

"There. How does that look?"

I gazed into the mirror and turned my head, examining her fast handiwork. I couldn't help but smile. "It's beautiful."

"Don't underestimate the little things, Skylar." Idris squeezed my shoulders, giving me a kind smile. "Celebrate the small gifts we're allowed to give ourselves. Don't forget it's not truly living if you only strive to survive."

Her words resonated deep within my middle, and my animal gave me the same warm, comforting feeling I had with Captain Fjorda. I knew she was telling me that Idris was someone we could trust.

"Sound advice," I said in agreement.

"All right, now let's get a move on." Idris took my hand and led me out the room. "The others will be waiting for us."

We entered the vast hallway that seemed more like a balcony. The opening on one side overlooked Crimson City below us, while the tanned wall to my right held natural ivy-like vines intertwining in a beautiful natural design. Their home was built on a raised hill or plateau, with the city expanding around all sides below. The rustle and bustle below were the opposite of the peaceful quiet of Solace and the surrounding forest. This place thrived and behaved like I imagined the human kingdom would. Detached from nature yet still alive in its own unique way.

I admired the differences between our two cultures as I took in the beauty of all the life surrounding us. We walked until a corner forced us to turn right and follow a narrower corridor toward the center of their home.

"It's a giant square," Idris said. "You can't get lost, and if you do, then I'd worry about your mental capacity."

"Lady Idris!" a call came from behind us. "Lady Idris!"

We stopped and turned toward the High Fae running down the hallway. I found it interesting that he didn't refer to Idris as *princess* even though she was the mate of High Prince Adohan.

Idris paused and turned, giving the High Fae who called out her attention. "Yes, what is it?"

"Astro is asking for you."

She rolled her eyes and scoffed, planting a palm to her face and shaking her head as creases formed between her brows. "Don't tell me ... He's trying his hand at the red colt again?"

The High Fae nodded nervously, looking down at his feet. "He refuses to work with any of the others until he is broken."

"Stubborn male, just like his father." Idris huffed, walking past me in the direction we just came from. "Oh, Skylar, dear, keep heading toward the center. There is a large outdoor seating area in the heart of our home. You can't miss it. Adohan, Daxton, and the others will be there. It's our family sitting area where we host ... well, everything." I nodded, understanding the directions she was giving me. "Tell my mate I'll join him shortly. I need to help our son Astro with his obsession project."

"His project?" I murmured with a questioning look that Idris didn't seem to notice. "All right got it. I'll let Adohan know."

"That's the spirit, and don't worry, I'll introduce you to the herd soon. How else did you imagine we would arrive in Aelius in such a short time?" Her brown eyes softened as she squeezed my hand and departed with the other High Fae swiftly following behind her.

Herd and colt. Hmm, it sounded like she was describing a group of horses or something comparable to that. At least riding would be a faster and easier way to arrive in Aelius. I was worried that we would be running to get there in time.

I continued down the corridor, admiring the intricate carvings and different landscape portraits along the walls until I heard voices up ahead.

"Who knows, Dax?" If I had to guess, I wagered that it would be Adohan's voice. I froze in the hallway, pressing my back against the wall and closing my eyes to try and concentrate on what they were saying.

"No one else." That was unmistakably Daxton's voice. No doubt there. My animal piqued her awareness inside me in response to hearing him, and I couldn't help feeling a warming glow in my chest. "But there are moments when …" His voice trailed off for a second before returning once more. "I don't know …"

"It's obvious to anyone who has eyes to realize what's going on," Adohan said. "I must warn you, though, my friend … this needs to be handled delicately and with extreme caution. There's so much at stake—"

"I know, Adohan. I know." Daxton sighed heavily, and I could tell he was contemplating something. I just didn't know what. "Is it even fair to add this burden? I can work through this … I don't care what happens to me."

"I scoff that you would even think of this as a burden, but then again … what about our lives is ever truly fair, Dax?" Adohan asked in a tone meant to comfort a friend in need. "I've seen you sacrifice everything for the sake of others for far too long. Trust me, this is not something you can turn away from or ignore."

"I don't want to turn away from it, Adohan," Dax said with a firm confidence that left no room for doubt.

"Well, that's a good place to start, then. Have you considered what may happen if …"

"There's a plan already set in place regarding Minaeve. If I'm … If it comes to the choice—"

"You don't have to say any more. I'm just glad you have thought of every possibility in this situation."

"I just want Skylar to be safe," Daxton said. "I know she can win the trials and unlock the Heart of Valdor, but it doesn't mean I'm not worried for her safety."

Well, that answered the "who" question. They were talking about *me*.

What was this burden that Dax and Adohan were referring to? I was sure I could handle any truth they needed to tell me, and I didn't think it was fair that I was somehow being kept out of the loop with something this important.

"There's nowhere safer than by your side, brother," Castor's sing-song voice chimed in.

Ugh, males. I groaned. *Females are so much better at gossiping.* They were missing key details, and I was beginning to run out of time. I couldn't lurk in this hallway much longer without my presence being noticed.

"But she has to enter the trials alone—"

"Well, this first one, at least," Adohan replied to Dax, and the room filled with an uncomfortable silence. "The others are still a mystery; we don't know if we can aid the champion in the other trials. This first one will test you just as much as it challenges her."

I couldn't afford to wait much longer and risk having Idris reveal my eavesdropping.

Making my presence known, I cleared my throat and began descending the steps of the hall once more, making sure my treads made a little extra noise. As I rounded the corner, all three males turned their heads toward me as I entered.

A clear blue sky with wisps of white stream-like clouds shone through a skylight. Carved from the stone above us with a sheer white fabric canopy draped over the sitting area. It provided the comfort and protection of shade from the blistering sun above and allowed natural light to encompass the entire area. There was a shallow pool of red-stained water in the center that flowed around the outer edge of the opening. Strange green plants with thorns decorated the space with vines that sprouted an array of orange and yellow flowers. Couches lined the walls with different luxurious seating options near the center.

Castor was lounging comfortably in a chaise off to the side in the direct sunlight. An arm lazily draped over his eyes as he barely flicked his wrist, waving to greet me.

"Good morning, Skylar," Castor mumbled. "I'm glad you decided to remain with the living and finally wake up. Have a nice cat nap?"

Yup, Castor was back to his usual self. I rolled my eyes at him and stepped over the trickling crimson water that encircled the space.

"How and why … is this water red?" I asked, looking toward Adohan. I did my best not to glance at Daxton. He would be able to read me like an open book, and my private eavesdropping would quickly become public knowledge.

"We're in Crimson City, are we not?" Adohan beamed and stood to offer me a seat between the lounging lazy Castor and my Silver Shadow, Daxton. I accepted his offer and tried my best to relax as I sat down.

"The red clay beds and sandstone that help shape our landscape influence the coloring of this infamous treasure of ours," the high prince said, pride beaming in his hazel eyes. "The minerals collected by this river are said to revitalize your spirits, and many choose to bathe in the red waters to help rejuvenate themselves."

"Does it actually work?" I asked.

"Look for yourself." Adohan hummed as he motioned toward his frame. "This is the face of beauty and wonder, while Castor, on the other hand …" He then flicked his wrist in Castor's direction on the chaise. "Is cold and off-putting like his ice and snow." His expression morphed into a beaming grin that contrasted stunningly against his darkened skin tone.

"Ha!" Castor laughed, still covering his face with his arm. "Good one, Adohan. It's nice to see your sense of humor hasn't dried up in this blasted hot box you call home."

"Is he wrong, though, Cas?" Daxton raised his brows as he glanced back at his brother. "You've been known to be a bit frigid at times. Especially when it concerns the morning after you've bedded a female."

I couldn't help chuckling lightly at Daxton's comment. Even he was joining in on teasing Castor, who, more often than not, deserved it.

"The two of you can shove off," Castor murmured while he held up his middle fingers to both of them.

"Good to see Castor's still in high spirits," a sharp feminine voice sounded from behind the shadows.

I jumped up, but Dax was there in an instant, his hand caressing my back, trying to help calm my nerves.

"It's all right," Dax said evenly. "That's Zola."

"Zola?" I repeated as I turned to the shadows cast along the corner of the room. I regained my composure as I returned to my seat.

"When did the *Shadow Stalker* get here?" Castor groaned as he turned over onto his stomach.

"She's been here the entire time, Castor." Dax shook his head and sighed, placing his head in the palm of his hand, looking exhausted. "You clearly need some rest, brother."

Castor lifted his arm and glared at Daxton. "Pot calling the kettle black again, brother?"

Gods above. Even I could see how worn down and exhausted Castor was from the dark circles that enveloped his eyes. Dax told me he was working with the fallen I had healed, and it was clear that neither of them had acquired much sleep since our time in the wilt.

"I'll take this as my cue then." Castor flung his arm to the side and slouched over his bent knees before pushing himself to stand. "I'll go check on her."

"Her?" I asked as Dax moved closer to me on the cushioned couch. The heat I felt radiating from his body ironically sent chills across my skin.

"The fallen High Fae you healed," Daxton said in a whisper.

Oh, *that* her. This was going to be an interesting meeting indeed.

Daxton's arm lightly brushed against my thigh and settled on my knee. My core tightened as I crossed my legs to try and alleviate the tension I felt pulling me toward him. I was still mildly upset about his comment earlier in my room, along with the unknown topic of their conversation I had overheard just moments ago.

"This is her, then?" Zola asked from the corner as she scanned over me with cunning dark brown, almost black oval eyes.

I tilted my head to the side, watching Zola step into the sunlight for the first time, unveiling herself from the shadows. At first glance, she had the typical stunning beauty of any High Fae, but when I took a closer look, I could sense something different about her. Her dark, tawny skin was marked with wisps of black ink extending along her arms and exposed neck, reminding me of tiger stripes. I imagined the markings traced along her back as well, possibly covering the rest of her trimmed muscular frame. Someone could assume that she was thin or frail, but then they would be sorely mistaken. Zola was average height with a thinner build, yes. But I could see that below the black leathers she wore, hidden strength lay underneath her thin frame. Zola flipped her long black braid over her square shoulder as she approached Dax and me.

Dax met Zola's gaze and nodded, his left hand still gently resting on my knee as she approached us. He squeezed it before releasing his hold on me, brushing his hand along my back to encourage me to greet Zola.

"Hi, nice to meet you, I'm Sky." I stood and held out my hand. Zola seemed skeptical at first, but she eventually reciprocated and accepted my greeting. The second her skin touched mine, it felt like a burning flame engulfed our flesh, causing both of us to gasp and release one another instantly.

"What ... What was that?" I exclaimed, examining my hand for any burn marks.

Zola looked just as confused as I did for a moment but then quickly regained her composure. "Hold out your hand again," she said in a firm tone, narrowing her dark brows.

"I'd rather not," I said as Daxton arose to stand at my side. "No offense, but that wasn't pleasant."

Zola didn't seem amused with my response as her lips pressed into a firm, thin line. "Give me your hand again," she said, her gaze not once wavering. Her dark, ominous eyes were all-consuming, firm, and demanding. I doubted few beings alive today would refuse one of her commands.

I hesitated, contemplating whether I should follow her lead. My animal didn't give any alarm inside my head, and with Daxton protectively standing beside me, I knew I would be safe. In the end, it was the spark of curiosity inside of me that turned into a blaze, and I reached out my hand to meet hers.

The same burning sensation ran along my skin, but it quickly dwindled into a simmer until, finally ... there was nothing. Zola grabbed my other hand to test her theory further, but strangely, there was nothing.

"Interesting," she murmured. "It must be my magic reacting to yours. I've never encountered a response like that. Including the previous four shifters that came before you."

"Me either ..." I said. "Glad I'm not the only one."

"Your magic has a different effect with mine as well, Spitfire," Daxton said.

Zola looked to Dax and then me again as he guided me back to our seats on the couch. Zola shifted around to my other side and took a seat next to me. She glanced at Daxton and then flashed me a half-grin that I believed was meant to comfort me, but in reality, it was slightly terrifying.

"Zola!" Idris's cheerful voice announced her arrival as she openly flung herself across the room and into the Shadow Jumper's arms.

"Good to see you, Idris," Zola grunted, and I saw the hard exterior of the warrior soften to embrace a trusted friend. It was remarkable to witness Idris bring out this side of Zola, and to be honest, it helped me relax a little more in her presence. There was more to this spymaster than her hardened exterior and mask of shadows—just like Daxton.

"You didn't come find me first when you arrived?" Idris asked. "I'm hurt. Truly hurt."

Zola shook her head and rolled her eyes. "This wasn't just a social call, Idris, and you know it."

"Doesn't matter," Idris said. "When my closest friend comes into *my* realm, I expect an audience." Her attention swept toward Daxton, and she raised a suspicious brow at him.

"*Whose* kingdom?" Adohan asked. Idris waved her hand, ignoring her mate.

"Glare all you want, Idris. But when I summon *my* spymaster, she reports to me first. You know this, so don't try and intimidate me or Zola with that look of yours. It won't work—*this time.*"

Idris cocked a grin that stretched across her face. "Very well. *This* time."

Then, a younger High Fae male entered the room.

"Astro," Idris said with a smile. The male nodded to his mother in greeting.

Astro's eyes were darker like Idris's, and he lacked facial hair on his chin, but he was the spitting image of Adohan. Astro's hair mimicked his father's with long brown dreadlocks, almost black at the roots, that slowly changed into red along the bottom.

Adohan glanced toward his son with a questioning look. "Finn is right behind me, Father," Astro said. "I stressed the urgency in the message, just like you asked. He replied right away that he was returning."

Right on cue, another male, physically identical to his brother, joined us. The only difference between the two High Fae males was how they styled and possibly dyed their hair. Finn's hair, which had a deep red color like their mother's, was shaved on one side with the other side folded over and draped to his pointed ear.

"I'm not late, am I?" Finn panted, glancing toward his father. "I swear I came back as soon as Astro sent word to me."

"I'm aware, Finn," Adohan said, greeting his other son with a nod. "Am I not in the center of our kingdom for this exact purpose? I know what is happening at all times inside and around my borders."

"Really, Adohan?" Idris asked. "Are you trying to sound like an arrogant know-it-all just because we have company or what?"

"Only because I know how much it pleases you, my love," Adohan's eyes softened as his wife— no, excuse me, his *mate*—joined him.

Idris smiled happily, curling into Adohan's side and molding her body into the perfect puzzle piece meant only for him. They shared a short yet passionate kiss before turning their attention back to the group.

Their bond was truly different, and I was beginning to understand why Castor corrected me back on the ship. There was a deeper soul connection with a High Fae mate bond, just like shifters. It reminded me of Magnus and Julia— then of Rhea and Talon. I smiled to myself, knowing that regardless of the differences between shifters and High Fae, the mate bond rang true.

My animal stirred once again in my chest, and I finally gave in to her pestering and turned to look at Dax.

"I can trust them," I said in a hushed whisper. "I can trust everyone gathered here with us." I knew because the same comforting warmth was present in my center.

He gave me one of his warm, charismatic smiles that made the floor drop from under me. His square jaw shifted to the side as his dimple appeared in his bearded cheek.

"Everyone here has earned my trust. I'm glad you feel the same." The way he smiled at me made me want to throw away every fear I was holding on to and take a leap of faith in his strong, steadfast arms.

"Good to see you up and about, Uncle Dax," one of the twins announced as he approached us. "Hi, I'm Astro," he said, turning his attention toward me.

"Nice to meet you, Astro," I said with a kind smile.

"And this is my twin brother, Finn." He motioned to the male standing just a few paces behind him.

Dax gave me an encouraging push, and I stood to greet them. Astro extended his hand first, followed closely by Finn. They each grasped one of mine and quickly kissed the backs, giving me a slight bow.

"She's hands down one of the more beautiful shifters, I imagine," Finn said with a sly wink, matching his father's charismatic charm and ego.

Astro quickly elbowed his brother in the side. "Only because she's the only shifter you've ever seen."

Adohan cleared his throat before speaking. "My sons are only forty-eight years old, Skylar. This is the first trial they have been alive to witness. Please excuse their rash remarks," Adohan said with a hint of a warning coating his words. "At twenty-five, our magic settles, and our immortal aging begins. They may appear younger in their years, but they're old enough to know better."

"What?" Finn shrugged as he looked over my shoulder, connecting with Daxton's stare.

The smug grin on Finn's lips vanished and he blinked a few times to try and steady himself.

Astro chuckled. "You stepped in it now, Finn."

Daxton placed a hand protectively on my shoulder. It was a little much, in my opinion, but after being in a shifter's sleep for nearly four days, I would allow it. After all, I was his *ward*.

"All right … all right. Sorry." The twins said, taking a few steps back with a slight bow and their palms facing forward. They acquired their seats on either side of their parents as I dared to glance at Daxton.

"She's more than just a beautiful shifter that you two can gawk at," Dax said with a deep, authoritative tone. "Skylar is the first champion to *ever* volunteer for the trials. Her actions and perseverance through everything she's been through in these past months alone have instilled a sense of hope, once more, in the Inner Kingdom. The strength of her heart and her

fighting spirit surpass any that have dared come before her. I trust that she will defeat the trials, and she will unlock the Heart of Valdor. I ... believe in her."
Everyone in the room was silent for a moment, including me.

Daxton's genuine declaration of his belief in me touched my heart. That warm feeling was spreading in my chest once again as I looked at him—really looked at him. Without a shadow of a doubt, I could see that he wholeheartedly believed every word he had just said. He trusted me with the fate of not only his life but that of his people and all of Valdor.

Zola was the first to speak. "If Daxton believes in her, then I do as well. Thank you, shifter, for inspiring hope once again in our people and my high prince." She tilted her head to me and gave me an affirming nod of acceptance.

The others all nodded in agreement, and I blushed as Daxton brushed his thigh up against mine. A zap of his ice magic floated over my skin. My heart fluttered along with a gush of power from my animal. As much as I wanted to, I couldn't deny the spark and the feelings I had developed for Daxton—however, I knew I needed to be cautious with my heart. The unknowns were beginning to pile up, and I was afraid of being hurt again. The last thing I wanted to do was foolishly fall for another person who only sought to use me.

"Well, if the eldest one here agrees, then it must be true," Castor said, announcing his return. He entered the area alone and leaned against the sandstone wall with a heavy, invisible weight resting on his shoulders.

"She's resting—finally. I couldn't bring myself to wake her. I'm—" He rubbed his sunken eyes before scratching at the nape of his neck, giving Daxton a pleading look.

"It's fine, Cas," Dax replied, sensing his brother's silent request. "Why don't you join her and rest?"

"Seriously?" Castor's eyes widened as he sagged his shoulders, releasing all the pent-up tension in his body.

Dax nodded, his own shadows forming under his eyes.

Adohan agreed. "I can see the exhaustion on your face from here, Castor. And yours as well, Daxton. *Both* of you should be resting before we leave for Aelius tomorrow morning. We will need you at your best before the high queen's ball."

My breath faltered as the timeline of this all hit me like a dive into an icy river. Silently, I forced the panic down in my throat and braced my hands on my knees, clenching my fists tightly against the fabric of my skirt.

There is no reason to panic, I told myself. *I traveled here for this. I knew the trials were coming. Panic will only get me killed faster. Ground my fears ... face them instead of running. It is all right to be afraid, but don't give in to your fears.*

I took deep breaths while conversations prolonged in a blur around me, allowing my panic to fade into fear and then finally acceptance.

"You know where to find me if you need me," Castor said as he took his leave down the hall. I had missed the conversation leading to his departure entirely, but thankfully, it didn't seem too important.

I turned to Dax, who I knew was watching me the entire time. He gave me a small grin followed by a slight nod, telling me he knew exactly what I was doing. His exhaustion, however, was no less than Castor's. I boldly reached up and cupped his cheek in my palm, gently brushing the scruff along his jawline that was remarkably soft to my touch.

"You need to rest, Dax. I believe I can manage without you for half a day," I teased.

Daxton leaned into my touch and locked his gray eyes on me for a moment before releasing a heavy sigh, allowing his shoulders to relax. He entwined his fingers in mine and kissed the back of my hand before reclining against the couch. Leaning his head back, he closed his eyes and finally allowed himself a moment to breathe.

"I have a perfect idea!" Idris sprang up from her mate's arms with a beaming smile. Daxton's eyes cracked open as Idris's expression became almost giddy.

"Uh-oh. Mom has that look in her eyes," Astro muttered.

"Yeah, Dad's funds are about to be emptied," Finn snickered, and Idris shot them both a fiery stare that silenced their laughs.

Idris strode over to me and Zola, grabbing both our hands and pulling us to our feet. "We're going shopping! I can't tell you how many times it's just me with all these overbearing males without any female company … And I don't intend to waste a single second of it!"

"I don't—" Zola started to protest, but Idris quickly cut her off.

"No. The fallen female is finally resting after keeping poor Castor worried and awake for the past four days straight. We know he won't let anything happen to her with that premonition sight of his. It even works in his sleep," Idris said. "Besides, you can't move her until we leave in the morning anyways. It would be too suspicious."

"That's fair reasoning," Daxton murmured. "Just a reminder, though, we're the only souls alive that know what Skylar was able to do with the fallen, and it needs to stay that way. I don't want to imagine what the queen would do with this knowledge."

I was relieved to hear that the knowledge of what I did in the wilt would be kept a secret. This new twist was almost too much for me to comprehend on top of the first trial taking place only two days from now.

"And Zola …" Idris said, "I know Daxton has been paying you and Gunnar extra wages while he and Castor have been away. You have the money to splurge, and you know that Crimson City has the finest jewelry merchants in all the Inner Kingdom."

The Shadow Jumper narrowed her eyes but shrugged and gave in to Idris's plea. "You'll need someone watching over you. I won't allow any harm to come to my godchild you're growing in there." Zola didn't outwardly smile, but her tone was softer when she mentioned the babe growing in Idris's womb. "And why not add another gem to my collection if I find one special enough to come home with me."

Adohan groaned and mumbled something under his breath, causing Daxton to burst into a booming laugh. "My love, don't empty our entire savings today, please," Adohan practically begged.

"Oh, hush," Idris said, waving her hand to silence her mate. "I saw the gown Daxton had made for Skylar, by the way. Don't make me add that to the tally!" She said it as a threat, but the look in her eyes said she was just teasing him. "And you …" Idris said, turning her attention to me.

I raised my brows with unease, not knowing what to expect next. "What about me?"

"Daxton told me all about your passion for reading along with creating and preparing different delectable meals in the kitchen. Did you know we have a plethora of book merchants and some of the finest herb and spice markets in all of Valdor? We can pick out anything you want to sample for the mind and the palate."

Food and books. Well, I was sold.

The trip might actually be a perfect distraction, and if I was honest with myself, I was dying to experience the city. Viewing it from the balcony of my room just wasn't enough to satisfy my curiosity. The thought of tasting the different spices and ingredients they had in the Inner Kingdom had my mind spinning with a variety of recipe ideas I wanted to try.

"All right, I'm in," I said, and Idris squealed with excitement. She didn't hesitate for the males to protest, instead leading us down the hallway and into Crimson City.

Chapter Three

"This is so good! You've got to try this!" I extended a sugary cinnamon dough dessert to Zola, who gave me a skeptical sideways glance. "Oh, come on, it's amazing."

To describe Crimson City as glamorous would not do it justice. Idris led Zola and me through numerous shops, parlors, and merchant stands, where we found everything from clothing, jewels, gadgets, and more.

The cobblestone roads were smoothed for easier travel and carts or carriages with decadent finery and details matching the architecture of Adohan's home. Illustrations of the crimson river were seen in the decorations on the walls and shops, with varying shades of red adorning the sandstone trim along the buildings. There were stores filled with instruments that sang beautiful melodies along with children dancing in the streets. Merchants sold sculptures and paintings that seemed to come alive through the oils and fabric of the canvas. The hustle and bustle of the city was far beyond anything I could have ever imagined. The High Fae here thrived on a life of luxury that I could only compare to the stories in my books back home.

Hell, give me a good old-fashioned bonfire in the woods with nothing more than a blanket of stars shining overhead, and I was one happy shifter. Our people were in animal form half the time anyway, so we tended to need space and allowed nature to dictate the layout of our homes. I wondered if the main kingdoms or cities were all like this. Dax seemed easygoing and more relaxed, but Castor did have a flashy personality that seemed to pair with the energy of Crimson City.

Out of all this glamor and luxury, however, what caught my attention the most were the new smells and delectable foods served in various restaurants and food stands. We had a few local pubs and eating-type venues in Solace, but nothing compared to this. Idris and Zola laughed at how I stopped at practically every store that was giving a sample of their specials for the day, devouring each one with never-ending joy.

"Zola, come on," I said with a mouth full of sugary delight. "I can't possibly eat this whole thing myself."

"Doubt it." Idris laughed. "I recall the appetites of the other shifters."

"I will not be eating … *that*." Zola's nose scrunched like I was trying to force her to eat something foul.

"What? Why not? Not even a taste?"

"I prefer to eat … *other* things."

"Oh," I replied, taking another bite of my indulgent treat. "Like what?"

"Nothing that you would find appealing, trust me."

"Zola only eats raw meat," Idris said. "Not cooked or frozen. She simply must consume it raw and fresh …" Idris's skin paled, and she looked queasy, turning down an alleyway and trying to fight back the wave of nausea overtaking her small frame.

I rushed to her side, pulling back her auburn braided hair. "You all right?" I asked, rubbing her back in concentric circles.

"Yes, I just need some air. Sorry, Z. I love you, but not your taste in food. Especially now with this baby doing flips in my belly." Idris bent over and covered her mouth as another wave of nausea hit her. She tapped my hand on her shoulder and straightened up with her back pressed against the wall of a shop.

"I'll be fine, I promise," she said. "Zola, take Skylar over to the jeweler on the corner. I know you've had your eye on that overly flashy sapphire in the window for years."

I watched Zola give Idris a skeptical glare. "I'm not sure leaving you is the smartest plan at this moment, my friend."

"This is not my first pregnancy, Z. I know how this works."

"And this is not my first time watching over you, so *I* also know how this works." There was a silent standoff with glares and raised eyebrows, but eventually, Zola groaned and threw her hands up in defeat. "All right, you twisted my arm enough. I'll go spend my hard-earned money on something outrageous. Happy?"

"That's the spirit." Idris gave Zola a bright, beaming smile of victory as she braced her back against the wall. "Go with her, Skylar. This shade will help. I promise I'll see you two in a few minutes."

Not wanting to be in a similar stare-down, I nodded and followed Zola to the jeweler around the corner.

"So why do you only eat *raw* meat?" I asked with earnest curiosity.

She gave me a skeptical squint, her dark eyes scanning my expression for hidden answers to the Gods only knew what. Allusive like the shadows she wielded, that could whisper secrets only she could hear.

"You don't hesitate like others do," Zola said quietly. "And it appears that you boldly jump into situations with a curious mind."

"I'm always eager to learn everything I can." I smiled at her, trying my best to get a read on what she was thinking. "If I offended you, please let me know I've gone too far. Back home, my friend Rhea was always the one to remind me if I was prying too much." Zola didn't respond nor change her features. So, I decided to take it as a good sign.

"You didn't offend me." Zola sidestepped a group traveling past us to scurry along the side of the bustling street. "This is who I am, and I'm not ashamed or embarrassed by it," she said with confidence. "Approximately five hundred years ago when I was *altered* by the wilt, my appetite also changed. Consuming raw meat was one of the side effects created by the death magic that marked me."

My eyes slid to the black swirling marks along Zola's tanned arms that also danced around the base of her neck. This close to her, I was able to admire the patterns painted across her caramel skin, and if they didn't carry such painful memories, one might call them beautiful.

"I have a question for you now."

"Happy to answer any you have. Fire away." I jumped over the curb and was once again at her shoulder.

"Why did you, Skylar Cathal, volunteer to compete in the trials?" Zola asked as we rounded the corner.

A female with questions of her own. I do admire inquisitive minds.

"I didn't plan on volunteering. I just knew it was something I had to do," I said.

Zola nodded, reached for the handle of the glass door, and stepped inside. She was a cunning, calculating creature with a vast world of knowledge ready at her disposal. My animal seemed cautious, but I didn't have a sinking feeling or a drive to run the other way.

As we entered, the glass windowed door closed behind us with a chiming bell that hung overhead to announce our arrival. The noise from the busy streets faded inside the shop, and I took a moment to revel in the quiet atmosphere. It wasn't the natural chime or calming sounds I treasured from my forest home, but it would do.

Zola meandered around the glass displays, meticulously admiring the jeweled pieces as I followed. I glanced at the various glimmering gems and trinkets that rivaled the finest crown jewels of the human kings and queens. She stopped at a solo display that held a deep blue sapphire necklace shaped into a teardrop setting with a singular diamond at the top.

"What drove you to make the decision? And before you answer," Zola added, "I would appreciate honesty, Skylar. Above all things, I strive to find the truth in this life, and I assure you I'm very good at my job." Her fingers danced along the glass casing, admiring the stunning sapphire beneath. "Otherwise, Daxton wouldn't employ me, and Castor wouldn't tolerate me, despite my promise to their mother to look after them."

That last part threw me for a loop. "Their mother?" Zola nodded, returning her stare to the gem in the display. I inferred that I wasn't going to get more out of her than the nod.

"Queen Minaeve," I said, "she first chose my younger cousin, Neera, as the champion. I couldn't let her go. I knew she didn't want to leave." The sheer look of terror in Neera's eyes that night in the meadow flashed in my mind. I had never seen her so scared or her complexion that pale. My heart had practically leaped out of my chest at the sight of her, my instincts driving me to protect her.

"It's normal for the chosen shifter not to want this task. So, I ask again, what made you take her place?" Zola asked as she cast her stare toward me. Her bluntness was harsh, but it was also a welcomed breath of fresh air.

I paused for a moment before answering, trying to interpret any hidden meaning behind Zola's question.

Why did I volunteer?

I realized I never truly answered that question other than the obvious response to save my cousin. I thought back to the night in the meadow and ran through all the events that led to my decision. So much had happened since then that it was difficult to piece all the details together. I traced back to the start of the gathering and remembered that Alistar had sent out a command for all of us to shift. But my animal and I fought against his magic.

"I didn't follow my alpha's command."

Zola stopped admiring the jeweled necklace for a moment, and I could tell I had her undivided attention as she tilted her head to the side. "And?"

"I begged for anyone to help stop my shift. I prayed silently to the Gods … to anyone listening to help me stop it. I remember the burning of my magic inside me—I thought I was going to burst into a ball of literal flames due to resisting the call of the alpha and the pull from the full moon."

"Shifters are naturally more powerful with the influence of certain astrological events, like a full moon,"

Zola said, exposing the depths of her knowledge concerning my kind. "What helped you ultimately stop your shift?"

"I felt …" It finally dawned on me what magic helped me in the meadow. I cursed at myself for being so blind and not realizing it before. It was Daxton's magic that helped bring me back. "Ice tamed the roaring flames from tearing me apart."

Zola nodded and gave me a genuine half-grin. "Then what happened?" It was like she was leading me to discover my own truths. Clever …

I smiled, knowing Shaw would've done the exact same thing if he'd been here with me.

"I heard the high queen speak to me. She warned me how the trials would test my mind, body, and soul. That no others have been successful or have been found worthy to unlock the Heart of Valdor."

"And what makes you think that you are worthy?" Zola calmly asked.

"I—I don't."

The reality of that truth hit me square in the chest. I didn't believe I was worthy of anything, not yet anyway. Maybe these trials were a test for me just as much as it was for Valdor.

Zola turned, spinning the necklaces over in her dark, tanned palm. "You don't?"

"I don't believe I should be idolized or placed on a pedestal for merely stepping in to lend aid when it was asked for. That's something any decent person should be expected to do. I came here … I volunteered because I was willing and able to do so. If, in the end, I can save the lives of those I love regardless of my own outcome, I will happily accept that as my fate."

"You're willing to put your life at risk to save all of our lives as well?"

I could read between the lines of her question. I knew she was asking about *all* of Valdor. I could say no. I could say I was doing this for *just* my people, but in my heart, I knew I wasn't. Even though I didn't know many humans or even fae, I believed in respecting all life. We should all be allowed to have the chance to make our world better. Everyone deserved that opportunity, regardless of who they were.

"I am. I'm willing to do this for—*everyone.*"

Zola gave me a full, cunning grin at my reply. "You, indeed, are different. Not many creatures in this world would think in the way you do. You're *more*, it seems, compared to the other four champions I have met." She paused, looking around for the shopkeeper before continuing. "I do believe, however, that you've entered the trials to answer more than just a calling of your own. I believe you'll determine the outcomes of not just your fate but all those in Valdor." Zola chuckled deeply. "Fate is a fickle bitch. Welcome to the game."

The bell chime signaled the door to the shop opening, and Idris entered frantically, waving a makeshift fan made of parchment. "Thank the Gods!" she declared. "The sun is finally beginning to set. I love you, Mother, but the heat of your love is sometimes just too much."

Zola and I both looked at each other and shared a small chuckle at Idris as she found a seat in the corner near a display. The hard exterior of the Shadow Jumper was still present, but I was able to see a glimmer of vulnerability that hadn't existed moments ago.

"You need to choose something," Zola instructed Idris.

"I don't need Adohan's heart to stop beating before the trials begin, Z. I love my mate, and I intend to mock and adore him for a long time to come … Or at least until his child is born, that is."

"It's my treat," Zola said to Idris, then glanced at me. "You need something as well."

"What?" I exclaimed. "I don't have any money."

"Daxton has paid me generously over these past few months, and he's also asked me to find something special just for you, Skylar."

"Really?" I stammered. "I-I don't know. This all seems too much. I've never dreamed of owning, let alone seeing, beautiful pieces of jewelry like this." Zola and Idris glanced at each other with mischievous grins, exchanging unspoken words. "What?" I demanded.

"Nothing!" Idris said.

I narrowed my eyes. She had to be hands down one of the worst liars I had ever seen in my entire life. "Idris."

"You deserve something for the ball tomorrow," Zola added as she stepped between us. "Daxton insisted."

"Yes." Idris immediately jumped to her swollen feet and ran her hand along my long-flowing hair. "With the ball tomorrow, you'll need something that highlights your natural beauty. Take a look over here." Idris motioned to the far side of the store. "I think a beautiful hairpin would give you just the right touch!"

"And it wouldn't likely break," I added.

Both stopped and looked at me with a confused stare. I lightly laughed to myself as I pushed past them to examine the beautiful variety of combs and hair accessories.

"There's a reason why shifters don't wear jewelry or keep such fine clothing in our wardrobes. It's why we mark our mate's flesh instead of wearing wedding bands on our fingers, necklaces, or earrings." I looked over the sparkling displays, entranced by the beautiful works of art crafted into various trinkets.

"Care to enlighten us?" Idris asked as she moved beside me.

"This is disappointing to hear, actually," Zola mumbled.

"When we shift, our bodies alter completely, the structure of our skeleton, our skin … everything changes. Most of us shred through clothing when we take our larger animal forms, so imagine what a ring or a bracelet would do if my hand suddenly transformed into a paw or disappeared entirely."

"Well, that's dull—" Zola huffed, and Idris elbowed her in the arm.

"It's … It's practical," Idris said. "It's also refreshing to hear." Idris gasped as she looked at the glaring expression on Zola's face. "My comment was not intended for you, Z. Calm down."

Zola crossed her arms with a tight scowl.

"Miss Treasure Trove over here has one of the grandest collections in all the Inner Kingdom. And she never likes to share."

Zola laughed, shaking her head as she flung her arm around her friend's shoulder. "I only acquire the best and brightest gems, and you are most definitely one of my most treasured."

"Good grief," Idris bellowed. "You are too much, Z."

I browsed the moon and star hairpins, but none of them stood out to me. I meandered to the selection dedicated to a variety of different plants and animals. I saw various elegant birds, which made me think of Gilen, so naturally, I passed over them as quickly as I could. The wolf reminded me of Rhea, but then I thought about how cliché it would be to choose an animal. Sighing to myself, I continued on to the flowers. My eyes scanned over the glimmering diamonds, emeralds, and rubies that represented a delicate rose, and I was about to pick it up until the sight of another stole my breath away.

The room seemed to disappear as my eyes scanned over the long ebony stem of shiny obsidian rock, leading to black oval leaf that framed brilliant silver and orange petals inside. This was the flower from my dreams, and it was somehow *real?*

"Do you like it?" the merchant from behind the counter kindly asked.

For a moment, I had forgotten how to speak. I smiled and nodded to the kind shop owner, who reached into the glass display case to hold it out for me to examine. I held it in my hands, gently stroking the colored petals that I believed to be a figment of my dreams.

"What is this flower called?" I asked, gaining Zola and Idris's attention.

"It's a rare beauty," the merchant said, looking at me with kindness in his weathered eyes. "It is known as the moondance flower. And it only blooms—"

"In the moonlight," I said.

"How did you know that?" Idris asked. "I didn't think you had these flowers in Solace or the mainland."

"We don't," I said, never taking my eyes off the divine trinket. "I've seen ... No, I've dreamt about this flower ever since I can remember. It always makes me feel safe, like nothing in this world can hurt me."

I was lost in the beauty of what I was holding in my hands. I couldn't believe that this flower was real, and I wished more than anything to be able to, someday, truly witness it bloom.

Zola and Idris glanced at each other with questioning looks over my shoulder, but I paid them no attention. I was lost to the beauty of this jeweled hairpin, which embodied the very real flower of my dreams.

"How much?" Zola asked.

The merchant's eyes dropped to my left forearm, where my champion's mark of three black outlines of eight-pointed stars was branded into my skin. "For our champion, it's a gift."

"We have the coin," Zola protested.

The merchant held up his hand. "Please, it's a gift."

I cradled the hairpin in my palms before clutching it tightly against my chest. I carefully slid it into a secret pocket tucked away at my thigh along the slit of my skirt.

"Thank you." I truly was grateful for not only his kindness but for Idris and Zola's as well. This day had turned out to be a perfect distraction for what was to come.

"It will look beautiful on you, Skylar!" Idris beamed as we exited the merchant's jewelry shop. Zola had her small trinket box tucked under her arm with a satisfied look plastered across her expression.

The sun was beginning to set, and we knew it was almost time to venture back to Adohan and Idris's home. However, there was one final stop Idris wanted to make before we returned, and of course, Zola and I allowed her to drag us along. As the city darkened, new lights began to illuminate the different streets, posts, and homes as we passed by. They were mesmerizingly bright and beautiful with no sign of fire illuminating them inside.

"What? How do these work?" I asked.

"These are fae lights," Zola answered me. "Summoned by magic and far more useful than torches, lanterns, or candles. They won't burn a house down."

"Remarkable," I said as I reached out to touch one. There was no heat radiating from the light source, so I picked up the lantern to begin examining it closer.

Zola reached out her open palm to me and called forth a glow into her hand. "Fae light."

"Wow! How'd you do that?" I set the lantern aside and examined the light forming in her palm.

She huffed a laugh to herself. "Magic, Skylar."

"Oh, right." The reality of this wild magic was still new to me, regardless of how natural it was to the rest of them. "Could I learn to summon one?"

"I imagine shifters could summon them utilizing the same magic you apply when changing into your animal forms, channeling it into something different."

"I agree. I don't see why not," Idris said. "You have both shifter and healing magic. I assume it stems from the same place. You just have to focus your mind on what you wish to accomplish."

"I wish I had time to practice before the labyrinth," I admitted.

"It wouldn't help you," Zola said.

"Why?"

"Because the labyrinth is warded. No magic can be used inside. Your mind is the only weapon within its walls."

I rolled my eyes. "That makes things more interesting." I had more questions about what I would encounter inside, but unfortunately, anyone who knew those answers was dead.

"Here it is!" Idris announced to Zola and me. "I'll be just a minute."

Zola watched Idris skip inside the garment shop and then shot a narrow glance at me, telling me she did not believe in Idris's timeline. "I'd better go in after her or else we'll be here another hour at least."

I covered my mouth, shielding my laughter. "Please do. I don't want to stay out too late."

Chapter Four

Alone, I patiently waited outside the clothing shop as a strange, anxious sensation trickled along the nape of my neck. My animal perked up, immediately alerting me. My eyes focused on scanning every inch of my surroundings, searching for anything out of the ordinary.

The evening quieted to an almost unnatural calmness. A fair number of High Fae were passing through, but the numbers were dwindling. I couldn't pinpoint the threat lurking in the darkening streets, but my instincts told me something was out there. I bent to reach for my dagger but realized I had never armed myself before leaving.

Shit—this is not good.

Zola and Idris emerged from the shop, and the Shadow Jumper immediately noted my alertness. "What is it, Skylar?" she asked, her posture stiffening as she reached inside her leather corset to extract hidden daggers from within the folds of her clothing.

"Something doesn't feel right," I said, admiring the ingenious design of her fighting leathers. "Can you shadow-jump back to the house with more than one passenger in tow?"

"I can manage the trip carrying one … but not two." She pressed her lips together in a thin line, and I knew she was anticipating what I was going to ask next.

"Wait just a second here—" Idris tried to step in, but I cut her off.

There was no way in Valdor I was going to leave Idris here alone. There was a baby to think of, and I wouldn't dare risk Adohan's wrath if anything happened to his mate and unborn child.

"Zola, take Idris back to the house right away, then come back for me." I could see Zola hesitate, but I wasn't going to allow Idris to encounter even the whispered threat of harm. The Spymaster grunted with disproval; I could tell she was on the verge of arguing with me, but I refused to allow her the ground to do so. "Go now, Zola," I commanded this time, allowing power from my animal to flow into each word I spoke.

Zola flinched, feeling the magic pulse within my command, and pulled Idris into the shadows of the alley. Her dark eyes met mine, giving me a firm nod of understanding. "I'll be right back," she said, and they both disappeared.

I spun around to search the darkening street for the unidentified threat I knew was nearby, but oddly enough, there wasn't a soul in sight.

"Well, there you are," an unnerving male voice taunted me from behind the corner of the alleyway.

I spun to my left to investigate when two pairs of strong hands forcefully grabbed ahold of my shoulders. Catching me off guard, they forced me backward into the shadows, out of sight from anyone passing by on the main street. My back smacked into the solid stone wall, with the rest of my body quickly following suit. They were pinning me down and making it impossible to move.

No matter how much I tried, I couldn't manage to break free of their hold. The two cloaked figures gripped me tighter as I uselessly fought against them. To my surprise, I was beginning to gain some ground and wiggle free, but they each moved a leg between my thighs to spread mine apart and force their weight onto me. Gods, they were heavy, like two stone statues plastering me to the wall and rendering me immobile.

"My, my. You're a feisty one. I'll give you that. But without being able to shift and access your animal's strength … you're no match for my guards. You're simply wasting precious energy by fighting this." The same voice from before spoke again.

A third cloaked figure appeared from the darkened corner of the alleyway. The stranger practically glided across the cobblestone, stopping mere breaths away. Their scents were hidden, indicating they held some magical abilities to create a barrier against detection.

"Clearly, you haven't spent much time around shifters," I growled. "Fighting is in our nature."

The guards' hold on me tightened, their grips now twisting my arms and pinning my legs to the point of pain. *Outstanding*, I grunted to myself, refusing to allow the thread of fear to build in my throat. There was no way out of their hold, but I sure as hell wouldn't give up this easily.

A stray fair-skinned hand emerged from under the dark green cloak and wound its way into the center of my chest, pressing down firmly between the peaks of my breasts and causing me to gasp.

"So, this—is our *champion*." His voice was vile, making my stomach turn. "I didn't realize a shifter could be this enticing."

I heard the swish of his hood fall back, and I snapped my head up to try and view the identity of my captor. A gorgeous yet menacing face stared back at me with a deep-seated hunger burning in his calculated glare.

His high cheekbones outlined a clean-shaven, narrowed jaw that was, of course, gorgeous and yet, a tad gentler looking than I anticipated. He stood just a hair taller than me, with a slimmer, less muscular build than Daxton. However, I could detect the deep well of thrumming power emanating from within him. This male was not to be underestimated. His haunting forest-green eyes stood out from under the hood of his cloak, tracing over my body like I was some kind of prized possession or delectable dessert.

"Let me go!" My eyes burned with hatred as I fought against my captors. My animal was screaming inside my head to fight back and to get as far away from this male as I could.

He bit his bottom lip and moved his head down toward my ear. "Now, there's that fire I've heard so much about. I was wondering when you would come out and play with me." He stood straight, trapping me against the wall with his body, and tilted his hips forward so he was flush against me. "Your beauty and power are so deliciously wild. I don't believe I've ever been this excited to capture one of your kind before." I squirmed against him, but he released a low chuckle at my efforts. "Please, by all means, continue." He rolled his hips as one of his hands migrated over to cup my breast. "I'm enjoying this encounter more and more with each passing second." His minions on either side of me snickered, but I ignored them.

"Screw you," I spat.

He was toying with me. My blood began to boil, rage bubbling to the surface, threatening to overtake the rational side of my mind.

Physically I was outmatched, and as much as I hated to admit it, it was fact. I had to try to use my whit to best them, or at least stall for time.

"What do you want with me?" I demanded with a fiery tone. I had been through worse—survived worse. This disgusting excuse of a male wouldn't get the satisfaction or pleasure of seeing me cower before him. I refused to be afraid.

"Oh, so many things, Skylar Cathal. There are seemingly too many to count." His grin widened as his veil of magic lifted around him.

His scent reminded me of willow shrub, with just a splash of citrus swirling through my senses, causing my stomach to jump into my throat.

"Who are you?" I growled. "What do you want with me? What games are you trying to play here?" I asked, deciding to resort to what I did best.

I had to keep my wits about me. Questions took time to answer, and I needed as much of that as I could get. Zola should have reached the house by now and would be on her way back to retrieve me. I just needed to distract this male for a little bit longer.

"I'm appalled," the male High Fae gasped.

He used his free hand to remove the rest of his cloak and stepped back, thankfully releasing his hold on my chest. Light blond ruffled hair adorned a charming yet deceptively cunning beauty that smiled wickedly. "I could simply read your mind, but alas, that would spoil all the fun in a hurry. And I intend to take my time with you." He bent his head closer to my ear and whispered, "Minaeve said I could have you as a prize if it pleased me. And by the grace of the Gods above, I believe you do."

My chest rapidly rose and fell as uneasiness rolled through me, realizing who this was. "Seamus."

"High Prince Seamus Duran," he corrected his eyes glimmering in the fading light. "I'm quite fond of the title and the power that comes with it … among other things that I'll happily share with you once we no longer have an audience. Or—" He paused, a devilish grin snaking its way across his lips. "Perhaps you would enjoy an audience, Champion? It has been a while since I have had a good fuck in public. I remember it can be quite the rush." He attempted to caress my face, but I turned my head away just in time. I couldn't allow him to come into direct contact with my skin. "Ah, so you've heard of me. Your caution towards my touch is flattering."

"What are you doing here?" I roared through clenched teeth.

"Retrieving you, of course. Queen Minaeve sent me and two of her guards to bring you to Aelius before the ball tomorrow. She heard of your encounters with the harpies and the hounds near the wilt border, and she now doubts the competence of the Silver Meadows princes' ability to bring you to the trials safely. You're to be handed over to me, and I will personally see to all your *needs*." His eyes scanned me from head to toe, oozing with lust that coated the corners of his cunning stare.

For a moment, I was relieved to hear that only the news about the harpies and the hounds reached Aelius. The queen didn't know about me healing the fallen fae. That secret was, at least for the moment, still safe.

"Just *my* needs?" I spat back at him with a venomous tone. "Shame to leave yourself out of the equation. Or is going solo simply the norm for you?"

His sinister grin widened, stretching from ear to ear. "Well, not just yours. You're correct, shifter. There must be some reward for all my hard work." Seamus spoke in a low, sensual purr as he reached to twirl a strand of my hair around his finger.

"Well, sorry to disappoint you, but I'm perfectly fine. I don't need anything from *you*."

He stepped forward once again, his eyes dropping to my chest as his fingers danced along the open slit of my skirt before meeting my eyeline once more. "Yes … I can see that." He tilted his head and narrowed his gaze, inhaling a deep breath near the base of my neck. "I didn't detect an increase of fear in your scent when I mentioned your encounter with the creatures or the wilt. Pray tell, dear Champion, what do you fear if not death itself?"

"Get off me!" I demanded once more, fighting against the hold of the guards, even though it didn't seem to make a difference. Their grip on me twisted, and if it hadn't been for my increased pain tolerance from my capture, I would dare say it hurt a little.

"If you won't tell me, then fine. My patience is running thin. I'll have to take a peek inside that pretty little head of yours myself." Seamus sneered with sadistic glee as he pressed the palm of his hand onto my temple and dove into the confines of my mind with his magic.

I couldn't help releasing a searing scream of pain through the confines of the darkened alleyway. A red-hot iron was digging into my skull and trying to split my mind in two. I crumbled under his touch, unable to fight against him as he tore through my memories. My animal surged inside me as my own power began to build. Doing all she could to fuel me with magic, encouraging me to find some way to fight back.

"Ah, there it is," Seamus whispered in a voice that reminded me of a venomous viper.

My body collapsed like a limp doll, held upright by his minions on either side. I heard a sickening chuckle as he dove inside my head again, his intentions set on recalling what I feared most. I could feel the memories surging to the surface of my consciousness, and as much as I tried to resist, they all came flooding back.

There was a flash in my mind's eye, and once again I was in the underground dungeon with Blade hurling the iron-tipped whip at my back. The vision was so real ... the sounds, the smell. Everything.

My arms and legs were bound with iron shackles that dug into my skin, making it impossible to heal and reducing my power to a mere whisper. I was hanging between the two posts, beaten, bleeding, and dying. Worst of all, I was alone, without a single ray of hope in the world that someone was coming for me or that I would survive.

With out warning, Seamus pulled his magic back. I could feel my body convulse as tears freely streamed down my cheeks. I could barely breathe, but I still managed to scream at him. "Gods-damned sadist!" I cursed.

"There's that fire I crave. You're like a drug that I can't seem to get enough of. Something in you is calling out to me, your scent is so ... *enthralling.* How intriguing." Seamus's voice rumbled as he inched closer.

My animal roared inside of me to fight back. Through everything in my life, I never backed down from a challenge. Was I scared? Yes. But I learned at an early age that running away solved nothing.

I summoned my courage, unhinging the confines of my magic. I focused my mind on creating a shield to push back against Seamus, and to my surprise, it worked.

A shimmering green barrier appeared between us before I shoved it at the High Prince of Aelius, pushing him backward and colliding with the opposing wall.

Laughing to himself, he said, "Ahh, I believe our *pet* has learned some new tricks." With a half-cocked grin he easily shoved himself forward through my wall of magic.

Pet? Fucking. Hell. He saw—He knew.

That name caused my breath to still as my eyes widened with a deep-seated hatred that drained every rational thought in my mind. That was what Blade had called me. Indicating that I was nothing more than an animal he wanted to keep as his own... *pet.* Bastard.

"I always did enjoy a challenge," Seamus said, moving closer toward me once more. "Something I see we have—"

"Touch her again, and you die!" A deep, commanding voice boomed from the opening of the alleyway.

There was a blast of ice-cold wind and a flash of silver light that made everyone pause with looks of dread painted across their faces. They knew that Daxton, no—They knew Silver Shadow was here.

Without hesitation, Daxton teleported between Seamus and me, plunging his dagger into the neck of the guard to my right. Blood spewed from the gaping wound as the High Fae's grip on my arm disappeared, his body falling lifeless to the ground. With my free hand, I moved to wipe the blood spatter from my forehead just in time to see Daxton create a weapon with his ice magic that impaled the chest of the other guard standing to my left.

Their deaths happened in less than a second. The look in Silver Shadow's eyes was dark and menacing. I could see that he held no regret for ending the lives of the two High Fae guards who now lay dead at my feet.

Silver Shadow coated his skin with a layer of ice as he shot forward and pressed his forearm against the base of Seamus's neck. The High Prince of Aelius grunted and groaned, trying to fight against Daxton's hold, but he wasn't strong enough to break free. Daxton was clearly the superior of the two. In one swift movement, he lifted Seamus off his feet and snarled at him with his exposed sharpened canines mere inches from his face.

"Hello there, Daaa—" the Silver Shadow pressed harder on Seamus's throat. "Pity you aren't allowed to kill me, right?" Seamus somehow managed to pull back against his arm just enough to speak. "Wouldn't want to start a war before the lines are clearly drawn."

Silver Shadow released a menacing low growl that made the hairs on my neck stand at attention. His eyes were frosted over with a wicked intensity that would strike terror in the hearts of even the bravest warriors. I had never seen someone so fearsome in my entire life. It was a firm reminder of how ruthless and dangerous he could be if pushed to the limits of his self-control.

"Daxton!" Adohan yelled, appearing at his side.

He draped himself in a thin layer of flames to combat Daxton's ice and shield himself against Seamus's mind-reading abilities.

"You *cannot* kill him," Adohan warned, echoing Seamus's earlier statement.

From his expression, I could tell Adohan hated every word he had just spoken to Daxton, but someone had to step in and be the voice of reason. From the looks of it, Daxton was still locked in a blind rage, and his wrath was fixated on the fae male dangling in his grasp. "Daxton!" Adohan shouted once more before lowering his voice. "You can't start this ... not now."

"If you *ever* harm Skylar again, Seamus," he said in a deathly calm whisper that chilled me to the bone, "I will end your miserable excuse of a life. I don't care if I must tear down your entire realm and the world crumbles beneath me. I will ensure your heart stops beating by my hand if you ever come near her again."

"What if she," Seamus gasped, trying to find his breath, "is the one who asks for *my* company?" He somehow managed to wink at Daxton, and I knew all hell was about to break loose.

Adohan leaped into action, his fires blazing as he fought to pull back Silver Shadow's arm that was now *crushing* Seamus's windpipe. The gurgling sounds of his mangled breath echoing across the cobblestone.

I whimpered, bracing myself to witness another death as the strength in my limbs disappeared. I barely noticed Zola's hands holding me upright against the wall as she tried to speak to me.

I didn't hear anything she was saying, my attention focused solely on Silver Shadow—my protector. His eyes flipped back to me, and there was a soft flare of concern that crossed his gaze. Then they immediately returned to stone as his focus shifted back to Seamus.

"Daxton!" Adohan screamed once more.

"*Grahhh!*" Roaring with frustration and rage, Daxton reluctantly released Seamus, allowing him to crumble to the ground, gasping for air.

"How did you manage to bypass my wards without me knowing, Seamus?" Adohan demanded.

"Since Queen Minaeve's last offering from the oh so generous High Prince Daxton ..." Seamus lifted his brows to me, and I returned his stare with a narrowed glare of pure hatred. "Our queen has been able to siphon enough of his magic to begin experimenting with portals. She can now summon them for instantaneous travel. Granted, they are not as quick or strong as Daxton's teleportation, and each portal needs an intended destination. But it is a successful doorway for a short period of time."

"Then you can leave," Daxton snarled as Adohan placed a flaming hand in the center of his chest. "Now. Before Adohan's reasoning runs dry and your blood stains my blade." A long silver sword appeared, strapped to Daxton's back. He reached for the hilt, drawing it clean from its sheath.

"No need to be rude now," Seamus taunted. "I intend to leave right away … with *her*." Seamus pointed a finger in my direction.

"Do you have a death wish, Seamus?" Adohan spat, putting himself between the males once more. I could see pure hatred and wrath in Daxton's expression, and I knew Adohan would not be able to hold his friend back much longer. "I'm accompanying them to Aelius tomorrow. Tell Minaeve she has my word and that she will receive my offering at the gathering as well."

That seemed to get Seamus's attention. "Yours—Ekon? Freely?"

"No," Daxton said.

Adohan steadied his breath. "Only if you leave my realm now, Seamus."

"Very well," Seamus said quickly, extending his hand out to Adohan, but the Crimson City high prince merely glared and crossed his still-flaming arms in front of his muscled chest. "Glad to see your mind is still sharp, and the mating bond hasn't dulled your senses completely." Seamus strutted out to our left and casually wiped his green jacket clean of any dust or residue. "Until the ball, beautiful Champion," he said in my direction and dashed away into the darkness.

Dax turned to Adohan. "You can't be serious, Ado—"

The High Prince of Crimson City held up his hand, respectfully silencing his friend. "We both know I would have too regardless. My mate bond wasn't going to spare me forever, and I knew that this time around, I would be forced to submit my power publicly to Minaeve." Daxton's eyes softened with sorrow and regret. "You cannot sacrifice yourself for me this time, my friend. It'll be all right. We'll all get through this," he added. "Now, tend to her."

Daxton turned toward me in the shadow of the alley and reached out to take my hand. I gladly accepted it, and he didn't hesitate before scooping me into his arms and teleporting us back to Adohan's home without another word.

I felt so raw and shaken from my encounter with Seamus that I didn't know what to think or feel. All I knew was I wanted to scream, yell, and possibly break things. I wanted to thrash out at the world and roar until my throat was raw and my eyes could no longer create any tears.

"Spitfire," Dax whispered, clutching me tightly against his chest as my body shook with rage.

"No!" I screamed as I pushed him away.

Leaping out of his arms, I landed firmly on my feet, sprinting toward my room without looking back. Memories bombarded me from all sides. Once again, I was trapped in the hunter's keep.

I loathed the fact that Seamus had done this to me, that he *could* do this to me. And I detested myself for allowing it to affect me like this.

I was weak.

How would I ever defeat the trial of the mind if this mere memory almost broke me once again? This kernel of darkness that I tried so hard to vanquish was rising like bile in my throat. I needed to block out the world so I could fight to breathe once more. I didn't want to burden anyone with this trauma, let alone have anyone else see it and judge me for my failure.

Soaring down the hall, I flung open the door to my room before turning around and slamming it shut. I reached down to bolt the locks so no one could enter after me. Tucking my knees to my chest, I collapsed onto the cool marble floor. Roaring, I pounded my fists against the door frame. Screaming into the emptiness of my soul, trying to cleanse my body of the pain I was forced to relive once again.

"Skylar ... Skylar," Daxton pleaded from outside my door. "Please, let me in."

I couldn't bring myself to unlatch the lock. I couldn't allow him to see me like this. "I need to be by myself," I whimpered, loud enough that I knew he heard me. "Please, Daxton." I cried out. "I have to do this alone."

"No, you don't," he said. I could hear his labored breathing on the other side, and I knew he desperately wanted to break through the divide between us. "I'm here, Spitfire. Remember, you're *never* alone," he said in a pining whisper. "I'm not leaving... I will *always* find you."

I didn't say the words that I now knew by heart.

No, instead, I shut him out, dragged myself away from the doorway and toward the bed. Burying my face into a pillow I screamed and yelled without fear of others hearing me. After what felt like hours, I caught my breath. I curled my knees inward and rocked my body back and forth, trying to calm down. I recalled my training with Shaw and began grounding myself in that safe world. I would not be a victim of my fears. My animal's presence lightly drifted in the back of my mind, trying to comfort me.

I refused to be weak. I couldn't afford to be.

Something sharp poked me in the leg, and I reached into my pocket to find the hairpin the merchant had given me earlier that day. I closed my hand tightly around the flower before kissing the silver and orange petals.

More silent tears fell, but I stubbornly ignored the comfort I knew was still waiting on the other side of my door. Utterly exhausted, I laid the pin next to me on the bed, praying that it would give me serenity and allow me to forget my nightmares.

Chapter Five

That night, I didn't wake to the sounds of my screams as they tore through the peaceful silence of Adohan and Idris's home.

My back bowed and arched as I thrashed in my night terror, feeling the sting of Blade's whip tearing through my flesh again and again. The blood from my wounds caused my feet to slip out from under me, hanging lifelessly from my iron-bound chains. The pain was not the worst of it. It was the image of his cruel, self-satisfied grin of amusement as he circled my limp, lifeless body. It was the sound of his rapid breathing as he relentlessly tore into my back. The merciless smile of delight that was seared into my memories. I screamed until my voice was raw. I screamed for someone, anyone, to find me so I wouldn't die in this prison consumed by darkness.

"Spitfire!" Daxton's voice drifted into my nightmare, pulling me out of the abyss and isolation that was tearing me apart from the inside out. "Wake up. It isn't real. Wake up, Skylar. Please!" he begged.

I had never heard him plead like this before ... like my pain was somehow also his. I felt his hands pressed firmly on my shoulders as my eyes fluttered open, trying to focus on the reality of the world around me. "You're *not* alone," he said in a commanding voice that was impossible to ignore. "You will *never* be alone like that again. I promise, Skylar. It was just a nightmare."

My stomach churned as I looked over to the bedside, trying to find anything to catch the bile that was rapidly rising in my throat. Daxton anticipated this and handed me the waste bin before I ruined the sheets. I knelt on the bed, hurling my guts out, trying to breathe while Daxton remained at my side, quietly holding my hair back—not uttering a sound.

"I-I was ... I was there, Daxton." I wept as another wave of nausea took over. "His whip ... The cell. It all seemed so real," I cried out uncontrollably. "Seamus. That bastard tore through my memories and found them. He ... He made me relive every gruesome detail, Dax." I openly sobbed, lacking the strength to hold anything back.

Every muscle in Daxton's body seemed to stiffen, and I swore he was shaking almost as badly as I was. He clenched his fists and moved to fetch me a glass of water. I tilted my head back, quickly draining the contents before dropping the cup to the floor as the backs of my eyes stung.

Daxton immediately wrapped his arms around my shoulders, tightly cradling me against his chest. Allowing my walls to crumble, I melted into his embrace. I should've fought against this, but I couldn't bring myself to turn away. I felt safe in his arms, like nothing and no one in the world could dare harm me.

"You're stronger than this, Skylar," he said. "Please, let me help. You're not alone—Remember this." His hand rubbed my back in small concentric circles. "I don't care how many times I have to keep telling you. I'll gladly keep doing it until you start believing it yourself." Daxton moved his hand to stroke my hair, helping calm my sobs and steady my emotions.

I could feel the presence of my animal stirring inside me, reminding me of the same thing. Shaking my head, I moved in his lap and pushed back to look at him.

"How can *I* do this, Daxton?" I sniffled with rasps scarring my voice. "How can I possibly be the one champion that can defeat the trials if I'm this ... weak?"

I had never doubted myself like this before, but my encounter with Seamus left me feeling helpless, causing my turmoil of guilt to continue to spiral out of control.

Daxton adjusted me so I was sitting between his legs and held my face firmly between his hands. I reached up to clutch onto him, trying to feel grounded in anything I could find. His hold on me sent a warm sensation through the cold limbs of my quivering body. It was the same feeling my animal gave me whenever I felt scared or lost, calming my trepidations and granting me a moment of serenity so I could find my way through the darkness.

"This will *not* break you, Skylar Cathal. It didn't before, and it won't now." He sounded so confident. His expression was unwavering as he spoke to me, without any trace of fear or uncertainty.

"How can you be so sure?"

I turned my gaze away, unable to look him in the eyes. I was so scared and not just of the nightmares. I was terrified of opening myself up to someone, of opening my heart to another.

Daxton gently turned my chin, encouraging me to meet his luminous gray stare. "Because I know what it's like to be held against your will. I understand that kernel of fear and darkness that you are now burdened with carrying. And trust me when I tell you that this will *not* break you."

My eyes widened with shock at the realization of his confession. "What do you mean?" I dared to ask him.

He nervously licked his lips, guiding my hands through the opening collar of his shirt to discover twin scars across his chest. "These," he whispered as he slid my hands over the crisscross marks. "These are some of the visible scars I carry from Minaeve's imprisonment."

My heart stopped as I traced over the thick scars on his body. They were old, perhaps from centuries ago, yet they never truly healed.

"It was iron." Daxton sighed, staring off to the side of the bedroom with a depth of horror in his gaze that was difficult to swallow. I gulped a heavy breath, sensing the pain that he tried so hard to keep buried beneath his armor of bravery. His fingers tightened around mine. "Minaeve hung me from the ceiling with barbs threaded through my chest."

I gasped, my hands moving to cover my mouth. "Oh, my Gods … Daxton. What? Why?"

"Because I refused to submit to her rule as high queen and freely offer her my power. When Minaeve cast back the first surge of the wilt, and the veil appeared, she demanded the three realms acknowledge her as our high queen. Adohan's father and Seamus knelt before her, but I refused."

"Why did you refuse?" I asked him.

"Because —" There it was again. A blank stare into an abyss like he was missing a key memory from his past. However, he quickly composed himself, blinking a few times before resuming his tale. "I didn't believe her claim was just or her rule fair. Despite the fact that her magic was… and still is the only thing that can siphon the wilt, I didn't trust her to protect and care for her people as a ruler should." His shoulders hunched forward as he fisted his hair in his hand. "The Inner Kingdom suffers, and my people struggle under her reign. They are starved, frightened, oppressed. Living like this for far too long. The shreds of basic decency she shows them are viewed as divine kindness," he said in a low tone full of discontent. "A ruler should never have loyalty out of fear alone." Darkness crossed Daxton's face as he dove back into the suppressed memories that he fought so hard to forget.

I reached out to grasp Daxton's hands, his grip tightening around my fingers as he continued.

"It was only a few months after the endless battles and war against the humans and shifters when Minaeve assumed the throne despite Silver Meadows' refusal to support her claim. Minaeve called for a truce with my realm and asked for me to attend a meeting for all of us to strategize a defense against the wilt. Only it wasn't a meeting at all." Daxton cursed to himself under his breath as I quietly waited for him to continue, never once letting his hands fall from my own.

"I was young and fucking foolish. Naive to this role and responsibility, and to be honest, I was distracted. Since our mother's passing, and my father dying in my arms on the battlefield, I was also Castor's sole guardian."

I nodded, trying to encourage him to continue.

"But," Daxton rasped with a twinge of regret, "I was also arrogant. Believing that with my father's strength and title that passed to me, I was too powerful to succumb to anyone's will. I didn't recognize that Minaeve was setting a trap. She drugged me with a potent weaponized iron dust. That, combined with the help of her siphoned magic from Seamus and Adohan's father, left me outmatched. I was Imprisoned beneath Aelius until I willingly swore fealty to her crown and offered her my magic."

The depth of Daxton's revulsion for Minaeve was coming to light. He resisted her tyranny, and as punishment, she tortured him. "How long? How long were you kept a prisoner in her hold?"

"Years." He tensed as he leaned backward on the bed, his features cast in both shadow and sorrow.

"Zola," I said remembering the mention her loyalty to their mother, "did she help look after Castor when…?"

"Yes, and I will forever be grateful for her aid in watching over my brother when I couldn't."

Silence passed between us, the tales of Daxton's past clutching the threads of my heart and threatening to shatter it to pieces.

"I would still be there if she hadn't threatened Castor's life and the salvation of Silver Meadows. I would give anything to protect my people. It's my duty and honor, with the power I inherited, to ensure they're safety." There wasn't a single piece of me that doubted his confession. "So, when my kingdom was threatened and Castor's life hung in the balance, I was forced to accept her rule." He threaded his fingers with mine, trying to steady himself. "I still have night terrors from my imprisonment, and unfortunately, every century, I'm forced to relive them all over again."

"Does the queen —" I stopped, swallowing a pain that cut me so deep it was hard to breathe.

"During my offerings, and then when it's time for the trials…" Daxton became deathly still, his hands clutching mine. "I'm forced to sleep with her, yes." The pain of his confession struck my core, my soul aching in ways I never knew it could. "It's her revolting way of attempting to control every gods-damned thing in my life." He turned away, and I knew there was a wall of shame keeping his gaze hidden. "She'll make a public spectacle of our submission at the gathering before the trials begin. Since I've recently bedded her, I pray to the Gods I won't have to do it again. Seamus is more than happy to fuck his queen; he should be able to appease her appetite."

I now understood the depth of Daxton's rage when I mentioned his kiss with the queen in Solace. My own wrath began bubbling to the surface at the thought of Minaeve with Daxton, but I forced myself to shove that ugly jealousy aside. He was forced to sleep with her, and the knowledge of that damn near broke my heart.

We both carried such horrific pain and suffering. It was hard to fathom how either of us was still breathing—let alone surviving.

"And Adohan?" My chest tightened with putrid disdain for Minaeve. Forcing this treatment upon her people so she could absorb their powers was wrong. There was nothing about her that seemed right, in my opinion.

"He's mated. Thankfully, she will not command him to bed her since it's taboo to force a mated High Fae to do so. But she'll expect his submission and an offering of his magic."

"Daxton," I said his name softly, hoping he would be able to bring himself to look at me. To my dismay, he stared off into the darkness, lost in a never-ending well of spiraling shame and sorrow. "What can I do?"

If Daxton could manage to combat his living fears, then so could I. Maybe not alone, but possibly together, we would be strong enough.

"You, Spitfire —" He braced himself on the edge of the frame before daring to meet my gaze. "You don't need to do anything more than you already have. You've given me a reason to hope again. I was *dying* inside before I met you, with no end in sight to the life I was forced to lead. You're my salvation, Skylar. Always challenging me to keep fighting despite the odds. If you can manage to defeat your demons, then I know that I can, too."

I slid closer toward him, settling between his legs once more, and encircling my arms tightly around his neck. I threaded my hands into his free-flowing hair, pulling him close. A deep, sensual humming sang through my body as he sank into my arms, molding his frame perfectly around mine. My animal's power surging to the surface in response to my proximity to this magnificent male.

Power pulsed between our bodies as we molded together like two halves of a whole. Daxton's hands tentatively glided over the curves of my hips before resting on the small of my back. I clutched onto him, reveling in his embrace, trying desperately to comfort him like he always did for me. His arms moved to encircle my middle as my legs straddled his waist.

Even still, I needed him closer. I craved his touch like a drug, and I couldn't stop my memories from racing toward the kiss we shared on the bow of the ship. I raised onto my knees to cradle his head against my chest, feeling him sink into my embrace and desperately grasp onto me with everything he had.

"You're so brave, Daxton," I whispered, resting my cheek on his brow. "Every day, you somehow manage to stop the world from crumbling around you. Always sacrificing yourself for the sake of others. You inspire resilience in the face of fear and never stop defending those you care for." I spoke the words I knew he needed to hear. What I knew and believed in my heart to be true. "I see through your mask of Silver Shadow, I see *you*, Daxton Aegaeon."

He took a deep breath as his hold on me constricted. "I'm sorry," Dax mumbled against my chest, catching me by surprise.

"What for?"

"I'm sorry I offended you earlier today." He gripped my hips tighter, his fingers digging into my sides, refusing to let me go. I could feel the tension and angst through his touch, and it worried me.

"What do you mean?" I managed to pull back, searching for an explanation hidden in his unspoken words.

"I know I disappointed you when I spoke about Silver Meadows," Dax said. "I *never* want you to feel like a prize or a trophy, Skylar. When you win the first trial, I want to bring you to Silver Meadows, not because you were victorious, but because I want to share my home with you."

I bent to gently kiss his cheek just above his hidden dimple. "I would love to see your home."

It meant the world to me that Daxton had recognized my reaction from this morning. But there was still an unknown truth wedged between us that made me hesitate.

What were they discussing before I entered the gathering this morning? What didn't I know?

Daxton grinned softly as he tilted his head to look at me, his hands caressing my back until they rested comfortably on my waist.

"What is it?" he asked as his smile evened out into a thin line of concern.

Curse him. How did he know?

"I don't want there to be any secrets between us, Daxton," I confessed. "I want to …" *Shit.* I didn't understand exactly what I wanted with him, but I knew I needed honesty to begin figuring it out.

Daxton shifted backward, giving me his undivided attention. "Ask."

I bravely swallowed the fears that were holding me back. If I could survive my night terrors, torture, and betrayal, then I could do this. Right? It made sense. I just had to take the leap and try.

"What were you talking about today with Adohan and Castor just before I arrived?"

Dax tensed, moving me from his lap and swinging his feet over the side of the bed. He gripped the edge of the mattress, his fingers digging into the sides with ice forming at his fingertips.

"What don't I know? What would be a burden on me if I knew?" I paused for a moment, allowing my questions to sink in. "Daxton, I need to understand what's going on."

"Spitfire." His voice trembled as he spoke. "I-I can't tell you. Not right now."

"Dax!" I sighed with frustration. I couldn't believe he was admitting to hiding something from me.

"I can't," he exclaimed as he turned, his brows pinched, creases forming in his forehead. He was fighting against the urge to tell me, and I knew this was not an easy decision for him to make. "Please … Please, Skylar. I'm asking you to trust me. I know you have every reason and right in the world to demand this answer from me, but I'm begging you to wait." His breathing quickened. "I promise, when the time is right, I'll tell you." He moved to kneel on the floor beside me, looking up at me with a desperate plea in his eyes. "Don't ask this of me right now. Please," he said again.

"I won't be able to deny you the truth if you ask me again." He bent his head forward, resting it on my knee.

This is it, I told myself. Would I take the leap of faith and trust him, or would I retreat inside myself and go at this alone?

My heart raced as my animal surged inside my middle, responding to Daxton's trembling nerves. Then an important lesson I learned long ago from Magnus surged into my mind.

A pack is stronger together. Someday, Sky, you'll find someone that you can truly rely on. Someone you can trust with your life. My advice to you, my daughter, is to never let them go. They're a gift from our creators, and regardless of who they are or where they come from, they are family. They're ... pack.

My pack.

Like me, Daxton wasn't a shifter, but he was someone I trusted. Someone I cared for. Someone I—

Gods, there it was again. That warm, tingling feeling inside my chest, and I knew what my response would be.

"I trust you, Daxton," I said tenderly, running my fingers through the free-flowing hair at the base of his neck.

He lifted his gaze to find mine and sighed with relief as he kissed my hands. "Promise me that you'll ask again when the time is right ... and I swear I'll tell you. Trust me. There isn't anything I wish I could do more." I could sense he was teetering on the edge of telling me right then and there, but he kept his secret locked away—for now. "Another time, ask me again?"

Me asking a question? Was he seriously nervous about that? I coyly grinned, leaning forward. "That's practically a guarantee, Princey."

Daxton smiled as he pulled back, adjusting his weight so he was kneeling upright at my eye level. I tentatively licked my lips, turning the bottom one in and biting it, fighting the longing to taste his again.

Daxton's eyes became heavy with something stronger—perhaps even deeper than pure lust or carnal need. My breathing quickened as heat surged through my middle.

He planted his strong, muscular arms on either side of me and spoke in a low rough voice. "You seem to have something else on your mind right now, Spitfire."

"That a guess? Or is it something you know?" I teased, aware that he could detect the scent of my arousal that was steadily rising under the heat of his gaze. "You know it's not fair, right?"

"What is?" Daxton asked, never taking his eyes off the lip I was biting.

"You have your magical shield, barrier thing, up. I can't sense anything changing from your scent."

Daxton playfully raised his brows and grinned. "Do you want to?"

"I—" This was dangerous territory. Did I want to do this? Was it wise to cross this line with him?

"Well?" His voice dropped even lower as he pushed forward onto his hands, towering his muscular frame over the top of mine. A body that was perfectly designed by the Gods themselves, carved to perfection in every way possible.

This male would be my undoing.

"What do you want, Skylar?" His words were laced with a heated passion that caressed my skin without him ever having to touch me. Through the open collar of his shirt, I could see the muscles on his bare chest flex as he shifted forward, his mouth hovering inches from the base of my neck. "Tell me what you want."

I was done for.

"I want you," I said, my chest rising and falling in rhythm with my thundering pulse. "I want to experience blissful pleasure to counteract this pain. I want to forget about the darkness... my fears, and just be here—with *you*."

Daxton released a low affectionate growl that reminded me of a purr. "I'm at your disposal, Spitfire."

Rough hands ravaged the curves of my body as Daxton's lips latched onto the base of my neck, lightly scraping my skin with his teeth. I moaned as he kissed the most sensitive places he could on a shifter's body, where we would mark our mates with a bite, forever scarring the skin.

His hands migrated to fondle my breasts, as his fingertips played with my nipples, causing them to harden into firm points. I reached under his shirt to feel his chiseled muscles with one hand while I clutched the base of his neck with the other. Daxton's mouth released my neck and eagerly found my lips, taking control and swallowing our shared moans of pleasure.

Holy—Gods. He was the most delicious thing I had ever tasted. His lips reminded me of the sweetest dessert, paired with a fine wine that I couldn't seem to get enough of. I pushed my hips forward, angling them just right to align with his hardening length as our kiss deepened. It felt like he was starving, and I was the only thing that would satisfy his ravening hunger.

I opened my thighs, wrapping my legs around his waist as he thrust forward, grinding his erection into my apex that was throbbing with need. My sheer skirt and his thin training pants created a practically non-existent barrier, allowing me to feel every inch of him. Daxton pressed his hard length against me, moving his hips in a mind-altering rhythm that ignited a pulsing need in my center. I rolled my hips in sync with his thrusts, desperate for the friction created between our thriving bodies.

To my surprise, my animal responded with her own wave of desire that pushed me over the edge of my control, driving me wild. This was different from Gilen. Different from anyone I had ever been with. It was almost like she was giving her approval for Daxton to claim us and fill us with his seed. *Fuck*. I was desperate, the need to have him inside me becoming almost uncontrollable.

He moaned against my lips, and I was frantic to do anything to hear that sound emerge from him again. Daxton then paused, pulled back for a brief second, and suddenly, I sensed it.

"Dax!" I gasped as I inhaled the scent of his arousal for the first time.

It was the most delectable aroma I had ever encountered. It carried me away, like I was running free through the forest mountains with luscious pine trees surrounding me on all sides. I was wild ... free. His arousal drove me into a heated frenzy, and my animal responded with her own flush of power and excitement.

Daxton gave me a wickedly playful grin as his mouth devoured mine once more. This time, the kiss intensified as I parted my lips for him to taste me fully. Our kisses driven by deep seeded hunger that surpassed all reason. I tilted my hips, aligning the head of his cock perfectly between my thighs.

"Fuck. Spitfire," Daxton growled with a heavy voice laced with desire.

My body burned with intense need. And I knew I wanted all of this ... with *him*.

Daxton was the epitome of everything I had ever hoped or dreamed of finding. I trusted him, and I knew he trusted me. We had formed a bond together before ever expressing one physically—and I knew, even though I had fought against even admitting it … I knew I was falling for him.

He moved to reach for the bottom of his tunic and quickly pulled it over his head. I sat back in awe, fawning over the sculpted physique that towered over me. I couldn't help reaching out my hand to trace over the tattooed design that adorned his left shoulder, ending on the mark I made from my arrow the first night we met.

Daxton closed his eyes, his head tipping back as my palms glided across the taut muscles of his chest and shoulders. As I followed the ink over his pec, down toward his rigid abdominal muscles, and then lower still, a low sensual gasp escaped his lips. My fingertips tracing over the V in his hips that pointed toward his pulsing cock that was angled directly at me.

I desperately craved to feel the weight of his naked body pressed on top of mine. The thought alone made my center throb with anticipation, as my desire for him only intensified.

Daxton eagerly helped remove my shirt, lifting it over my head as my hair cascaded over my shoulders. His heated gaze lingered on my body as the intense stare in his eyes silenced any doubts about his desire for me.

He was staring at me like I was a masterpiece. Like I was something he had only dreamt of and never imagined he would get the chance to see. I knew this because it was the same way I was looking at him. Daxton bent to kiss me deeply once more, before he slowly pulled away. His hooded eyes dropped to the bindings on my breasts as I reached back to unhook the clasps. I watched as the hunger inside his gray stormed eyes shone with intense longing and anticipation. His throat bobbed as his breathing quickened while he waited for the fabric to fall away.

"Are you going to just tease me?" he asked before turning those alluringly gorgeous eyes back up to meet mine. The intensity of his stare stole my breath away. I bit my bottom lip and purposefully stalled my fingers from untying the strap that would unveil my breasts.

My High Prince of Silver Meadows flashed me a sinister grin. "You're truly ... a wickedly cruel female. Taunting me like this." His smile widened as a dimple appeared along his cheek. "Spitfire ..." My apex throbbed as he purred my nickname in a husky, lustrous voice.

"Whatever do you mean, Princey?" Slowly I unlatched the final hook and tossed my bindings aside. Dax didn't bother to say anything more. There was no need for words right now.

He pushed himself on top of me and pinned me onto my back. Sprawling me across the bed, Daxton took one of my breasts firmly in his grasp while dropping his head to take my other pebbled peak into his mouth. I arched my back as intense waves of mind-altering pleasure washed over me. He slowly sucked on my nipple, worshiping my body with his lips and the tips of his sharpened canines, building me up higher and higher. He migrated over to the next breast while his free hand moved toward my soaked entrance that was begging for his attention. Daxton's fingers reached under my waistband to stroke my sex, and my body began shaking with pure delight.

Daxton stilled and adjusted his positioning, releasing my hardened nipple with a popping sound that made him grin. I eagerly took advantage of the space between us and reached down toward the fastening on his pants. Dax tensed as my fingers worked the strings, keenly aware of what we were about to do.

I was ready for this, but it didn't stop a wave of nervousness from crashing to the surface.

Daxton sensed my second of hesitation, reaching out to intertwine our fingers before bringing them to his lips and gently kissing each one.

"You're nervous," he said as a fact and not a question. I gazed at the breathtakingly gorgeous male in front of me. His naked torso taunting me to reach out and lick my tongue over every peak and valley I could find. Gods...I could spend all night just kissing him.

"Spitfire?" he said, adjusting his weight so he was hovering over me.

"I haven't ..." I wasn't overly excited to admit or have *this* conversation right now. But ... Gods be damned. "I-I've never had sex before. I'm—"

Dax silenced my rambling with a passionate, all-consuming kiss that made my toes curl. He pulled away and I barely remembered what I was saying seconds before. "Have you ever been pleasured to orgasm by someone other than yourself?" Dax asked as he continued trailing kisses along my jawline before nibbling on my earlobe.

"No," I rasped, my insides melting from the glorious sensations of his lips on my heated flesh. Gilen had been close, but no. I hadn't before.

"Perfect," he whispered as he nibbled on the base of my neck once more, lightly scraping his teeth while he pinched my nipple between his fingers. The intense surge triggered from both areas combined into a passionate wave of heat that had my apex soaking with need. "Then that's where our journey together will begin."

Daxton moved to kneel above me, his eyes deep and heavy with desire. "You have no idea how long I've dreamed about tasting you, Skylar. *All* of you ..."

Holy shit. My undergarments were officially soaked through. Daxton tilted his chin and sniffed the air. A low possessive growl of approval combined with his amused devilish grin sent butterflies flying in my stomach.

Gods, above... This male was going to devour me. And I couldn't fucking wait.

Daxton slid backward, hooking his fingers into the waistband of my skirt, slowly sliding down the length of my legs, casually discarding everything onto the floor. He had seen me naked before, but this was different. He appeared mesmerized, with a glossed-over expression that made me feel like I was the most breathtakingly beautiful creature he had ever seen in his immortal life.

A wave of embarrassment overtook me, as I moved to try and cross my legs. "No," Daxton commanded, reaching out and grasping my knees. "Don't hide the beauty of your body from me, Spitfire. You're the most gorgeous female I have or will ever lay my eyes upon. And I intend to taste every inch of you before the night is done."

He moved my legs apart, lowering himself to feast on the apex between my thighs. I flung my head back and gripped the bedsheet as his tongue flicked and vibrated against me.

It felt *so* good. I thought I would pass out from the pleasure, but instead, it only continued to build. I raised my hips and widened my knees, granting him a better angle to continue devouring me. Giving me the most intense build-up of pleasure I had experienced in my entire life.

That was, until he began using his fingers.

First, it was one. Then slowly, two as his mouth continued to work its magic on my clit. He released his hold on me with his lips, stroking his tongue across my sex as he thrust his long, thick fingers deep inside me.

"Oh, fuck! Daxton!" I moaned, my hips bucking up from the bed and my body shaking from his touch and delicious mouth.

I was teetering on the edge. I didn't know if I could take much more. Daxton slowed and devilishly grinned at me from between my thighs.

"Please … don't stop, Dax. Please," I begged.

"Do you enjoy it when I devour you like this, Spitfire?" He swirled his fingers, applying pressure with his thumb where his mouth was only moments before. "Because I would remain here… between your legs forever if I could."

"Oh, my—" I rasped. "I need more. Please, I'm so close. Daxton, don't stop."

"We'll get to that soon, Spitfire. I want to make sure you're ready when it's my cock and not just fingers that are soaked with your release."

I shuddered as he plunged his fingers back inside me, careful not to give me more than I could handle. It didn't take long for me to adjust to him, and then I was quivering, desperately yearning to find my release.

"Good," he growled as he continued fucking me with his hand.

"Yes!" I screamed as my body stiffened. I threw my head backward, spreading my thighs wider so he could have access to every part of me.

Dax bent down once more, replacing his thumb with his mouth, sucking on my clit with his fingers slickened from my arousal. I had never felt such intense pleasure in my entire life, the friction of his touch creating an intoxicating high. This male was everything, and gods ... he was good with his mouth

"Gods, you taste so fucking delicious. Just like I knew you would. Just like I dreamed you would."

My release was winding up like a spinning top, threatening to burst apart at the seams. With his free hand, Daxton reached up and roughly grasped my breast. It was almost too much. I was on the verge of shattering in his hands and desperately needing to come. I lifted my head and saw that Daxton's eyes were open, watching me soar with the pleasure that he was giving.

I was done for.

"Daxton!" I gasped and cried out as the most intense orgasm of my life barreled through me.

I could feel the walls of my center tighten around his fingers as he slowly pulled them away. He gently kissed the insides of my thighs before moving to my hips, stomach, and neck. Not stopping until he found my lips once more.

This kiss was different from the ones we shared earlier. It was slower, filled with intent and a deeper connection that I could no longer deny. I wrapped my arms around his neck, pulling him closer as I molded my naked, trembling body around his. Daxton turned onto his side, delicately running his hands across my exposed flesh. Tantalizing me with his touch, his tender caress forming goosebumps across my skin.

I didn't want this to end. I didn't want him to ever leave.

"Will you stay with me tonight, Dax?" I bravely asked, pulling back.

The High Fae prince took my chin between his fingers and possessively bent to kiss me once more. "The threat of the entire population of fallen creatures couldn't pull me away from you tonight, my Spitfire," he said with a satisfied grin that exposed the dimple on his right cheek. "I'm yours."

I kissed that masked dimple, following his lead as he turned me around to tuck my backside into his front, encircling me within his strong arms.

I was very aware that I was still naked, but it didn't bother me. In fact, I enjoyed the thought of nothing but Daxton covering me tonight. I shifted and pressed my back up against him, feeling his hard shaft pulsing against me through his pants.

I tilted my head up, giving him a questioning look. "Don't blame me for being attracted to you," he teased. "Tonight, however, was meant just for you, Skylar. I hope I was a decent enough distraction this evening?" Daxton asked as he leaned to kiss my brow.

"*More* than decent," I said as I reached back to pull his lips to mine. His hand moved to grasp my breast, and I could tell by the hardness of his erection that he was enjoying this almost as much as I was.

"Sleep, Spitfire," Daxton commanded with a heavy tone, biting his lip to try and remain focused. "I won't leave you tonight. I promise." He grabbed the sheet, pulling it over us both and snuggling in to hold me once more. I struggled to keep my eyes open as he pulled me in tight against his chest. "Sleep," he instructed once more. "Together, we'll help keep both our nightmares at bay."

I nodded and nuzzled into the nook of his arm. Daxton's presence granted me the feeling of safety, something I doubted I would ever find in this lifetime. I closed my eyes, and for the first time since my capture by the hunters, I found a peaceful, restful night's sleep.

Chapter Six

"**K**eep trying, Spitfire," Daxton encouraged. "You were able to form a barrier with your magic when Seamus was invading your mind. Try to focus like that again and create a shield around yourself. It will help protect you from other forms of magic and detection."

"But that was instinct," I murmured. "I wasn't thinking. I was just … reacting."

Daxton propped himself on his elbow and cocked his eyebrow at me. "It doesn't mean you give up. Try again."

"How?" When he didn't reply, I grunted in frustration at his stubborn silence. "Fine, I'll *try* it again."

"There she is," he said with a saccharine grin that I knew I could never be angry at for long.

Dax and I awoke well before dawn, and although we hadn't left my bed, we were still relentlessly working on accessing my magic. He told me that all I had to do was *will* my magic to perform a new task. My powers should adapt and change if I was stubborn enough to see it through. Easier said than done.

My magic thrummed through me, trickling along my middle like a babbling brook, where my animal's presence always seemed to spring from. Luckily, the task of summoning my magic was not difficult, and Dax said that this was the trickiest part. Well, for him it was anyway. I just couldn't seem to figure out the connection of pulling from my well and altering the intent of it. Shifters were not trained to manipulate their magic like this, but I had to adapt. If I wanted to survive in the Inner Kingdom, I had to equip myself the best I could.

My will. My will, I repeated, and suddenly, it clicked.

Alphas utilized magic with their command, and lucky for me, I had some experience in that. With a new spark of determination, I called upon my power, imagining it coating my skin, creating a protective bubble around me that mimicked a shield of armor.

Daxton reached up and gently stroked the hair along my brow, allowing his finger to caress my neck as his lips followed suit. My eyes rolled back in my head, loving the feeling of his touch, longing for him to continue what we started last night.

He unexpectedly pulled away, and I snapped my eyes open to see his cocky grin. "You did it, Spitfire."

"What, really?" I sprang up with the biggest grin on my face as the sheet I was holding freely fell to my waist. Daxton's eyes widened, and I could see the hunger of arousal shine as his eyes roamed over me. I quickly remembered that I was naked and reached down to cover myself.

"Don't," he said, reaching out to pull me on top of him. "I'm very much enjoying this morning's view."

I straddled Daxton's hips, planting my hands on his firm chest, before running my finger through his tangled mop of silver and black hair. "Are you, now?" I teased as I bent lower to whisper in his ear. "It's hard to tell when you conceal *your* scent. You know … Shifters love utilizing our sense of smell. It heightens everything for us."

His grin widened enough for his dimple to make an appearance. "Very well then." Once his scent hit me, my body melted on top of his. I couldn't—wouldn't—resist the pull toward Daxton. The drive to be near him was practically instinctual. I followed his lead and lowered my barrier next., watching his eyes spark with lust as he recognized the change.

"You wicked ... breathtakingly beautiful female," he growled as he captured my mouth with his. Our kiss deepening as—

"Knock, Knock." The sound of Castor's voice put a halt to our kiss as he banged on the frame of my door. "I hate to interrupt, but we're leaving for Aelius within the hour."

Daxton grunted and tried to ignore his brother as I shifted my hips over the top of his hardened shaft. "You're not helping," he whispered to me as I giggled, and he nibbled on my ear.

"Says who?" I whispered as I turned to nip at his bottom lip. "This is all part of the fun." I gently kissed his cheek, moving onto the base of his neck. Daxton tensed as I pressed my hardened nipples into his bare chest, creating the friction I craved from last night. He firmly grabbed my ass and caressed my backside, moving his hips in rhythm with mine. Gods, this was amazing, and I hadn't even had my full taste of him yet.

"Daxton!" Adohan's voice joined Castor's.

Daxton growled with disdain this time as he held my hips firmly in his hands, halting my movements. "We're coming."

"Oh really?" Castor laughed half-heartedly. "Coming already?"

I chuckled and to my surprise, Daxton grinned as well.

"He's jealous. But, you do need to get dressed." Daxton looked me over, his lingering eyes burning with hunger to continue what we started. "And please, be quick about it. Or else—" he coughed to clear his throat. "I'm a patient male, but you're testing every ounce of my willpower." He paused and leaned in closer.

"Or else what?" I grinned.

"Or else I'll have to devour that sweet pussy of yours and have you screaming my name over and over again."

"Are you trying to convince me to get dressed?" I asked. "Because you aren't doing a very good job of it."

"Never," Daxton said with a twinkle in his eye. "But for now ... Unfortunately, yes, I'm asking you to get dressed."

"Fine," I huffed as I lightly kissed his lips. I could tell from his reluctance to pull away that he wanted this to continue just as much as I did.

"Also, conceal your scent," Daxton added, and like the good student I always was, I obliged. "It'll help."

I could tell he didn't truly believe it would, and it made me purr with delight, knowing I had the same effect on him as he did on me.

Wrapping the sheet around me and gathering my clothes, I moved toward the washroom. Pausing at the screen, I turned around and winked at him with a sly smirk, and Daxton returned my playful smile with one of his own, making my heart flutter.

"How are we traveling to Aelius?" I asked stepping to the other side of the divide. I heard something drop to the floor, and I noticed the flower hairpin that the merchant had given me yesterday in my pile of clothes.

"Idris didn't tell you?" Daxton hollered, still resting comfortably on the bed by the sound of it.

"No," I said as I reached out and placed the flower hairpin on the counter. I splashed water on my face to cool down and dabbed it dry with a towel.

"Then I'm not going to ruin the surprise."

I peeked around the corner of the screen as he flashed me a beaming grin. "Please?"

He shook his head. "Hurry along, Spitfire. The longer you take to get ready, the longer you have to wait to find out."

I narrowed my eyes, to try and intimidate him into answering me, but it didn't work.

"Fine," I cursed under my breath as I returned to the washroom to finish getting ready.

I found new undergarments and fresh travel clothes neatly folded in the corner near the screen. Like magic, they appeared out of nowhere, and I knew Dax had summoned them for me. I playfully wondered if he could magically remove clothing just as easily as he could summon it.

"Remember … don't drop your barrier," Daxton called out, and I immediately refocused on concealing my scent with my magic.

I pulled on my leather pants paired with a fitted long-sleeve tunic and corset, which was surprisingly comfortable. I tucked my hairpin into a pocket next to my chest, making sure it was secure for the journey to Aelius. There was a thick cloak lying next to the stool, and I hesitated before picking it up.

"Isn't it a little hot to be wearing this?" I asked as I held up the cloak and walked out of the washroom. Then, as I turned the corner, I was met with a sight that took my breath away.

Daxton was leaning against the doorframe, patiently waiting for me to return with his shirt casually flung over his shoulder. It only took him a second to notice me gawking at him, but when he did, a serene smile curled at the side of his luscious lips. Desire flooded through me like water bursting through a river dam.

I couldn't help it, and to be honest, I wasn't sure I wanted too anymore. Daxton tilted his head, holding out a hand to encourage me to cross the distance separating us.

Gods, was this real? Did last night actually happen? I wasn't just imagining this all in my head, right?

I strolled across the room toward Daxton, linking my hand with his and leaning into his open arms. With his free hand grasping my waist, I looped my other arm behind his head as he tucked our linked fingers toward his chest. He might have a dozen fancy titles and nicknames, but my personal favorite was *Dax*.

"Your riding leathers fit you perfectly," Daxton said as he caressed the smooth leather along my outer thighs, admiring my curves in a way that made me feel treasured.

"So, we're riding! Ah-ha!" I grinned wildly, discovering a clue as to how we were traveling to Aelius.

Daxton huffed a laugh and bent to kiss me, practically lifting me off my feet with the touch of his lips on mine. "I named you well, my Spitfire."

The lock on the door suddenly turned, and our secluded retreat from the outside world came crashing down. The door swung open with Adohan and Castor impatiently waiting on the other side.

"You'll need this," Castor taunted, extending his hand with Daxton's cloak and a new shirt hanging from his fingertips. "Remember, this isn't the nudist shifter colony of Solace. You're expected to be clothed when you're around others outside your bed chamber."

Daxton grunted with discontent as he released his hold on me, donned his shirt, and pulled his cloak over his shoulders.

"I see you taught her to mask her scent, at least," Castor snipped. "That's a relief because I can only imagine that I would be able to smell you all over her, brother. You might want to try and do the same before anyone else confirms what's already suspected."

Daxton shielded his scent, unable to stop the grin that curved at the side of his mouth as he winked at me. "In a mood today already, Castor?"

"Hardly," Castor answered as he crossed his arms and slouched against the wall.

"We've all had the pleasure of his unpleasant company this morning, and it still hasn't improved despite my efforts," Adohan said.

There was something different about Castor, but I couldn't figure out what it was. He wasn't his normal chipper self, and a mild mockery from him about what he and Adohan had clearly interrupted this morning was off-putting.

"Everything all right with you, Castor?" I asked with genuine concern.

"I'm fine," he muttered as he waved away my worries and stuffed his hands into his pockets. "Zola already left with the fallen female."

Daxton nodded. "Good. I instructed her to depart before us so she could slip away without anyone knowing."

Castor pursed his lips. "You couldn't have told me that?"

Daxton paused and sighed, scratching the back of his head, "I-I didn't think about it, Castor. I'm sorry. Zola is returning to Silver Meadows. You'll see her again soon."

Castor grunted and looked off toward the open walkway. "You know how difficult it is, Dax. Of all people … you should know better." Castor closed his eyes and stepped away from us. "I need a minute."

Daxton grasped his brother's shoulder before he left and met his gaze. I could see Daxton was conflicted about the decision, but I was unsure about how it affected Castor. Dax nodded to his brother in silent understanding. "We'll meet you at the stables."

Adohan gave Castor a pat on the back while I was left standing there with my hands on my hips, clueless as to what was going on. Nothing, and I mean nothing, seemed to get under Castor's skin. What the hell was going on with him? Daxton tilted his head for me to follow them.

"But—" I started to protest.

"I'll be fine, Skylar," Castor said, pausing before rounding the corner. "I'll be along in a moment. That'll give Dax and Adohan a chance to explain the ruse you and I will be orchestrating once we arrive in Aelius."

"Wait … ruse? What ruse?" I repeated, narrowing my brows as Daxton and Adohan began walking in the other direction. I dashed after them and sprang in front of Dax, stopping him in his tracks by poking him square in the chest. "All right. Time to talk. We were up all morning practicing my shielding, and you didn't think to mention a *ruse*?"

Adohan held back a sneering laugh, trying not to seem overly amused. "I never thought I would see the day Silver Shadow would allow someone to stop him with the might of a single poke."

Dax grunted in annoyance and narrowed his eyes at the Crimson City high prince. "I believe Idris is already impatiently waiting on you, my friend. Don't you have somewhere else to be?"

"Low blow, Daxton. Low … blow." Adohan scowled but managed to flash me a confident grin as he passed us by.

I turned back to Dax and gave him a look, which meant I was serious and that nothing he could do was going to make it go away this time. "What is Castor talking about, and what parts do he and I have to play?"

I didn't like this one bit.

"Talk." I poked him again.

"All right, all right." Dax grasped my wrist and pulled me to his side. We continued walking together through the halls with his arm draped around me. "You'll arrive alongside Castor today, and tonight … you'll attend the ball as his companion. You two will create the illusion that you are a pair."

"*What?*" I exclaimed as I cocked my brow at him. "That—What? Why?"

"It's to protect you," Dax said swiftly in defense.

"Protect me? From what?" I was already entering the 100 percent failure rate trials. My life was already hanging dangerously in the balance. What more did he have to protect me from? Then it dawned on me. "Queen Minaeve?" Daxton's nod was all the answer I needed.

After what I learned last night, I felt sick speaking her name out loud. I'd disliked her before, and after hearing everything she did to Daxton and the other royals—let alone her people—I despised her even more.

"But why? Why do I need to be protected against her?" I still didn't understand, and I needed him to elaborate on his reasoning.

Daxton stopped and gave me a soft half-smile as he reached to push a strand of hair out of my eyes. His hand lingered on my cheek as I leaned into his calloused palm. I reveled in the roughness of his hands when they touched my skin. He wasn't just some highbrow royal with a title. He had fought and earned everything he had in this life, and it made me admire him more for it.

"Do you really have to ask that question, Spitfire?"

I could assume that Daxton's own emotions mirrored everything I was feeling, but I had been burned by that blind belief before. I didn't want that to happen again. "Why?" I asked.

"If Minaeve discovers that I've grown fond of another … she'll use you to manipulate me or worse, threaten to harm you. Champion or not." Daxton's brows pinched together. "At the end of the day, all she cares about is her crown and power. Anything that stands in her way she cuts down without a second thought. I don't want to test the limits of her self-control. My feelings for you threaten her hold over me and Silver Meadows. I won't forgive myself if I'm the reason anything happens to you."

Feelings for me?

"Do you believe she would have me killed if she found out?" I didn't necessarily want to ask the question, but I couldn't help it. I needed to know everything before entering the Aelius court.

"She would try," Dax growled. "And she would fail. But I don't want to take unnecessary risks if we don't have to. Regardless of what happens to me, *you* will not be touched or harmed."

I squeezed his hand, demanding his attention. "You mean besides the trials?"

He sighed as the corner of his mouth curved to the side and he gave me a nod. "Once you defeat the first trial and we are out of Aelius, we can drop the ruse. Silver Meadows will be the safest place for you inside the Inner Kingdom."

"So, you're *fond* of me, huh?" I asked with a coy grin. It wasn't a full disclosure of his feelings, but I would take what I could.

He arched his brow and bent to kiss my cheek. "*Very* fond of you, actually."

All right, he added the *very*, which was helpful. I would accept it for now, but if and when I survived the trials, I'd ask him again, and perhaps I'd have my own answer as well.

"What're you scheming?" Dax speculated.

"Wouldn't you like to know?"

"I always want to know what you're thinking, Spitfire." He inhaled a deep breath near the base of my neck. "Your progress with your magic is remarkable. I imagine it's because you already had experience utilizing your healing powers." His lips brushed against my skin, causing my knees to wobble. "Sadly, though, I think it's backfiring for me. I can't pinpoint exactly what you're feeling when your barrier is up."

"Sucks, doesn't it?" I taunted as I playfully turned my head to stick out my tongue.

"Careful," Dax warned. "You remember what *my* tongue can do." I blushed and bit my lower lip. I knew exactly what it could do. "Then again," he said in a rasped voice, "I'm beginning to understand your subtle quirks and hints. I don't think you'll be able to deceive me for long." He shifted closer to me as I looked up into his luminous eyes.

I saw his desire threatening to break through the shield of self-control he kept as a facade for the rest of the world—but not with me. He was opening up and sharing who he was.

"I could argue the same thing," I said. Dax grinned softly as I reached up to pull on the base of his neck, longing for his kiss. "Dax," I said, tensing, "I'm entering the trials tomorrow and—"

"Shhhh." Dax steadied my nerves as he wrapped his arms around me. "Everything will be all right. We came up with this ruse because we believe you will succeed. I'm planning to see you enter and come out of the trials alive. In fact, I've already wagered gold coins in favor of you doing so."

"Against whom?"

"No one in particular."

"Do I get half the trove?" Daxton chuckled as he bent his brow to mine. "It's only fair, as I'm doing most of the work."

"It's only fair," he repeated.

"All right then," I said, swallowing my fear and lifting my chin with the confidence that Dax instilled in me. "Let's go."

"Good," he said, hesitating to release his hold on me. "We better hurry along before the others come looking for us."

"So, why Castor?" I questioned as we continued walking along the open walkway, the hot morning air slowly becoming sticky and thick.

Dax held my hand as he led me outside the confines of Adohan and Idris's home, meandering down the sandstone steps toward the stables. "Castor is known for his wandering eye and holds the reputation of stealing the hearts of young females. The ruse is that he has wooed you, and you are head over heels for him. That's what others will believe and won't question."

"But I—" I shook my head. I didn't think this was going to work. Hiding how I was feeling for Daxton seemed impossible.

"I also want him with you because, with his gift, he'll be able to detect any threats toward you when I can't be there."

"I see."

"It'll be difficult for me as well, Skylar," Daxton admitted as we continued toward the stables. He paused as he turned and looked up at me from below the steps. "I'll have to force myself not to rush to your side when you enter a room. Your beauty and ferocity undoubtedly will draw the attention of everyone around you, and I'll have to simply stand idly by and watch," Dax said with remorse. "I won't be able to smile as you catch me watching you out of the corner of your eye. I'll have to refrain from laughing at your witty remarks or even admiring the beauty of your curious mind as you ask a million and one questions to everyone you meet."

"Dax—"

He delicately brought my hand to his lips. "Whenever you see me tonight, please remember that I must become someone else. I won't be—"

"Well, there you two are!" Idris bellowed, interrupting our conversation. "All right, we're all set. Sky, I have the perfect mare for you to fly on. She's already saddled, and your pack with your things is strapped to her back."

"I—Wait, what? Did you say 'mare' and 'fly' in the same sentence?" I stammered for a moment.

"Of course!" Idris exclaimed. "Oh wait! I forgot to show you! Sorry, I hope you are all right with flying, cause that is the fastest way to get to Aelius."

"Flying … on?"

"Pegasi, of course."

My jaw practically dropped as Daxton wisely moved aside, allowing me to sprint around the corner to see the paddock of horses. No, excuse me—*winged* horses.

"I told you it was a good surprise," Dax said as I stared in awe at the magnificent creatures that were prancing and kicking up dry dirt beneath their hooves.

"Oh, my Gods!" I exclaimed. "They're magnificent, Idris!"

"My own herd," she said, beaming with pride. "Didn't think Adohan mated with a nobody, did you?" She winked. "My family has been caring for this pegasi herd for as long as I can remember. We've cared for and supplied Crimson City with these fearless mounts in battles for centuries."

"All right, so we're going to *fly* to Aelius then?"

"Yes!" Idris smiled as she walked over to a pair of black pegasi, holding the mare's reins out for me to take. "This is Nisha. She's one of the most graceful fliers I have, and I believe she'll be the smoothest ride for you."

"Well, hello there, Nisha," I said to the pegasus, who bobbed her head in reply. "Can they understand me?" I whispered to Dax, who went to greet his own midnight-black stallion.

"Yes," he answered. "They're very intelligent creatures, and although they don't speak like we do, they can communicate in other ways."

I held out my hand so the mare could smell me, releasing my shield for a second before turning it back on again. She whined and flipped her ebony mane, snorting and pawing at the ground with her hooves. I noticed Idris stopped to observe what the pegasus was doing but didn't intervene. I stood still, watching her pound the dry earth, kicking up dust before she released a loud, high-pitched sound that startled the rest of the pegasi in the paddock and the stables.

"What did you do, Spitfire?" Daxton asked as he tried to calm his own mount.

"I don't know. I let her smell me. I lowered my barrier for a second; that was all, I swear." Idris tried to calm her and Adohan's colts while Castor rejoined us and quickly jogged over to try to stop his painted mare from flying off into the sky.

Then, all of a sudden, Nisha raised onto her hindquarters and crashed onto her powerful front legs, breathing heavily yet remaining utterly still. My animal awakened inside me, bringing forth a wave of magic that flowed like liquid heat in my blood. I knew my eyes were glowing with the amber haze as I boldly met the mare's midnight-black stare. She snorted, gentler this time, and bent down onto her front legs. Lowering her head in a bow, she remained steady before me as the other surrounding pegasi did the same. Everyone stared at me with the same puzzled expression.

"Well, that's a first," Adohan commented to Idris.

"It must be her shifter half. The pegasi are led by a matriarchal society, but Nisha is still so young," Idris added. "What animal are you, Sky?"

I shrugged. "I don't know. Maybe my animal is a horse, and that's why they recognize me?" A spark of power ignited through my middle in response. "Or maybe not?"

"Well, they're calm now," Castor added. "We need to get going before Skylar riles them up again."

I moved my hand against the soft velvet coat of Nisha's shoulders, careful not to touch her delicate feathers. Swinging my foot into the saddle, I sat comfortably on my mare's back as she spread her midnight wings, preparing to lift us into the sky.

"Ready?" Daxton asked as his stallion trotted beside my mare.

"Absolutely," I answered as our mounts flapped their magnificent wings, running toward the fence and taking off to soar into the sky.

Crimson City was beautiful to behold from the air, just like it was from the ground. Adohan and Idris's red square-painted home in the center of the city was perfectly framed by their people's buildings and houses. It fanned outward for what seemed like miles on both sides, with the winding crimson river cutting through the various twists and turns of the streets, bringing water and life to their home. The main city center with all the shops Idris dragged Zola and me through was quiet in the early morning. Merchant owners were just beginning their day, with the fae lights flickering inside the buildings.

The vast desert covered with sagebrush and patches of smaller tree outcrops disappeared in a blur behind us. We flew in a streamlined pattern through the air with Idris leading the way, Castor and Daxton surrounding me in the middle, and Adohan bringing up the rear. The speed and grace of the winged horses were remarkable. They were ten times faster than traditional steeds that would run across the ground. These beautiful creatures never seemed to tire as they flew with the wild winds, changing course with the Inner Kingdom passing us below.

Idris pulled on her reigns, guiding her mount higher up into the sky as the rest of us followed suit, making our way through the clouds. "Why are we flying so high?" I asked to the wind.

"The wilt," Adohan hollered back. "This mountain area divides Crimson City from Aelius, the most infected region of the Inner Kingdom. It has progressed in the last century with the new decay appearing near the coast where you first arrived."

I glanced over my shoulder, toward the ground, and realized what Adohan was explaining. The map of the Inner Kingdom that Castor had drawn appeared in my mind, and I understood why flying was our safest route. From the northeastern tip, around the black sand beach, the wilt was encroaching on the borders of the town of Niamh. This was why Daxton teleported us directly across the bay so that we could avoid any dangers—that didn't happen, of course. But it only proved that the wilt was indeed growing.

It was growing … and somehow, I could also heal it.

It had almost killed me, though. My magic was not a solution to curing the wilt itself. Not now anyways.

I secretly hoped I would at least get to see the fallen fae before leaving, but Zola had already begun her journey back to Silver Meadows before I had the chance. A part of me knew it was likely for the best. I didn't even know what I would say or do when I saw her.

Castor had been watching over her, trying to find ways to communicate and help her in any way he could. They said she hadn't spoken a word since she was healed, and really, could anyone blame her? Who knew how long the wilt's magic infected her? Naturally, other questions came to mind as we flew amongst the clouds. Would my magic somehow flare to life in her presence? And the trials…

Oh Gods. The trials would begin tomorrow. It was one of those *Hello, Sky, did you not realize this was happening?* moments.

As we bobbed and weaved through the white puffs of fluffy air, my mare seemed to playfully kick at the clouds, almost like she was bouncing on top of them.

"I guess we all deserve a little fun, don't we," I said to her as I stroked the black velvety coat along her neck.

Gradually, a massive body of water appeared through the haze of clouds. "Sterlyn Lake," Daxton called out.

"The home of the water nymphs, right?" I asked, recalling the short but important lesson about the different types of creatures that lived in the Inner Kingdom.

Castor's pegasus came to my other side. "Yes. Nasty creatures, but they do have fascinating mating rituals that I encourage everyone to try for themselves." He flashed a cocky smile.

There he was. The good old sultry, borderline inappropriate, overly confident Cas was back.

"Personal experience?" I asked into the whistling winds.

Castor grinned. "Skylar … it's the only way to truly know."

I caught Dax shaking his head, but there was a lightness to his gesture that made me relax. "Is anyone safe from that wide charismatic net you cast everywhere you go, Castor? Do you ever come up empty-handed?"

"Never!" He melodramatically gasped for effect. "I would never dream of denying the ladies of the courts—or anywhere—the pleasure of my company. I must admit, I do miss the lack of clothing from Solace, Skylar. It was so much easier to frolic in the brush or a nearby shop when there was literally *nothing* in the way. Gunnar would have a field day in your shifter lands."

"Seriously, Castor?" I shook my head and couldn't help but laugh. "You do realize when we shift into our animal forms, we have to undress or else we shred our clothing? There are piles of clothes stashed away in various hideaways near homes, trees, or bushes."

"I know." And something told me he did. "It was quite the view in the meadow when all the ladies shifted, and then again when the alpha's son was yelling at you with nothing but—"

"Enough," Daxton bellowed at Castor, his jaw flexing at the mention of Gilen.

"One day," I said to Castor, "I bet that'll change for you. Mark my words … someday, someone will make your world stop, and you'll be powerless to resist them."

"*If* that happens, Skylar—and that is a very big *if*—I would lay the world and all I had and am at my chosen's feet—And I expect nothing less than perfection when it comes to understanding all the different ways I can please them. So, until that day arrives, I shall practice with any willing party."

"Practice?" I arched my brows.

"Practice makes perfect," Castor said as he kicked his pegasus to fly ahead.

"Castor is such a—" Honestly, there was no comparison when it came to Castor. He had a knack for blending in with whomever he was with while still being true to himself. It was impressive, to say the least.

"Castor is never shy," Dax said as we continued to fly over the lake. "His bravery shines through in his self-confidence, and it's one of the attributes I admire most about my brother. It's also one of the reasons he attracts the attention of so many nightly or, in some cases, daily companions."

"Not *all* females swoon over him," I said.

Dax released a trivial, vibrating chuckle. "Oh really?" He steered his mount closer to Nisha. "What attributes do *you* find attractive then, Spitfire?"

I glanced at Daxton and bravely decided to step on the cliff edge I had been teetering on since he pulled me from the waters on the green sand beach.

"I agree that Castor's confidence is appeasing, but personally, I'm attracted to a different type of bravery." I seemed to grasp Daxton's attention as he tilted his head in my direction, carefully listening. "I admire a male brave enough to treat their female as their equal. Someone who values them as a true partner in every aspect of their life. A male of my choosing would validate and encourage me to make my own choices while supporting me on my journey of navigating them. A true leader who not only inspires greatness but shows it in every aspect of his life. Someone I can depend on. Someone I trust with all my heart, and that trusts me the same."

I could feel my heart thundering inside my chest. I had no idea what I was doing or where I thought I was going with this, but there it was. Everything I said to Daxton was the Gods' honest truth. The feelings I was beginning to have for this male were real, and it was terrifying to admit to myself—let alone begin to speak them out loud.

What if I was wrong to assume his fondness for me went beyond my role as champion? What if Dax didn't feel the same way? What if I took this leap only to fall once again? And to top it off, what if I died tomorrow in the first trial?

I took a deep breath and dared to gaze at the male I believed I was beginning to fall for.

The way Dax looked at me just now made my world stop turning. There it was again, the glazed-over heart-melting look that swept me off my feet and warmed my middle. My animal stirred, emitting a gentle song inside my head. His gray eyes locked onto me with such wonder and hope.

"Have you had any luck finding a male that meets these unique qualifications?" Daxton asked.

"You know, they just don't make them like that anymore. If you find one, please let me know. I'm kind of on a tight schedule, though, with the trials, possible death, and the world collapsing—but no rush." I smiled as I watched him laugh at my joke.

"No pressure then," he said.

"None whatsoever." I winked as Dax flashed me a carefree smile that sparked a light of joy in my heart.

Chapter Seven

"There it is," Idris called out at the head of our traveling party.

The pegasi relentlessly carried the five of us across the Inner Kingdom without ever tiring along the journey. The pegasi were well trained and had the stamina of what seemed to be ten horses compiled into one body. I could feel Nisha surge forward, recognizing the change in landscape as we approached our intended destination. Aelius.

The palace of Aelius stood on an isolated spit of land surrounded by water from Sterlyn Lake on all three sides. As we descended through the clouds, an unsettling feeling began trickling across my skin. Similar to the warning I felt in the alley with Seamus, causing my senses to be on high alert.

Elevated towers on each corner of the palace were connected by a protective wall laced with spikes pointing skyward that stood well over thirty feet tall. The center of the massive structure overlooked the surrounding walls, with every rooftop decorated by ornate white paint against gray cobblestone and a black swirling outline. This place was an absolute fortress, complete with heavy metal gates guarding the only entrance or exit. A wide stone bridge walkway connected the royal residence to the sprawling city that surrounded the shoreline and continued into the rolling hills to the east.

Aelius was larger compared to Crimson City, with High Fae residing in homes that were stacked on top of each other near the center. From my mount in the sky, I could see shops on the bottom, with people living on the second, third, and even sometimes a fourth level of the structure above. While sandstone and other white or natural tan clay rock built Crimson City, Aelius appeared cleaner, almost crisp. Many of the structures were made of stone or wood decorated and painted white to match. It gave the appearance of perfection, or at least trying as best they could to do so. In the distance, a long winding road connected Aelius to the sea, where a harbor was posted with the sails of dozens of ships visible from the air.

I couldn't put my finger on it, but this kingdom gave me a rainy-day vibe. There was an underlying feeling of melancholy that seemed to be intertwined with the realm itself. Aelius reminded me of cold spring days in Solace, when I would snuggle into my loveseat with a good book because venturing outside into the downpour would be miserable. Even today, as we arrived, Aelius was shrouded in clouds, with rays of sunshine barely able to peek through the overhang.

We dove through the sky, first reaching the rolling pasture fields before circling back over Aelius. Even this late in the day, the city was awake, with countless citizens still gathering in the streets, decorating their homes with white banners that held three eight-pointed stars painted on the design in the middle.

I looked down at my champion mark and realized this was the same pattern. At first, only a few doors swung open with curious eyes peering up at us. I could hear shouts echo through the streets below as we soared over the towering buildings. Then windows burst open, and more people began gathering in the streets. Our presence igniting Aelius. High Fae citizens gathered in clusters at the shoreline and near the bridge to the palace, watching our descent onto the cobblestone path. Idris landed first, followed by the rest of us, as our pegasi finally tucked in their wings on landing.

"Thank you," I whispered as I stroked Nisha's neck. "You were amazing." She neighed in return and swished her head. I smiled, interpreting this as her saying you're welcome.

I glanced around the gathering crowds, stunned that there were almost too many for me to count. I held my breath as I peered in their direction, meeting the people of Aelius for the first time.

There was an array of hair colors paired with fair skin features amongst the crowd. Shades ranging from black to dark blond, with an impressive number of hazel and green eyes speckled among them. And surprise, surprise, they were all either handsome or beautiful, with an air of grace that seemed to flow with their movements. I swear, if I ever saw an ugly High Fae, that would be something to take note of.

Castor guided his mount next to mine and gracefully swung his leg over the front of his saddle. He came to my side and extended his hand to me. "Let's put your training to the test. Shall we?"

I gave him a confused glare before remembering the ruse we were supposed to be playing. I held my breath and stole one final look toward Daxton. He gave me a final reassuring nod before his mask reappeared, and Dax transformed into Silver Shadow. His expression lacked any softness as his jaw clenched and his eyes narrowed with an air of ice that would chill you to your bones.

Despite his facade, I could see the muscles in Daxton's shoulders tense as he cracked the knuckles in his right hand. He was anxious.

Silver Shadow took a deep breath in preparation for what was to come, and my heart ached to see him like this. His gaze was hard, like stone standing against a raging storm on the open seas. There was no trace of the magnanimous, carefree smile I loved. Standing before us now was the fearsome, hardened warrior of legend who led the High Fae armies into the war of Valdor five hundred years ago. The most powerful high prince ever born to the Inner Kingdom, Silver Shadow.

And ... Gods help me; he was captivating.

Others might turn away or cower from this vicious, ruthless side of him, but not me. I wasn't afraid. After witnessing him in spurts of battle, I noticed how he was always able to control his rage. Never teetering over the edge and into madness. This highlighted his ability to control his emotions and not abuse his power over others, which was something of note, in my opinion.

My people always respected power. It was our way of life, and Daxton's sang to me like a siren's call to a sailor at sea.

"Let the games begin," I said to Castor as I donned my mask of deception. I accepted Castor's hand and adoringly stood by his side.

Idris whistled to our mounts, and the pegasi flew off into the hills. "They'll return with the same tune. If you need your pegasus, they will come on that call."

"Good to know," I said.

I saw a grimace of concern flash across Idris's face as Adohan, her mate, stepped to her side. He looped his arm in hers and affectionately grasped her hands, kissing her before guiding her to stand at Daxton's left. I recalled Adohan's promise to Seamus to offer the queen his power, which made my stomach churn. They couldn't deny her this offering, and every ounce of my being hated Minaeve for what she was forcing them to do.

"Focus, Skylar," Castor whispered in a warning as he looped his other arm around my waist. "I won't bite ... unless you ask, of course."

I rolled my eyes as he smiled and winked at me playfully, trying to play his role.

"Does that usually work in your favor?" I asked, moving to stand closer to him, adding to the appearance of the closeness. Our proximity made my skin crawl, but I swallowed my unease and plastered on a brave face. I knew what Daxton was being forced to do, so I could at least manage this.

"Typically, I don't have to work *this* hard to charm a female," Castor said, his gaze never wavering from mine.

"What exactly do you do then?" I asked. "A simple bat of your chocolate eyes at someone from across the room ... and they're helpless? Falling head over heels into your lap and then your bed?"

"Well, not always my bed. Other areas suffice when one is not readily available." Castor grinned, flashing his elongated canines. "Then, I bite."

"Gods help us all, Cas." I flattened a palm to my forehead, trying to conceal my slight embarrassment at his unfiltered descriptions of his sexual conquests.

"You'll see, eventually," he said. "Most certainly not with you," I whispered. "I do value my head attached to my body, Skylar. I'm not an idiot. Even imagining you as a possibility would not end well for me."

I raised my brow with a smirk, biting my lips to conceal my amusement. He was referring to Daxton, and it made my heart flutter with excitement. There was no official claim Dax or I had to one another, but knowing that Castor would never follow through with his vividly animated suggestions made me grin with satisfaction.

"Let's move," Daxton ordered in a cold, flat command. It caught me off guard at first, but I had to remember that this was not the same person I had come to know. Silver Shadow was here with us … a hard, cunning, calculating warrior who would cut you down faster than you could blink. A deadly weapon of the High Fae queen that would eradicate his enemies without a moment's hesitation.

My heart raced as I watched Daxton march forward with his strong shoulders squared and his head held high. His hair was neatly pulled back, highlighting his square jawline and ebony-trimmed beard that framed his formidable, rugged features. He was the definition of a warrior prince. There was no doubting his role or place in this world in anyone's mind when they laid their eyes on him. And somehow, I had become someone he was *very* fond of. Memories of the other night flashed through me, causing me to sigh and my knees to weaken. *Gods above help me. This male would be my undoing.*

"Remember that I'm the one you're supposed to be fawning over, Skylar, love," Castor whispered so only I could hear him. I blinked and refocused on Castor, crimson flushing my cheeks. "Focus on small aspects of the truth when you're speaking to others within the Aelius court. Use that wild imagination of yours and play the part of *my* companion. It's not just you that could feel the wrath of the queen's jealousy if she knew about your other activities ... especially last night's."

I nodded. "Sorry, it won't happen again. I understand what's at stake."

"Good. I doubt you see the entire tapestry we're weaving, but I believe you know enough to get the picture."

I gritted my teeth and bit my lip as I shook off Castor's remark. I had to focus and buy into this ruse if we would survive an audience with the queen. It wasn't a guarantee she would harm me, but then again, I wasn't willing to test it if Daxton was cautious. Besides, whatever this was between us, I needed to push it aside for now. I needed to focus on my mission and why I was here.

The trials.

This was the seed of truth I needed to cling to while visiting the Court of Aelius and in the presence of Minaeve.

As the gates opened, Castor's eyes darted to the figure on the other side. "Shields up, love." He gently kissed my cheek before interlocking my hand with his and guiding us forward across the bridge.

Seamus.

I allowed myself a quick glance ahead at Daxton. Pure hatred flowed from his stare as Seamus simply stood at the entrance with a wide grin of satisfaction. I knew Seamus would be here, but it was still jarring to see him again. I was able to construct a basic shield to mask the scent of fear I knew I was emitting, but I didn't think it was enough to stop his magic from invading my mind if he touched me.

"So far so good," Castor said to me. "Now keep going."

As we walked together, each step seemed like a hundred. "Easier said than done," I whispered.

As we crossed through the gate, I realized that it was constructed entirely out of iron. My magic seemed to buzz inside my head as we entered the palace, and it made me wonder what else was lurking below this fortress.

"I'm pleased you've arrived safely," High Prince Seamus greeted us with a melodramatic bow, casting his arms out wide in a ridiculous sweeping motion.

As we entered the palace, I was taken aback by the ornate, elaborate decor surrounding us. Dramatic fae lighting and vibrant colors created illusory effects within the architectural features of the palace to make it seem like we were in another world entirely. Above our heads were ceiling frescoes depicting different floral designs that were all connected by entangling black vines. The vines themselves twisted into spiraling patterns with thorns protruding outward along the curves that gave the plant a deadly front. The feeling of unease spread through my limbs as I continued to stare upward at the paintings. My animal surged to the surface, comforting me as best she could, letting me know I was not alone.

"Please, follow me." Seamus's eyes snapped toward me with a far too interested glimmer, causing me to grip Castor's hand tighter.

"Easy," Castor warned me in a hushed murmur. "Follow my lead." He drew the attention of anyone in earshot of us and loudly announced, "Don't worry. We shall retire to our room together soon enough. I am more than willing to assist you in changing *out of* … and into your new attire for the ball."

Our room? Oh, right. I was supposed to be helplessly swooning over him. I quickly recovered and looked up at Castor with a fake girlish smile I had seen far too many females in my pack don over the years.

"How thoughtful of you, Cas. You're undeniably handy when it comes to unfastening all the buttons on these bindings." I reached up and tugged on his collar, releasing one of the hooks on his shirt to expose the skin at the base of his neck and tracing my fingers against his collarbone. "Just as long as I'm able to assist you as well."

It felt *wrong* to touch him like this, and I could see Castor sense my hesitation. He grabbed my hand from his neck and turned it around to kiss the back of it gently.

"Leave some things a mystery," he added, trying to help ease my discomfort. I didn't dare allow myself to glance in Daxton's direction.

Seamus scoffed at our interaction as his eyes darted to Daxton. "Your brother, it seems, has attracted the attention of yet another? However, I didn't know he favored the stench of dirt and grime. Pray tell, what is that other smell coming from her besides Castor's?"

"Burning cedar and the winds of the sky, obviously. It's typical of shifters to have an earthy scent mixed with the air of their homeland, or did you forget? Wait … no, my mistake." Dax laughed darkly. "You haven't ventured to the mainland since the veil. The queen's most loyal subject mustn't risk his well-being for the sake of others," Dax bit out coldly, looking away from where Castor and I stood together.

"Is there a chill of jealousy in the air?" Seamus stepped toward Daxton and narrowed his eyes with a speculating stare. "From your outburst in the alleyway the other day, I was almost convinced that it was *you* she would be on the arm of tonight."

"I'm at our queen's service, Seamus." Daxton turned his stone-cold glare toward the Aelius high prince. "You know she commanded me to protect the shifter as my ward and ensure her safe arrival. You bringing forth a tortuous memory that pushed her to the brink of insanity seemed to be doing the opposite. So, I defended my ward, and Castor comforted her in a time of need."

"How lucky for the second-born prince of Silver Meadows." Seamus scowled at us with his dark, skeptical eyes.

"Very lucky," Castor said as he pulled me in closer.

I played along, wrapping my arm around his middle and placing my hand over his chest. The act made my insides cringe because, well, this was *Castor*. But it also pained my heart knowing Daxton was standing there watching.

Seamus huffed a laugh. "This follows the trend of shifters and humans alike. They easily fawn over our beauty and forget the teeth that lay behind the cunning smile."

"I believe *that* is jealousy, Seamus," Castor taunted. "Is the queen tiring of you so quickly nowadays that you're seeking out warmth from another's bed? From what Dax and Skylar told me … you were moments away from trying to take her maidenhead before I was able to claim it for myself."

My cheeks flushed as I tilted my chin downward in utter embarrassment. I shifted my feet so I could move closer to Castor while conveniently digging the heel of my boot into his toes. I watched his jaw tighten as his gaze bent to meet mine.

Reaching up, I pulled on the base of his neck so his ear was close to my lips and whispered,

"Congratulations … you found the line. Don't cross it again." I kissed his jaw and caught a glimmer of understanding shine in his eyes. I was fine with playing this ruse, but boasting about taking my virginity was not something I was comfortable with at the moment.

"Careful with how you address me, Castor. I'm a *high* prince and the queen's favorite. You'll show me respect." Seamus pumped a wave of power through the room as he glared at Castor with a deep-seated hatred burning in the darkened depths of his stare.

"Can you please … lead us inside, High Prince Seamus," Idris chimed in, purposely stepping between the males and rubbing her rounded belly. "Some of us need to rest after such travel. I can feel the babe kicking, and I would greatly appreciate the time to recover before tonight."

Seamus stepped back, and his menace seemed to melt away with the presence of Idris. He acknowledged her with a genuine look of awe and dipped his head to her, which surprised the hell out of me.

"Yes, of course," Seamus said as he turned on his heels. He led us through a long hallway that opened into a beautiful foyer surrounded by a large grand staircase that divided the two different wings of the palace.

"What was with that sudden change of mood from Seamus?" I whispered to Castor.

"I forget how much you don't know sometimes, Skylar." He shook his head and sighed deeply. "High Fae children are, at times, difficult to acquire. It can take couples half a century to conceive, and everyone cherishes them. But a High Fae child born of a mated pair holds a special tier all on its own. They're precious—highly treasured. The child is typically born with special gifts or powers."

"I see," I said as we stopped at the base of the stairs. "Like you, Daxton, and the twins?" Castor nodded his head as we came to a stop.

Idris and Adohan's twin sons were able to manipulate fire as they could, and I could only assume there were other strengths or abilities they had as well.

Seamus paused on the steps, turned to us once more, and lazily leaned against the golden railing of the grand staircase behind him. He reached up and ran a hand through his tousled blond hair, clearly a fan of the messy, rolling-out-of-bed kind of style. He was cocky, arrogant, and he had an air of unpredictability that kept me on high alert when I was in his presence.

"Your rooms are located on the eastern side of the palace, as I'm sure you remember," he said to Castor and me. "Daxton and Adohan, you are summoned to Queen Minaeve's chambers in preparation for tonight's festivities."

This time, Castor gripped my hand, and I could see his jaw tighten with concern.

"Queen Minaeve," Daxton said, but Seamus silenced him with an upturned hand.

"She commands the presence of all the high princes of the Inner Kingdom. We will accompany her this evening like always. She insists we present a united front before those in attendance here at court tonight, in preparation for the first trial tomorrow."

No. I forced a blank expression, but on the inside, I was screaming. *No, no, not Dax. Not Adohan.* What was the queen intending to do with them? I shuddered, imagining the sick, twisted games she could play with the help of Seamus's magic.

Glancing toward Adohan, I saw he couldn't hide his dismay, nor could Idris. There was nothing they could do. He could not refuse their queen.

"I'll see you tonight, my mate." Adohan took Idris's hands and kissed them both before taking her lips with his own. The embrace was soft and tender with love and compassion beaming like a ray of light around them. Adohan then knelt and affectionately rubbed Idris's belly, kissing it softly before rising to find her lips once more. "I can't wait to see how beautiful you look in the gown you made for the occasion."

"You won't be able to keep your eyes off me," Idris quickly said. I could see the longing look of concern lingering behind Idris's brave illusion of confidence.

Adohan reluctantly released Idris's hands and ascended the staircase behind Seamus, followed by Daxton. I clutched onto Castor as tightly as I could. My legs shook as I watched our companions reluctantly march toward Queen Minaeve's chambers in the western wing. Each step they took forced them to retreat further into themselves and don the mask they needed to survive. They had to play the part of devoted subjects or else risk raising suspicion.

Seamus stopped at the top of the steps, leaning over the railing as he watched Daxton pass him. "She's especially anxious to see you … Silver Shadow." He had the audacity to chuckle and roll his head to the side, turning to glare at the three of us who remained on the main floor. "Pick whichever rooms suit your needs, Castor. The lower-level bedrooms on the other wing are all available."

Castor nodded, refusing to give any hint or sign of his displeasure that I knew was raging like a sandstorm beneath his calm, dark brown stare. His composure, like Daxton's, was utterly astonishing. My animal, on the other hand, was the opposite of calm. She was raging inside my chest, sending waves of aggression and fury that were pulsing inside of me, making it extremely difficult to remain composed.

Daxton didn't even bother reacting to Seamus's comment. He kept his stoic expression plastered on his face. He simply continued on his way to the western wing of the palace, silently marching toward what I knew he dreaded and despised most in this world.

"They both will be all right," Castor said aloud to Idris and me.

I looked to Idris, who fought to hold back the tears coating her eyes. She encircled her growing belly and fought to steady her shaking limbs. I released Castor and rushed to her side, looping an arm over her shoulder to try to comfort her.

"Idris—"

"Don't," she snapped.

I didn't take offense to her reaction. She was forced to watch her mate heed the call of a female who, in the past, had forced him to sleep with her and siphoned his magic from him. Queen or not, this was wrong. We didn't know what her intentions were for Adohan or Dax, but we knew that tonight, she was planning to make a public spectacle of their submission.

"Come on," Castor encouraged us. "Our rooms are this way."

The ornate decorations of the palace entrance continued through the halls as Castor guided us to the opposite wing, where we would stay for the evening. Gold, green, and black were the three main colors of note in the decor with a hint of dark turquoise hidden amongst the swirls of gold. Tapestries adorned the halls with Minaeve as the main focus of each centerpiece. Even without her physical presence, she plastered herself across this entire palace, making sure everyone here knew she was the sole power in charge. The pictures without her in them also held a symbolic presence of her power and sole rulership over the Inner Kingdom. Even the vines growing along the windows, I now realized, reminded me of the High Fae queen herself. Deadly, beautiful, and treacherous.

At the end of the hall, Idris somberly opened the door to her room, which was directly across from mine and Castor's adjacent lodgings. "Idris?"

She turned and glanced toward me in the doorway, her vibrant smile gone as heartbreak overshadowed her joy. "I just need a moment. I will kick Castor out and help you prepare for the ball in an hour. I just need to rest …"

"You don't have to. I'm sure I can manage," I protested, not wanting to ask any more from her.

"No, I do," she said firmly. "I need to keep busy. If I just sit here and do nothing, I'll go mad."

I nodded. "See you in an hour."

The door closed to the hallway, and I swore I heard the faint sound of her cries whisk through the cracks under the door. My heart broke hearing her sorrow, knowing that this was not the first time she had to endure seeing her mate like this. It was wrong. There was no other way to describe it.

"We're in here," Castor said as he opened the door to my room. No, excuse me, *our* room.

I stepped inside and marveled at the vast splendor covering every inch of this place. This room was vastly different, with light blue walls framed in gold accents, decorated with a gold textured ceiling, and vast arrays of different floral arrangements. The large, white-sheeted canopy bed was pushed against the wall on the near side, and vast open windows looked out onto the crystal-blue water of the lake.

My heart longed for my home in Solace. The log cabin house felt connected and open to the nature surrounding it. This palace room was unnatural, like an over-the-top display to try and distract someone from seeing the true horrors beneath.

Castor strode to the opposite side of our quarters to reveal a doorway leading to a smaller adjacent bed chamber. "This is where I'll sleep," he said. "I'll ward the room so no one can hear inside or enter without my knowledge." Castor kept his gaze turned away from me as he leaned against the wall, sighing heavily as he crossed his arms. "It'll help the illusion of our boisterous lovemaking smokescreen."

"Right." I sighed as I sat on the edge of the pristine white bed.

"We also each have our own washroom. Luckily, these rooms were built to house private servants' quarters," Castor said.

"Servants?"

"Yes, that or consorts."

"You mean ... whores?" I asked, uneasy with the thought of anyone having to sell their body for profit or status. A wave of disgust and anger rolled through me that I didn't fight to suppress.

"More or less," Castor said. "Even before Minaeve took her mantle, the high princes of the three realms did not share their title or power with their significant other. They take wives—even, at times, multiple consorts—hoping to continue their line of succession with an heir. But they never shared the title."

"Wait. Not even your parents shared the title in Silver Meadows?" That fact surprised me.

Castor shook his head. "No. Our mother held rank and a position of power from Aelius. Then, once our father married her, she gained status in Silver Meadows, but she didn't hold the title of *high princess*."

"Interesting. Why is that?"

"Power is difficult to share." Castor's face was calm, yet his eyes danced with curiosity. "I imagine I would ask my father that very question if he were still alive, but alas, it's an answer I don't believe we will ever truly know."

I nodded, not agreeing but understanding.

That was why Idris was referred to as lady instead of princess. For shifters, the alpha didn't always have to be a male, but it was rare for a female to possess enough power to take on the role.

In our pack's history there had been less than a handful of female alphas. One of them was an ancestor, but her reign was short-lived because she died in childbirth. Even so, there was only ever one seat of power, never two.

I had to admit the idea never sat well with me.

In my opinion, if it ever mattered enough to make a difference or influence change, a mated pair should rule together, strengthening each other in ways they couldn't on their own, either as king and queen on the same throne or sharing roles as alphas. Like the Gods, two were stronger than one.

"I'm worried about him, Cas," I whispered after minutes of silent contemplation.

I heard Castor's footsteps stride across the room as he gracefully sat on the bed beside me. "Dax is the bravest and most powerful being I know, Skylar. And because of that … unfortunately, he's forced to carry what others cannot."

"I know, Castor, but …"

"He told you, didn't he?" he asked me plainly.

Behind our closed door, Castor was able to tear away his veil of deception and show me a glimpse of what he tried to hide from the world. The sorrow and guilt for his brother lingered behind the shadows of his somber brown eyes, which weighed heavily upon his heart.

"He did," I said.

Castor nodded and sagged his shoulders, leaning forward on his forearms. "Trust me, I hate this. I carry the guilt of his bravery and sacrifice like a heavy stone in my shattered heart. Each time he is forced to submit on behalf of all of us, to protect us, it shatters a little more. I just hope he is right about this."

"What do you mean?"

Castor stared out the window at the seemingly endless, tranquil water of the lake, his mind running a million miles a minute, always thinking ten steps ahead of the rest of us. "Yes. Dax knew from the moment he first saw you in the meadow that you were tied to all of this—tied to *us* in a way. He has been strategically plotting and planning in the only way he knows how."

"He knew what? Explain."

"Dax knew you were special, Skylar. He told me right before you appeared at our rooms in the alpha's house, ready and willing to help heal his wounds … that, ironically, you caused." He huffed a small laugh of amusement before continuing. "But regardless of that fact, he was certain there was something unique about you, even before you were marked as the champion. And I must admit," he said with a half-smile, "I believe he's right. You may be the one to finally break the cycle of abuse we are all forced to endure from a spiteful, narcissistic ruler. You very well might conquer the trials and free our world."

"When … When did he tell you this?" Castor's confession pulled at the swell of emotions stirring in my chest.

"After he found you in the hunter's cell underground. We scoured the hideout, searching and killing any of those filthy creatures foolish enough to think Dax or I would grant them mercy after what they did to you."

I never asked what happened to the hunters or their lair after my capture, and I wasn't sure I was ready to. "What did Dax tell you exactly? Why did he believe I could do this?"

"Because of what you have already endured and overcome, Skylar." Castor's expression turned melancholy. "You might think you failed. But Dax and I saw how much you fought. How you refused to give up." I blinked rapidly; my attention solely focused on each word the silver tongue High Fae spoke to me. "I saw it," he confessed, and I knew he was referring to his premonition gifts. "And Dax told me, about how he cradled your lifeless frame in his arms. How broken and bloodied your body was … How close you were to death's door and the crossing. I saw it all unfold." Castor went still, taking a steadying breath to try and calm himself. "It's an image that kept Dax awake at night and still does to this day. When you finally awoke in Solace, you were terrified and hurt, but your answer about the trials was still the same." Castor stood up from the bed and sauntered over to the open window. "The trials are a test of the mind, body, and soul, but ultimately, they determine if your heart is true and worthy. No shifter has ever completed the first trial, but we believe you can because you already have, Skylar."

I didn't know what to say. It touched me to know that Daxton felt this way all along. That he had faith and belief in me even before I did. Before I even accepted the champion mark, he thought I was something special. "Do you know what awaits me inside the labyrinth?"

"Not exactly," Castor said, still glancing out the window. "The door of the labyrinth will appear only for the champion who wears the mark. Opening when the sun is at its apex in the sky and closing once it sets along the horizon."

"All right ... so, there is a timeline attached to this trial, then?"

"Yes, that is a component of it. We honestly don't know if the previous shifters have actually finished or simply ran out of time trying to reach the center."

"Where *is* this labyrinth? I didn't see anything from the sky as we flew over."

"That's because it is under the palace itself," Castor said, pointing below his feet.

Dammit. Underground? I squeezed my eyes tightly as I fought the urge to scream.

"Luckily, it's almost impossible to get lost in a labyrinth," he added.

"Wait, what? I thought that—"

"Remember, a labyrinth differs from a maze because it has only one pathway leading to the center."

"Then what's the challenge? If I don't have to figure out which way to go, then that sounds simple enough."

"That's the twist. You see, this is a test of the mind. Following a winding path is a simple concept to understand. But ... to continue on, regardless of the obstacles that lay in your way while you're alone, in an underground tomb with the Gods only know what lying in wait, can test the mental capacities of even the brightest minds. The challenge, I believe, is not to turn back."

I cringed. "Yeah, that makes sense."

"That and there is a ward preventing any magic from passing through the gates. Once you enter, no one else may follow you. The other trials may differ, but this first test is for you—and you alone."

"No one knows exactly what's inside, do they?"

Castor shook his head. "No, but I remember hearing ..." His lips pressed into a hard, thin line, almost like he regretted speaking the last words aloud.

"Hearing?" I jumped up and raced to the window. "What did you hear?"

"Do you really want me to tell you, Skylar?" I could feel his unease as he hesitated to answer, nervously threading his hand through his silver hair and flicking it over to one side of his head.

"I have to know."

"The last shifter to enter was a male, about your age, named Stark. We believe he made it the furthest of all the others, but he sounded absolutely crazed." Castor closed his eyes, recalling the memory of the last champion. "Toward the end, I remembered hearing him screaming so loudly I swear it shook the walls and the ground beneath my feet. He kept screaming, cursing to the Gods that he had lost something ... until we didn't hear him anymore." Castor's face paled. "He was searching for something stolen from him, turning away from the center and doubling back through the labyrinth pathway."

"He ... He turned back?"

"Yes, we believe he almost made it back to the entrance when ..."

"When what?" I had to know if I was going into this tomorrow. I needed to learn everything I could to prepare myself.

"When the crunching sound of bones silenced his screams of death."

"Something killed him … or *ate* him?" I couldn't help but hear the quivering sound in my voice. It might not be the best question to ask. I realized that, but the fear of the unknown was at times worse than knowing.

"Not sure."

"Great." I slumped against the windowsill, looking out onto the lake. Castor shifted nervously on his feet, and I realized for the first time since I met him that he was unsure what to do or say next. The sun was beginning to set, turning the sky a brilliant orange color that warmed my heart.

"This is one of his favorite colors," I said, looking off into the sunset. "It reminds me of Dax."

"It's where he got the inspiration," Castor murmured.

"Inspiration for what?"

Castor widened his eyes for a second as he stumbled back a step, trying to right himself. "Ah, nothing. Forget I said anything."

I glared at him. "Uh-uh. Why do I get the sense you're lying to me?"

"I don't know what you mean." Castor waltzed over to the secret door. "I'll leave you so you can get ready for tonight. Knock when you and Idris are ready."

Well, I didn't get an answer to that question, but I did learn more about what to expect from the labyrinth. I knew it would be a test of the mind, but preparing for it seemed almost pointless. I figured I either had the mental capacity to beat this trial, or I would fail trying. No amount of training I could do in these next few hours would prepare me for this. This trial was built to test our inner strength. The courage we developed from true struggle and rising above to accomplish the impossible.

I was not going to walk into this with fear in my heart. If I did that, I knew I wouldn't survive.

Unable to sit still and wait, I decided to keep my body busy to try and quiet my mind. I moved about my room and decided to work on the balance movements Daxton taught me on the ship. Slowly, I worked through each exercise, focusing on my core strength to keep me stable as I flowed from one pose to the other. I heard Dax's voice in my mind, encouraging me to perfect each motion before continuing to the next.

Eventually, my movements became fluid, and I progressed through each one, repeating the cycle over and over again. I became lost in the repetition of the exercises. The physical exertion gave me something to focus on, and I was grateful for the time to practice and allow my mind to drift into nothingness. Sweat coated my brow as I spun and shifted my footing midair to land a fearsome kick in the chest of an imaginary enemy.

Knock, knock, knock. "Skylar?" Idris echoed on the other side of the door, and I rushed to open it.

"What in the Gods' names have you been doing?" She looked me over from head to toe, gawking at the sweat dripping from my brow and coating my clothes.

"I was training," I panted. "I don't like to sit still. I had to do something ... I—" I stopped because Idris understood, and she didn't need another reminder about where her mate was at this very moment.

Idris shook her head, pushing past me to enter the room. She held two gowns in her arms and delicately draped them over the white sheets of my bed. "Thank the Mother and Father you have me. This is going to be my toughest work yet. Now strip down, clean up, and get ready to put those acting skills to the test. You, me, and Castor will all be playing the role of dutiful subjects tonight, and it won't be easy."

Chapter Eight

"**A**re we finished yet, ladies?" Castor's foot impatiently tapped against the floor on his side of the secret door. "The festivities have already begun, and our absence will be noted if we don't hurry along soon."

"Perfection takes time!" Idris snapped back through the wall. "If anyone makes a fuss, you can blame it on me. They won't sneer or ask questions as to why I'm moving so slowly." The final pieces of my hair fell into place as Idris stepped back. "I have to say, Skylar, this is my best work yet!"

I grasped the bottom skirt of my deep purple fitted gown and walked over to the mirror next to the doorway.

"I-Idris. Is that me?" This was hands down the most glamorous gown I had ever seen, let alone worn. I was practically speechless, and the fact that Daxton had given instructions to have this specially made for me made it all the more special.

I twirled in the reflection, gawking at the beautiful, vivid amethyst and silver sparkling gown that hugged the curves of my hips perfectly before flowing out behind me in a long, delicate train. The sheer glittering fabric mimicked a second layer of skin around the neckline and sleeves, holding microscopic gems that made my fair skin sparkle to life in the reflection of the fae lights. The slit along my right leg ended just above my upper thigh, adding a sensual, captivating aspect to the bewitchingly beautiful design. The purple fabric opened in a deep V between my breasts, highlighting them in an elegant yet still alluring way that would undoubtedly catch the attention of any eyes glancing my direction. Idris pulled half of my hair back using the hairpin I was gifted in the marketplace as the accent to finish her design.

"You love it?" Idris asked, circling me.

"How could I not?" I gasped. "You look amazing as well, Idris."

"Obviously," she said with a brazen smile.

Her flowing gown was a deep crimson color, tightly fitted and stretching wide over her very pregnant belly. It dropped into a similar deep V-cut, exposing the entire length of her back from the nape to her hips.

"Ready?" she asked.

"Ready," I answered, steadying my nerves and preparing myself to enter the Aelius court. And trust me, I knew it was not for the weak of heart.

I opened the secret door to find a handsome, debonair Castor waiting impatiently for us to join him. He was dressed in a black shirt layered with a fitted silver jacket and elegant black stitching along the seams. Paired with black pants and a silver cloak draped over his right shoulder. The emblem of the three silver mountains hovering proudly above his heart.

In Silver Meadows, if anyone wished to join their army, they had to successfully master the Gauntlet to become a Silver Meadows warrior and earn their first peak. Another was added when the warrior defended their realm, and the third was earned when their actions honored their people. Holding all three peaks was considered a treasured distinction beyond measure.

"You look handsome." I looped my arm through the nook of his elbow. He grinned and held out his other arm for Idris, who happily accepted and stepped to his other side.

"I'll be the envy of every male and female in attendance tonight. I have no doubt we'll likely steal all the attention this evening— Gods above, how lucky you two are to have *me* as your stunning escort," he teased.

On cue, Idris and I both smacked him firmly in the chest.

"Ouch." Castor chuckled. "I didn't know you enjoyed rough foreplay. That can always be arranged ..."

"Castor," I said in a low warning tone.

"What? I have to get these in while I'm out of Dax and Adohan's hearing range."

"He has a point." Idris laughed as she gripped Castor's arm tighter.

I could see a look of concern flash across her face, so I tugged on Castor to wait a moment longer before exiting our shared room. I watched as Idris straightened her shoulders, embodying her inner strength and grace.

"Let's join them," Idris confidently said, holding her chin high as the three of us walked down the long corridor to where the sounds of music, mingling, and laughter lured us.

Guards at the entrance to the main ballroom stood watch, adorned with lightweight deep green armor. They held up their hands, recognizing who we were, and asked us to wait before entering.

"What should I be expecting?" I whispered to Castor and Idris.

"The usual," Castor said. "Dancing, conversations, lies, deception, scandal. Oh, and perhaps the occasional fucking in a secluded room out of earshot from the music and conversation. Or perhaps just outside the—"

"So, everything you live for, then, I assume?" I arched my brow at him, and he gave me a half-grin, turning to brush his lips against my cheek as one of the guards switched his gaze toward us. I tried my best to fake my enjoyment, but all Castor would get out of me was compliance. I couldn't bring myself to return that kind of affection.

"Alright, time for a confession," I said, swallowing my nerves.

"And that is?" Castor asked, leaning in close. Luckily, he wasn't much taller than me, so it made our hushed conversations easier to hide. From the outside looking in, it appeared that we were whispering sweet nothings to each other.

"I've never been to a ball … or any fancy party like this before." Judging by the look on Castor's face, this didn't seem like a surprise to him, and that somehow put me at ease.

Castor rolled his eyes. "Shifters. It had to be shifters …"

Deciding to ignore Castor's remark, I was still a bundle of shaking nerves, and my hands began to sweat. Thank the Gods, Castor didn't notice, or he was trying to be nice and not taunt me about it for once.

The guards motioned for us to enter, and for the first time, I stepped into the Aelius court. The space was decorated with gold splendor that would put even the human king's treasure vaults to shame. The floor-to-ceiling arched windows gazed out onto the surrounding landscape and Aelius, which was glowing with fae lights that sparkled against the darkening evening. The high vaulted ceiling was painted a deep blue, almost black, with dustings of gold specks that danced along the textured surface. The starry sky decorated above our heads trickled down into the white walls, slowly fading into gold designs that flickered like starlight. Large columns stood between the windows, and the same black thorny vines decorated the spiraling pillars. As we entered the massive room, the music slowly sank into the background while all the High Fae in attendance turned their attention toward me.

"Did I mention I don't do well in situations like this?" I murmured while Castor released Idris and wrapped an arm around my middle, practically dragging me forward into the room.

"You'll learn," he said. "I'm a fabulous teacher, and I won't let you tarnish my reputation. Now walk, one foot in front of the other. There you go."

We passed through the crowded space, and each High Fae who met my gaze immediately dropped their heads in a show of respect. I blushed, "I still don't understand why they're all looking at me like this."

Idris leaned in from Castor's other side. "You still don't get it, Skylar?"

"Clearly," I mumbled, but she didn't seem to hear me.

"You represent *hope* for all of us. For the first time ever, a shifter has volunteered to enter the trials. News of your resilience from your experience with the hunters has traveled with you here to the Inner Kingdom. For the first time in centuries, our people dare to dream of a life without the wilt." She paused to look down and lovingly caressed her growing belly. "We have *hope* that our children will be born, never having to live in a world filled with fear, never being locked in a cage."

My heart stilled at her genuine words and heartfelt confession. I had become a beacon of hope for our world by simply doing what I believed was right.

"Are you beginning to understand?" Castor turned to look at me as reality of this finally sank in. I was about to say something when a grand melody erupted around the space, drawing our attention.

Idris removed herself from Castor's company as she marched to the far side of the room. We both hastily followed in her footsteps, and I could see what she was pacing toward. At the opposing end of the ballroom was a raised platform with a set of five steps leading to a single golden throne where Minaeve, the High Queen of the Inner Kingdom, sat with her three high princes surrounding her.

Minaeve's elegant black dress flowed alongside her golden throne, decorated in vibrant green and golden gems that sparkled when she shifted in her seat. The exposed front of her gown dropped below her navel, clinging tightly to her silhouette, highlighting the seductive feminine curves of her thin frame. Her luminous turquoise eyes popped against the colors painted on her tanned skin that shimmered with a magical glow. Wavy jet-black hair held a golden crown with three small glimmering translucent gems that sparkled like stars in the night sky.

There was no denying the high queen's beauty, but I knew it only ran skin deep. The singular throne was a reminder to all those in attendance that Minaeve was the sole ruler of the Inner Kingdom. She alone was the leader, and although each prince held their own territory and power, they were all at her mercy.

"Very subtle," I said under my breath.

As the crowds parted, I noticed Adohan seated on the lowest step. He wore the same-colored attire as his mate with an elongated open-chested vest and fitted black pants. His golden armband matched a gilded crown on his brow that shone in the glimmering fae lights as he leaned forward, sensing his mate's presence.

Adohan's hazel gaze shot up from the floor as soon as Idris entered his line of sight. I watched him tense as Idris marched straight across the room without hesitation and reached out for him. She knelt next to Adohan on the steps, intentionally ignoring the glares from Minaeve, who sat above them on her throne. It was bold, perhaps stupidly brave, to ignore Queen Minaeve's presence like that. They shared a sweet, longing kiss, and I smiled at the love they truly shared.

The next high prince on the middle steps directly at the feet of the queen was none other than Seamus. His dark green fitted coat was paired with black pants and knee-high boots, giving him a clean-cut look that I would deem handsome … if it were not on him. Gold thread accented his attire in elegant swirls paired with the same golden crown resting atop his tousled blond hair as Adohan's.

Seamus's forest-green eyes were locked on Idris and Adohan with keen interest and, possibly, *longing*. Was there a hint of jealousy for what they shared?

A mating bond amongst High Fae was highly regarded, sacred even. Could it be that Seamus covertly longed for a connection this deep and profound?

Crossing one ankle across his knee, Seamus leaned back and boldly ran his hand up Minaeve's leg as he glanced her way. The longing, lustful look hung heavy in his eyes as he reached higher, stroking her inner thigh with his fingertips.

Then—Gods. Mother and Father, help me. I couldn't bring myself to look past the queen's throne to the final high prince at her side tonight. I purposely kept my eyes tilted down, not wanting to find the male that would tear away the mask I had worked so hard to build.

Castor was muttering pleasantries to the queen and guided me into a low bow that I executed with absolute perfection. As we rose, however, I could no longer look away.

Discreetly, frost brushed against the nape of my neck. The ice-cold caress on my skin sank into my middle, igniting a blaze that spiraled through my limbs. I recognized his magic instantly and couldn't fight the pull from my animal that pushed me to meet his gaze. So, I bravely braced myself for the inevitable.

Time stood still as I lifted my amber eyes to the High Prince of Silver Meadows, stoically standing beside the high queen's throne.

Handsome would not do him justice. He was the epitome of grace and power, something I imagined even the Gods would envy. Daxton's hair was pulled back, framed by a crown of golden thorns that highlighted his square jaw and jet-black trimmed beard. He shifted on his feet as a lock of his midnight-streaked hair fell across his brow. I waited on bated breath as our eyes locked on to each other. His lips parted as he took in a deep, silent gasp, causing my knees to tremble underneath my skirt. One look from him and my whole body hummed with a melody that spanned across the distance that separated us. It was a song that only we could hear, a tune so sweet and lovely that it made you stop and listen.

This is dangerous. For him. For me. For all of us.

A depth of regret and shame lay hidden behind his storm cloud eyes that stole the breath from my chest. I longed to leap into his arms and kiss away his pains, comforting him as he had done for me countless times before. Fighting the urge to run to him, I forced myself to remain where I stood. I needed to be strong, not merely for him but also, for me. If Castor wasn't holding onto me, I believe I would have.

"Daxton," the queen's voice snaked through the room, snapping us out of our trance and hurling us back into reality.

"Yes, Queen Minaeve?" His words were vacant and distant. Secretly laced with wild disdain and hatred beneath a calm exterior.

"We'll lead the first dance together." This wasn't said as a request.

Silver Shadow stepped to Minaeve's side from behind her throne and held out his arm. His midnight silk dress shirt was unbuttoned at the top of his collar, revealing an opening down toward the center of his firm chest. Gold stitching, not silver, adorned his attire. It dawned on me that it mimicked the same design Minaeve was wearing tonight. She was purposely putting him on display. Flaunting the fact that she was claiming him as hers.

I could see his muscles tense as Minaeve accepted Daxton's arm, tracing her hand up his shoulder and lacing her fingers into his hair. She tugged on the base of his neck and pulled him in to kiss her.

Don't fucking touch him! I desperately wanted to scream.

Watching them ignited an explosion of fury inside my chest. I clenched my fists until they turned white and gritted my teeth so tightly, I thought they would crack. My animal surged with rage and pumped power through my limbs, making me visibly shake against my escort's steady hold.

Castor gripped my waist, sending waves of his ice magic through me to try and settle my wrath. His hold on me, was the only thing keeping me from charging up the steps and throwing myself between Daxton and Minaeve.

My eyes were ablaze with raw power as my animal continued to supply me with more and more of it, pushing me to help save him. To help in any way I could. Gods above, I was going to …

"This way. Let's go," Castor said.

Silently, I refused to budge.

"Now, Skylar!" Castor fronted me, blocking my view of the queen and Daxton. His eyes were black, a premonition of impending death taking hold. He blinked rapidly as the whites of his eyes returned.

"If you walk up those steps …" His jaw clenched. "Champion or not, Minaeve will see this as an insult and kill me as punishment for both you and Dax. Trust me, I've seen it."

"Fuck," I cursed.

"Fuck, indeed. Now let's move onto the dance floor."

Castor twirled me around in step with the vibrant music filling the ballroom. My temper continued to simmer, unable to erase the image of Daxton and Minaeve from my mind. Even with the music and dancing as a distraction, when I closed my eyes, all I could see was them.

I hated Minaeve. I even dared admit that I wanted to kill her. I wanted to win the trials so she could no longer call herself high queen. Dax and all the realms wouldn't have to bow to a ruler who treated them like playthings or possessions.

Our world was dying, and the people of the Inner Kingdom were suffering from more than just the wilt.

"You're falling behind, Skylar," Castor said as he lifted and spun me around in the air before gracefully placing me back on the floor.

"I can't—"

"You can. And you will." He spoke as if there was no other option. And to be honest, I couldn't argue. I knew there wasn't.

"Look at me," Castor commanded, and I snapped my eyes to meet his. "Not like that." He sighed and twirled me around again. "Imagine I'm Daxton."

"What?"

"Cute." He rolled his eyes. "I've seen the way you look at each other, and despite your reluctance to admit the obvious … I know there's a connection forming between you both that goes beyond mere physical attraction." I glared at him, but it didn't seem to do me any good. "I'm sure I wasn't the only one who noticed how my brother had to physically brace himself behind the queen's throne as you entered the room on my arm." I almost stopped dancing, stunned to hear this, but Castor gracefully countered, dipping me back into a low bend. "We both need to pretend tonight, Skylar. We both must imagine the face of another we wish to see."

The sincerity in his words caught me off guard. "The face of another?"

He nodded as the music slowed, and he grasped my waist, pulling me close to his chest while holding out my other hand. "Place your right arm on my shoulder, around my neck." I silently nodded and followed his instructions as we began blending in with the other couples dancing about the room.

Across the way, I saw Daxton dancing with Minaeve until Seamus approached them and bowed to cut in. He respectfully excused himself and retired to the side of the dance floor near the throne. He looked to be far away, finding whatever sanctuary he could inside his mind to guard himself as best he could.

"Focus, Skylar," Castor cursed under his breath. *Right. Focus.* I gazed at Castor, trying my best to imagine he was Dax. "That's a slight improvement."

I rolled my eyes as Castor turned me around toward another male dance partner, waiting and ready to take my hand. Castor accepted another female, so I followed the pattern, dancing with an array of different companions throughout the rest of the song. The music's melody was beautiful and relaxing, helping calm my temper.

The final loop of the song began as I was guided to my final dance partner. I stopped, frozen in place and unable to turn away.

Why is my luck always this Gods dammed horrible? I moved into step with my new partner, keeping my eyes cast downward because one look from him would completely unravel me.

Daxton.

I knew I couldn't just run away. Wandering eyes might suspect something if I picked up my skirt and sprinted from the dance floor.

Daxton took me in his arms and coldly regarded me as a mere nuisance or stranger. He casually grasped my hand, spinning me around until we stepped into frame, moving with the rhythm of the music and other dancers around us. If I didn't know any better, I would have guessed that my presence aggravated him.

Right now, I was simply a burden ... his *ward*. I was anything but a ray of hope for their world.

Slowly, the melody halted. I slid my right hand from his shoulder and pressed it on his chest to steady myself. I could feel the smooth, sculpted muscle beneath the fine silk of his formal attire as my pulse began to race. I was barely able to move, let alone breathe. His body was rigid like the ice he commanded—but never cold under my touch. I forced myself to tilt my chin up, glancing into the eyes that swirled me into an endless sea of emotions.

There was a glimmer of softness underneath the iron-cold stare, unlocking his hidden world and showing me a window into the depths of his true soul.

I knew the person concealed within—the true High Fae prince who sacrificed himself time and time again to the will of the queen, the sole saving grace of his people.

Daxton was the most powerful High Fae born to the Inner Kingdom, which is why he had to give so much. He was the prince who was promised to unite his people, a selfless ruler who strived to put others first. This was the male I knew.

Dax ... *my* Dax.

"Daxton, Adohan, and Seamus," Minaeve called out as the music finished.

I clung to the silk collar of his shirt, my fingers curling in the fabric, refusing to let him go. "Dax, I ..." The words stopped on the tip of my tongue, but the emotion rang through my gaze as I stared at him.

Quickly, Daxton moved to turn his back toward the queen's throne and grasped my right hand in his. "Thank you for the dance, *Champion*." He took one step back but hesitated to take another, unable to release me just yet.

To everyone else in the room, this seemed routine, mundane even. But to us, this was *more*. Daxton held my right hand close to his chest as he gave me a respectful bow. Then, as he rose, his lips moved toward the scar just above my wrist—the scar he gave me the first night we met—the scar that never healed, even under the magic of the mage that held me captive.

His mouth pressed into my skin, covering the permanent mark he had embedded into my flesh. Sparks ignited against his touch accompanied by a lick of fire spreading through my center.

Daxton straightened, hesitating to return to the queen's throne. His back, now turned to me, carried heavy shoulders with the weight of five centuries of torture. Each step he took felt like the world was spiraling and splitting in two.

My mind raced, unable to focus on anything besides the feeling of his lips as they caressed the mark he had made on my wrist. *Did I mention before that I have a knack for the worst possible timing in the world? If not, this is evidence of just that.*

A hand suddenly grasped my waist, guiding me away from the dance floor amongst a flurry of High Fae that were enthralled in their drinks and conversation. I was so consumed with the thought of Daxton that I didn't even notice who was leading me away from the gathering.

"Hello, Champion." His smooth voice had a calming essence that aged him beyond his physical appearance. "I need to show you something," he said, leading me toward a doorway in the forgotten corner of the ballroom off to the side of Minaeve's throne.

I called upon my animal to help me assess his intentions while searching for Idris or Castor, but as luck would have it, they were nowhere in sight. To my surprise, I didn't feel anything from her. *Great, thanks for the help.* I cursed under my breath.

"You don't need to fear me, Skylar Cathal. It would be foolish to threaten the life of the shifter who is trying to free us from the wilt."

"Logically, yes, I agree with you," I said as I matched his pace. "So, you know my name. Is it not polite that you share yours with me?"

"Curious, are we?" He released a lighthearted, humorless chuckle. "Care to take a guess?"

I looked him over, carefully calculating how to navigate the game of the courts with this key player. *All right, Castor, let's see what I can do.* "You're wearing a long green dress coat that matches Prince Seamus. That tells me you're a member of the Aelius court and likely high on his list of trusted associates due to the intricate fine detail of your clothing."

"You catch on quickly."

I attempted to detect his scent, but realized it was shielded. "And due to your magical barrier protecting you, you have other gifts as well."

"Can you infer what they are?"

"You're from Aelius … so naturally, you possess a power of the mind."

"Yes," he said as we reached a door.

I stepped away, uncomfortable with the idea of going somewhere alone with him. "Your name," I said. "Give me your name, and I'll consider going with you."

"You've already assessed enough information to take a guess at my identity, have you not?" He interlocked his hands behind his back, cocking an eyebrow of anticipation in my direction.

His lean, muscular frame that gave him a unique sense of gracefulness I hadn't seen before. His deep-set blue eyes were cunning, ever calculating, and draped under a mesh of midnight-black hair hanging below his brow. I took note of the softness of his hands. Indicated that he was not a battle-hardened warrior but possibly a warrior of a different kind.

A scholar.

"Rhett Parmeet."

A moment of silence passed between us as an unabashed grin adorned the corner of his mouth. "Very clever, indeed." He reached for the handle of a door and opened it. "After you."

What would it say about me if I blindly followed his lead?

So, I tried once more to listen for my animal. Nothing—*Really? Seriously? Come on.* I sighed, gritted my teeth, and pushed back my shoulders to give the illusion that I held no ounce of fear. "How long will this take?"

"Long enough to go unnoticed, if you don't dawdle," he said in a calm, even tone. "And enough time to accomplish our intended task."

"Which is?"

"You'll have to step inside to find out," Rhett said, his hands still folded behind his back.

I nodded and boldly followed his direction, entering the doorway and stepping through. Rhett followed, waving his hand to illuminate fae lights that hung along various columns. Endless stacks of books and trinkets lined the shelving on the walls, surrounding a single stand in the center. I was overwhelmed by the vast collection of texts that towered over my head, seeming to continue with no end.

I gasped as I raced toward the books on the shelves, delicately tracing my fingers over the spines, reveling in their presence. I could spend years here and never tire of the endless stories and knowledge I could learn from the pages of wisdom I eagerly wished to devour.

"You're an admirer of knowledge as well?"

I nodded as I inhaled a deep breath to take in the delicious aroma of the room. Awakening a feeling of peace and fullness inside my soul. Books always had a distinct essence that called to me. The knowledge locked away in these pages was a gift. Something to be cherished and protected.

"You're their keeper?" I asked with a piqued interest.

"Yes," Rhett said as he strode to the center of the room. "That, along with various trinkets I've collected over the years. Each has its own story to tell, and not only the written words."

"Your gift." I recalled that Rhett could see the past of an object just by touching it.

Rhett nodded as he moved to the stand in the middle and beckoned me to join him. "This is what I wanted to show you."

I rounded the book stand and gazed upon a scroll that appeared to be centuries old. "What is this, exactly?"

"Pull back the left sleeve of your gown. You seem to be a clever female—I'm sure you'll notice the similarities."

I did as he said and exposed my arm where the champion's mark flared to life across my skin. "It matches the seal." I slowly reached out to touch the scroll.

Rhett moved in a flash and firmly grasped my wrist. "Please, don't touch it."

Although he was firm, I knew I could free myself if I wanted, and his grip didn't cause me harm. I could sense that this was merely a warning, and he didn't intend to hurt me.

"What is this?" I asked again.

"This, dear Champion, is the scroll of the Heart of Valdor." Rhett released my wrist and very gently waved his hand over the scroll, using his magic to unroll the parchment so it was fully exposed to the fae light.

"The Trials of the Heart of Valdor." I gasped at the black star design that adorned my skin and how it was identical to the three on the scroll. Next to each star held a title, alluding to aspects that each trial would entail.

The trial of the mind. The trial of the body. The trial of the soul.

"This enchanted parchment is linked to the Heart of Valdor," Rhett said. "The first trial is described here." He directed my eyeline to the writing near the star closest to the top.

Alone, you will enter the world of the labyrinth. It will invade the confines of your mind and test the strength of your resolve in the face of your fears. Your logic will be tested along this singular path, but the challenge is that you must never abandon your goal nor turn back. A choice must be made against the terrors that haunt your waking dreams. Once you reach the end, the true limits of your sanity shall be tested, and you must cross the divide. The choice will be yours to decide ... obtain the key—or die.

I read the passage over and over again, trying to memorize each word written and decipher the meanings behind them.

"We've studied this for nearly five centuries. I doubt you'll uncover anything new in the minutes we have remaining here."

"I'd hate to blindly agree with you ... and we both end up being wrong." I shot Rhett a menacing glare as I read the scroll one final time. "Why show me?"

"I have my reasons," he said plainly. "Once you complete the first trial, the first star will fill in. When the trinket or key is retrieved and touches the parchment, the second description will appear." He pointed to the second star in the middle of the page.

"How do you know that?"

"Because the last shifter, Stark." Rhett became still as he cleared his throat. "The last champion was the most successful thus far. Reaching what we believe was the *divide* dictated at the end of this description."

I recalled Castor's retelling of what happened to Stark, knowing they all heard his grotesque, agonizing screams of death. I understood Rhett's unease with the subject. Hearing anyone's final screams of agony was unnerving.

"How do you know the previous champion almost made it?"

Rhett pointed to the outlined star of the first trial on the scroll. "Because the first star on the page began to fill in."

There were countless questions spilling into my mind. I didn't know where to begin. This scroll was connected to the magic of the trials, and apparently, after each key was retrieved, the next clue was revealed.

"What—"

"Skylar!" Castor's voice cut into the room. He shot Rhett and me a frigid expression that sent a chill down my spine. Daxton might be the terrifying Silver Shadow, but this was a firm reminder that Castor wasn't far behind.

"Hello, Cas. I didn't know I was going to enjoy your company this evening. What a treat," Rhett said.

My eyes darted between the two of them, sensing unspoken tension brewing in the room.

"Rhett," Castor sneered as he strode toward me. "Come on, Skylar. Your absence has been noticed." He glared at Rhett with daggers in his eyes that reminded me of a scorned lover.

"Such hostility," Rhett snickered with a calm demeanor, which I had no idea how he was able to pull off. The look on Castor's face made me uneasy. "You know I only have our champion's best interest at heart. I show each of them this scroll before the trials."

"Yes, but never alone," Castor rebutted.

"True." Rhett moved from behind the stand of the scroll and fronted Castor. "I apologize. I should've asked you *privately* first if she could accompany me. I was unaware of your ... attachment to her?" A sly grin appeared on the side of Rhett's mouth.

Privately? What was he aiming at here?

"There's no need for that, Rhett."

"Oh, why? It was such fun last time," Rhett said as he boldly stepped toward Castor and me. "We both seemed to be enjoying ourselves amongst the mass entanglements of our various companions. I certainly have fond memories of the occasion."

Castor's jawline tightened. "As I said before, there's no need for *us* to speak privately."

Rhett scoffed, frowning like a disappointed child. "Such a shame. Your reputation in the bedroom did precede you."

My eyes widened. *Oh shit. Okay, then.*

Castor growled a low, threatening warning at the back of his throat in reply.

Yep, that answered my question.

The music changed in the other room. Trumpeting sounds consuming Rhett and Castor's undivided attention. "Well, the nightmare of a spectacle is about to begin," Rhett muttered under his breath. "You two better hurry along. This night is just beginning."

With out saying another word to Rhett, Castor gripped my arm and led me out of the hidden library.

"What was that about?" I couldn't help asking, even as Castor threw me a glare that told me to keep my questions to myself. "Cas—"

"A regret from a drunken night with barrels of wine and multiple willing partners wanting to lose themselves in each other's company." He cocked his head in my direction as we continued our way. "Do you really need me to elaborate on this? Do you truly not know what an *orgy* is?"

My brow shot upward. "Nope!"

"*Ha, ha, ha.* Such a prude." He snickered. "We can address this later, but right now, we need to find Idris."

"Why?" I asked as we re-entered the ballroom.

"Because the offerings are about to begin."

Chapter Nine

"There she is," I said, pointing toward the gathering crowd. "In the front."

"What in the Gods' names is she doing so close," Castor cursed. "Hurry, we need to move."

Sensing the panic in his voice, I followed the frantic pace of his footsteps as we weaved through the crowd.

I knew Queen Minaeve was going to make a public spectacle of Daxton, Adohan, and Seamus this evening. She would force them to bend their knees and grovel to her rule in front of everyone in attendance. Seamus, I assumed, was overjoyed to bow and obey like the good lap dog he was, but not Daxton and Adohan.

To say I was nervous was an understatement. I couldn't imagine what Daxton and Adohan were feeling.

"Idris!" Castor called out as we reached her side.

"I need to be here, Castor," she said. Her demeanor reminded me of a slow, crackling ember. Hot enough to burn the skin off your flesh, yet quiet under the raging flames above. Her mate was about to be drained of his magic while she was forced to watch helplessly from the sidelines. She was like a sleeping volcano, ready to erupt and unleash a death sentence on the queen.

"Idris, no, you don't."

"Yes, I do." She answered Cas in a low, quiet tone that only a mother could master. The steadiness of her voice was matched by the fire burning behind her deathly, terrifying stare. There was no moving her. She was not going to leave this room unless she wanted to, and we both knew that it was not going to be without Adohan.

I went to her side and grasped both her hands in mine. "Dig in if you need to." I motioned to our clutched embrace. "I'm pretty tough."

She gave me a half-smile in return before turning her attention back to the throne. Queen Minaeve had all three of the High Fae princes standing below the steps, facing the crowd. She glided to stand in front of them, and the hairs on my neck stood straight. Daxton was in the center with Adohan on his right and Seamus to his left. Minaeve slid between Daxton and Seamus, lightly caressing both their arms and receiving a cunning, sultry smile from Seamus, while Daxton continued to stare blankly at the wall beyond the crowd.

The silence in the room was deafening. The tension becoming so suffocatingly thick that it could be sliced with a knife. I glanced around at the furrowed brows and grimaces that adorned almost every face in the ballroom. No one wanted this. They all understood that this was a sacrifice unwillingly given, and this time, the queen was making a unique spectacle of it.

"Welcome, my subjects," Minaeve announced with a soft, sweet voice that lured all eyes to her. I wanted to turn around and hurl into the nearest wastebasket. "Tomorrow, during the new moon, our shifter champion will enter the first trial. As our mother, the sun, is at her apex, the gates to the labyrinth will open, and we shall wait to see if her mind is able to overcome the obstacles." Minaeve's turquoise stare slanted toward me, and this time, I refused to buckle or show any sign of fear.

Fucking bring it on, bitch.

Idris's grip on my hand tightened in silent encouragement, causing me to grin. Minaeve narrowed her eyes, but other than that, she showed no sign of unease.

"If the shifter is able to best the trial of the mind, then she will be the first to do so, bringing our people and our home one step closer to salvation." Minaeve kept her gaze locked on me as she spoke.

I didn't know if she expected me to cower or show her praise, but neither was happening tonight. I refused to incline my head or bow to her stare. She was not *my* queen.

Minaeve curled her arms in front of her and opened her palms to her people, sending a blast of her magic out through the room. Everyone felt the strength of her power pressing on their minds, and I could detect the faint smell of fear sweeping across the crowd.

I watched through gritted teeth as she grinned. She gods-damned *grinned*. Sickly enjoying tormenting us all and using her magic to force us into submission, ruling over the people with fear instead of love and respect.

Yep, I definitely was not a fan.

"If the shifter fails, however," she said with an all too confident smirk, "we must wait another century for the trials of the Heart of Valdor to open. To ensure our continued safety, I will accept the submission and offerings of power from the three realms of the Inner Kingdom. Each high prince will freely grant me access to their magic, sharing their life's blood and powers with me so I may continue to combat the wilt with my magic.

Without this sacrifice, I would not be strong enough to continue protecting the three realms, and the wilt would consume us all."

Wait. Life's blood? What did she mean by that? What was she planning to do?

On cue, Minaeve summoned a golden chalice and withdrew a long, slender dagger from her thigh. She turned to Daxton, beckoning him to hold out his hand. Daxton's expression remained unchanged as he reached out and gripped the blade of the dagger himself, slicing his palm and squeezing it over the opening of the cup. Even though Minaeve's back was to me, I knew she was smiling with her victory. She was truly wicked … a grotesque excuse of a queen. Adohan didn't falter as he followed Daxton's lead, with Seamus slicing his palm last.

"With the offering of their life's blood, a connection is made. The link forged by magic to transfer from their vessels into my own." Minaeve tipped back the chalice and drained their offerings, not allowing a single drop of their blood to fall to the floor or remain in the cup.

"What now?" I whispered to Idris.

She bit her lip, hesitating at first but eventually whispering a hushed reply, "Now … Now, she uses her siphon abilities to link with each of them and absorb their magic. Their essence, their lifeforce in a sense, is taken from them."

Memories of Daxton in Solace flashed across my mind, and I squeezed Idris's hands tighter. "She wouldn't kill them … would she?"

Idris's eyes widened, and I knew I had just spoken her fear out loud.

"She wouldn't dare be that foolish," Castor cut in. "Killing Adohan or Daxton would instill a civil war.

Wilt or no wilt. They have the loyalty of their people and their realms. Silver Meadows warriors would gladly fight and die to avenge either of them." He smirked, lowering his voice so only we could hear him. "On the contrary, they would greatly enjoy tearing this place apart and shattering the golden throne of the queen."

"And what about Seamus?" I asked.

"I would throw the party myself if she drained his life away," Castor said with a humorless laugh. "But that wouldn't happen."

"Why?"

"Because he's Minaeve's lap dog, her king consort in all ways but the name and title."

"Why not the title?"

Castor looked around to see if anyone was listening in. "Because Seamus isn't the most powerful high prince, even though he is powerful ..." Castor bit his tongue, struggling to finish his thoughts. "Seamus is the closest to rival Daxton's strength and power, but my brother is still her main prize. She wouldn't settle for anything less than the best. And, unfortunately for Dax, that's him. She's obsessed with power, Skylar. My brother has always been her desired target for marriage and *breeding*."

"But he refused her, right?" My chest tightened as my heart froze. I found it difficult to draw in a breath. My eyes were transfixed solely on Daxton.

"Of course." Castor huffed, and my heart began beating once more. "Please don't insult him by thinking otherwise."

"Adohan will be the first to give his offering," Idris whispered, trying to hide the fears she refused to voice.

Minaeve turned to Adohan and reached up to cup his dark-skinned chin in her tan, golden hued hands.

Idris clutched onto me tighter, practically breaking my skin with the sheer strength of her grip as the queen stepped closer to him, drawing his lips into her own. The kiss was quick, unnatural, and a second later, I understood why.

Minaeve pulled her lips from Adohan's and inhaled a deep, all-consuming breath. Swallowing in wisps of a red-shadowed figure resembling the Crimson City prince himself. She continued to inhale as she siphoned the traces of Adohan's magic, devouring the beautiful fire that ignited the depths of his soul.

Adohan dropped to his knees as the queen consumed his essence.

"That's too much!" Idris yelled as she stumbled forward. I refused to release my hold, preventing her from climbing the steps.

"No. He's stronger than this," Castor insisted.

"I'm not leaving my mate's life to chance!" Idris tried to break free, but Castor stepped in and hugged her to his chest. "No, Cas—" Idris groaned, struggling against his hold as tears pooled in her eyes.

"Idris … Dax won't let him fall." I didn't know what Castor meant exactly, but it seemed to calm Idris down enough for him to keep her in place.

Adohan groaned in pain and collapsed onto shaking hands.

"Enough!" Dax demanded. Minaeve released Adohan and turned her attention to him. "Take from me whatever else you need. I'm at your disposal, High Queen."

Castor released Idris, and she sprinted to the steps, clinging to Adohan with everything she could. She refused to allow her tears to fall as she tilted her chin up to glare at Minaeve with hatred steaming from her dark, ominous eyes.

"Take your *mate*," Minaeve spat at them. Like Adohan was nothing more than a toy she no longer had an interest in playing with. "He's given all he can, and I need more."

And that more was Daxton.

Idris draped Adohan's arm over her shoulder as a path cleared for them to depart the ballroom. He was weak, stumbling from his loss of energy and power, but his mate was there to support him. The loving looks exchanged between them were heart-wrenching. They were partners, and when one fell, the other was there to pick them up.

Castor and I stayed behind. There was no way I was leaving without making sure Daxton survived this. Even with Seamus eagerly awaiting Minaeve's kiss of death, I knew she was planning on taking all she could from Daxton. The temptation was too much for her to ignore.

In a flash, Minaeve reached out and pulled on the base of Dax's neck, bringing him to her lips. Her kiss was more sensual compared to the one with Adohan. She pressed herself up against Daxton, possessively tracing her hands up and down his body, making me smolder with rage. I could see him stiffen as her fingers scraped against the smooth skin on his chest. His palms curled into fists as Minaeve deepened the kiss. Her hands entangled into Daxton's hair, pulling at the tie and letting it fall freely around his face. She was clearly enjoying this more than she needed, and Minaeve was not afraid to show her people how she could make the High Prince of Silver Meadows bend to her will.

Slowly, the queen pulled away from Daxton. Drawing in a deep breath, just like before with Adohan, she inhaled the wisps of his silver essence. The amount of swirling energy coming from Daxton was brighter and much greater compared to Adohan. It was evident that she was taking more of Dax's power simply because there was more for him to offer. Minaeve's skin glowed with a golden hue, becoming even more vibrant as Daxton's seemed to dim. She was literally sucking the life out of him, and there wasn't a damn thing I could do but watch as she tore him to pieces.

No! I screamed inside my head.

I didn't know how it was possible, but I could have sworn that I felt Daxton's pain as my own while the queen siphoned his magic away. Daxton's groans of pain echoed as he crumbled to the floor, but Minaeve continued drawing from his pool of power. My heart galloped inside my chest seeing this, feeling like I was going to shatter into a million little pieces.

My animal surged inside my chest as Castor frantically threw his arms around me, hauling me toward the back of the crowd.

"Castor! No. Please!" I grunted as he lifted me off my feet, carrying me backward through the gathering and away from Daxton. "Castor!" He muffled my voice with his hand across my mouth.

"Do not scream," he whispered in a harsh tone. "Do not draw attention our way. Follow me out the back, Sky. I'll come back for him, but we need to get *you* out of here now."

I was prepared to tear through Minaeve myself to help free Daxton if I had to, which was exactly why Castor was forcing me to leave. My heart and my animal were begging to stay with Daxton—to do anything in our power to help save him.

Castor wrapped his arms around me, sneaking toward the wall in the back and finding a side door that allowed us to leave unseen. With everyone's attention locked on the queen and Daxton, our departure went unnoticed.

Outside the ballroom, Castor dropped me onto the ground and forcefully pushed me up against the wall. His arms framed my head as he stared at me in silent outrage. I could see the look of pain etched into his features, and I realized I wasn't the only one who was angry. I cursed at myself for being so selfish.

"Cas, I—"

"Don't." His dark brown eyes were an endless sea of regret and guilt that suffocated the words I was trying to form. He pushed off against the wall and paced along the hallway before speaking to me. "Go to the room."

"What? Like hell I'm leaving." How could he think that I was going to simply drift into the background and stand idly by as *that* was happening in the next room? It wasn't in my character to just ignore this. I wasn't a fully trained healer, but I still had a gift that could help. I needed to help. There wasn't any other choice for me in this matter, especially when it concerned someone that I cared for.

"Do I need to haul you out of here and tie you to the bedpost?"

"You wouldn't dare."

"Try me." Castor glared, backing me up against the wall once more. "Skylar, I like you—I really do. But right now, I don't give two shits about what you want. It's not about you right now."

"You think?" I roared back. "It's about Daxton. I don't care if I'm safe. I need to help him." Castor's stare bore into mine, and for a long, silent moment, neither one of us moved or uttered a sound. I knew this look, all shifters did. This was a dance of dominance. To see who was willing to back down first and bend to the will of the other. Well, sorry, Castor. I was never going to back down when it came to protecting those I cared for. He should have known that by now.

"Please," Castor finally asked, dropping his challenging gaze. "Just go to the room. Can you do that?" Castor asked with a stern, flat expression.

"I can't explain it," I confessed, shaking my head. "I just can't leave without knowing Daxton will be all right."

"That's exactly what I'm trying to do, Skylar!" If we didn't have to keep our voices down, I knew he would've been screaming. "Your death will only kill him faster," he growled, this time flashing his elongated canines as he did so. "Daxton is *my* brother. *My* high prince. It's my duty to follow and uphold his command, and I was sworn to keep you safe above all else. Do not push me on this and force me to uphold a promise I made to my brother."

I pushed back the tears from forming in my eyes. Not out of fear from Castor, but from the terror I saw in his eyes for Daxton. Without saying another word, I picked up the skirt of my dress and sprinted down the corridor to our room.

Thankfully, there were no other souls in sight as I stormed through the hall. Reaching the heavy golden framed door that led to our shared quarters, I grasped the metal handle and threw it open, quickly spinning around to slam it shut once more. Racing toward the window across the blue and gold room, I twisted the latch open, desperate for the fresh night air to help calm my shaking nerves. I held my breath as the seconds ticked by for what seemed like hours, and the minutes seemed to stretch on for days. Pacing through the room, I became restless, wringing my hands together and eagerly waiting for my shifter hearing to alert me to anyone coming my way. I hated this, but there was nothing else I could do right now.

My ears picked up the sounds of footsteps in the hall, followed by the scent of fresh pine and mountain air. *Daxton.* I sprinted across the room and leaped to turn the handle.

"Castor," I gasped as he and another High Fae male carried an unconscious Dax through the doorway.

"To the side room." Castor motioned to the other male. They both gripped Daxton's waist with an arm over each of their shoulders, carrying him carefully across the threshold. "Bastard gave her too much," Castor cursed.

"Why?" the other male asked. His hazel eyes contrasted against the whispers of silver that highlighted the dark brown hair hanging just below his jawline.

Castor glanced my way, and instantly, I understood why Daxton had freely offered so much to Minaeve. "Adohan."

I opened the secret door to the smaller adjacent room as the males carried Dax through, carefully laying him on top of the bed. This room held the bare minimum compared to the other, with only enough space for the bed, a small side table, and a dresser on the other side. The walls were a stone-gray color, matching the outside of the castle with an open doorway to the adjacent washroom with a large, plain white bathing tub.

I didn't hesitate to find my place, kneeling at Dax's side on the edge of the bed. Reaching up, I brushed the hair away from his face and trailed my fingers across his bearded cheek, waiting and watching for any sign of him waking up.

"Prince Castor, what more can I do to assist you or our high prince?" the male asked, looking at Daxton and then at me.

"Nothing more this evening," Castor said with pursed lips, clearly more concerned for his brother's well-being than he was letting on. "Thank you for stepping forward to help, Reece. Dax has all he needs for tonight."

"Yes, thank you," I said, reaching out to grasp his hand in gratitude before returning my attention to Daxton. Reece seemed to blush at my thanks, but I didn't give it much thought. My world was locked on the male lying unconscious next to me.

Bowing slightly, Reece quietly took his leave. Once he was gone, I released my own magical barrier, allowing my scent to fill the room. Castor shifted uneasily, taking a step toward the doorway as my scent swirled and combined with Daxton's. I hadn't paid much attention to my own scent before, but it was just as Daxton described it. The warm aroma of burning cedar combined with his pine and winter air, creating a unique balance.

"Dax?" I leaned closer, caressing his cheek in my palm. He twitched, and he released a quiet groan. "Castor!" I gasped.

Castor was lightning fast as he knelt by his brother's side next to me. "Hey. Looks like I'm still retaining the title of the *smart* brother."

"I'd say I agree with you, but then we would both be wrong." Daxton grinned. He actually grinned, and I couldn't help but shake my head and release a small laugh of gratitude. "Fuck," he groaned, "please tell me you have whiskey or something stronger to take the edge off. This feels worse than Gauntlet training days."

"Males," I muttered, trying to smile as he turned his gaze toward me.

Daxton lifted his quivering arm and placed his calloused palm on my cheek. "Found you ... Spitfire."

"Why am I not surprised by this anymore," I said as I moved closer, trying to assess his condition as discreetly as I could. "You're ice cold, Dax."

"That's not a very nice thing to say," Daxton said, closing his eyes and wincing as he moved to sit up on the bed. "And here I thought we were starting to spark something. Not the other way around."

"Good grief. You've lost it." Castor rolled his eyes, reaching out a hand and placing it on his brother's shoulder. "You gave her too much, you gods-damned idiot."

"Careful," Daxton warned. "I *will* remember how you keep insulting my intelligence the next time we're sparring. You know why I did it, Cas." He winced. "Did Seamus ...?"

"Yes."

I looked at Castor as I leaned closer to Daxton, sitting on the edge of the bed next to him. "What about Seamus?"

Castor grunted as he moved to stand at the foot of the bed. "You want me to tell her?" Dax didn't protest, so Castor interpreted his lack of objection as encouragement. "Seamus will be the one bedding his queen tonight, with perhaps a few others joining them," he said with a look of disgust. "She gets an erotic high from all the power she siphons. Daxton gave her a larger offering of his magic to not only help Adohan ... but to make it impossible for her to expect anything more from him tonight."

"Smart plan." I sighed, relief rolling through me knowing Daxton wasn't going to be forced to spend the night with Minaeve. "Just not the life-draining aspect of it."

"Well worth it," Dax muttered, and I didn't hesitate to agree.

Sitting up on the bed, I began preparing my healing magic. "All right, start getting him undressed, Castor. I'm going to heal you tonight, Daxton."

"No." Daxton's eyes shot open, his stare burning a hole through me. His body trembled with violent convulsions as he forced himself to sit forward, pushing himself upright on his strong arms that held a tenth of his normal strength.

"Yes," I fired back at him with the same unwavering glare he was shooting at me.

"Skylar, the trials are a little more than twelve hours from now. The last time you healed me after the queen siphoned my magic, it put you into a shifter's sleep."

"And?" I countered, defiantly crossing my arms in front of my chest.

"*And* I can't let you jeopardize yourself like that for my sake."

I stared him down. "What makes you think I'll be able to focus in the labyrinth knowing that you're suffering and I didn't help?" I asked. "I'm beginning to agree with Castor's insults to your state of mind because you are a gods-damned idiot if you think I'm not going to heal you."

"Gods be damned, Skylar. This is not a joke," Daxton argued.

"Do you see me laughing?" I pursed my lips together, raising my brows. "I know it's not, Dax!" I yelled, this time rising on the bed, so I was even with his eyeline. "I'm well aware of what lies in wait for me tomorrow. I understand the burden I carry not only for *my* home and *my* people but for all of Valdor." His lips pursed together as he silently listened to my ranting.

"I know that no shifter has bested the logic of the labyrinth. That Stark, the last champion, made it to the final obstacle and then turned back … swallowed by some unknown madness or fear that ultimately killed him." Dax stiffened uncomfortably, his brows pinching together, realizing I knew what happened to the last shifter. "I also know that if I fail, *this* sadistic cycle of nightmares continues for you and everyone here in the Inner Kingdom. I know that another shifter in one hundred years must leave their home and step into this role I am in now. I know all this, Dax." I stared him down, unwilling to budge. "And *yes*, I will still heal you."

The room went silent. Neither Daxton nor Castor said a word or muttered a sound as seven seconds ticked by like seven hours.

"I can't enter the labyrinth with the clear mind needed to win if I'm …" I was fumbling over my words now. Great. I swallowed and tried to steady my shaking hands. "If I'm worried about *you*, Daxton." I turned away from his burning gaze. Afraid of what he might see or perhaps what I wouldn't see in return. "I'm sorry," I muttered. "I'm sorry that I'm not strong enough to push the thought of you aside and pretend that it means nothing."

"Castor, leave us," Daxton commanded in a flat tone, his eyes never leaving my face.

Castor nodded and went to the door without arguing. "I'll ward this room along with the other. If anyone comes looking for either of you, they won't be able to detect your presence." Dax gave him a nod of thanks as Castor slipped outside, latching the door shut behind him.

The fae lights in the high corners dimmed, casting us in a shadow that concealed the strong features of Daxton's tired, weathered face. I braced myself to turn to look at him.

Gods, this demanding drive to protect him was overwhelming, and I didn't want to fight it anymore. My animal stirred in my center, encouraging me to give in to my feelings and allow all logic to fall to the side. If tonight was my last night in this world, I wouldn't want to spend it anywhere else.

I held up my hands as I slid closer next to him. "Will you let me heal you? Please, Dax," I practically begged. "Just enough so I won't lose my mind with worry while I'm in the first trial."

I could see him grimace, struggling to accept my request. I knew I was asking him to put aside his reservations to appease my own, and although it was selfish of me, I had no choice.

I saw him nod yes, and I didn't hesitate to act, fearful he might change his mind. I called upon my healing magic and placed my palms under his silk shirt, resting them on top of his bare chest, concentrating on healing his energy levels.

After a minute, Daxton firmly grabbed my wrists in his hands. "That's enough, Spitfire," he said. The fact that he could lean forward without trembling meant I had done my job. "I can manage from here."

I nodded in agreement, content with the amount of damage he allowed me to repair.

"All right," I said, but he didn't release me, nor did I move away.

"Skylar," he whispered, and I imagined what deeper meaning lay beneath. "You don't ever have to apologize for who you are or how you feel when you're with me. The more time I'm gifted to spend in your presence, the more your strength and beauty—both inside and out—transcends past all my hopes and dreams."

"Dax, I-I …" I was speechless. His quivering hand released my wrists and intertwined our fingers together. "If Castor hadn't hauled me out of there tonight, I would've … I would have tried to kill her." *Gods. Above.* I didn't know if I could, but at that moment, watching him writhe in pain with his life being sucked out of him, I knew I wanted her dead. Seeing him and Adohan suffer like that bore a deep hole in my heart.

"I know," he said softly as he pulled me closer. Daxton moved his shoulders, bringing himself into the dim light and drawing me in until his lips were mere breaths away from mine. "Trust me. I know."

I didn't dare move or even breathe. I couldn't bring myself to kiss him, even though every fiber of my being was screaming inside to do it. I would wait for Daxton to take the lead, giving him control tonight.

This close to Daxton, I could feel his heart drumming inside his chest. Despite the coldness of his skin, I could sense a flicker of heat radiating from within his center. It sang to me, to my animal, and we were anxious to answer its call. His eyes scanned my features before finding the flower hairpin from Crimson City.

"This is beautiful," he said.

"Remember asking me what my favorite flower was?" I watched Daxton's eyes soften as he gave me a shallow nod. "This is it. I didn't even know it existed until I saw it in the shop."

"The moondance flower," Daxton said the name with familiarity and ease.

"You know it?"

He reached up and stroked my cheek, bringing my gaze to meet his. "More than you know." The way he looked at me stole the breath from my lungs.

Gazing into his entrancing eyes, I could feel the longing building behind his stare. "What do you want, Dax?"

It was the same question he asked me the night before. I allowed my fingers to trace over his arms and dared to move them toward the opening of his shirt against his chest.

"You," he rasped with heavy, heated breath. "I want *you*, Skylar. I'm tired of fighting against my desire to have you, and so gods-damn sick of denying it." I immediately pulled up my skirt, straddling his waist as his hands cupped my backside, possessively hauling me into his lap. "But …" he whispered.

Well, that's one way to dampen a mood.

Chapter Ten

I froze and swallowed a gulp of regret for being so bold. Leaping into his lap and straddling him like this was impulsive. I tried to move back, but his grip stopped me.

Confused, I shook my head at him. His words and actions were not matching up. I cocked a suspicious brow toward him, silently asking, *What the hell are you doing?* He returned a deep, sensual grin paired with a chuckle of amusement that vibrated deep within his chest.

"But …?" I boldly asked.

Deciding to test a theory I rotated my hips, grinding my apex against his growing shaft. His immediate moan and heavy sigh in response were encouraging.

"Gods … Fuck, Skylar," he cursed, his scent changing with his rising need. The aroma of his arousal was mind-altering, only making me crave him more. "You know, your arousal smells just as sweet to me," Daxton whispered. "The calming yet wild nature of your burning spirit is a remedy I can't seem to get enough of. The mere hint of your arousal makes me want to fall on my knees before you and worship you like the queen you are."

"Tempting offer, Princey," I teased, giving him a wicked grin as I threaded my hands into his hair. I tugged his head to the side as I bent to taste the nape of his neck. A low growling purr emanated from Daxton's throat, urging me to continue tasting him. I began gently trailing my lips along the curve of his chin down to his ear. I then paused, feeling his entire body tense.

"But …?" I repeated, halting my progress.

Daxton encircled my long hair around his wrist and pulled me upward. "But—" His breath was staggered, and the entrance between my thighs dripped with anticipation. He was forceful and aggressive with his hold on me, controlling me in a primal way that sang to the animal thriving inside my middle.

"But …" He slowly released his hold on my hair and grasped the base of my neck with one hand while the other began working its way underneath my gown. "These are not the proper conditions for the first time I have my way with you, Skylar Cathal. You deserve better than this—better from me. But it doesn't mean we can't enjoy *other* things tonight."

"The *first* time … huh?" I playfully mocked, twirling a finger around a strand of his luscious hair.

"Yes." He grinned, catching my play on words. "The *first* time I fuck you, I'll have you shaking and trembling so immensely from the intensity of your orgasms that you'll be unable to leave my bed. I intend to make that beautiful voice of yours hoarse from screaming my name over and over again as I make you come with my mouth, my fingers … and then, finally, my cock buried deep inside you."

My eyes widened with pure elation, my apex throbbing with a deep-seated need that could only be fed by his touch. I didn't care which one he picked to please me with first. I already knew what his fingers and mouth could do, and selfishly, I needed more.

"That a promise?" I breathed heavily, my chest rising and falling in deep swells. He nuzzled his face into the nook of my neck, kissing the sensitive spot near my collarbone that drove me absolutely wild. "*Daxton*—"

Hearing his name on my lips caused him to release a pleasing rumble from deep within his chest. In response, he thrusted his hips up between my thighs, slowly releasing his lips from my skin.

"The moment you first entered the ballroom tonight," he rasped, "I became lost in your beauty. You're an absolute vision, breathtaking in rags or riches, and even more so naked." I bit my lip, blushing at the last remark, but Daxton's smirk only grew. "You shined brighter and more beautiful than any alluring diamond or rare jewel tonight. I couldn't, nor do I want to *ever* take my eyes off you."

"I heard you had this dress made for me."

"I did." He leaned back, examining the delicate handiwork of the tailor. Slowly, Daxton traced his hands over my curves, his fingers skimming along the bottom of my breasts and lingering along the deep V of the dress. "It needs to come off, though. I'd hate to see it torn to shreds."

"You first." I smirked.

He flashed me a wicked grin that exposed his long, sharp canines. "What're you playing at, Spitfire?"

Oh, the places I want him to use those teeth. I had an idea in mind, but I needed to make sure he was well enough to enjoy it with me.

"Care for a bath?" A spark of lust ignited my words. I wasn't going to let tomorrow's trouble interfere with tonight.

His hooded eyes slanted as he peered at the washroom. "Alone—or with you?"

"With me," I said as I unfastened the clasps at the top of my gown. "I'll need your help, though." I stood and turned my back toward him as his fingers meticulously unbuttoned the delicate clasps that ended near the base of my spine. I held onto the edges of my gown and stepped toward the direction of the washroom. "Get undressed, and I'll fill the tub." I passed through the opening and heard the creak of the bed not long after I rounded the corner.

I knew he was still recovering, so I planned to move cautiously at first, allowing him to set the pace and take charge of how far we could go.

One of the benefits of the fae magic and, apparently, a rich, decadent palace was that there was a supply of scalding hot water that you could summon with the turn of a single knob. I adjusted the dial, getting the temperature just right as it filled the tub to the brim.

The sound of bare feet stepping onto the washroom tile caught my attention. Without turning around, I stood up from the water's edge, dropping the sides of my gown and revealing my naked flesh.

Daxton rushed to cross the distance between us, his chest against my bare back as he brushed my hair to the side, slowly tracing his fingers across my shoulder. Heat flushed my cheeks as I tilted my head to rest it against the crook of his neck. His firm, muscular frame molded against mine, making me tremble with desire as his pulsing cock pressed against my backside. My fingers reached up to thread into his midnight and silver hair, pulling him toward me while he cupped my exposed breasts in his large hands. He used his knuckles to tantalize my nipples, making them harden into perfect peaks.

"Daxton," I moaned as his lips hovered over the skin along my neck.

"I'm a gods-damned fool," he swore. "I can't believe I haven't kissed you yet. Since I saw you walk into the room tonight, it was all I could think about doing."

"That can be fixed." I dropped my arms and turned around to see all of him.

The sight of my high prince standing unencumbered was exhilarating. He was absolute perfection, sculpted from head to toe with rippling muscles that mimicked marble. My eyes devoured the sight of him with a hunger roaring in me that I didn't know how to describe.

Admiring his broad shoulders, I traced my palms over his muscles, moving inward toward his firm pecs and down along his rippled, taut stomach. Then, ever so slowly, I allowed my fingers to migrate further down his body, along the V cut in his hips that pointed directly at his large, hardening shaft. I swallowed an audible gasp, my eyes widening as I took in his sheer size for the first time. I had seen my fair share of shifter males in Solace, but Daxton was indeed a sight to behold.

Dax watched me taking in the sight of him with a cunning smirk stretching across tempting lips I needed to taste. A ravenous hunger lurked in the depths of his stormed gaze that I wanted to lose myself within. A strong pulse of desire flooded my body, fueled by the cunning spark of excitement that shone beneath his hooded eyes. His cock throbbed at my light touch, hardening even more as I continued to admire him.

I bit my lip as the apex between my thighs ached.

Daxton released a deep, dominating growl that erupted from within his throat. "Come here, I need you. Tonight, Skylar Cathal, you're mine, and mine alone."

"And *you*, Daxton Aegaeon, High Prince of Silver Meadows, prince who was promised," I said, reciting the titles I knew. "My Dax ... You belong to me." With the dimple appearing against his bearded cheek, I knew my response was well received.

Daxton greedily pulled me into his arms, giving me the most passionate and heated kiss that I had ever felt in my life. My body hummed with pleasure as his lips parted, inviting me to explore his mouth with my tongue while his hands traveled along the curves of my body. I molded myself to him, feeling his hardened length pulse against the soft skin of my stomach.

I wanted him. There was absolutely no denying this fact. I was desperate to explore every inch of his body as he did to me the previous night.

Our rapid breathing increased as we kissed, ignoring the world outside our room and falling into each other's touch without a second thought. I dared to open my eyes as I slowly broke away from our embrace, my heart racing along with my need for him. I placed my hands on his shoulders, pressing down on them to guide Daxton toward a seated position on the tub's edge. I knelt before him, my hands on his knees, guiding them open so I could settle between them.

"I want to taste you," I said as I slipped my hand around the base of his girth. I took hold of him before moving my lips to the tip of his pulsing head. "I want to feel you come deep inside my throat." I licked his sensitive tip first, testing his reaction before parting my lips to taste him. I heard Daxton moan as I relaxed my jaw and devoured him whole.

Dax tilted his head back and aggressively gripped my hair, holding me in place as I blissfully choked on him, reveling in the slight pinch of pain that combined with pleasure. My saliva coated his length, allowing me to stroke the base of his shaft while I pulled away to catch my breath.

"That better not be all you intend to taste tonight, Spitfire. I didn't mark you for a tease."

I greedily began sucking his cock once more, taking him deep into my throat and loving the taste of him. Utilizing my slickened palm to work in tandem with my mouth. I grinned with wicked excitement, his roars of pleasure only encouraging me to continue.

Daxton groaned as he reached out with both hands and gripped my hair, holding me in place. His hips thrust upward, sending the head of his cock colliding with the back of my throat. His entire body began trembling with his release building.

This was so fucking erotic. I couldn't help touching myself, riding waves of pleasure along with him. I moaned as I reached down with one hand between my legs to rub my clit, the other hand now running along the seam of his balls.

"Gods above, Skylar!" Daxton yelled with pure ecstasy. "Yes. Touch yourself. I want you to play with yourself while I fuck your mouth."

I managed to catch my breath and pull my head back, pumping him faster. A bead of precum dripped from the tip, so I bent forward to lick it clean while moving my free hand between my slickened folds. Greedily, I vibrated my fingers across myself as Dax reached down to fondle my breast, rolling my nipple in between his fingers. It felt so euphoric having his hands on me with his cock buried inside my throat. I swallowed, taking him deeper as I released another moan, sending vibrations of pleasure rocketing through him.

"Don't stop. Gods above … Skylar, you're— Keep going. This feels incredible." He groaned in delight.

Daxton's entire body tensed. His grip holding me in place as he vigorously thrusted his hips forward. My animal sent a wave of power through me that crashed against Daxton's. He moaned, and I knew he was close.

I glided my fingers inside myself as Daxton teetered near the edge of his own release. I desperately wanted to see his reaction when he reached the top, so I snapped open my eyes to watch him come. This put Daxton on the verge of exploding. When he opened his eyes to look at me and saw me eagerly watching him fuck my mouth, he couldn't hold back any longer.

He threw his head back and emptied himself deep inside my throat, compelling me to swallow his warm seed.

I slowly pulled away, deliberately never taking my eyes off him. I wiped my lips with the back of my hand to clean up any lingering seed and boldly stood before the trembling male I had just devoured.

"Come here." Daxton reached out to pull me toward him, wildly kissing me, even with traces of his seed still lingering. "That was the best fucking head I've ever had in my life," he rasped between our kisses. He shifted and placed his hands on either side of my face, pulling me back. "Now, it's your turn, Spitfire."

Gods. This male would be the end of me.

Daxton moved to the floor and pulled me to sit in his lap. Even though he had just come, his length began hardening against me as he settled himself between the seam of my backside. He reached around my front to replace my hand with his own, fingering my apex and possessively fondling my breast while his sharp teeth scraped against my neck.

"Oh my ... Daxton," I moaned as he pinched my nipple harder, causing me to gasp.

"You enjoy a bit of pain with your pleasure, my Spitfire?"

If it meant him doing more things like this, then … "Yes." *Hell, yes.*

"What about when I use my teeth on the base of your neck, right here?" His lips parted as his sharp canines scraped against my skin.

"Ahh. Fuck!" I moaned as my body trembled with rolling waves of pleasure crashing into me. Daxton moved his hand to my other breast as he slipped two of his slickened fingers inside me while his thumb rubbed my clit. I was ready for him this time.

"You're so wet, Spitfire. It's taking every ounce of control not to fuck you right now. I need you to come for me," he rasped with a hint of demand in his voice. He kissed the corner of my mouth before saying once more, "Come for me, Skylar."

No problem. I could feel my orgasm rising to the edge, already building when his cock was buried deep within my throat. I recalled the image of him moaning and rolling his hips in pure bliss with my mouth sucking on his manhood.

"I'm close." I could barely speak.

Daxton purred in delight as my body tensed in response to his magical touch.

He swirled two fingers inside me, while quickly vibrating his thumb across my clit. Then, his mouth opened, and he scraped his teeth along the base of my neck, his lips sucking on my flesh.

"Daxton!" I screamed his name, holding nothing back as I shattered to pieces in his grasp.

Thrilling, mind-blowing sensations thrummed through me while my orgasm ravaged my body from the inside out. I collapsed into his embrace, and thankfully, his shaking limbs were strong enough to hold me against him as I came down from the high of my release.

"I couldn't leave you unfinished," he whispered, lightly kissing my brow. "That wouldn't be proper."

"I don't think anything we just did was proper." I laughed.

"Just wait, my Spitfire. Wait until I show you *all* the improper things I want to do with that fiery little mouth and soaked pussy of yours."

"I'm always up for a challenge," I said. "Especially when the reward is this sweet."

"I'm far from sweet," he said with a low growl. "But you seem to be my exception."

I laughed softly and happily reclined in his lap. The smell of his scent became intoxicating as it drifted over my senses, somehow slightly different from before. Dax noticed my shift and adjusted his hold on me. "Something on your mind?"

"Always." I flashed him a coy grin.

"Fair enough," he chuckled. "What *is* on your mind then?"

"Well, I did promise you a bath," I said, looking toward the tub, which was still steaming with fresh warm water. "It would be a shame to allow it to go to waste."

"Indeed, it would. What did you have in mind?"

"Join me," I said. "This time, *you're* allowed to peek."

Dax smiled, his saccharine grin exposing the dimple on his cheek that I coveted and always craved to see. "All right. After you."

I eagerly stepped into the tub, leaving room for Daxton to slip in behind me. The warm water seeped into the pores of my skin as I leaned back into the strong embrace of Daxton's steady arms. We bathed in silence, enjoying the quiet intimate moments while we helped clean one another. After a while, the water cooled, but I still didn't want to leave.

"Your skin is pruning," Dax said.

"I know." I sighed. "I don't want to get out just yet. A few more minutes."

"Very well." He pulled me against his chest and tenderly kissed my brow before finding my lips once more. I sank into his touch, closing my eyes and melting further into his embrace. "Skylar?"

"Yes?" I answered.

"Tell me something about yourself."

That question caught me off guard. "Like what?"

"Tell me about your family … about your friends. I want to know everything about your life before coming here to the Inner Kingdom."

"What specifically?" I asked.

"Everything."

I turned and swiftly kissed his cheek. "All right then." I stood up and grabbed two towels for us to dry off. "We should move this to the bedroom. This could take some time, Princey. And you've already pointed out that my skin's beginning to prune."

"Happy to give you all the time I have." Daxton smiled as he pulled the drain and dried himself off, tucking the towel securely around his waist and not missing my lingering eyes for one second.

We moved into the small bedroom—both blissfully unaware of how late it was, and frankly, we didn't seem to care. I found a slip in a nearby dresser that hung just below my bottom as Daxton donned shorts that clung tightly to his strong thighs. I could see that Daxton was still a bit shaky, and I moved to help him relax under the covers of the small but cozy bed.

"Remind me to kick Castor's ass for taking the larger bed in the other room," Daxton teased, even though I knew he was serious about doing just that.

"I'm happy to help," I said as I curled up next to him, placing my head on his chest and my leg over his.

"All right," he said, tucking his arm around me. "Tell me about your life before the trials ... before *all* of this. I want to know everything."

I settled in close. "Long, long ago ..." I chuckled, knowing my few years of life were just a mere blink in time compared to his. "I was just a baby when Magnus found me on the outskirts of Solace."

I told him everything that night. At least everything I knew about my past, my upbringing, my family, and my friends ... about my life and my pack.

He listened intently, never interrupting, only encouraging me to continue for what seemed like hours on end. I could feel my eyes begin to flutter as the late night slowly turned into the early morning.

"Sleep, Skylar," Daxton whispered as he stroked my hair. "I'll wake you when it's time. The Father still watches us from above in the sky, waiting for his mate to shine her rays down upon our morning."

I could feel my breathing slow as I clung to Daxton, feeling the warmth of his body returning. He held me close and gently stroked my hair until the world around me turned black, and I drifted into a deep, restful sleep.

From a high window near the ceiling, sunlight peeked through the tinted glass, shining directly on my eyes and waking me from a dreamless sleep. I tried to move, but Daxton's arm was draped over me, and I didn't want to disturb him.

I glanced at his sleeping face and melted. Dax was so strikingly handsome that it was hard to believe he was real. While he slept, it was downright sinful. I reached up and stroked his cheek, waiting patiently for those storm-gray eyes to open and greet the morning with me.

"Hello."

Daxton blinked when he found me looking up at him. "Hello, Spitfire." He affectionately bent to kiss my brow before finding my lips, looping his other arm tightly around my waist. "Wasn't I supposed to wake you?"

"I'm an early riser," I said. "Can't help it, but it is well past morning by now …"

Gods Above. Past morning.

Daxton stilled as the reality of today came crashing through our bubble of tranquility. I shot up and practically jumped from the bed, pacing the floor as he raised himself up onto his elbows. I held my hand to my head, racing through a million thoughts and questions pinging around my mind.

What if I fail? What if I win? Crossing the divide … what will I choose? What fears or mind games will I encounter? What logic will be tested? What will I face inside the labyrinth?

"Skylar." Daxton's voice was steady, commanding my attention with just the use of my name on his lips. "Stop spiraling."

Dax swung his feet over the edge of the bed and stood up. "You can do this." I stared blankly at him, clinging to the strength and stability he had always given freely to me. "Remember, the courage of your heart is more important than physical strength. You have the ability to defeat the labyrinth, Spitfire." His stare bore into me, and I became enraptured by the confidence pouring out of his eyes. "Repeat my words," he commanded. "I can do this." He moved to grasp my hands, resting his brow against mine, and inhaling a deep breath while he closed his eyes.

"I can do this," I repeated, sinking into his rhythm and matching my breathing with his.

"I will defeat the trial of the mind."

"I will defeat the trial of the mind."

"When hardship and fear threaten my victory, I will not turn back. I will continue forward."

The certainty of his voice was overpowering, and I knew he believed every word he spoke to me. "When hardship and fear threaten my victory ... I will not turn back. I will continue forward."

"I carry the love and strength of my pack and the hope of all fae that live in the Inner Kingdom."

With power pulsing from my animal within my chest, I repeated, "I carry the love and strength of my pack in Solace and the hope of all fae that live in the Inner Kingdom."

"I am Skylar Cathal," Daxton began, but I didn't need him to finish the words I knew I needed to say out loud.

"I am Skylar Cathal, champion of the Solace pack, and I *will* conquer the trials. I *will* unlock the Heart of Valdor. And I *will* cleanse our world of the wilt."

Chapter Eleven

The first trial is here.

And I am ready.

The stone steps below the palace of Aelius echoed with the sounds of our boots as we slowly descended into obscurity. Fae lights hung along the low ceiling of the passageway, guiding our way through with light from one beginning just as another ended. The shadows that crept along the sides didn't dare approach us as we marched into the depths of the dungeons—one forced step at a time.

Regardless of the outcome today, I would never regret taking my cousin Neera's place as Queen Minaeve's chosen participant. Saving her from the fate of leaving her home and entering the trials of the Heart of Valdor was worth the cost of my life if I failed, though that was not my intention. I was determined to win.

My thoughts drifted to the family I left at home in Solace. Knowing I carried each one of them with me as I marched forward with my head held high.

I wondered what had become of my pack. Was Gilen now our alpha? Would he lead our people with the strength and courage I knew he carried?

Despite my vendetta toward his intention to claim me, I understood why. However, fate held a different path for me. My heart didn't belong with Gilen. And even though I was likely marching down the steps to my death, I was relieved that destiny decided to bring me here.

As ridiculous as it sounded, I began counting the steps as we descended further into the darkened stone hallway beneath the palace of Aelius. I did my best to swallow the inner demons that were clawing away at my nerves as we continued underground, these steps reminding me of the ones I was dragged through in the hunter's lair.

A stray wisp of cold air brushed against the nape of my neck, sending me a silent message of comfort that stirred the sleeping animal spirit inside my chest. His ice igniting liquid fire throughout my veins.

Daxton, the Silver Shadow, High Prince of Silver Meadows, the prince who was promised, followed close behind. His footsteps echoing in perfect sync with my own.

I could sense a connection forming between us that I hadn't noticed before. I was keenly alert to Daxton's every movement, almost sensing him on an instinctual level. I was beyond denying my affection. From the moment I decided to kiss Daxton on the ship, I knew I cared for him.

Daxton insisted, ruse or not, that he was accompanying me as I entered the first trial of the Heart of Valdor.

"This isn't a good idea," Castor protested.

"I'm walking with her," Daxton said. "I'm not asking your opinion on this. I'm telling you."

And that was that.

I led our group, with the others in step behind me. Castor descended with a disgruntled march alongside Daxton. Adohan and Idris followed, walking hand in hand, supporting me with a confident silence as we made our way to the labyrinth's entrance.

The Crimson City couple emerged from their room at the same time we left ours. Adohan was shaky, but he could stand on his own feet without much trouble. Idris was steady by his side.

The fae lights gathered along the ceiling as the stone steps came to an end. I swallowed a gulp of fear as I shut my eyes and clenched my teeth so hard I thought that they would crack.

One hundred and thirty-six.

That's how many steps I had to take to see the light of day again—to feel the fresh, clean air cleanse my lungs and my restless soul once I was victorious. It was not a number I would likely forget.

As we reached the end of our descent into darkness, I moved aside, letting the others pass through the stone-arched entrance to an open foyer leading to yet another underground tunnel. I placed my hands on rough gray rocks, pressing my forehead against the stone, trying to steady my quivering limbs.

"Breathe." Strong hands rubbed my shoulders and back. "You're not in the hunter's lair. You're not alone … Remember, you won't ever be." Daxton moved closer to me, wrapping his arms around my shoulders and turning me toward his chest. "You're stronger than your fears, Spitfire. You're the towering mountain that never bends and never breaks against the strength of the fiercest winds." His lips dared a soft brush of a kiss on the crown of my head as I encircled my arms around his middle. "I've got you, Skylar Cathal." Daxton took a deep, steadying breath and I followed his lead, absorbing his courage and molding it into my own. I could feel his magic building, mine rising to the surface in response. "I will find you."

"We will always find each other," I whispered, burying my head into the nook of his collarbone near the base of his neck.

Those were the words Daxton told me in my dreams when I was tortured and dying underground in the cell of the hunter's lair. I still don't know how he managed to send me those messages, but I didn't dare question them. Instead, I decided to succumb to the magic they somehow possessed.

"Dax," Castor warned in a hushed tone. "We're not alone."

I felt Daxton tense, yet he didn't release his hold on me. I was thankful for this because, without his strength, I wasn't sure I would be able to stand on my own just yet.

I lifted my gaze to the entrance of the tunnel to see a dark-haired High Fae staring at us from across the way. He was a silent threat. I knew all too well that the power of the mind was never something to overlook.

"What are you doing here?" My words were meant to have more bite to them than they did, and I cursed my shaking nerves for their obvious hold over me.

The male casually leaned against the wall and crossed his arms along his chest. His fitted forest-green tunic with gold embellishment shimmered against the fae lights of the underground passageway. "Would you expect me to be anywhere else?"

"Rhett." Daxton said the fae's name, but his cunning deep-set blue eyes remained locked on me. "You should already be with the queen."

"And shouldn't the shifter be finding comfort in the arms of your brother?" Rhett countered as he cocked his head to the side, his elegant, alluring features still unreadable behind a mask of porcelain.

Shit. Well, there goes the ploy of our little ruse.

"Don't even attempt to concoct a rebuttal, Castor." Rhett held up his hand, finally turning his gaze to Daxton. "I'm not a fool, and I can see well enough to infer what is here … even through the lack of daylight in this underground tomb." Blue eyes darted across the distance to collide with gray steel.

A moment of stillness passed between Daxton and Rhett. I watched as they stared at each other, not in aggression or fear, but almost like they were sizing each other up—testing one another like predators dueling over territory or a fresh kill.

"How?" Daxton asked aloud.

"Besides the obvious?" Rhett replied, tilting his head up to assess the air around us. I wasn't worried. I had my shield up, and I knew Daxton did as well.

"You see it," Adohan said, addressing Rhett in a softer tone instead of one fit for a sworn subject of Aelius. The comprehension twinkling in his hazel eyes reminded me that Adohan was more than just a handsome face. "Because this isn't foreign to you." I had no idea what Adohan was referring to, but from the looks of it, Rhett sure as hell did.

"Stop," Rhett said sharply.

There it was. A flash of shock and perhaps sorrow crossed the unreadable, emotionless mask of the illusive male fae. His unruly dark hair aided in concealing the dwelling sadness that anchored a forever lingering pain inside his beautiful cold eyes. I would have missed it if I blinked, but it was there.

Rhett immediately concealed his emotions, as he reached into the shadows. "Here," he said, clearing his throat, "I've brought this trinket to help aid our champion." In his hands, he held a chest plate of black armor, plainly decorated yet humming with magical power. "The bottom half of this armored suit is still proving difficult to locate. I'm unsure of what you may combat inside the labyrinth, but if this helps protect you on your journey, then it was worth the trouble bringing it down here."

"What is it?" I asked as I moved in Daxton's arms.

"It's the armor of Aegis, Skylar," Daxton said as he accepted the chest plate from Rhett's outstretched hand. "You've been searching for this for—"

"A century, give or take a few decades."

"What is this exactly?" I asked again, hesitant to accept aid from a sworn subject of Aelius.

"It's a magical object, Skylar," Castor said, unsheathing one of his thin blades at his hip.

Once the armor was delivered into Daxton's outstretched hand, Rhett wisely took a step back. Castor swiped his dagger at the armor, the blade coming to a swift halt with no indent or scratch on the material.

"It was rumored to be forged with the magic of the Heart of Valdor itself, a gift of protection for its first shifter guardian," Castor said. "This armor will protect the wearer from any physical harm where it covers you."

"It's impenetrable," Daxton said with a suspicious undertone. "And thought to be lost to the depths of the Blue Hole." I flashed Dax a questioning look, with my curiosity spinning like a top.

Rhett cocked his brows upright with an intelligent sparkle in his eyes. "You have your resources, Silver Shadow, and I have mine."

"Is this some kind of trick, Rhett?" I asked.

"Now, why would you think that of me, shifter?"

"Self-preservation," I answered him coldly. To my surprise, Rhett released a small laugh under his breath as he glanced between Daxton and me.

Dax tensed. "Even before meeting us here, you intended to bring this for Skylar. Why?"

Damn, that was a good question. Why hadn't I thought of asking that? Gods, this labyrinth was throwing me off my game.

"Hope."

"Hope?" I repeated as I found the strength in my shaking limbs to release my hold on Daxton and confront Rhett.

"Yes. Hope that you do not feel the sting of death, young champion. For I fear that it is not only your life that hangs in the balance here today."

"Cryptic much?" I sneered. "Can you speak in anything other than riddles?"

Rhett seemed amused with himself as he looked to Daxton. "You nicknamed her *Spitfire*, yes?" I crossed my arms and gave him a narrowing glare. "Fitting," he said as he flipped his gaze back to me.

Daxton moved to my side, pressing himself securely beside me. "Don't, Rhett," he warned with a low growl.

"You don't need to worry about any of this," Rhett said, waving a wide arm around the foyer. "I'm a master of deception that challenges even your second, High Prince Daxton." His eyes cast sideways, meeting Castor's. "I'll wander ahead with Adohan and Idris, giving you a private moment to help her don the armor. The leathers alone won't be enough to stop talons, teeth, or whatever monster she may have to combat in there.

It's a labyrinth … after all. The mind has the ability to turn our nightmares into reality."

I pursed my lips in frustration, still not understanding why Rhett was lending me this aid. Was there a hidden agenda behind his seemingly good intentions? What was I thinking? Of course there was. He was a High Fae from the Aelius court of all places. There was *always* a hidden agenda.

"You're running out of time," Rhett said.

"I'm well aware of the timing of the trials," I answered, mustering more fire than before. "Why don't you run along to your queen's side? I'm sure Prince Seamus is anxiously awaiting the trusted members of his court to arrive."

Rhett turned the side of his mouth upward, but I could see a hint of displeasure at my snide remark. This fae was a wild card, perhaps an undecided party member, teetering between two opposing forces at play. Or he was simply out for what I'd guessed in the first place—self-preservation.

"Knowledge is sadly just out of reach at times for the youth," Rhett sneered with a half-smirk, "but not courage or character, it seems. Thank the Gods above." Rhett kept his cunning glare locked on me as he nodded for Adohan and Idris to follow his lead.

"We'll see you at the labyrinth," Idris said as she quickly hugged me and kissed my cheek before joining Adohan at the tunnel entrance.

The Crimson City high prince bowed his head to me and then to Daxton. "Minutes … would be pushing it, my friend."

"I know," Daxton said.

"I will be on the steps," Castor announced as he moved out of sight. "Don't want any more surprise visitors for today."

Then, it was just the two of us, surrounded by nothing but the fae lights that glistened in the shadowed passageway.

Daxton spoke more with his actions than his words. The meanings behind his gentle touch, his mannerisms, or his demeanor spoke for him when words could not. Me, on the other hand, I tended to fill the silence with a never-ending sea of questions or wonderings.

But now … just mere moments before the first trial, I was uncharacteristically silent.

"Hold back your hair," Daxton said softly. "I'll help you fasten the chest plate. It might be large right now, but once you set it in place, it will mold to fit your frame."

"Magic?"

"Magic." He nodded.

"I thought magic was unable to enter the labyrinth."

"Magical objects tend to play by their own rules at times," he said. "And wearing another layer of protection won't hinder you—magical or not."

I turned around so he could help fasten the leather straps of the black armor around my back. It was loose, mainly around my shoulders, while cutting into my hips and narrowing around my chest.

"Apparently, a much larger male wore this before me."

"Clearly," Daxton huffed in agreement as his hands traced over the curve of my hips and rested for a moment on my backside.

I arched my brow at him, giving him a playful smirk. "I don't think there are any clasps that far down."

"My mistake." He chuckled.

"You, Daxton, High Prince of Silver Meadows, are admitting to a mistake?"

"Are you referring to my wandering hands?" Daxton asked as he snapped the last tie into place, the armor molding perfectly around me, just like he said it would. "Or my lingering eyes?"

I turned around to glare at him. "Both," I teased. "But please, feel free to continue making them." There it was, that sweet smile that kindled the fire in my heart and stirred my animal to life inside my chest.

"I needed to see that," I said as I reached up to cup his face in my hand. He leaned into my touch as I caressed his cheek. "Answer me this …" I asked with a hint of playfulness in my tone.

"Anything."

"Careful what you promise, Princey."

"Care to test the limits of my words?" he asked.

The corner of my mouth turned upward as I formulated my grand question. "How do you keep your beard so trimmed and yet still so soft?"

Daxton bit his lower lip, and his eyes closed with a laugh hiding behind his lips. "That? That is the question tumbling around in your inquisitive mind?"

"Why not?"

Daxton shook his head and reached to grasp my hand in his, uncaging his smile so it reached his pointed ears. "Magic."

"But of course!" I said with an air of lightness that I knew we both needed before I tumbled into the suffocating unknowns of the labyrinth.

Daxton pulled me closer, wrapping his arm securely around my middle. "What else do you need, Skylar?"

Well, that is the question of the century now, isn't it?

I gazed up into his luminous storm-gray eyes, never wanting to forget them or how I felt when he looked at me like this. What did I need? Was he asking what I needed to succeed in the trials or what I needed in the silent moment wrapped in his cocoon of strength? Was the answer one and the same?

"I can tell you're spiraling," Daxton murmured as he pressed his forehead against mine. "Don't overthink it. Just tell—"

This time, I silenced *him*.

I surged forward, crashing my lips against his and entangling my fingers into his free-flowing hair. He shifted against me, pressing his body against mine and lifting me off my feet with the sweep of his tongue across the inside of my mouth. His hands migrated over the armor he had just helped me fasten, fondling me through my layers of protection that I hoped to the Gods I wouldn't need. I knew this kiss couldn't last much longer, so I savored every second of it.

We both paused, regrettably breaking our embrace as we possessively wrapped our arms around each other. "I'm not scared of the labyrinth, Dax," I boldly whispered.

"You never cease to amaze me, Spitfire," Daxton said as he nuzzled into the nape of my neck.

Sadly, we both knew our moment together was gone.

"Dax. Sky ..." Castor's warning echoed from the staircase.

"There's not enough time," Daxton murmured as I pulled back to look at him. "Skylar—"

"Shh," I said as I quickly pressed a light kiss to his lips. "I said I wasn't afraid, but if you start talking like this is the last time I'll see you, then ... Then I'll start second-guessing my chances of coming out of this alive." I flashed him a reassuring grin, trying to give him the strength he had always shared with me.

"Wise for someone so young."

"Rhett can eat his words," I said with a coy grin. "It's okay," I whispered, placing my hands on his chest. "Elders in my pack say the mind is the first thing to go with old age. I'm here to keep you all on your toes." I couldn't help teasing him. I needed to see his smile once more before Dax had to disappear, and his Silver Shadow mask needed to be worn once again.

"Again, you never cease to amaze me." He hugged me tight, giving me exactly what I needed to take the next steps forward.

Castor's footsteps were hesitant at first, but we all knew time was not on our side. "I'm sorry," he said in a reluctant tone.

"Don't be," I said. "I'm ready." I turned to Daxton with power blazing in my amber eyes that fueled me with strength. He nodded and bent to kiss not my hand but the scar beneath my right wrist.

Castor glided silently next to me, extending his arm. "Ready?"

"As I'll ever be," I said, staring into Daxton's comforting gaze for what could be the last time.

"Then let's go. If we spend any more time lingering, Minaeve may send Seamus to retrieve us."

"He's the last thing I want to deal with right now."

"Agreed," Daxton said as he turned and began leading Castor and me through the fae-lit hallway.

Thanks to my shifter half, I was able to see perfectly in the dark and didn't need the fae lights to see what lay in wait for me ahead. Queen Minaeve wore a deep green gown embroidered with gold stitching that shimmered against the three sparkling gems on the crown that grazed the top of her flowing ebony hair. Her turquoise eyes, painted with gold, narrowed as she watched us approach the entrance to the labyrinth. I didn't know what she was trying to speculate over or infer from our arrival, but Castor only drew me in closer to keep the facade of our intimate relationship.

Seamus was armed with a long sword at his queen's side. His dark forest-green armor matched his queen's and contrasted against his light blond hair. He wore a skeptical expression on his face that made my insides twist in on themselves. Seamus reminded me of a snake, always lurking and yet still unpredictable in when they would strike. I imagined if he were a shifter, that animal would fit him perfectly.

"You gave her the armor of Aegis?" Minaeve said to Rhett, who stood off to the side, cloaked in shadows underneath the arching fae lights.

"Of course," Rhett replied. "I followed your request, my queen, and sought out the trinket myself." Oh, great. This was somehow her idea? I was now regretting putting this on.

"I don't recall giving you the directive of arming the shifter," Minaeve sneered, and I couldn't help the look of surprise that crossed my features.

Rhett shifted out from the shadow and faced Seamus and High Queen Minaeve. "I believe you instructed us to do all that was in our power to help aid the champion and ensure her arrival at the first trial. The poor creature was shaking so badly the other night at the thought of facing this trial, and I thought of something that would help ease her worry."

"But this is a trial of the mind," Seamus cut in as Castor and I reached them.

"Yes," Rhett countered, "and the mind is a powerful tool that can force the body to succumb to wounds and vice versa. This adds a layer of protection to ease the strain of the mind, knowing the body is well guarded."

Seamus grunted with annoyance and rolled his eyes, but I could tell that he was not going to argue against Rhett's logic. Rhett might not be a hardened warrior like the rest of them, but his knowledge and wit were just as sharp as their blades.

"Very well," Minaeve muttered. "Shifter." Her attention snapped to me, and I felt a curl of darkness laced in her words as she pushed her power throughout our surroundings. "The labyrinth entrance is through the black fog. It will only allow the bearer of the champion's mark to pass through. Once inside, you have until sundown to complete the unknown tasks that lie ahead."

I knew all this, and I didn't see why she needed to repeat herself. "I understand."

"Then don't waste any more time. Say your goodbyes and enter." Her venomous words struck me with force, but I refused to flinch against them. "Daxton," Minaeve said as she tilted her head in his direction, "stand by my side." Daxton nodded and moved to hover near the queen's shoulder, joining Adohan and Seamus.

Anger churned in my middle, my animal sending flickers of our own power throughout my limbs.

"Good," Castor murmured. "You're going to need every ounce of that."

I tilted my head toward him. "Meaning?"

"Anger … rather than fear. I would remove the latter before entering."

I knew from training with Magnus that fear led to panic, and in the labyrinth, if I panicked, I was dead. "Anger it is then," I said, allowing my hatred for the queen to fuel me.

"Come here," Castor said as he wrapped his arms around me. Ruse or not, I felt the sincerity in his embrace. This was real. "Do me a favor, will you?" he whispered so only I could hear.

"Aren't I already doing you and everyone in Valdor a favor?"

"It's a small one, I promise," he teased as he squeezed me tighter, placing a gentle kiss on my cheek. "Don't. Die."

"No pressure."

"I only ask of my students what I know they can achieve. Nothing more, nothing less," he said as he moved to kiss my other cheek.

"Again, no pressure."

"That's the spirit."

"You're not getting any premonitions of my impending death, are you?"

He grinned. "None! You're in luck for once, it seems."

"Don't jinx it," I countered. Castor swiped his fingers in front of his lips, silencing any additional comment he planned to make.

I released Castor's hands and boldly turned to the alluring fog that shimmered against the fae lights. I couldn't make out any details of the labyrinth, only a dense blanket of midnight clouds. As I stepped closer to the entrance, tendrils of the mist bent and twisted around my outstretched hand. I could feel the thrum of magic caressing my skin, searching out my identity as it encircled my body.

Well, that is my cue, then.

I picked up one foot and then the other, slowly entering the fog and walking toward the entrance of the first trial.

I dared a glance backward just for a second before the world I knew disappeared. The only thing I longed to see was already staring directly back at me.

Gray eyes that mimicked the storms over the mountain peaks softened, flooding me with unspoken support he never failed to give me.

Daxton's face was the last thing I saw before the fog encased me in the world of the labyrinth. It was an image I would never forget, and one I would carry with me as I entered the first trial of the Heart of Valdor.

Chapter Twelve

This place was cold as if death lingered in the cracks along the gray stone walls. It was desolate, isolated, and, above all else, petrifying. The hairs on my neck stood on end, with my animal spirit restlessly stirring inside me. She was warning me. Not to run but to keep my guard up, to see what my eyes alone couldn't. Nothing was as it seemed in here. Our minds would be tested in this place, and if I had any hope of surviving, I knew I had to rely on her primal instincts and my own.

The same stone that encased the staircase on our descent from the palace adorned the walls along with the spiked vines of some kind of ivy-looking plant.

There was no ceiling above my head, only a haunting abyss of endless night that I could not see through, despite my keen eyesight. I knew the labyrinth was underground, and it would be dark here, but this was something else. The air surrounding me smelled foul and putrid, doing little to settle my pounding heart and shaking nerves.

A singular path stretched out before me with only one direction to wander. I squared my shoulders, swallowed my reservations, and turned to take my first step on the broken cobblestone path. My animal's presence surged inside my middle, reminding me that regardless of the terrors that lay before me, I was not alone in this fight. I smiled to myself, knowing I always had her with me, a gift inherited from my father that never ceased to amaze me.

As I took my first step forward, a flash of bright light blinded me from above, forcing me to shield my eyes and turn away.

Why, hello there.

What was that? I spun around frantically, looking for the source of the voice I heard. "Who's there?" I said. Was there someone else in here with me? I thought only the champion bearing this mark could enter the first trial.

Such a twisted yet beautiful mind you have … Oh, the games we shall play.

"Who's there?" I screamed again into the emptiness. Shivers crawled up my spine as I realized my ears hadn't heard the voice. It echoed inside my mind.

I would not dawdle if I were you, sshhhifter. Time, as you know, is not on your side. The key you seek will only be freed if you can meander the pathway and reach my center. If you reach this point before the Mother seeks her rest and the Father takes his turn watching us from above, you may leave here alive.

I realized this inhuman, cold, decrepit voice speaking directly into my mind was the labyrinth itself.

Must another fall so soon? The voice of the Labyrinth gave an audible sigh of pity. *I had such high hopes after the last champion. He made it so far, but alas, his mind was ultimately lost.*

Suddenly, I felt the floor beneath my feet tremble, forcing me to stagger and fall to my knees. I braced my hands against the wobbling stone, praying for the shaking to stop. I had never felt anything like this in my life. The rolling shockwaves vibrated the earth, forcing me off balance and preventing me from moving onward.

Hurry along, the labyrinth taunted as the sounds of crumbling stone echoed around me. Was the labyrinth collapsing?

I twisted my head to look behind me as the floor began to disappear. "What the—"

Never say I didn't warn you.

Adrenaline surged through my veins as I sprang to my feet, sprinting as fast as I could down the path. Each time the heel of my foot lifted from the cobblestone, it vanished into nothing, disappearing into a bottomless chasm.

My animal pumped power through me, urging my limbs to move faster than they ever had before. Drafts of vile-smelling air wafted from the empty abyss that chased after me, reminding me of death incarnate and what awaited if I faltered in my steps. I pumped my arms as fast as I could, trying to encourage my trembling legs to follow suit.

Daring a glance over my shoulder, I could no longer see the entrance or the fog I passed through to enter. I took a sharp turn to my right, grabbing the corner of the wall with my outstretched hand to help continue my momentum along the corridor. The labyrinth shuddered and shook once more, throwing me off balance, and I crashed hard into the ground. My chest collided with a protruding piece of stone, but thankfully, the armor of Aegis kept me from cracking my sternum.

Lucky break for you, it seems …

Rubbing the center of my chest, I silently thanked Rhett for giving me this armor. Then, to my surprise, I noticed the halt of the vanishing cobblestone floor during the earthquake. Thank the Gods; this gave me time to think and get my bearings, but my relief was short-lived. Crouched on the ground, I heard a faint growl and screeching sound from beneath me, under the labyrinth itself. I bent to place my ear on the ground to listen but soon regretted my decision.

"What in the Gods' names is that?" I exclaimed. The sounds of teeth and claws vibrated beneath the layer of cobblestone, steadily growing louder from the empty pathway behind me.

My children are hungry ...

Well, fuck ... this was not good. "For what?"

For you. And, yes, I agree, not good at all. They only awaken and are granted an opportunity to hunt and eat once a century when my gates open. They absolutely love the taste of fresh shifter flesh.

"Sorry to disappoint them, but they won't be dining on me tonight."

It's actually the bones they enjoy the most. The flavor lasts longer.

"Or any other shifter ever again!" I yelled at nothing and everything all at once.

The soul-rattling scraping of claws against stone amplified. The echoes of jaws opening in anticipation of a meal quickened my frantically beating heart. They were mere inches away, hiding in the darkness behind me where the stone path once stood. I gasped in pure terror and scurried from the gaping hole filled with deadly creatures. In all my life, I had never heard such monstrous sounds. These creatures, or children— whatever was lurking down there, were not something I wanted to meet.

So brave. The other champions thought that as well. But in the end, fortunately for my children, they were wrong.

"Well, I'm not like the others that have come before me." The walls and floor finally stopped shaking, and I regained my balance enough to jump to my feet and continue running.

No ... The voice of the labyrinth paused for a moment, making my insides turn. *You are definitely not. You are* more. *Interesting. This shall be a treat.*

"If you say so." I wasn't planning on sticking around long enough to find out.

I sprinted round another corner, bearing right. My feet pounded against the cold stone with relentless resolve. I was determined to distance myself from those monsters as much as possible. As I rounded another turn, the fog from the entrance reappeared along the straightaway, forcing me to skid to a halt. I shuddered with surprise and fell backward, thrusting my arms in front of my face to try and shield myself. The mist encased me, encircling my limbs and brushing over my skin with its magic, almost like it was tasting me.

Ahh—there it is. You're not just a shifter; you're also human. This is a first. I'm genuinely intrigued.

It wasn't the first time I'd heard that. "Happy to hear the trial of the mind has some intelligence present. I was curious when you'd discover that hidden gem about my origins."

And a quick wit as well. Oh, what a delight.

"You've got a sick way of describing something as—*fun*," I said to the emptiness as the fog slipped away into the cracks of the walls. I pushed up onto my feet once more and jogged along the straightaway. I could keep this pace all day if I had to, but the air in the labyrinth was different. Each breath I took was labored, almost like the thinning air was disappearing as time slowly ticked.

Wise to keep up the run.

"Thought so, considering I have no way of telling how long this labyrinth is. And as you kindly pointed out, I don't have time on my side."

I'm not sure how long it will last.

Stopping to try to catch my breath, I panted heavily, sweat dripping from my brow onto the ivy-covered cobblestone path beneath my feet. No matter what I did, I couldn't manage to catch a full breath. I knew the lack of air was causing my muscles to fatigue faster than I had anticipated. "Why ... am ... I ..." I panted, struggling to speak. "Why can't I catch my breath?"

Why wouldn't you be struggling to breathe? The labyrinth is ... underground. Do you see any specks of daylight that lead to the open air above? The magic of the trial can only hold air for so long.

"Prick," I murmured.

Now, that was rude.

"You're trying to suffocate me! I believe *that* is rude," I said with quiet fury, lifting my arms over my head and gasping as I leaned against the wall for support. I focused on breathing in through my nose and then out through my mouth, trying to steady my mind and regain my senses.

True, but what if I told you the floor wasn't disappearing at the start and that my children were not real?

"W-what?" I stammered, glancing backward. My eyes widened as the cobblestone path behind me magically reappeared before my eyes. *What now?*

Welcome to the trial of the mind.

"Fucking prick," I cursed again, forcing myself to continue forward and meander around another corner of the nightmare I was trapped in.

Well, congratulations.

"For what?" I sneered with hardened words.

One of the four shifters before you fell into the abyss and fed the monsters below your pounding feet.

"I thought you said the floor was not disappearing and that your children were not real?"

The floor did not disappear as it has now returned. And the monsters below are not my natural-born children. I am merely their keeper. I fondly call them my children, but they are no such thing.

"A play on words ... fan-fucking-tastic," I groaned as I jogged down the path. "So why are you giving me congratulations again?"

Because you ... have forced my hand.

"Didn't know you had any."

Clever.

"You still didn't answer my question," I said as I leaped over an ingrown patch of thorny vines protruding from a seam in the cobblestone.

Watch your step.

Before I could think of a rebuttal or slight back, the vines I was stepping over parted to reveal ... *nothing.* I tumbled forward, unable to stop myself from falling into a darkened pit.

Always a good idea to be mindful of your surroundings, the labyrinth said, followed by a sinister chuckle.

I screamed as I fell through an opening in the cobblestone floor, desperately reaching out for anything to grab onto. The thorny vines that encircled the opening were my only salvation. I reached out, desperately curling my hands around them as my body somersaulted and plummeted into darkness. The thorns tore into my flesh, penetrating the skin on my palms and shredding them to pieces. Still, I held on for dear life as I dangled helplessly in the opening of the labyrinth floor.

Nothing clever to say now? the voice inside my head taunted. *You better think of something quick because I can hear one of them approaching.*

"Outstanding," I grunted as I looped a vine around my leg. The thorns dug into my calf, but I knew I had to sacrifice a slight wound to find leverage to hoist myself out of this crater of death.

The snarling, grotesque echoes of grinding teeth snaked their way through the depths below, slithering closer to my dangling feet.

Oh, you won't enjoy this monster, I'm afraid. She relishes the screams almost as much as I do.

The scorching hot breath of the shadow-cloaked creature encircled my dangling feet as a long serpent-like tongue curled around my ankles. It licked at the trickling blood that dripped from my wounds with a low purr of satisfaction. A pang of fear shot straight through my core. My animal fluttered to life, warning me to run, desperate for me to do something to get us out of there. The monster patiently lingering below, but it wouldn't be long before a vine snapped or I lost my grip.

She's drooling from the mere taste of your blood. How remarkable. The voice almost sounded joyous, making me sick.

I struggled to hoist myself up; the fatigue from my run along the path and the thinning of the air put me at a disadvantage. The labyrinth had been taunting me this whole time. Purposely distracting and weakening me so I would fall into this opening and be unable to escape.

What shall you do, Champion? Give up?

No. Never. I gritted my teeth and pulled myself up along the thorny vine.

What is this? Is there some stamina remaining in the shifter-human hybrid?

Ignoring the labyrinth, I used my leg as a base to help hoist myself closer to the opening. Blood soaked my pants and dripped freely from my hands. Underneath me, I could hear the screech of dismay from the monster concealed in the darkness. The screams echoed off the stone wall, tearing into my mind with a piercing, high-pitched ringing sound. I screamed as I sank back down to my previous position, my blood-soaked hands unable to fasten a firm grip on the vine.

My mistake.

No, it couldn't end like this. It wouldn't end like this. I sought out every ounce of my strength and sheer stubborn will to push through the pain and ache of my muscles to pull myself free. I thought of everyone depending on me back home and here in the Inner Kingdom. And then, I thought of him.

Interesting, the labyrinth snickered.

I tried once more to pull myself up, using my legs as much as I could to help lift me. My limbs shook as the reality of my death sank in. I was going to fall.

"Skylar!"

My head perked up as I scanned across the opening above my head.

"Skylar!"

My name echoed again from above. Was this some kind of trick? The voice of the labyrinth was only inside my mind, but this ... This sound was real.

"Daxton?" I couldn't believe it. I shook my head, trying to right myself, but when I opened my eyes, he was still there.

"I'm going to get you out. Hold on!" he yelled as he disappeared for a moment before returning. "Grab onto this." He threw down a line of rope, wrapping the other half around his torso as an anchor.

"H-how?" I stammered, so dumbstruck that I didn't reach for the lifeline dangling next to me. "How are you here?"

"Come on. Don't give up and die on me now. Grab the rope, and I'll tell you." I released my thorny vines and grabbed the lifeline that Daxton was granting me.

"Hold on," he hollered as he began pulling me up. My bloodied hands made it difficult to keep my grip, but I refused to let go. Once I reached the top, I collapsed into Daxton's open arms. He ignored the fact that my hands were drenched in blood and scooped me into his lap, holding on to me just as tightly as I was to him.

"You're hurt," Daxton murmured with concern as he gently released me to examine my hands.

"Just a few scratches."

His brows arched as he shook his head, telling me that he was not convinced. "Here, I believe it's my turn to heal you." Cradling my hands in his, he allowed his ice magic to flow over the top of my burning wounds, caressing my bleeding skin and binding together the cuts and scrapes that were inflicted by the thorns. "There ... That should do it."

"Strange turn of events—you healing me this time around."

"I'm merely striving to meet the standard you mentioned on our journey here from Crimson City," he said with a coy smile as his lips gently kissed my healed skin.

"A lot of good this armor did to protect me."

Daxton either ignored or shrugged off my remark and turned his attention to my calf. He gently guided his magic over the wounds and healed them with ease. Then, without warning, Dax unsheathed a knife from his belt and thrust the tip against the side of my torso.

I gasped and flinched backward. My eyes widened in surprise. "What the—"

"The armor protects what it covers."

"Gods, Dax! That would've left one hell of a mark."

"I believe I'm owed one from our first encounter." His dark brows arched upward as he sheathed his dagger. "With this armor, you're safe, Skylar. Besides … you know I would *never* harm you."

I nodded and gave him a soft smile. My animal, however, remained silent. "Dax," I murmured, almost forgetting where I was for the moment. "How the fuck did you find me?"

His storm gaze met mine, and a playful gleam shone from within. "Do you really have to keep asking that?"

I couldn't hide my smile even if I wanted to. I reached out my hand to thread my fingers in his hair while he held my other close to his chest. His trimmed beard was the same, which magically felt soft against my touch. His eyes were his—and I could feel his strong beating heart beneath my palm as he tucked a strand of hair behind my ear. His fingers traced the outline of my face, migrating to my chin as he gave me a rushed, hurried kiss, pulling me to my feet.

"How are you here, Daxton?" I dared to ask again. "The labyrinth said only one may enter this trial."

"Always with the questions, Spitfire." He chuckled, stealing another kiss before moving to stand. "Come on. Follow me." Without hesitating, I followed.

After what seemed like an eternity of him dragging me along the path, I asked again. "Dax … how are you here?"

He tilted his head to the side, pursing his lips in a thin line as we turned around yet another corner. The turns seemed to be occurring more often now, indicating we might be nearing the center. Glancing sideways at him, it seemed like he was wrestling with the same question I was asking. It dawned on me that he may not even have a reason why he could teleport into the labyrinth and find me.

"There was an opening," he said softly. "I could feel the magic of the fog separate, and I heard your scream."

"My scream?" I paused, tugging on his hand. "You heard me from the outside?"

He nodded. "It was the same for all the other champions before you. Those on the outside could hear what was happening inside the stone walls, but we could never come to their aid."

"Until now?"

"Until now."

"Could you hear everything?" I asked.

"No, not everything," he said with a firm expression that I couldn't seem to crack. "Imagine you're in a closed room. We can hear loud noises, but your normal conversations are muffled."

"Dax, wait," I said, forcing him to stop and look at me. I was relieved that he was here, but I was also scared for him. "This place is a nightmare. I don't want to see you get hurt on my account. What will Minaeve think if we manage to get out of here? What will happen to you?"

"Shh," he whispered, pulling me close. "All will be fine. Don't burden yourself with those thoughts. Let's just focus on surviving this place and obtaining the key."

"Right," I said with determination. "How much time had passed before you were able to teleport here?"

"Too much, I'm afraid." Concern flashed across his features, making me tense. "We'd better hurry. Smart to keep up the run."

"Keep up the run," I repeated slowly, "right."

We took off down the hallway, keeping pace with each other and making sure not to step near the vines. Every so often, I could hear claws clicking or the deep growl of the monster's hunger lurking from beneath. It was a reminder of what lay in wait if I misstepped again.

Glancing ahead at Daxton, I was amazed by his stamina and speed as we zipped through the labyrinth. It didn't even look like he was breaking a sweat while I, on the other hand, could soak the floor with my brow alone. The heat was somehow intensifying down here, along with the thinning air. Daxton's cloak swept aside as he came to another right turn, but unlike the others, I came crashing to a stop, colliding with his backside. I landed with a firm thud against his solid frame, practically bouncing off and ending up on the ground. He looked back and quickly reached out a hand to steady me.

"What's with the sudden stop?" I asked.

Daxton's brow furrowed as his eyes narrowed and darted to the space behind him. He swallowed a heavily weighted sigh. "Take a look for yourself. I believe there's a challenge for you ahead."

I peered around his wide shoulders to see what had caused him such alarm. In the center of the labyrinth pathway, a raised pedestal blocked our route. "What in the Gods' names is that for?"

"I'm afraid you, Skylar, are the expert of this place. Not me."

"Oh, joy," I groaned as I meandered around Daxton to approach the pedestal. I was cautious, looking for any sign of trickery or a hidden trap. A sense of normalcy had already fooled me, and I wouldn't want that to happen again.

Why, hello again …

"What was that?" Dax shouted as he spun around and extracted a long dagger from his belt. *Why didn't he summon his silver sword?* Maybe there was not enough room with these close quarters to do so safely. I knew Dax carried an array of weapons, always armed to the teeth, ready to counter any threat of danger lurking, and this place was the epitome of danger.

"That's the voice I've been hearing since I entered this place," I said.

"A voice?" Dax stammered, clearly shaken by the labyrinth. "That's unsettling."

"Keep your dagger out and watch my back. I have a feeling we may need it."

He nodded and stepped in closer, shielding my backside while I concentrated on moving forward. As I reached the pedestal, I noticed a small divot in the stone, reminding me of an offering plate.

I have an offer for you, hybrid. A bargain.

Fantastic, I thought, not enjoying the idea for one second. I did not trust the labyrinth.

"What is your offer then? Besides stalling me from reaching the center?"

Not just you, it appears. Hello, High Prince Daxton Aegaeon of Silver Meadows. So kind of you to join us.

I glanced at Dax, who held a stern, cold look that could kill an enemy where they stood. The look I knew he had given time and time again as the Silver Shadow moments before death swiftly followed. He remained silent with his jaw clenched and his dagger at the ready.

"What offer do you have?" I repeated into the abyss.

Eager as always.

"Aware of the time is more like it."

Well, so as not to waste the little time we have remaining together ... here's my offer that I believe you both will find intriguing.

"Both of us?" I shifted and glanced at Daxton. "Don't buy into its game," I whispered.

It's far too late for that. He's already inserted himself into my world, and if either of you wish to leave here alive, I suggest you listen to my proposal.

"I'm waiting ..." I said in a harsh, gruff tone. I would risk my own life in this place, but I was not willing to leave Daxton's life to chance. Too many relied on him outside these stone walls.

A circular opening appeared to our right with blinding light encased by outer edges of swirling magic. I shielded my eyes and felt Daxton come to my side. As my eyes adjusted, I lowered my arm to see a tranquil, majestic forest with a calm, winding river between various rocks and trees inside the swirling magic. It was so peaceful, so serene. The labyrinth had just opened a portal—an actual doorway out of here.

Take this exit with your companion, the labyrinth suggested. *And free yourselves from the burdens of this life. I don't have to worry about losing a key; you have an escape. This is what you might call a win-win scenario.*

"What's the catch?" I knew better than to blindly accept this handout. Throughout my life, I had always fought for everything I had. Nothing was ever freely given; it was earned. I knew the labyrinth would be no different.

You're freed from the burdens of this task, and you may pass to a new beginning. You can escape the worries of this life, and be free together.

"What's the catch?" I demanded this time.

"Skylar," Daxton growled. "Why are you questioning this? We're being offered a chance to leave! Let's take it and run." Daxton stepped toward the portal, tugging on my hand, but I held steady, refusing to follow him.

"Skylar," he said my name again, the creases in his brow forming lines of concern that mimicked rivers cutting through a stone canyon. "What are you waiting for?"

"What happens to the Inner Kingdom? To Solace? The wilt?" I asked. "It will spread everywhere, Daxton. What will become of the trials? Of our world?" Only silence followed my questions.

Why does it matter? The task will simply fall to another in one hundred years' time.

"Dax," I pleaded, urging him to stop and consider the consequences of taking the labyrinth's offer. "We can't let this happen. You know the state of your realm. The Inner Kingdom won't last another hundred years. What … What if …" I paused for a moment, thinking this through. "What if Daxton is allowed to leave while I continue onward?"

"No!"

Slowly, I turned to look at my high prince. "I won't put you in harm's way. I would rather die before I let anything happen to you, Daxton." I snapped my mouth shut to keep it from falling to the floor. I surprised myself with the sincerity of my confession and for how bold I was being in spite of all this danger.

I now understood what this ache in my chest truly was, why my breath stilled every time I saw him, and why I asked him countless questions just to listen to his voice for a few moments longer.

I was in love with Daxton and had been for some time now.

He was the steady voice that calmed the rage inside—the castle walls that never wavered in support when I was forced to combat my darkest memories. I was too scared to admit it before, even to myself.

"I won't leave without you. The fate of the world means nothing to me," Daxton countered, and I felt myself step away, taken aback or maybe just too stunned by my own realization to comprehend what he had just said.

"What—What do you mean?" I asked.

"Without you, there is no world for me, Skylar."

My beating heart stilled and ached inside my chest. In my mind, there was no other option in this scenario. I would do everything, even give my life, to ensure he survived. Too many people depended on him, regardless of my success or failure.

I said you both *would escape the burdens of this world. Your partner sees the truth in this and knows I have the power to ensure it.*

"Why are you offering us this?" I cursed at the labyrinth. I refused to believe this was nothing more than a ruse.

You summoned another inside my walls. How? I do not know. But what I do know is that this is not something I wish to put to chance. You could call others to your aid with your unique magic combined with your ferocious will. You may, in fact, best this trial, and then I will cease to have a purpose. Being locked in a prison with no purpose—Now that is just maddening.

"So, in the face of uncertainty, you offer a coward's escape. I hate to break it to you, but that's not something I see myself doing."

"Enough of this!" Daxton roared. "Skylar, you're coming with me, and we're escaping. You don't have a choice in this. *I* am making this decision for you. We can be together. Isn't that what you want?" The plea in Daxton's eyes made me hesitate.

Yes. It is clouded, but even a blind man could see it, if not feel it. Hmm, interesting, I believe that is how you called him here. A force as fickle as fate, it seems, and just as powerful.

"I-I ..." I couldn't believe this was happening, and I hated that Daxton was putting me in this position. I searched for my animal's presence, but she was silent. No, she was absent. There wasn't even a whisper of her guidance, making me feel isolated and alone. I had never felt this lack of connection with her before, and I couldn't help but wonder if this was a warning.

"Daxton," I pleaded once more. "I want this. I do. But this is not the way to do it. I have to see the trials through. And I know you. We couldn't live with the guilt of abandoning everyone we care for just for the sake of our own happiness."

"Fuck the world, Skylar," he roared. "*You* ... are my world." His confession was earth-shattering but also deathly frightening. "You're coming with me," he demanded as he reached for my arm, his grip tightening like a vice.

"No!" I countered, ripping my arm out of his grasp. "This isn't you, Daxton! This isn't right ..." And then suddenly, it dawned on me. "You ... You're not really Daxton, are you?"

A sheepish grin crept to the side of his trimmed beard, his square jaw cocking to the side. I gritted my teeth as anger boiled inside me.

"Daxton wouldn't force my hand. This ... This is all some kind of sick trick!" I silently cursed myself. How had I missed it before? The absence of my animal's presence, the shift in his demeanor, and the way he tried to force his hand. It all made sense now.

This was *not* Daxton.

It was a damn good impersonation of him, but it wasn't him. "Who are you?" I roared, my power flaring out around me in a pulsing wave.

"It's still just *us* in here, I'm afraid." Daxton was still standing before me, but now, his voice was different. "All I've done is taken a new form ... One that I thought would've convinced you to freely turn away from the path and ultimately grant me a victory."

"Labyrinth?" I breathed.

"Why, hello there."

Sheer horror took my breath away as I realized that this *was* the labyrinth. It had the ability to take a physical form. It could shapeshift.

Chapter Thirteen

The grin on imposter Daxton grew wider, almost inhuman, as the gray coloring of his eyes turned crimson.

"Well, well. Clever indeed. It's pleasing to see that your beauty is not just a front. You have a precarious mind to match." His menacing chuckle sent chills along my skin, my animal finally returning. "Your mind effortlessly ventured to this figure," he said in a sweeping motion, addressing Daxton's form. "In your extreme duress, the details were so astonishingly exquisite that it took little to no effort to duplicate his appearance based on your memories alone."

Black fog encircled Daxton's figure as his shape changed into none other than Gilen. "I wonder ..." The voice was now an exact match to Gilen's, making me gasp. "Would this person have convinced you?" He flashed me a wicked grin that was anything but sincere. "No? Perhaps this, then?" With a wave of its hand, Shaw's form suddenly appeared, and then Rhea's.

"No, based on your memories, I was correct the first time," the labyrinth said with a perfect imitation of Rhea's voice. "The prince is the only one that could have tempted you through death's door *willingly*." The black fog rearranged and conjured Daxton once more, but instead of the stormy gray that I longed to see, his eyes were as red as blood.

"Death's door?"

"Why yes," it sneered. "This was a gateway to the great crossing. One that two champions before you willingly took. Yes, some trickery was involved that ultimately ended in deception … But some temptations are often too difficult to ignore. Was it not warned on the scroll to not abandon the path?" I paused, recalling the line in the writing Rhett had shown me. "Very good, you do remember. Now, if you could ease my curious mind, I wonder … what gave me away?"

The creature that I now knew was the labyrinth approached me with an inquisitive spark in his red glowing eyes. He still held Daxton's physical form, his grin reminding me of a child anxiously waiting to play with their favorite toy.

"Your kissing was abysmal and lacked luster," I said, bucking my chin and refusing to cower or back down.

"*Ha, ha, ha,*" he bellowed, folding over with amusement. "My my, you most certainly are a *spitfire.*" I narrowed my eyes and growled with displeasure.

"Move aside," I demanded, trying to meander around him.

"Not yet," he answered, rematerializing at my side and then appearing again at my front.

"What do you want?"

"I require an offering," he stated, sweeping his arm toward the pedestal.

"What kind of test of the mind is this?" I said with a scowl. I didn't have time for these games, and the air was getting thinner by the minute.

"Make me an offering worthy enough to pass."

I looked into the red glowing eyes inside Daxton's body, and my stomach churned. "Take your true form. Leave Daxton out of this so I can think." His eyebrows rose, and he pondered my request momentarily before nodding and disappearing into the fog. "Thank you."

You're welcome. Now, there are the manners I believe we have been missing.

"You just tried to trick me into walking through death's door at the fucking crossing into the afterlife!"

Trial of the MIND. I never said I would play nice.

"And the part where I was dangling above an abyss with monsters ready to eat me whole if I slipped from the vine? How was that of the mind?"

You volunteered to be here. No one forced your hand. I was about to argue, but as much as I hated to admit it, the labyrinth was correct. *You had to mentally push past your physical limitations to surpass the pit of monsters. Now, give me an offering. Our time together is approaching an end, and I would hate to see your demise due to the ticking of our clock.*

I stared at the pedestal for a long moment, contemplating what offer I could give that would allow me to pass. "How about a wager?"

Intriguing. Enlighten me.

"What if we make a bet? Care to test if fate is in your favor? Clearly, it's not in mine, so what do you have to lose?"

Go on …

"I wager that I'll win the trial of the mind."

It's absurd! Even if you make it to the center, no shifter can pass the final test—none have.

"I wager I will."

And if you lose, we both know you die. But I wonder … what more is there for me to gain? What else do you offer to entice me?

"My soul." Silence followed my words, telling me I had the labyrinth's undivided attention. "If I lose, I will not travel to the afterlife with my ancestors. I will remain here, forever, with you. I offer you my soul if I fail the trial of the mind."

That ... is some offer.

"But if I win ..."

You earn the key and are one step closer to unlocking the heart.

"But since I am potentially binding my afterlife to you and this *delightful* place, surely you see the reason for giving me something in return. As you've said before, no shifter will be able to pass, so what is the harm in humoring my offer?"

Very well. What is it you seek?

"A favor."

Elaborate.

"I can't see the future. I'm not an oracle." I swear I heard the labyrinth's eyes roll—if it had eyes. "All I ask is that I can call upon you for a favor, and you must grant it."

Hmm, the labyrinth hummed.

"What's the harm in a favor? You said it yourself. No shifter can pass the final test. So, is this not a win-win scenario for you?"

Very well. Just for fun ... I'll accept your offer. The last champion offered me the sanity of his mind, but a soul? Now, that is truly a treasure.

Suddenly, a pit of despair opened in my stomach, but I refused to let it show. "It is struck, then?"

With blood binding, of course.

I nodded, stepped forward to the pedestal, and sliced my hand once more with a thorny vine to seal our bargain with blood. The magic of our deal swirled around me, and the fog dissipated, allowing me to enter the path again.

Tick tock, tick tock, little shifter.

As I raced along the corridor, I cursed myself for allowing Daxton's false impersonation to cloud my judgment. How could I have been so foolish to believe that Daxton was here with me?

The mind is a clever tool, the labyrinth countered, reading my thoughts. *Many things can be made real if the mind believes them to be true. The shifter champion worthy of the Heart of Valdor must be strong-minded and willing to choose what is right above all else. To prove your worth--- to do what must be done when the time comes.*

"What else must be done?"

Perhaps you'll be able to find out, but likely not.

"Humor the dying, would you?" I mocked. "Consider it a final request."

The true champion, the one who could conquer the trials, must be unique and brave above all. They must embody what the heart represents and be able to guard and protect the people of Valdor with everything they are or ever could be. To be worthy enough to wield the power it holds.

"Outstanding," I muttered, rolling my eyes. "Not cryptic at all."

Must I remind you again ... that this is a trial of the mind? It's getting ever so tiring having to repeat myself. Shall I simply open the floor and release my monsters to end this here and now?

"Where's the challenge in that?" I asked.

True. What good is a trick already used? Besides, my final obstacle is one that is too good to miss.

"Good to know," I said. "Now, butt out of my head and let me focus."

One last thing—my pet.

Every nerve in my body and hair on my skin sparked with a sickening fear buried deep inside my soul. The voice of the labyrinth suddenly changed into the unmistakable sound of my most hated nemesis ... Blade. I froze, collapsing onto the ground, the strength of my limbs vanishing like a drifting puff of smoke.

Ah, there she is. My prized experiment. Do you like how I am able to tap into your greatest desires and now dabble in your darkest fears?

"Stop," I whispered, paralyzed with fear, trembling as my breathing became erratic. The air disappearing from the walls of the labyrinth.

Where would the fun be in that? We never did get to finish our final experiment. Do you recall the one right before I lashed you with my iron whip? I gulped as my hands began to shake despite my fingers digging into my palm. *You do. I fondly remember it as well. During nights alone or when I am fucking a lowly mage or servant—I'm fondly imagining that it is you I am thrusting into, the fire dimming in those savage amber eyes. It saddens me that I never got to truly taste you.*

"Enough!" I screamed as I pounded my fist into the ground, cracking the stone and cutting gashes into my flesh. "I remember the last time that thing tried to touch me. I broke his nose, or did you not see that in my memories?"

You can give up, you know. That is also an option others gratefully took at this point.

"I don't have that choice," I wheezed, my chest caving in like the walls of the labyrinth that began swirling around me. The never-ending hallways becoming a blur.

It would be so easy. Just like you did before in the prison cell. I know your secret. Your shame. You gave up once before ... you died in my keep.

My body convulsed as I folded over onto my stomach, my breathing becoming heavy. Regretfully I remembered each second alone in the dark underground prison when I welcomed the brush of death and embraced the call of the afterlife. At that moment, I had given up. I didn't want to admit it to anyone, but I could not hide here inside the labyrinth.

Yes, my pet. Allow the memories to flood your mind. You performed valiantly in this trial, but let's be honest, we all knew you would not make it out alive.

Tears pooled on the ground as I rested my cheek against the stone floor, immobilized by the fears lurking inside my head. The mists slowly gathered as my breathing became heavy. My will to fight faded once again. The connection to my animal dwindled as I struggled to find the strength to fight against my darkest fears. It felt like I was drowning on solid ground.

That's it. Your mind now belongs to me. Soon, the rest will follow. I blinked slowly, closing my eyes for what very well might be the last time. *That's right. Just like before in the hunter's lair —you are alone. No one is here. Give in to your fears. Death is the only escape for you, now, my pet. Unburden yourself. I promise you will not feel a thing once you give in.*

The greatest weakness for a shifter was just that—isolation. The labyrinth knew it, and Blade knew it, too. Our people were stronger together, united as one. But divided, we were weak. I reached for my animal, but she was somehow being blocked. Our connection was muffled by the labyrinth's magical control. My mind drifted into blackness as I tumbled into a dark abyss.

I will find you.

What was that? The labyrinth's voice seemed panicked.

I recognized that voice.

Forcing my eyes open, I gazed into the midnight mist that encased me. *I will always find you, Spitfire. We will always find each other.* His voice sang to my soul and shattered the magical gag on my animal, awakening my power from within. I knew this was no trick of the labyrinth. It was really him.

"Daxton," I sighed with relief.

Call it fate. Call it whatever the fuck you wanted. Titles didn't mean shit right now.

Since meeting Daxton, I'd felt a spark, a kind of electricity that surpassed all logic or reason. Even in my darkest moments, he was somehow able to find me and help bring me back, and this trial was no different. I forced myself to stand on shaking limbs, leaning heavily against the wall to try and escape the invisible shackles of my fears.

"Seems I won't be giving up so soon."

The labyrinth cackled, recalling the deafening fog. *Then, by all means, continue.*

I took off at a slow jog at first, trying my best to put some distance behind me. The turns became more frequent, which meant I was winding closer and closer to the center—to the end of the labyrinth. On the final curve, I entered a large circular opening with twin pillars surging up from the floor along a red-carpeted walkway.

"A tad dramatic?" I asked aloud.

Again, rude.

"What am I supposed to do now? Simply walk across this carpet, and then a key will magically appear?"

At times, the most logical answer is the simplest one.

"But never here." That was for damn sure.

Walk along the path. Once you reach the end, the trial of the mind will be complete, and you shall receive your first key to unlock the Heart of Valdor.

"What's the twist?"

Whatever do you mean? His singsong taunting voice was beyond annoying at this point, praying on my last viable nerve.

I glared at the blackened, non-existent ceiling. "What's the catch? You've been going on and on about how no shifter will pass the final challenge. So, what is it?"

You must not turn back, regardless of what comes next. If you do, our bargain will be in my favor. Your soul will remain here with me for eternity.

"I'm aware," I sneered. "No other hints?"

None.

"No pressure." I gulped. I glanced at the twin towering pillars that stood at the start of the red carpet. "What happens once I pass through these?"

Always with the questions. The other shifter didn't even have the intellect remaining or the audacity to ask. He simply stepped forward, and then well …

"Spare me the details, please."

Manners! For once? I'm shocked.

I scoffed. "What happens once I step through?" I asked in quiet fury, my patience now non-existent.

Tick tock … Tick tock.

"Shit," I cursed, realizing that I was running out of time to complete the trial.

I don't believe you have time to dawdle. My fog is encroaching behind you, and your air supply is practically gone.

"You don't say?" I countered. "I was wondering why my chest was burning, and I was beginning to see stars."

Eternity will never be dull with you around.

I rolled my eyes and shook my head. "Well, here goes nothing."

Throwing caution to the wind, I turned on my heels and took off at a sprint, deciding that a running start would be the best solution for crossing the threshold. The distance to the center of the labyrinth was in sight, only twenty or thirty yards at the most. I pushed my legs to move forward as I rapidly pumped my arms to keep pace. Leaping between the barriers, a pulse of magic tore a hole through the center of my body.

"Nooo!" I roared with a blood-curdling scream as I collapsed onto the ground. I screamed so loudly I swore the cobblestone walls and floor shook beneath me, as my very soul was ripped from my center.

I would have gladly broken every bone in my body, felt the iron tips of the whips tearing pieces of my flesh, or even the fiery pain of Seamus's magic rip through my mind—anything but this. Everything inside of me was silenced. My animal's spirit was gone.

This is indeed the best trick I have! Blissful pleasure and enjoyment rang through the labyrinth's voice, but I was too numb and torn to even think of a reply.

All I could do was scream.

I screamed until I had no air left in my lungs. Until my voice cracked and then disappeared. Until all rational thought was torn from me. I couldn't move. I couldn't even think.

My animal spirit was gone. She was gone, and I became an empty vessel. A story without an ending, a song without a melody.

What better way to test the confines of a shifter's mind than to strip away a piece of them while keep them physically whole? I rolled over onto my side, clutching my knees to my chest as I roared into the emptiness of the labyrinth.

They can hear you outside my walls of stone. I ignored his taunting as I struggled to catch my breath. *Just as the other before you. He made it this far ... only to fall exactly where you landed.*

I frantically looked around, trying to regain control of my mind as I succumbed to the emptiness of my animal's absence. She was absent, and there was no trace of her left inside me. It shattered everything I was.

I could feel nothing … *She's gone*, I repeated to myself. *She's gone.* The world around me faded away.

Such promise, hybrid. The voice shifted once again, no longer belonging to Blade but to the original cold, inhuman labyrinth itself. *You had such promise.*

Hybrid …

I gritted my teeth, focusing on that one word echoing inside the confines of my mind. I wasn't just a *shifter.* I was *more.*

I sucked in a breath, refusing to allow yet another scream to erupt from my torn throat. I pried open my eyes to see the end of the labyrinth only a handful of body lengths ahead. Near the edge of the crimson carpet, a glowing orb of bright red and orange light hung above a golden glimmering sun-and-moon-shaped key.

Your animal's spirit is now bonded to the key. If you would've succeeded, both could have been yours. But now you will die without either. Pity. I always thought you shifters were stronger-willed than this.

If I were just a shifter, this would've been my undoing. The loss I experienced from my animal's absence was blinding, but I knew I had to fight through it. There was no other option. My soul and the fate of all souls of Valdor were counting on me.

"Sorry to disappoint you—" I sneered as I crawled my way across the red carpet.

Fog curled around my feet, warning me of my impending doom. I dug my fingernails in the threading, causing my nails to crack as I dragged myself forward. Every muscle in my being shook with relentless suffering. I knew I would not survive long with my animal's spirit stripped from my own. The loss was proving too much to bear. I could feel the pull of death calling for me. Ahead, I could sense my animal, her essence swirled around the key that dangled on the edge of the carpet, begging me to reach them.

Power thrummed inside me. Not the strength of my animal, but one of a different kind altogether. The strength of my human heart and stubborn will carried me forward inch by inch.

This ... This is not possible!

I wanted to tell the labyrinth to fuck off, but I couldn't spare the effort it took to speak. I had to focus all my energy on crawling across the crimson floor.

No—

Ten yards, and then finally five. There was only a body's length distance between me and the end, but I stumbled as the pain seized my strength, bringing me crashing into the ground.

"Skylar," a soft feminine voice sounded to my right, causing me to lose focus for a second and turn my gaze away from the key.

She stood alone, masked in the ebony fog dusted with sprinkles of what looked to be starlight. She had tanned, sun-kissed skin with beautiful brown eyes and vibrant wavy golden hair flowing down to her hip. She smiled at me. A soft, tender expression that I recalled Julia giving to me and Neera countless times throughout our lives.

"Skylar," she said again, causing me to pause. Her features were so familiar, almost like looking at a reflection on a lake. Uncanny, how close they resembled my own. All but the shape of my eyes and brow, which I knew came from my father.

"Mother?" I whispered. I had always imagined what she looked like, sounded like—anything about her, really.

"Yes, my daughter." Her pink lips curled along her golden skin as tears began to form in her softening eyes. "Skylar, come with me. There's another way out of all this," she pleaded.

"What is it?" I asked, feeling myself rise onto my feet.

"You must relinquish your shifter soul. It can remain here per your bargain … Then, you can come with me. We can be together, my daughter—I can save you from this fate."

Gods, this place had tempted me beyond reason, but this … This was something I never saw coming. "You—You're not real!" I stammered.

Pain flashed across her face like I had slapped her. "I may not be alive, but I am real, Skylar."

"No. No, you're not!" I shouted, my voice cracking. "Because my mother, my *real* mother, wouldn't ask this of me. She might have abandoned me, but I know that she did it to save my life … to give me a chance to have one."

The figure of my mother stilled as the midnight fog drifted around her delicate, beautiful face. I wanted to run to her, wanted to believe this was not yet another ruse of the labyrinth, and give into a primal need to heed my mother's call. I had never once cursed my mother for abandoning me with the Solace pack, but I had never told anyone why.

"I was born a hybrid. A half-breed. Mixed blood. My mother gave me to the people she knew would protect me. To the ones that would nurture me to become what I am today."

I was done giving up pieces of myself to fit someone else's agenda.

Perhaps in another life, I would have fallen into the role as Gilen's mate. But there had always been something inside me that told me I was meant for more. I now realized that fate had always been leading me here. I was done wandering and being afraid of who I really was. Nothing was going to stop me from completing this trial. Not when I was so close to the end.

The deafening silence told me I was running out of time. Illusion or not, though, I needed to speak these words aloud.

I turned to look at the image of what I believed was my mother. I didn't know if this was real or some illusion, but regardless, the words needed to be said. "I forgive you for what you had to do. I was given a good life filled with love and a family. I knew true happiness, and even now, I know I'm never alone."

She silently nodded, a shimmer of tears soaking her deep brown eyes. "Never give up hope, my love. The strength of your heart will carry you through." Folding a hand to her chest, the sparkling starlight faded into the midnight mist. I forced myself to turn away from her disappearing figure and squared my shoulders to take my final steps forward.

The walls around me shook with anger. The monsters below growled with disdain and resentment at a meal lost to them. The fog encircled me as a coy smile reached my lips.

"Fucking low blow there at the end," I cursed into the mist. "You're really a fucking prick." These were my final words to the labyrinth, which I felt were appropriate considering what I had been forced to endure inside these stone walls.

The red-orange light of the glowing orb encircled a golden key with the shape of an intertwined sun and moon on one end. It blazed to life as I curled my fingers around the middle. On a deep inhale of breath, my animal's presence returned. She flooded my body with an overwhelming feeling of bliss. I couldn't hold back the tears of pure joy that trickled down my face.

The next thing I knew, I was in darkness. The fog encased me in its magic, with flecks of stabbing pain bouncing off my skin.

One moment, I was standing at the end of the labyrinth, and then the next, I was magically transported back to the entrance.

I couldn't believe it.

I had successfully completed the trial of the mind, and the labyrinth was in my debt. I held a favor from the most cunning creature of Valdor.

Until we meet again, hybrid.

Chapter Fourteen

I had bested the trial of the mind, or at least I thought I had.

Gods, Mother and Father, please tell me I won, and this is not yet another sick, twisted game, I prayed.

Sinking to my knees, I clutched the golden sun-moon key to my chest as I openly sobbed in the underground entrance to the labyrinth. I could hear gasps of surprise echo across the stone, followed by frantic voices fluttering around the edges of my conscious mind. I hadn't dared open my eyes yet. I didn't allow myself that thread of hope for it to only be taken away from me yet again.

Magic coiled around me, and all the voices underground suddenly turned into silence. "No one approaches her!" Queen Minaeve's unmistakable voice bellowed, causing me to shudder.

Great, another test, I thought to myself.

"She holds the key!" a female voice exclaimed in protest. "The trial is complete!" It sounded like Idris, but I wasn't holding my breath for any luck to start turning my way.

"But at what cost?" Minaeve rebutted. "She is to win the trial of the mind only to return to us with a broken one. No one is permitted to approach her until I assess what state the shifter is in."

Let me out.

All I wanted was to escape this prison and feel the brush of nature caress my skin.

"Skylar?" There it was again—the voice I had dreamt of in the labyrinth—the voice that belonged to the one being in this world that I would give everything to protect. "Let me make sure she's all right. Let me assess her." His voice sounded strained, like he was fighting to reach me.

"No one, steps—closer," Minaeve sneered, followed by groans of pain as her magic flared.

At the sound of knees colliding with the stone, I finally forced myself to open my eyes to find Daxton only an arm's length away from reaching me. Spirals of black mist forced him down as Minaeve stood over him, her hand outstretched, hovering over the crown of his head.

"It's unlike you to defy me like this, Daxton," she said in a low venomous voice.

"Let me out," I repeated aloud this time.

"I've sworn a vow to protect the champion as my ward. I'm simply striving to uphold that promise." Daxton's words were laced with half-truths.

Minaeve didn't seem convinced, but then Castor tried to inch closer. Her attention snapped toward him. "And your brother—he's quite driven to do the same, but for another reason, it seems."

"She holds the key!" Castor tried to appeal to logic as he fought against Minaeve's magic. "She's completed the first trial! You cannot hold her as a *prisoner*. She's a gods-damned savior!"

The air was different. It was less putrid compared to inside the labyrinth, but it still did not feel real.

"Let—me—out," I said in a low, firm whisper laced with fury.

The high queen turned her turquoise gaze to me. "What was that, shifter?"

"Let me out!" I roared. My rasped voice was torn to pieces, but still, I managed to speak without a drop of fear. Fuck. I just defeated the labyrinth. What more could this false queen do to me? I guarantee the labyrinth did far worse.

"I'll release you when I'm certain you're not a threat."

I bent my head down and released a low maddening laugh. "Threat to *your* subjects? Now that's a joke."

All the rage I held before entering the trial came rushing back. It filled my lungs like fresh air and swam through my veins like a gushing river, granting me access to a deep-seated power I knew was thrumming in my core. I called upon my animal spirit to help fuel my intention as I turned my amber-glowing eyes toward the high queen of the fae.

"Let me the fuck out!" I commanded with my animal's power pumping through each word I spoke. The ground beneath my knees shook, and the walls surrounding the entrance to the labyrinth started to crumble behind the swell of power I was sending out through my command.

My alpha command.

Minaeve stumbled back a step as her magic faltered, releasing its hold on me and the others who were trying to make their way toward me. Castor, who was the closest, reached me first, followed immediately by Daxton.

"Get us out of here, Dax!" Castor cursed, grasping my shoulders as Daxton slid to his knees before me and reached for my clutched hands. In a silver flash, we were gone.

I shut my eyes tightly as we materialized somewhere far away from the underground chamber that held the labyrinth. I remained utterly still, refusing to move or even breathe in fear of what was real and what wasn't. My mind had been bent and twisted. My deepest desires turned against me, along with my greatest fears. As much as I hated to agree with the queen, maybe she was right. I didn't know if I was sane anymore. Was I free of the labyrinth or merely locked in yet another test within the confines of my mind?

Is this real?

Castor's hands released my shoulders, stepping away from my side, but Daxton, my Dax, remained.

"You did it, Skylar." The steadiness of his voice was identical to the imaginary figure conjured inside the labyrinth. It twisted my heart, and I hated myself a little for being so foolish to believe the imposter I faced in the trial was him.

"No," I admitted in denial. "It's just another trick. Another test. You won't fool me this time." His hands tightened around mine, the one that still clutched the golden key. I refused to breathe. I was afraid to inhale the stench of death and decay that followed my every step inside the trial of the mind.

Daxton, being the ever watchful and observant creature he was, noticed my reaction and released his grasp on my hands.

Cupping my face, he whispered one single command, "Breathe."

In theory, it was *so* simple.

"Breathe, Spitfire," Daxton said once more, pressing his brow to mine. "Together, with me." I listened to him inhale a deep, steadying breath and desperately wanted to follow his lead. My hands trembled as my chest burned from the lack of air in my lungs. "Please, *my* Spitfire, just breathe with me."

My animal surged in my chest, pushing me to follow him. *Wait —She's alert*, I thought in a panic. When I encountered the imposter Daxton inside the stone walls, she was silent. But not now.

I parted my lips and inhaled a short, shuddered breath. "Yes, that's it." Daxton sighed with relief. "Now again. Fuller this time." I followed his instruction, allowing a grounding breath to fill my lungs as I tilted my head back and opened my eyes to the skyline above.

The sky. Gods above, it was the most beautiful sunset I had ever seen in my entire life. The purple, pink, and orange colors of the setting sun danced across the horizon like wisps of paint from the canvas of a masterpiece. Colors decorated the different edges of the never-ending sky, spanning outward amongst the cageless openness from above. The phase of the new moon was a whispered outline yet still ever watchful and present with the sun lowering below the western horizon.

"Is—Is this real?" I asked as a lone silver droplet formed at the corner of my eye.

"More than you know," Daxton said as his barrier lifted, and I was overwhelmed with his scent of fresh pine and cold mountain air. "You did it." He smiled softly, kissing my cheek where a tear had fallen.

In the labyrinth, I could only detect the scent of death, but not here. Gorgeous fresh air filled my lungs and caressed my fevered skin. The sky opened and then … Then, there *he* was. A dormant piece of me recognized this, recognized Daxton, as something safe. I dropped my magical barrier, allowing the feel of him to swallow me whole.

"You're … You're real," I gasped. Dax gave me a puzzling look, and I remembered that he had no idea what I was talking about. "I'll tell you later," I breathed.

His brows pressed together with obvious concern as Daxton moved to wrap an arm around me. "As real as you are." He reached up to stroke my face with a kind of tenderness only a lover could achieve. "You did it, Skylar," he repeated.

I tilted my head to the side so I could look at him. A hope-filled sense of joy beamed inside the stone-gray eyes of the male who unknowingly held my heart. And for a moment, I wondered if I wasn't alone in how I felt. I smiled at him, still shaky and confused, but in his eyes, I found the strength to fight against my wavering fears. "You … You were there," I said in a hushed confession.

"Where?"

"Inside the labyrinth … I—You—" I didn't know exactly how to tell him everything that had happened. My throat instantly dried, my breath stilling in my lungs. The rapid fluttering of my heart was now fueled by the fear of his rejection of the affections I could no longer deny.

"If it's too difficult, you don't have to tell me. It's all right."

"No," I said with a surge of emotion bursting through my chest. "I want to tell you." I wanted to tell him, shit, well, *everything*. Gods above, I didn't want to waste another second of this life pretending.

"Then I'm here to listen."

There it was again. The imaginary tether pulled me closer to him like a moth fluttering toward a flame. How could I have been so blind not to see this coming or foolish enough to allow myself to feel this way about him? Perhaps this was all just a false hope—a silly fantasy clinging to something pure in the face of so much hardship.

I sighed heavily, realizing I couldn't even think about confessing my feelings—not now, at least. I needed to keep a clear mind and focus on the remaining trials. I glanced down at my clutched hands and slowly uncoiled my fingers. Daxton's eyes never left my face. Even with the first key to the Heart of Valdor on display before him, his attention was solely on me.

Fuck, this was going to be harder than I thought.

"Later," I whispered. He nodded, never questioning and somehow understanding my reasons without ever having to speak them aloud. "This is it." He finally looked down at the key in my hands, but he didn't seem interested. "What is it?" I asked him. "Isn't this what we came here for?"

Dax seemed to shudder, and without warning, he wrapped both arms around me and held me close to his chest. "Not many things in this life have truly caused fear to enter my heart, Spitfire." He stilled, holding me tighter and inhaling a deep breath of my scent. "But when I heard your screams … a piece of my soul shattered at the sound of your pain."

"Could you hear everything I was saying when I was inside?" A memory of what the labyrinth said flashed inside my mind. *They can hear you.*

"No," Daxton said. "Only at the end, just like the other champion before you. I imagine your voice echoed outward when you reached the center."

243

I wrapped my arms around his middle and clutched him tighter, desperate to be closer to him. Desperate to ease his concern just as much as my own. When I thought Daxton was in danger inside the labyrinth, I knew I would do anything to save him.

"Please promise me," I said as Daxton held me tightly, "there are no red carpets anywhere in Silver Meadows."

"Is that supposed to be some kind of joke?"

"Kind of—but also a legitimate request," I said with a forced hint of a grin.

"There are no red carpets in Silver Meadows," he said in a soft tone. "And if there are, I will destroy them before you set eyes on them."

"Promise?"

"I promise."

I sank back into the warmth of his chest, needing to feel his touch against my skin and relishing in this moment of tranquility. I was keenly aware of every inch of my body that encountered his, the same electric spark tickling my senses where the heat of our bodies connected. Gods, he was like a warm sunrise, glowing, beautiful, and bright.

"We don't have much time," Castor said with hesitation. I had almost forgotten he was even here with us.

Daxton reluctantly loosened his hold on me, and I finally dared to assess where he had teleported us. "Where are we anyway?" I asked.

"The beach outside Aelius," Daxton said.

Sterlyn Lake stretched out before us, framed by gentle waves rolling onto the tanned shoreline with various pebbles and rocks scattered along the sand. The deep blue colors of the water darkened against the setting sun, giving it a breathtakingly alluring appeal that was difficult to turn away from. Stars above our heads emerged as the reflection of their shining light bounced playfully from the surface of the calmer pools of water.

"Can I have a moment to myself?" I asked. Daxton and Castor looked uneasily at one another before turning back to me. "I want to wash the stench and feel of the labyrinth from my skin. I need to cleanse my body of the trial so my mind can begin processing everything that happened."

Daxton looked to Castor. "You see anything?" I knew he was asking if leaving me alone would conjure a premonition of death from his brother's survival magic.

Castor shook his head no, thankfully.

"Can you help me remove the armor, Dax?" I asked as I pulled my hair to the side so he could unclasp the fastenings at the back.

"Of course," he said as his fingers began working at the attachments. "I wanted to ask, how did you hurt your hand?"

"I did it to myself." I said glancing back at him.

Daxton pursed his lips together tightly. His brow furrowed and pinched together. "Why?"

I couldn't give him an answer just yet, so I asked him the same favor he asked me when we shared our first night together in Crimson City. "I can't tell you this part of the story now ... But please, trust me enough to ask later?"

Someday, I knew I would call on my favor from the labyrinth. Someday, I would collect my winnings, but instinct told me that this secret would be best kept to myself until the time came.

A flash of concern glimmered in his expression. I knew he was not pleased with my request. Nevertheless, he gave me a firm nod and unclasped the remaining straps of the Aegis armor. "There."

The weight on my chest felt lighter as I moved my shoulders around and rolled my neck. "Thanks, that feels better."

"We'll be just on the other side of those boulders," Castor said as he meandered out of sight. "And that's we —Dax," he added from somewhere out of sight. "Give the female a moment alone to get her head straight. Stop with the brooding overprotectiveness. Skylar can clearly handle herself."

Daxton growled and glared in Castor's direction before returning to face me. "Are you sure you'll be all right?" he asked.

I knew all I had to do was ask him to stay or leave, and Dax wouldn't hesitate to do as I requested. "I'll be fine. I just need to be on my own." And that was the truth. I needed to commune with my animal spirit—just her and me. Daxton hesitated with every step he took away from me, but we both knew time was of the essence. Too soon, we would have to return to Aelius to face the high queen.

I stripped off the dark tunic first, gratefully freeing myself from the mangled fabric that was coated with my sweat and the stains of my blood from the ivy thorns. I glanced down at my hands. One still held a death grip on the key, while the other held the mark of the bargain struck. I had walked away from this with more than just a key.

I glanced toward the three star marks on my arm and noticed an alteration to the design. The top star—the one representing the first trial—was now different from the others. It was shaded black against my skin. The other stars, representing the final two trials, were still outlines.

Well, there you have it, I thought. The proof of my victory was written across my arm. I had won the first trial of the Heart of Valdor. A feat no other shifter has been able to accomplish, and now it was time to face the second—the trial of the body. I had no idea what awaited me there. My mind flashed to Rhett and the magical scroll he showed me the other night. The clue for the next trial would be revealed with the completion of the first.

Inhaling a steadying breath to settle my nerves, I removed my pants and tossed my clothes to the side. I wanted to feel the clarity of the clean waters on every inch of my skin. I needed to cleanse myself and connect to the nature of this land that I was fighting to protect. I waded into the water, letting it splash against my bare thighs before raising my arms above my head and diving into the blue abyss.

The lake's cold waters engulfed me as I swam out from shore, feeling all my stress disappear into the waters. My animal sang a calming, tranquil tune that relaxed every muscle in my body.

Surfacing, I swam toward the drop-off and positioned myself for a deeper dive. I planned to settle on the ledge overlooking the deeper sections of the lake and lose myself to the peaceful rocking of the currents. I needed to silence the chaos of the world above me. Taking a handful of deep breaths, I prepared myself for the dive. On one final long inhale, I ducked my head under the water and swam down toward the bottom shelf.

The silence I experienced under the water was peaceful. I swam further until I settled on the ledge overlooking the dark depths of the lake. I closed my eyes and listened to the world disappear around me, searching for my animal's presence amongst the stillness of the surrounding waters. In an instant, she was there, filling my center with a sense of comfort and fullness that I feared I would never feel again.

Thank you, I thought as I opened my eyes to the underwater world surrounding me. I floated in suspension, relaxing and cleansing every muscle in my body, trying to find my center.

In this tranquil state, I was unaware of the lurking presence slowly stalking me from the depths below, unaware that I was not alone in this underwater world.

Flashes of bubbles streamed past my face. The figures creating them were a blur in my sight underwater. I could hear the high-pitched laughter as a tail whipped in front of me before disappearing over the ledge I was floating over. I didn't need to think twice about my next decision. I needed to get out of here.

"Why the rush?" a soft female voice called out, followed by a sensational melody of music. The song was breathtakingly beautiful, making me pause in my pursuit of the surface. "Come with us."

The two figures swimming past me in a blur suddenly stopped, allowing me to see them properly for the first time. The top half of their bodies were human-like, with their bottoms disappearing into a colorful, large-scaled fin. I knew these creatures. These were the water nymphs Daxton had warned me about when we first entered the Inner Kingdom, and he hadn't exaggerated their beauty.

The water nymph singing to me had long, flowing light blue hair that curled around her midsection and matched the unique teal and blue scales that adorned her tail. Perfect ... and I mean absolutely perfect breasts were visible across her human chest, adding to her unique beauty that even I was having trouble turning away from. The other female swam next to her, the scales along her body transitioning from dark to light pink, which beautifully contrasted with the glow of her darker skin.

The third member of the group swam to the blue one's left side, and to my surprise, it was a male. He had dark ebony eyes, fair skin, jet-black hair, and a black-scaled tail to match the rippling muscles adorning the top half of his human body. He noticed my eyes dart to him, and he gave a soft grin to the females before beating his strong tail to propel him toward me.

"Greetings, land-dweller." I dumbfoundedly stared at him. My eyes opened wide as the song changed to his deeper baritone melody.

"Stay with us, I insist," he sang as he swam forward to clutch my chin with his fingers, bringing my lips to his.

Instantly, air rushed into my lungs. His tongue danced around my mouth, magically granting me a breath of air from underneath the water. I opened my eyes as he pulled away. His dark gaze matched his ebony hair flowing in the soft current of the waters. He flashed me a handsome smile that would make any female above the surface gladly jump in and take a swim. High cheekbones paired with a straight nose and an elegant, narrowed jawline combined in a beautiful masterpiece.

A surge of fire licked through my middle, warning me of the dangers of the beasts lurking behind the beauty. *I need to get out of here.* I beat my arms backward to try and swim away, but the male water nymph had other plans. He parted his thick lips and released another song that encircled me, halting my escape. His mouth turned upward as he watched me struggle against his hold.

No. I cannot stay.

Through sheer will, I forced myself to block out their song and used my own magic to create a barrier between us. I saw the two females snarl in anger near the ledge of the sea cliff. The male pulled back his lips, revealing an array of sharpened teeth meant for shredding and tearing through flesh.

"You're staying with us," he snarled, grasping my left arm and trying to swim away into the depths with me in tow. The water's surface broke with a splash. Daxton and Castor had arrived at the shore above, but they were too late.

I was already being towed away into the darkening waters when another water nymph appeared. He was much larger and more powerful looking with deep auburn hair, swimming toward us with a tail glimmering with yellow, orange, and red scales. His eyes were an iridescent blue that reminded me of the waters themselves. He approached the ebony-haired nymph, who halted in his watery descent but not yet his hold on me.

"You fool," the larger male hissed.

"She entered our territory. All land-dwellers know the cost if they are foolish enough to venture into our waters for this long."

"By right … she's ours to dine upon." The pink nymph licked her lips in anticipation.

Oh, joy. First, the monsters from the labyrinth and now the water nymphs. How did I get so lucky?

The auburn male glared at the nymph, holding me with menacing blue eyes that were as cold as ice. "Release your hold on her … and you will see the grave error you have *all* made." The three seemed shocked, but they all turned their heads toward the champion mark on my arm. "You see now?"

The dark-haired male seemed to gasp as he released me from his hold. "I—We had no idea."

"And see what she clutches in her other hand." I figured that was my cue as I released my finger just enough to reveal the head of the key I retrieved from the first trial.

All three water nymphs bellowed and released a heartbreaking song as they dipped their heads and swam away over the cliffs. "Forgive them. They're young. This is the first trial they have seen. They underestimated the value of your life and the miracle you have just achieved. I promise you will never have to fear my people, Champion."

I floated in suspension, scared to move but also keenly aware I was running out of air. I looked to the surface, and the male water nymph followed my gaze. "Let's return you to the land above."

He swam under me so quickly that I could have sworn he teleported like Daxton. Effortlessly, he scooped me into his arms, beating his long tail to propel us toward the surface. I opened my eyes and coughed while taking in a deep breath as we breached the water.

"There she is!" Daxton called, and I immediately turned, looking for him.

"Is this who I should return you to?" the nymph asked.

"Yes," I said with my gaze locked on Daxton. He was worried but also surprised at the sight of me cradled in the arms of this water nymph.

"High Prince Daxton Aegaeon," the auburn male murmured as he swam forward, "I imagine if I value my head being attached to my shoulders, I should return you as quickly as I can then."

"Probably a good idea," I said, not taking my eyes from Daxton, who aggressively marched toward me through the surf.

"How exactly are you going to carry me to him in the shallows? You don't have any—" As the nymph's chest breached the surf, his magnificent fin transformed into two legs, corded with strong muscles, with nothing else covering them.

I quickly averted my eyes and looked ahead at Daxton. "Give her to me." His tone was gruff and heated.

"Happy to oblige," the nymph said as he handed me to Daxton. "I wouldn't want my waters to freeze over."

"What happened?" The question was not proposed to me, so I tucked myself into his arms and pursed my lips together, for once not uttering a word.

"Forgive my young ones," the nymph said.

"Why are you here, Malek?" Daxton snarled. I was surprised by his aggressiveness, but then again, this creature's young ones were about to pull me into the depths of the lake and eat me.

"A mistake, High Prince. And one that is now corrected."

"That is yet to be determined," Daxton said in an even hushed tone that sent a chill of fear through me.

"The champion …"

"Skylar. Skylar Cathal." I shifted in Daxton's hold, placing my feet firmly on the sands to stand of my own accord. As I found my footing, a black slip of fabric magically appeared around me, interlacing behind my neck and flowing out and down my body until the hem of the skirt reached my shins.

"Cathal." Malek spoke my surname with a familiarity that made me pause. "That is a name I have not heard in centuries, but one I remember." I swallowed, unaware that my surname had any reverence. "Your sire's line, they were alphas."

"You … You knew my ancestors?" I asked, my heart thrumming like the wings of a hummingbird. I had always been curious about my family history, and I couldn't help but yearn for him to say more, to share anything he knew about my past.

"I did." His coy smile stretched wide across his face. "Water nymphs and shifters were friends before this wilt and the war."

"You recognize *my* surname, why?" Daxton shifted beside me, lightly brushing his hand against the small of my back. He stared Malek down with a stone-cold expression that dripped with menacing violence. I didn't always appreciate the firm hand he dealt, but right now, I think it was working in my favor.

"Because I value self-preservation, I'll make this quick."

"Wise," Daxton growled. I pursed my lips and glared at him, but it made no difference.

"Cathal shifters were a dominant generation of the alphas here in the Inner kingdom, living centuries before you were even a thought, I believe, High Prince." Malek said moving gracefully in the water. "Their bloodline is old and powerful, laced with the magic of the first shifters ever created. The Cathal bloodline was the first to receive the gift from the Mother and Father and granted the animal spirits with the magic of the heart to create your species. I find it most intriguing that she is now our champion."

"Wait, how old are you?" I asked. "And why does no one else seem to remember this about my kind?"

"I'm old enough to remember … yet still young enough to endure the future." Malek folded over in a laugh as he stepped backward into the lake. "We do not freely speak of the time before the wilt, young shifter. Not yet, I'm afraid. Perhaps you truly are the one to free us all."

"That makes no sense," I said as Malek slipped back into the waters. With a flick of his vibrant red tail across the surface, he disappeared without a trace into the watery abyss.

"Which part?" Daxton asked. "I think he wisely chose to leave as quickly as he did."

"The part about him being *that* old, Daxton. Or how he knows so much. What is he, their king or something?"

Daxton raised his brows. "Yes."

My eyes widened, and my jaw practically fell onto the sands of the beach. "Well, sure. Yep. That sounds about right, then." *Gods*, I groaned and crossed my arms.

"You're smarter than you give yourself credit for," Daxton said in amusement. "There are creatures older than the High Fae courts in the Inner Kingdom, but none are more powerful."

I simply met his stare and rolled my eyes, shaking my head. "Yet, when we first arrived, you warned me about them."

"Dangerous, yes. More powerful, no."

Gah, egotistical High Fae, I muttered.

"Well," Castor said as he meandered to join Dax and me in the surf, "your story just keeps getting better and better now, doesn't it?" He looked to Daxton and gently nudged his brother's shoulder. "You all right, Daxton?"

"I'll manage." Hearing the duress in his voice, I gently brushed my fingers against Daxton's clenched fists, his grip loosening to greet mine. His eyes were still as hard as stone, but at least he wasn't completely closed off.

Castor nodded and looked over his shoulder toward Aelius. "We need to head back."

I understood why Daxton was still uneasy—hell, I was too. "Do we have to?" I asked grimly.

"Unfortunately, yes." Daxton kept his gaze firmly on the dangers that his instincts told him were still lurking just below the surface of the water. "Rhett is the keeper of the scroll, which has the description of the next trial. And Minaeve …"

"I have to face her again.," I said as Daxton met my stare and gave a firm nod. "I'm not scared of her. I still can't believe she tried to imprison me when I reappeared at the entrance."

"The others won't either," Castor added. "Her actions went against everything our people have been fighting for over the past five hundred years."

"For the first time, I believe Minaeve was afraid." Daxton's magic whipped across my neck, giving me a comforting embrace. I welcomed the feel of his ice against my skin and flashed him a small smile of thanks.

"There were witnesses to not only her treatment of you, Skylar, but of your own power as well. Minaeve might fear that her control over the Inner Kingdom is slipping." Daxton's expression remained calm despite the worry I could see in the way he began cracking the knuckles on his right hand.

"I used an alpha command." They both nodded in agreement. "Well, no hiding that trick now, I guess."

"It's impressive if not somewhat terrifying. Mind control, it seems." Castor flung out his arms in a questioning manner. "Why in all of Valdor, would you want to hide it?"

"Because I don't know how to control it, Castor." That much was obvious. "I was reacting on pure instinct while I was underground."

It was just like the other times I had used it against Gilen and, ironically enough, against Castor as well. It was interesting that my ability worked not only on shifters, but also on High Fae. Maybe, it was because I was a half-breed? Shifters were once, very long ago before the separation of our species, fae.

"You'll figure it out with time, Skylar," Dax said, his ice magic continued caressing the nape of my neck. "Would you like to get dressed before we leave?"

I glanced at my bloodied clothes on the shoreline and a better idea popped into my mind. "Can you burn those instead? This slip is fine for now. I honestly don't care what I wear when I face Queen Minaeve, but I would prefer never to wear those again."

"Very well." Daxton placed an arm around my shoulder while Castor retrieved the armor of Aegis. Daxton magically summoned a spark that ignited the clothing I tossed in the sand. The blaze was short-lived but symbolic, nonetheless. I steadied myself, preparing for whatever lay ahead and ready to face the next trial lying in my path.

"All right, let's go back."

Chapter Fifteen

"**D**id either of you know about the history of my surname?" I asked as Daxton teleported us inside the walls of the Aelius castle. He grimaced from the strain on his magic but quickly concealed evidence of his discomfort. His expression relaxed as he released his hold on me and Castor.

"No," they answered in unison.

"But," Daxton added, "it does fit your history due to your father's status and your ability to produce a powerful command that can affect High Fae and shifters alike."

"I need to learn to control it," I said as we marched forward. I didn't want to waste any more time. I had to face High Queen Minaeve. I had to find out what the next trial would be.

Even if I was offered the tonic of the sleeping dead, rest wouldn't come for me. There was too much to do and so little time to do it. I didn't even bother to change out of the slip that Daxton conjured for me on the beach. I personally didn't give two shits about what I was wearing when I addressed the queen and her court. The scars of my victory were painted on my flesh, in my mind, and on my soul. No amount of finery was going to cover that. I would walk into Minaeve's court a different person from who I was only a night before.

My mind raced with the knowledge King Malek shared. My ancestors were the first ever shifters created by the Heart of Valdor and the Gods.

Throughout generations of our people, alphas fluctuated between a handful of different family bloodlines. The reign of a pack leader lasted until another shifter surpassed them. It could be decades or perhaps a handful of years. A shifter gifted with the strongest magic rightfully held the title of alpha. Power wasn't a privilege or a right. Instead, we saw it as a responsibility to serve our pack and family.

Opposite to how Queen Minaeve ruled over her people.

"You'll learn to control your powers, Skylar," Daxton said with encouragement. "All you need is practice. You need a chance to work with your gift instead of hiding it. It'll take time."

"We don't have time." I closed my eyes and shook my head in frustration.

"I'm not volunteering to be her test subject," Castor added. "I've experienced the effects of her alpha command *thing* before, and it's unnerving to lose control of yourself like that."

"I didn't mean to do it," I said remorsefully. recalling the night I used my magic to force Castor to answer my questions about Daxton's injuries. It wasn't one of my proudest moments, but I was grateful for the outcome.

"Right." Castor sighed. "Imagine what else you could have made me do in other scenarios. That would be exciting—" Daxton and I stopped in our tracks, and

Dax gave him a look that, for once, silenced his mockery.

"Don't push me, Castor," I said. "You're tempting me to use my gifts to command your silence."

"That would be the *best* day." Daxton laughed, clearing his throat before speaking once more. "We'll help you in any way we can, Spitfire." Daxton shot his brother a firm warning glare.

Castor narrowed his eyes and scoffed. "*Fine.* I may not want to, but I can't deny that this gift you seem to have may just, in fact, save your life. And in turn, all of our lives in the process."

"Glad your logic decided to take over, brother."

"I can still surprise you? *Oh joy*, lucky me," Castor taunted with a heavy sigh.

Daxton discreetly stroked my upper back with his fingertips as his hand came to a rest on my shoulder. "Ready?"

I nodded, and together, the three of us returned to the Court of Aelius.

The gold-plastered arching doorways leading to the throne room, where we had danced the night before, opened as we approached. The raised platform holding the singular throne of power held the fae queen, who waited patiently for us to approach. Disdain painted her menacing turquoise eyes, highlighted with faint purple accents and flecks of gold.

The High Fae crowded in from all sides, wearing elegant garments decorated in colors of green, silver, and red to honor the realms from which they hailed. Most fae from Crimson City had darker complexions but, not all wore red. Some donned silver as well.

Silver Meadows was an open realm, welcoming to anyone who pledged loyalty to Daxton and his crown. Since Adohan took the ruling seat from his father after he perished in the wilt, Crimson City began adopting a similar governance model.

Aelius, however, didn't. They remained isolated under the high queen's authority and power. Seamus hadn't seen a reason to share their practice.

This evening, males, females, and even children were in attendance. All three kingdoms had sent representatives to witness the trials, but from the shocked expressions and gawking faces, I could tell they had hoped but in reality none of them had expected me to survive.

I walked forward as the crowds divided, allowing us to pass through.

Daxton and Castor entered behind me, following my lead. This bold gesture was sure to be noticed by every citizen in attendance tonight.

Idris stood with Adohan, near the steps, securely holding her to his side. Her dark brown eyes were wet, not from tears of fear or sorrow but from joy. *You did it*, she mouthed to me, placing one hand on her very pregnant belly. *Thank you.*

I inclined my head to her and smiled kindly in return. *One down. Two to go*, I mouthed with a wink.

Idris held a powerful essence with a compassionate heart that could break down the toughest barriers anyone could think to build. I knew that was how Adohan fell for her. The High Prince of Crimson City was cocky, perhaps arrogant to a fault, but he had Idris to center him and set him straight when he needed it.

The Crimson City high prince and his lady wore triumphant smiles that spread across the entire room. I watched as Idris clutched her mate's hand and looked up at him with a beaming sense of hope that would encourage even the grandest pessimist to believe.

I didn't stop until I was directly below the steps to the lone throne that held the High Fae queen.

Seamus stood beside Minaeve, casually leaning against the back of her singular golden seat. His tousled blond hair and eyeline dipped to his queen as I halted on the final step before her throne. Despite High Prince Seamus's obvious devotion to his tyrant ruler, I sensed an unspoken tension between them.

Did Seamus truly love his queen? Was this devotion more than just a drive for power and control?

Minaeve's glittering crown lay atop her head with an elegant arrangement of white flowers braided into her ebony hair. Her outward appearance hid a power-hungry ruler who only held her throne because she siphoned magic from others.

My gaze flickered toward her crown, the three shimmering stones decorating her brow. They hummed with foreign magic that likely caused her tanned skin to glow or highlighted the turquoise color of her rounded eyes. Regardless, I dreamed of the day this self-proclaimed queen no longer sat on her throne.

I couldn't help but wonder how many of the High Fae supported her rule. What would happen to their lands if I unlocked the Heart? Even though I wasn't a High Fae, I cared about what happened to the Inner Kingdom and its people.

I paused at the bottom step, my animal stirring in my center in response to the queen's flaring magic. It spread out across the room, making everyone tense with unease.

"Before we reveal the second trial, there's an issue that needs to be addressed," Minaeve said slowly, her eyes shifting across the room.

Without warning, her shadowed vines of magic darted from her fingertips and spread throughout the crowd, whizzing around the High Fae in attendance, finding their intended targets. It happened so fast. Only the loud cracking sound of bones snapping indicated the deed was done. The limp, lifeless bodies of three High Fae in the court dropped dead on the white marble floor, two wearing green and one dressed in silver.

"Addressed," Minaeve said.

I stilled. Disbelief rushing through me, followed by pure blinding rage. "What ... What is the meaning of—"

"You don't speak or question my court, shifter." Minaeve's magic filled the room, pressure building all around us. A firm warning that at any second, the queen could and would use her magic to kill those who she saw fit to address.

Still, despite her vast well of power, my amber-glowing eyes met her turquoise gaze without fear or trepidation. Very different from our first meeting.

How naive I had been then, but not now.

I made a silent vow to the Gods that when I released the Heart of Valdor, I would protect the High Fae kingdoms and help all of Valdor heal.

"Now ... Champion," Minaeve spoke like nothing had happened, addressing me with an *honored title* even though her tone was far from respectful. "You are the first ... the only shifter to conquer the trial of the mind and retrieve the first key. We're all *honored* by your bravery and celebrate your success."

I highly doubted she believed I would survive. Maybe that was why she killed the others? Did they believe I would win and began whispering thoughts of a rebellion?

"Many of us are surprised that ... *you*, out of all that have come before you, somehow managed to win. I wonder if the trials have weakened over the years." Minaeve lounged in her golden throne, casually flipping her hair over her shoulder.

I clenched my fists, biting my tongue to prevent myself from lashing out without thinking. My knuckles turned stark white in my grasp.

"If High Fae could enter, I believe this curse would've been broken long ago," Seamus said.

No one is stopping you from trying, Seamus. I would love to see how the labyrinth would twist his psychotic mind.

"It's the first step to rectifying the dark deeds that are damaging our world and its people," I said in a flat tone that was neither harsh nor grateful to receive her praise. "It is my greatest wish for the wilt to disappear, and then *you* no longer have to strain yourself and others to combat against such a threat. Your magic will no longer be needed." Daxton moved behind me, and I caught the hint of a smile at the corner of his mouth.

The throne room became quiet, almost too quiet.

"Hand over the key," Minaeve commanded, her tone flat with a hint of anger bubbling beneath the surface.

"No," I said without pause. Was this bitch out of her gods-damned mind?

The high queen silently arched an eyebrow and leaned forward, glaring at me with daggers in her eyes. I had no doubt that had I been one of her subjects, she would have killed me on the spot for publicly defying her command. However, she was no queen of mine.

Minaeve, a look of displeasure on her face, placed her elbow on one of her crossed legs that opened to reveal the tanned skin of her upper thigh through the slit of her dress.

"I beg your pardon ... *shifter*," Seamus said, spewing the word "shifter" like it was something beneath him.

Seamus glided over to her side as his hand wandered over her exposed thigh. He trailed his fingers under her dress, venturing them higher as he sank to his knees at her side. His mood was a combination of excitement and amusement as Minaeve threaded her hand through her lover's hair and down to caress his chest.

"Do I need to remind you of where you stand amongst our kind?" Minaeve said coldly.

Rage seethed in my heart. The fae might be immortal and able to wield magic more freely than we could, but a full-grown shifter with control over their animal form made a formidable match.

"I said no." I drew my shoulders back and hardened my gaze. Daxton and Castor remained where they stood, lending me their unwavering support.

"I believe the champion has given her response," Dax said, and the queen's eyes snapped behind me to glare at him.

This was a dangerous game to play. Regardless of my hatred for her, she was still their queen. With her siphoned abilities, she held their power and a commanding rule over all her subjects. I knew Minaeve wouldn't kill me, but that didn't mean she would hesitate to make a show of her reign in front of everyone here.

"You must give the key to Rhett," Minaeve countered, keeping her emotions locked under a veil of tranquility that made me nervous. "Rhett is the keeper of the scroll, and he needs the key in order for the second trial to be revealed."-

On cue, Rhett entered the room with the scroll delicately lying in his open-palmed hands. "If the champion would kindly grace me with the key, I can then read aloud from the scroll." His demeanor was surprisingly indifferent. He did not balk at the three dead fae being carried away or the look of disdain on his queen's face~~expression~~. It was almost like he expected all of this.

I clenched my fist around the key but saw no point or advantage in refusing this request. "Here." I held out my hand.-

Rhett's dark hair brushed against his brow as his blue eyes scanned the trinket I held in my palm. His movements were swift and elegant as he glided across the floor to the steps below the queen. Once he reached me, he bowed to Minaeve before untucking the scroll and holding it out in front of him.-

"If you would touch the key to the second eight-pointed star," Rhett said.-

"You don't want to take it?" I asked.-

"No. I don't wish to see the horrors tied to the memory of *this* key."-

I nodded, recalling his unique gift of seeing the past through objects. I could only imagine what flashes of torment he would be forced to witness if he touched this key. It had dwelled in the ~~l~~Labyrinth for nearly five hundred years, witnessing untold horrors.

Reaching out, I brushed the key against the ancient scroll, and magically, the second description appeared.

"What does it say?" the anxious crowd behind us called out. "Read it!"-

Rhett seemed indifferent to the rantings and ravinges from the audience in the throne room. His eyes restlessly tracked over the writing on the scroll, undoubtedly putting the words to memory and analyzing what this task may hold.-

"Well," Rhett said softly so only I could hear him, "it seems now you have another monster to slay."-

"Read the scroll," Minaeve ordered with Seamus now casually leaning against the base of her throne. His hands stroking her leg through the slit of her skirt.

"As you wish."

Daxton stepped to my side and discreetly traced his hand against the small of my back as Rhett read aloud, turning to the court.

"*To find the key that you seek, you must first defeat the beast.*" Rhett turned toward the room, leaving the parchment clutched in my grasp. "*To look upon my white crest is to know true death. I'm the king of my world, and only my equal can dethrone me. In the waters, I hunt, and in the darkness, I wander ... now released from my silver cage of slumber. Between the slickened rocks, I creep, feeding on the weak and the meek. The first key will show the way to anyone who dares to come and play. My bars are gone, and now I'm free, but only the champion can take the second key. Two cycles of the Father shall pass and then I will forever be free at last.*"

I listened to Rhett's voice as I read the words again and again, trying to make sense of what monster lay in wait for me. "I have to defeat some kind of beast," I said, "in two months?"

"A monster that embodies death itself," Castor said, looking over my other shoulder. "Any ideas as to what this creature is?"

"I don't want to make any speculation without further research," Daxton said. "The library in Silver Meadows holds a collection on mythical beings thanks to our mother's fascination with them. The clues are there. We need to figure out what monster we are facing to work on a specific strategy for Skylar." He rubbed his chin, stroking his beard while reading the scroll again. "It also seems that *anyone* can enter this creature's lair."

"Who would want to willingly enter it is the better question," Castor whispered. "You have to be out of your gods-damned mind to do something like that."

"Thanks," I said, glaring at Castor. "But why is this trial different than the labyrinth, where only I could enter?"

"Maybe it's a test to see who's foolish enough to enter the lair in the first place," Castor murmured.

"Perhaps," Daxton said. "Or the Heart of Valdor is testing not only your virtue and strength but that of its people as well. Are we worth saving if we don't do all we can to help?"

Castor and I looked at each other for a moment before he scoffed and said, "Nope, I'm going with my first assumption. Foolish."

"Or maybe the creature is hungry," I said, recalling the monster from the labyrinth.

"Regardless, we still need to locate the lair," Daxton said, "and see if someone besides Skylar can also enter."

"Until we figure out what it is, no one will be safe, and *no one* besides me will be going in there to challenge it," I said in a hushed tone so only they could hear me. "I don't care if others can enter. This is my task. My responsibility."

I looked at Daxton, who I knew was stupid or perhaps brave enough to contemplate entering the second trial with me. I wouldn't have it, though. I couldn't allow him to put himself in this kind of danger. Too many others were relying on him to lead and protect them.

"We'll continue your combat training and ensure you're ready for whatever you must dethrone in the second trial, Spitfire," Daxton said with a proud grin. "Our warriors in Silver Meadows are the strongest fighters in the Inner Kingdom. We'll make sure you're ready. The trial of the body is a test of your physical limitations." I knew it would come to this, and I was relieved to hear that Daxton was already anticipating it.

"Daxton," Minaeve bellowed above the noise of the crowd.

We were lost in our conversation amidst the roar of the court doing the same. I almost forgot about her— almost. Again, luck wasn't always on my side.

"Kneel."

Daxton tensed as he lowered himself to a knee on the closest step before the high queen. I gritted my teeth in outrage for him. *What could she possibly want now?*

"Is it still Silver Meadows' intention to guide and oversee the champion through the second trial?"

"Yes," Daxton said. "As it was discussed beforehand. The trial of the body is a physical obstacle, and Silver Meadows holds the most skilled warriors in the Inner Kingdom. Bringing the champion to our lands to train prior to entering the second trial is the best plan for success."

"And there are no other reasons why you're so eager to take this shifter," she sneered, looking at me, "to *your* homeland? Could you not remain here and train her?"

"The second trial is in Silver Meadows," Daxton said.

"It is?" I whispered to Castor.

He looked at his brother, tilting his head to the side with narrowed eyes that suddenly widened with clarity. He nodded, his mind meticulously working through the possibilities Daxton seemed to have figured out.

"The silver cage of slumber refers to the silver ores that run through the ancient volcanic rock faces on the southern territories of my realm. No other land holds those magical threads," Dax said.

Minaeve pressed her lips together and narrowed her brow. It was clear she couldn't dispute Daxton's reasoning, and she wasn't happy about it.

"I must admit that I'm the eager one," Castor said, kneeling at his brother's side. "I wish to take Skylar to our home for reasons besides training. My brother has his role as guardian … while I confess to other less honorable intentions and an infatuation I can't escape." Castor's charming smile stretched across his face as he took a second to glance back in my direction.

"Infatuation?" Seamus asked. "From you, Castor? You expect us to believe that a shifter has kept your wandering eyes at bay?"

"Does her beauty not transcend that of the Mother herself?" Castor asked with a sly sparkle in his eye. "Or her courage and selflessness, perhaps? I believe these attributes add to her radiant beauty, only making this rare gem even more enticing."

"You speak of her as though she is an object," Seamus said.

"She's the object of *my* desire." Castor tilted his gaze upward, challenging Seamus to question him further.

I silently watched and waited, hating this dance of the silver tongues.

The turquoise gaze of the queen drifted between Castor and me. I had no idea if she believed us, and I didn't know what the consequences would be if she found out the truth. Her calculating stare bore into me like the tip of a sharpened blade, barely skimming the surface of my skin, pressing hard enough to leave a mark but not enough to kill. Then I felt it. The whisper of her magic circled around the barriers of my mind.

Be careful ... young shifter. The hearts of mated offspring are never fully sated without the bond of a true mate. I detect no magic of a mate bond emanating from you. You may have the dalliance of an Aegaeon prince, but it will never last. He'll soon tire or dispose of you. I suggest you guard your heart for what little time you have left in this world, mortal.

"Was that a threat?" I did my best to cage my rage as the queen spoke to me inside my mind. I was starting to get really fucking annoyed with voices in my head.

"A warning," she said before turning her attention to Castor. "Do you intend to wed this shifter after you have publicly flaunted your deed of bedding her? Or is this just merely a dalliance?" Her brows furrowed with suspicion. "As your high queen, I need to know the intentions of the royal bloodlines and succession of the realms should your action result in a child growing in her womb."

Concealing my outrage at that comment was the hardest gods-damned thing I had ever done in my entire life.

"The concept of my family line has yet to be addressed," Castor said, eloquently answering without so much as a hint of a lie. "This delicate topic has yet to be addressed due to the uncertainty of her living past today. But I can't deny that having her marry into my family name is tempting ... *if* she survives." Castor was earning his silver tongue today. I couldn't bring myself to glance anywhere else in the room, knowing I had to play my part.

"I can handle my personal affairs. I don't need guidance or permission from the High Fae courts," I growled. "What I decide to do with my life, who I decide to sleep with, and how I spend my days after the trials is *my* choice."

"A choice I intend to try and relentlessly persuade my way," Castor said with a sing-song tone that I knew all too well. He was executing our ruse beautifully. And, well, I was ... trying.

During this exchange, Daxton remained utterly silent. His expression mimicked stone, and his gaze was glued to the steps. I didn't dare look his way, or else the roles we were trying to play would fall apart entirely.

"You do know their kind is easier to breed, right?" Seamus snickered. "Perhaps you'll overthrow your brother with a fruitful line of succession while our high queen finally earns Daxton's vow and seed."

Utter disdain rolled through me. "I'm no one's prized breeding tool, nor do I condone others being treated as such," I said. "If I wanted a life reserved for child rearing and station alone, I would've stayed in Solace as the alpha's mate and allowed another to take my place."

"Interesting remark. And yet you feel it is appropriate to indulge with *Castor* of all people?"

"No one wishes to die a virgin," I said. Rapid blinks from Castor and coughs from the crowd indicated that I had successfully thrown everyone off a step. "Cas has a sparkling reputation and the most experience out of everyone here. I figured, why not go out with a bang?"

"My ... my!" Seamus bellowed with laughter. "I admit I'm jealous you got to take her maidenhead, Castor. It would have been so sweet to pluck her fruit from the tree." The floor and the air surrounding us began to freeze. Castor moved to make it seem like it was his magic, but I could feel the difference. It was Daxton's rage fueling this magical shift.

"Stand down, Castor," Minaeve commanded. "Enough of this nonsense bickering." And for once, I couldn't agree more with the queen. "The fate of this shifter will be discussed later. There are still two more trials for her to master, so this topic is a waste of time." Her gaze then turned back to the kneeling Daxton, who kept his head bent toward the floor. "When will you depart, Daxton?"

"We ... will—"

"Immediately," I interjected, pushing myself before the kneeling princes to confront the queen. "We'll leave immediately. There's no sense in waiting." I didn't want to be here any longer than I absolutely had to. Leaving tonight might be tortuous and tiring, but it gave us time that we desperately needed.

She glared at me. "It seems so. The gate to the second trial is already open, and according to the scroll, the creature inside is free. You must make haste to ready yourself for the task ahead. Two cycles of the moon will pass sooner than you think."

"We shall accompany them," Adohan announced with Idris at his side.

"That's surprising … with your mate's condition, Adohan," Seamus said.

"Indeed," Minaeve agreed. "Why do you wish to accompany them? Should you not be resting and preparing for the birth of your child?"

Idris affectionately touched her rounded belly, giving the room a soft smile. Adohan intertwined his fingers with his mate's before he addressed the room. "We appreciate the concern, High Queen. But our child still has time to grow. We wish to witness the success or failure of the shifter firsthand. Besides, Silver Meadows may have the strongest warriors and Aelius the cleverest minds, but Crimson City holds the slow-burning flame of resilience. My people have weathered the devastating attacks of the wilt more than any other region, and yet we continue. We still thrive. Our fires are always burning."

"Crimson City will help guide Skylar in preparing for this task alongside Silver Meadows," Idris said.

"I don't believe you were addressed, *Lady* of Crimson City," Minaeve spat, rising to stand at the side of the golden throne. This was a direct attack on Idris's lack of station in the High Fae courts. In their eyes, Idris held no true position.

"You do not speak amongst our circle unless spoken to first." The line between Seamus's brows deepened as he paused. It looked as though he wanted to say more, but something was holding him back.

Personally, I thought his opinion on this was complete and utter bullshit. Yet I held my tongue, taking in Castor's teachings and putting them to use.

I could see the fire in Adohan's eyes burn as flames licked across his darkened skin. "Be careful how you address my mate. Regardless of a formal title, I will not stand for anyone disrespecting her."

"She's not recognized as a royal," Minaeve said as Seamus stepped toward Adohan. From his body language, he intended to use more than just his cunning words to make his point. Daxton immediately arose from his kneeling position and fronted Seamus's approach. He didn't say anything—the look of death in his eyes did that for him.

Seamus's eyes widened. He was no match for Daxton, and he knew it. "You're fortunate in your allies, Adohan … But it won't save you in the end."

"Seamus," Minaeve said. "Don't allow him to get under your skin. This is below you, come here." And like the good lap dog he was, he dutifully returned to his master's side. He bent to kiss Minaeve's cheek and then trailed a kiss down her neck. I watched as she closed her eyes and curled her lip into a half-grin. "Hmmm, yes," she said in a soft moan. And suddenly, I felt the urge to dry heave.

"We'll take our leave then," Daxton announced, bowing to the golden throne.

"Go," Minaeve answered. "We'll travel to Silver Meadows in two months."

Daxton nodded before turning toward me. "After you, Champion."

Again, he was honoring me by letting me take the lead. I knew what the gesture meant, and above all, it showed his respect for me in more ways than his words ever could.

"Idris," I said, "call the pegasi. We fly for Silver Meadows tonight."

Chapter Sixteen

Thankfully, I was able to change and gather my belongings while Idris called the pegasi from the surrounding hillside. We mounted and took off at a boisterous pace without ever once glancing back. I wanted to put as much distance between myself and Aelius as I could. Daxton and his stallion led the way, with Castor and Adohan close behind. Idris and I were last, bringing up the rear of our traveling party.

No one had spoken a word since leaving the throne room in Aelius.

The trial of the mind was over, but I still had two more to face. The riddle on the scroll describing the trial of the body replayed repeatedly in my head. I was desperately trying to decipher what clues we needed to focus on to understand the type of creature I had to face. Training and preparing for the wrong opponent could lead to death.

I was lost in my thoughts when Idris called out next to me. "Adohan … Adohan!" The High Prince of Crimson City pulled back on his reigns, urging his steed to slow to his mate's side.

"What is it, my love? Is it the babe?" Idris nodded in distress. "Daxton!" Adohan called out into the wind. "We need to land immediately."

Daxton turned in his seat as he and Castor slowed. "It's not safe until we reach the border of Silver Meadows. Can you hold out for a little longer, Idris?" The brave mother nodded as she folded over her stomach, laying against her steed's thick neck.

I wasn't sure what was happening, but the look on Idris's face told me it was not good. "What is wrong, Idris?"

"I'm having ... contractions," she said through gritted teeth.

"How often?" I pursed my lips and glanced at Adohan's panicked face. "Can you speak through them?"

"N-n-not. W-well," she said through a grunt of pain.

Shit. This was not good at all.

"Dax, how much further?" I met his gaze and tried my best to communicate the severity of this situation without speaking the words aloud.

Idris had borne children before, and because they were twins, they would have likely come early. In this pregnancy, she carried only one, but her body knew what to do in labor. It would strike faster this time around. And if she was experiencing contractions, ones she had difficulty speaking through, the child could be on its way into the world.

"Can you teleport us to the border?"

Daxton nodded. "I don't see another option." Sensing my urgency, he steered his mount toward Adohan and Idris. "I can take us all to the river separating Aelius and Silver Meadows. It should be safe there."

"Do it," I instructed. "She needs to rest. I might be able to use my magic to help them."

"Everyone needs to connect," Daxton said as Castor reached into his bag and retrieved a long rope. "Hold on."

We each grabbed a portion of the rope, and we disappeared from the sky in a silver flash. The pegasi neighed and bucked as their hooves touched the ground instead of soaring through the open air. Adohan leaped off his mount and took Idris. He clutched his mate tightly, tenderly kissing her brow and cradling her against his chest.

"Castor, keep watch," Daxton ordered, shaking his head to try to right himself from the strain of his magic. "We're in our realm, but the border is not far."

Castor withdrew his twin blades and marched toward the river, scouting the area for any sign of trouble.

"Bring her over here," I instructed, unfastening my cloak and preparing a comfortable makeshift bed on the mossy earth for Idris to lie down on.

"Do you have experience bringing young ones into the world, Spitfire?" Daxton asked.

"Not much," I replied, remembering the two births Latte practically dragged me to watch. In hindsight, I cursed myself now for not allowing her to bring me to more. "But I know enough about the signs and progression of labor. This baby is likely in distress and will come faster than the twins because her body remembers childbirth."

"It's too early."

"I know," I replied with a grim look. "But there might be something I can do to stop the labor from progressing …"

"Then do it!" Adohan roared, the plea in his eyes taking root in the center of my heart. "Please." His last words were barely a whisper as silver lines appeared around the rims of his eyes. He was afraid. The proud high prince was terrified for Idris and his child. Through their mate bond, Adohan could sense Idris's distress as his own. All his showboating and air of confidence was stripped to the side as he clutched his mate's hands.

Idris's face tightened, and I knew the contractions were getting stronger with each minute. High Fae babies grew in the womb for twelve months … She was only eight months along. For a human or shifter, delivering this early would be worrisome, but for a fae, this was utterly dangerous. She still had four months before the fetus was fully formed and ready to enter the world.

"Lay her down on her back with her feet resting above her heart." I glanced around me, pointing to a nearby log. "Bring that over here. I've seen my pack's healer try this before, and it worked to reverse the natural progression of the baby exiting the womb. We're going to try and use gravity in our favor."

Daxton rolled the log toward a soft moss-covered tree, helping elevate Idris's legs and bottom while Adohan cradled his mate's head. "This is an odd position," Idris said between labored breaths.

"We're trying to let nature help keep that baby inside you," I replied.

"Clever," Idris rasped. "I can feel the baby shifting."

"Good."

Without warning, I reached out my palms to place them on her hard, swollen belly. Adohan unexpectedly snarled and roughly grasped my wrist. Fire crackled in his palm as it danced across my skin, searing my flesh and causing me to scream in shock.

"Ahh!"

Daxton responded in an instant. Faster than I thought possible, he surged forward and grabbed Adohan by the throat, throwing him against the base of the tree with his hand firmly around his neck. Ice coated the flames along the forest floor as Daxton's rage combined with his power to overshadow Adohan's magic. Both males pulled back their lips, exposing their sharp canine teeth while releasing low, threatening growls of violence.

"Idiots," Idris groaned. "Adohan, you paranoid, overprotective male. Skylar is trying to …" She couldn't finish her words as another powerful contraction rolled through her womb. This time, I was close enough to see the muscles around her belly contract as blood trickled between her thighs and stained her dress.

"Not good. Right?" Idris turned her warm brown eyes to me, full of fear for her unborn child.

"Dax," Castor yelled, rushing to his brother's side. "Let go of Adohan! Both of you are not right in the head." Daxton darted his gaze to Castor before returning it to his grip on Adohan's throat. "None of this is helping Idris or the baby!"

Daxton seemed to regain his senses and released his grip on his friend. The crimson prince gasped and rubbed his throat before widely meandering around Daxton and returning to his mate's side.

"No, it's not good, Idris," I whispered, and she gave me a grave look of understanding. She knew bleeding like this, paired with the contractions, was dangerous. "But I can help."

If there was blood, that meant the baby or the womb was in distress, and there was something causing the pre-term labor. I called upon my healing magic as my palms glowed.

"Sooner would be better, Skylar," Idris groaned again as Adohan cradled her head in his lap. "Sorry, that's just the panic setting in."

Gently, I pressed my hands to her stomach and allowed my healing powers to flow through me. My magic sought out the baby, sensing its distress from Idris's womb. I allowed my magic to heal the area around the growing baby, settling the trauma and speeding the infant's growth. The child was underdeveloped, needing more time to grow, and I was able to use my power to aid in the maturing of its lungs and ease the unborn baby's suffering.

"There," I gasped as I lifted my hands. "The labor should stop now, but you need to calm yourself, Idris, so the babe doesn't feel any more distress."

"Calm," she panted as she rested her head against her mate. "Right. Understood." I knew the stress of seeing Adohan at the offering, the trials, and then the audience with Minaeve and Seamus was difficult for her.

"And you should restrict your movements as much as possible, perhaps a limited type of bedrest if you can manage." I hated advising this, but it was the only thing that made sense. Walking and stress would progress her labor. Limiting both as much as possible would help ensure the baby and the mother would be closer to full term.

Idris tilted her eyes open toward me with a grim look on her face. "That's easier said than done, but I'll do my best." She affectionately rubbed her belly, with Adohan linking his hand with hers. "Looks like we will be on research duty then."

"Not a bad place to be," I answered with a reassuring smile. "Books can be the best company at times."

Wanting to give them privacy, I stood and walked around the corner of the trees. They had just had an intense scare and needed a moment alone. We could afford to give them that.

"The baby, and perhaps Idris, would've died without your help, Skylar," Daxton said. "Crimson City is in your debt."

"Unfortunately, they aren't out of the woods yet."

"Quite literally," Dax answered with a playful undertone.

I shook my head with an audible scoff, arching my brow as I turned toward him. "Really? At a time like this, you think it's appropriate to make a joke? You almost ripped Adohan's throat out a few seconds ago."

"That was a moment ago, and the danger of it has now passed. There is no sense in dwelling on what happened."

"But why did *you* react like that? Why did Adohan try to burn me?"

Daxton shifted his feet beneath him. Even though others would dismiss this small movement as nothing … I knew better.

He cleared his throat before speaking. "We all knew you were helping, but in his state of panic, you were a threat to his mate and unborn child. He reacted out of instinct to protect them, and as a result, he lashed out."

"He wasn't the only one reacting." I stared him down, but Daxton didn't answer or turn to look at me. I could see his mind working through something. What, though, I wasn't sure, but I knew asking about it would lead me nowhere right now. His blatant avoidance of my prying told me to try again another time, so I decided to change the subject.

"Idris will have to remain calm to keep the labor from progressing, but I did manage to support the infant's lungs and other vital organs. The baby may be born sooner, but she'll at least be stronger now."

"*She?*"

"Yes." I smiled brightly. "Idris was right. It's a girl ... but don't share that with anyone else," I warned, reaching out to grab his arm with my right hand. "Let it be a surprise."

Daxton smiled, glancing at my touch as the dimple on his cheek appeared, making my stomach flip and my knees wobble.

"I wouldn't dream of spoiling the surprise," he answered, placing his hand atop mine. "I'm happy for them and the newest addition to their family."

We stood at the bend of the river, listening to the creatures of the night scurry about and the calm waters trickle across the meandering turns. His touch lingered as his fingers brushed the back of my hand, moving down to my scarred wrist.

Daxton's voice trembled as if he were holding something back. "I'll teleport them to my stronghold in Silver Meadows. Idris shouldn't fly."

"I agree." I stepped closer to him, wanting to feel the heat of his body sink into mine. "Are you able to travel that far with multiple passengers? I honestly don't know what limits you have on your powers and the queen's siphon ..."

"My station as high prince allows me to draw from the land I govern. My gifts are stronger here than anywhere else in Valdor despite the queen's hold over me."

I cringed at the mere mention of Minaeve. "I would move them soon. What do you think—" I stopped as Daxton, sensing my unease, wrapped a protective arm around my middle. I couldn't help leaning into his hold. It felt so natural. Like I was home. Daxton's presence calmed and centered me unlike anyone else in this world.

"I wish we had more time, Spitfire," Daxton said as his lips discreetly graced the crown of my head. "I wish I had time to tell you *everything*."

Hesitation lurked in the back of my mind, but when he held me like this—when he spoke to me like this—all my doubts disappeared. "There's no time like the present," I answered, interlacing my hands around his waist and placing my head in the nook of his shoulder. "I promise I won't interrupt. I'll only listen."

His deep chuckle of amusement rolled through me, causing my heart to skip a beat. I tilted my head up to gaze into his luminous gray eyes, holding softness reserved only for me. His gorgeous features highlighted by the moonlight gave him an unnatural glow that quickened my heaving breath.

He bent to bring his lips to mine without warning as he cupped my face in his large, rough hands. I melted at the pure ecstasy of his taste. His lips parted as his tongue roamed my mouth, his whispered moan mirroring my rising desires. I moved to clutch his shirt in my hands, desperate to rip it away and feel the heated flush of his bare skin against my own. There were simply too many layers separating us from one another. He gently pulled back, and I immediately despised the absence of his lips. I wanted to kiss him until the end of time itself.

"There never seems to be an opportune moment … when all I want to do is let the world disappear and become lost in you."

"Luck has never really been my forte," I said with a sweet smile tinged with sadness. Daxton adjusted his hold, bringing me closer as a feeling of contentment settled within me. He reached up to gently tuck a strand of hair behind my ear, brushing his knuckles along my chin and down the nape of my neck. Goosebumps settled over my skin as his eyes darkened with a longing I knew all too well.

"Good thing we'll always find each other then."

"Very good," he answered with a smug grin. "I know it will be *hard* … trust me." He winked as I grinned wickedly, pressing my hips against his hardening length. He cleared his throat in surprise, followed by a satisfying dark chuckle escaping his lips as he moved in line with mine. "But we must resist falling into certain temptations when there is a potential for wandering eyes all around us."

"Is that a reminder for yourself or for me?"

"Perfection doesn't need a reminder," he answered with a gleam in his eye.

"Right," I teased, my playful smile mimicking his own. "I can see where your brother learned to inflate his ego."

"Who said I was talking about myself?" Daxton leaned in closely, meticulously caressing the curves of my body so he wouldn't miss a thing. "That is self-inflating." His teeth nipped at my ear as he whispered, "Besides, I would much rather have you take that role instead."

"Don't tempt me." I breathed heavily, the throbbing between my legs turning into an aching need.

"Why not? This is extremely … entertaining." Daxton's growl vibrated along my skin, reaching the base of my neck, where his lips hovered.

"Because I don't have as firm a hold on my self-control as you do, apparently," I said.

"And who's saying that's a negative trait to have?"

"You. Literally one minute ago … *you* did."

"Ahh, right," he said, nodding and turning his gray eyes to me. The heat of his desire lingering in his stare made my body melt. "It's hard to argue with such pristine wisdom."

"You're unbelievable." I laughed.

"Why thank you." His smile curled wildly across his comely face.

"Oh, Gods, Daxton!" I shouted, playfully smacking him in the arm and pushing him away.

Faster than I could blink, he spun me around, placing my back to his chest. He held me close as he bent to whisper in my ear, "I didn't know you could see the future, Spitfire, because that's exactly what I plan to have you screaming sooner rather than later."

My eyes rolled into the back of my head as his filthy words spun me like a top. Gods, I wanted him.

"Daxton." Castor's voice boomed from the trees where we left Idris and Adohan. "We need to move out."

Daxton tensed and immediately went on high alert, protectively draping an arm around me and holding me close to his side. "Did you have a vision?"

"No, but I didn't need to. When I was patrolling the river, a group of Dryads informed me that Anjani's spies have been lurking along our borders. They are requesting a meeting with you to discuss this issue once we've returned to Silver Meadows."

"Anjani wouldn't dare step foot into my realm without permission," Daxton replied in a deep, calm tone that would terrify anyone within earshot.

"It seems our absence has weakened our defenses."

Daxton narrowed his eyes and released a displeased grunting sound from his chest. "I'll have to speak to Gunnar and Zola about this."

"This does mean, however, that outside the wards or the Summit, we are never safe from the queen's wandering eyes." Castor said with his eyes darting between us, and Daxton's face fell grim. "If you recall, Skylar, Anjani is Seamus's kin. She can create illusions and conceal her troop of spies from detection."

"She's the one who masked your ships when you entered Solace pack lands?" I asked.

"Correct." Dax nodded.

"Would she dare enter Silver Meadows without your approval?" I asked.

"She can fucking try," Daxton cursed. "I'll inform Gunnar and send Zola to investigate this when we arrive. Then, I'll seek out the Dryads along the city boundaries. Any deception lurking in my kingdom will not be tolerated. I will not stand for spies within my home."

"Zola will have a field day hunting Anjani down," Castor snickered. "Can I be the one to tell her of this mission?"

"If you wish," Dax said before finding my worried gaze. "If her spies are following us, Spitfire …"

"Then we must continue our ruse." I didn't hide my displeasure, glancing Castor's way.

"You're not the only one," Castor argued. "While I'm beginning to find your company tolerable Skylar, I detest the death looks my brother gives me after I have to touch you."

I tilted my head and raised my brows toward Daxton, but he didn't bother acknowledging me. He was all business right now. "Inside the palace, we have wards barring entry. But in the training ring and in the city, I'm afraid we will have to be cautious about how we are toward one another."

"I hate this, Dax." I looped my arms around his neck and pulled myself up to kiss him. He greedily returned my affection, lifting me off my feet. "I don't want to hide."

And that was the truth. I decided right then and there that any doubts I had would stop. Even if the queen detected no mate bond, I would take whatever time I could with Daxton.

"Neither do I, Skylar," he said with a heavy sigh. "I want to make good on my promise to you the night before the first trial." Heat pooled in my center as my heart quickened in my chest. "But I refuse to jeopardize your safety."

"What if I no longer give a shit about my safety or what the queen might do to me if she finds out my dalliance with Castor is a lie?"

Daxton half-smiled before nuzzling into the nape of my neck, his lips grazing my heated flesh. "That's why you have me." He tenderly kissed my lips again, pulling me close to savor our fleeting moment.

"Not the best time, you two," Castor announced, unbashful at interrupting us. "I'll gather the mounts. Dax, you should teleport Idris and Adohan first and then return for us."

"Watch over her, Cas?" Daxton asked as the warmth of his embrace slipped away.

"On my life." Castor nodded as Daxton released me, never taking his eyes from mine until he was out of sight around the corner. "I don't like this threat to our realm," Castor muttered.

"Is Anjani truly that dangerous?"

"Yes. There's no telling where she could be. Zola thus far is the only one who has been able to track her whereabouts. Those two have had a grudge toward one another for centuries. But if Daxton ever found her … let's just say her death would have consequences that my brother would likely serve."

"I, for one, would not want to be on Zola's bad side."

"Not many remain there for long," Castor replied as we watched the silver flash of light around the corner. "Skylar," Castor said in a softer tone, and it piqued my curiosity. "I need to ask a favor. And understand that I don't ask this lightly."

"What is it?"

He took a deep breath, leaning his back against the trunk of a thick tree, staring off into the winding river. "It concerns my brother." I froze.

"What about him?"

"I need to—" Looking down, he fidgeted his feet and hands uncomfortably, taking me aback. "I'm asking you …" Castor began as his dark eyes snapped open to my amber gaze. "Please, don't hurt him."

"What do you mean?"

"My brother has guarded his heart in a gilded cage ever since Queen Minaeve imprisoned him in her hold. Those who truly see and know him understand his caution and still love him despite it. We understand why he must keep to himself and carry the burden of the crown alone. But ever since meeting you … he … He's changed. Daxton is vulnerable and yet somehow more alive all at the same time."

"Is that a good thing?"

"It could be," he answered, sweeping his darkened gaze across my face. "But it could also lead to his demise, along with yours. You've given him hope, and that's one of the most powerful weapons someone can wield. He has hope for a better life, a new beginning.

That gift alone is enough to shatter the chains of the darkest dungeon, and it's all tied to you."

"What are you getting at, Castor?"

"He is my brother—*and* my high prince. My duty is to serve and protect him, even if he always seems to do that for me. I ask you to please … Please use caution and trust your instincts. Do not leap unless you are ready to fall, for I fear my brother already has."

This … This was unreal. I knew I was falling in love with Daxton. In all honesty, I had been since we first met. But I wouldn't admit that to Castor, not before I had the courage to tell Daxton myself.

"I understand, Castor," I said. The muscles along his shoulder were taut, following his pinched mouth that unveiled his unease. I needed to do something. "How about this," I paused watching him closely. "I'm willing to swear allegiance to Daxton, just like the other citizens who come to Silver Meadows from other realms. Would that ease your concern and gain your trust?"

"Perhaps." He pushed off from the tree and walked to the water's edge. "What words would you speak?"

"I vow to honor and protect Daxton Aegaeon, High Prince of Silver Meadows, with my actions and my words. To do all I can to guard his heart and protect his soul."

Castor seemed pleased, giving me a single nod. "With magic, we will speak this together, holding the earth of our kingdom and binding it to the realm in which we stand."

Drawing on the power that swelled deep within my animal, I repeated the vow with Castor as he gathered a fistful of earth and poured it into my outstretched hand.

"I believe you have sworn allegiance to Silver Meadows with this vow to our high prince. You now have citizenship and recognition within our realm," Castor announced. "May the land recognize you as kin and treat you as such."

With Castor's words, a tether emerged from the ground beneath my feet, flowing from the sole of my boots to the top of my head. The winding and trickling waters through the river felt comforting, and the air twirling through my hair gifted me strength. The land and magic of Silver Meadows recognized me as one of their own.

"Castor, what did you do?" Daxton asked as he silently approached us. "Skylar?"

"I have sworn in a new citizen of our realm. Now, she can freely move about our kingdom, bypass the wards, and is recognized as one of us. She'll be treated as such as well. I believe you mean to say, *Thank you, Castor.*"

"I didn't wish for her to swear allegiance if she didn't want to, Cas. I was prepared to alter the wards or have her always enter the palace with—"

"I wasn't forced, Daxton," I interjected. "Please. Do you *really* think I could be convinced to do something like this if I didn't want to?"

He pursed his lips into a thin line. "No, you wouldn't."

"I freely pledged my loyalty to you and Silver Meadows. And I would gladly do it again if asked. Besides, if the second trial is indeed in your realm, this extra boost won't hurt. You said yourself you draw power from the land you govern … I imagine it is the same for your people as well." I knew I was winning when Daxton didn't argue. However, that didn't mean he wouldn't try. I needed to guide this conversation elsewhere.

"I think it's about time you brought me to Silver Meadows and showed me your home, Daxton Aegaeon."

Dax silently reached out and took my hand, looking at me with a mesmerizing gaze I couldn't bring myself to turn away from. Electricity crackled along my skin when he touched me, our magic reacting to each other's presence like it always did. Did he feel the same way I did? The queen warned me that an offspring of a mated pair would never settle for anything but a mate. Even with the lack of a mate bond, could Daxton *love* me? Was I enough?

"Let's go," Daxton said as Castor placed a hand on his brother's shoulder.

"Welcome to Silver Meadows, Spitfire," Daxton said with pride beaming from his expression. The scent of mountain pine and cold air reminded me of him, and I realized he smelled exactly like this city ... like his home. This was, without a doubt, where Daxton belonged.

Silver Meadows was tucked away within the sanctuary of towering mountains and a channel to the ocean along the eastern horizon. Starfall Island, which Captain Fjorda and the crew of the *Opal* called home, was breathtaking, highlighted by the morning sun. My eyes widened as the mountains to the west and south glistened with silver ores along their snow-capped peaks. The beauty of this realm took my breath away. Aelius and Crimson City had no hold over Silver Meadows.

The bulk of Silver Meadows was built atop steep rolling hills leading to three towering silver-streaked mountains to the north, where their main palace resided. The hanging valley at the base of the tallest mountain caught my attention immediately, and I made a mental note to visit there as soon as I was able. The gleaming silver mixed with the deep shades of green highlighted the natural beauty embedded into the wilderness.

Rolling hills were divided by a broad, winding river the color of the brightest turquoise and rarest sapphires. The waters snaked across the landscape, leading to the channel dividing the mainland from Starfall Island. Tucked between patches of thick wilderness with various brush and green pines, three distinct market squares emerged. The city's buildings were crafted out of white marble intermixed with patterns of warm red and tan stone and wooden frames. I recognized that the same red sandstone designs from Crimson City adorned some of the rooftops, giving the city an array of alternating colors.

From our vantage point on the palace steps, I could see other sections dedicated to townhouses with green copper roofs and white chimneys. The fae lights illuminating the cobblestone streets dimmed as the pink and yellow sunrise kissed the landscape below.

"I can't believe how beautiful this all is."

"I'm glad you approve."

"Just wait until you see inside," Castor boasted.

I turned where I stood, my head tilting upward, taking in the immense sight of a gray stone palace that loomed behind me. Built at the base of the three towering mountains, the palace resembled a rectangular fortress, with different sections branching off from the center.

"Our father designed this stronghold to host large gatherings and various visitors. Since our mother was from a different realm, he wanted to ensure she could invite her kin without fear of overcrowding. We fondly call it the Summit," Daxton said.

"Even though it is not at the top of the mountain … it's at the northernmost edge of the city, so it fits," Castor added.

"What do you do with all your space now if you're not hosting visitors?"

"We get creative," Castor said with a smirk.

I rolled my eyes. I did not want to imagine how Castor used the abundance of space in his home.

"Guest wings are near the base, with our main rooms on the center and top floors. Castor's rooms are on the western side, while mine lie toward the eastern wing. The training area and healers' quarters are also on the center floor, on the western side," Daxton explained.

"Near the training and sparring grounds, I assume." I glanced toward the mountain's base, which held a large clearing.

"Correct. The formal throne room and gathering areas are unique. They are directly at the entrance. The library, of course, is at the far end of the eastern wing."

My eyes widened as my excitement jumped. "Show me!" I practically squealed with delight. "Can you show me the library? Please. Please!"

"I never thought I would see the day someone was more anxious to read than you, brother," Castor snickered. "She might as well get started researching the clues we have from the scroll."

"Castor's right," I replied with a grin. "*For once*," I added under my breath.

"Very well." Daxton nodded. "Skylar, I'll take you to the library, but then I must tend to my duties as high prince. It's been some time since I've been home, and the news about Anjani and the Dryads needs to be addressed."

"Don't worry. Leaving me in a library surrounded by books is no trouble. Just don't be upset with me if I put up a fight when you try to get me to leave."

A small grin tugged at his lips as if he were almost as excited as I was to show me his treasure trove.

"Cas, find Gunnar and Zola. Tell them to meet me in the War Room with Adohan within the hour. I need to hear the reports they gathered while we were away and address any concerns our people have raised. Also, Cas," Daxton said to his brother, "send word that I will meet with the Dryads' leaders within the week."

Castor nodded, giving us both a slight bow before making his trek toward the training grounds on the other side of the palace.

"Alright, close your eyes," Daxton said, guiding me through the entrance. "I want the unveiling to be special. The library is one of my favorite places to dwell when I have time." I smirked, unable to hold back my excitement any longer, and happily obliged his request. Before I settled my nerves, Daxton whisked us away.

"All right, open them."

The two-story library in the Summit held stacked shelves filled with countless volumes spanning every topic imaginable. If I wandered from one side to the other, I would become lost within the spanning aisles and tempting tales. It was a reader's paradise, unmatched by any I had seen. The smell of this place was bewitching, with sections leading to cozy corners tucked away from sight and the musty scent of aged books that seemed to transport me into a different time and place. I was transfixed by the amount of knowledge I knew this sanctuary held. Majestic marble columns surrounded the intricate frescoes adorning the arched ceiling, and rows of beautifully bound books were calling me.

"Daxton," I gasped, "this is unbelievable."

His smile was serene as he guided me to the spiral staircase leading to the second floor. "The second level is the best place to begin searching for the creature you will face in the upcoming trial. There is also an area dedicated to different plants and other wildlife you might encounter here. I can show you different sections about history on the lower levels and possibly our archives in the city center if you believe it will help."

"This will do for now," I answered, half-hearing what he said—still mesmerized by the sheer size of the library. "Wait, there are archives as well?"

"Yes, this library is our family collection, began by my mother. But the archives in the city's center are for all of us to share. They hold the scrolls of our history that are looked after and kept safe."

"You must show me the archives later, but for now ... this is a good place to start."

"Very well. I'll leave you to it then." Daxton chuckled, realizing I was more than happy to be left alone. "I'll come back for you as soon as I'm able."

"I'll be here," I said, motioning to the stacks of manuscripts I was ready to rummage through. I traced my fingers along the spines of a few books along the first row, reading the various titles and deciding where I should start. "You gave a secret bookworm an entire library to themselves ... good luck ever getting me to leave."

"I'll take that challenge," Daxton answered, giving me an amused look that had my toes curling. "Good luck." In a silver flash, he was gone.

I began diving into the section describing the different types of fae creatures, then decided to indulge in a volume dedicated to the land's geology. The riddle described the creature's lair, so the clue identifying it could lurk in where its cage was held.

The charm and allure of the library proved to be a good distraction. Most of the day had already passed, and the sun hovered closer to the seas in the west through the skylight windows.

I finished rummaging through a fae creature book and made notes about the landscape of Silver Meadows but then meandered to a different section dedicated to folklore. I grabbed a few titles and searched for a nook to curl up in and begin researching. In the second story, where Daxton had left me, I found a chaise in the corner, near a picture window. As I sat down, I realized his scent was embedded in this place. My animal stirred as I relished in the feel of him, even in his absence. I would wager that this spot, in particular, was his hideaway. Draped by a tapestry on one side with the other hidden by a large potted plant. It was perfect.

Kicking off my boots, I lay down on the large chaise and tucked a pillow on my lap to begin reading. I became lost in the pages, blissfully ignoring the lapse of time and diving head-first into the folklore tales of the Inner Kingdom: It wasn't until the fae lights appeared that I realized what time it was. The snacks I stored in my pack were almost gone, but surprisingly, it hadn't deterred me from my reading. I had almost finished the second book when I could no longer seem to hold my eyes open. Exhaustion tugged at every aching muscle and dark corner of my consciousness, and still, I could not bring myself to sleep. I leaned over onto my side, resting with the book still open and my eyes skipping over the words, trying desperately to keep awake.

I didn't stir or flinch when the weight of the book disappeared because it was immediately replaced by his hand intertwining with mine. Daxton silently slid in behind me, tucking me in close to him with a hand possessively curled over my waist. It seemed so natural that I didn't even think to second-guess how or why he was here.

"I see you found my reading spot."

I smiled softly as I sank into his warm embrace. Somehow, his presence allowed the rest of the world to slip away. With him, everything was different. There were no lingering dangers or fears when he was with me. It was just us.

"You need sleep, Spitfire," he whispered as his scruff brushed against my cheek. "Tomorrow will come soon enough."

"What if I can't sleep? What if I'm too scared to close my eyes and realize this is all a dream? That I am still locked in the labyrinth and my soul …"

"Your soul?" He was deathly still, his grip bringing me closer. "What happened in the labyrinth, Skylar?"

"I want to tell you … but it's something I'm having a hard time believing myself," I whispered. I still couldn't believe I had dared to bargain my soul. I shuddered as the monster from the deep crept into my mind. Daxton reacted to my fears like they were his own, moving over me and cupping my cheek. I slowly opened my tear-soaked eyes to find his.

"Skylar." His voice was calm despite the concern lingering in his gaze. "It's over. You don't have to—"

"But I do, Daxton," I practically yelled as my facade of strength shattered. Daxton moved back against the chaise and cradled me in his arms. I sobbed for everything I went through—and everything I still had to overcome in order for our world to be free. "What if … What if I can't do this, Daxton?"

"What if you can?"

I turned to look at him. His expression was so soft and comforting that it made my heart skip a beat.

Gods above, he was so ridiculously handsome it wasn't even fair. His hands softly stroked my arms before moving to my shoulders and making small circles against my back as he cradled me in his embrace.

"What if you can, Spitfire?"

His chin rested against my brow as I inhaled a deep, calming breath. His scent came crashing through my senses, the pine and winter mountain air reminding me of the open sky and wilderness that grounded me and my animal. A warm sensation spread through my chest, allowing the tether of a connection with Daxton to open and consume me.

"Can—" I stumbled forming the question on my lips. "Can you feel that?" I asked.

Daxton paused before answering me. "There are many things I'm feeling right now, but I don't possess the experience needed to accurately express them. This ... What I feel with you is foreign to me. Even in my past relations, I've never—"

"Never what?" I questioned, turning to look at him as my chest rose and fell in heavy labored breaths. *What was he feeling?*

"I've never been willing to be so open with someone before. It's never been this effortless to do so. I have a tendency to keep even those I care for at an arm's length, but not you, Skylar." He paused and I held my breath, anxiously waiting for him to continue. "Since the day you scolded me for almost dying, I've been at your mercy." Daxton's smile was soft as he ran his finger across my cheek, his finger twirling in the ends of my hair.

My thoughts ventured to what Castor had said before I made my vow and allegiance to Silver Meadows. *But ever since meeting you ... he ... He's changed.* I realized he was likely just as lost as I was, and to add the weight of the trials to all this? It was utter madness.

"I—I saw you in the labyrinth." I confessed.

I watched Daxton's expression stiffen, yet he remained quiet despite the endless questions no doubt rattling inside his head.

"You were there inside the labyrinth, and you helped rescue me from being eaten alive while dangling over a blackened abyss of doom." I watched Daxton's reaction carefully, yet he remained silent. "The labyrinth it … it was a living thing. And he created himself in your image, trying to trick me into leaving. I didn't take the offer, though. Obviously."

"How did you figure out it wasn't me?" Daxton asked.

"Because the labyrinth couldn't replicate the real *you*. There were tells, small mannerisms that seemed different."

"No one can truly mimic perfection. They can try, but it will only end in failure."

"Oh, Gods, don't let your ego inflate like Adohan's." Daxton laughed and curled his lips inward, nodding for me to continue. "My animal didn't react to your presence. Your magic seemed off, and you were joking at the time, but you tried to stab me."

"Stab you?" he repeated, shaking his head with a more serious tone now. "Skylar, you know I would never …"

"Clearly," I said with a half-smile to try and comfort him. "But that wasn't what did it for me."

"I'm intrigued to hear what my ultimate tell was."

"You tried to force me through a portal and leave. You said that you were making this decision for me and that I had no choice." I purposely omitted the part about the imposter confessing his feelings for me and the desire for us to be together. While I knew Daxton was fond of me and desired me, I was cautious. "In our time together, Daxton, you've never once forced me to do anything. You've respected my decisions."

"And I always will." He tucked my hair behind my ear, causing me to lean toward him. I desperately wanted to kiss him. Hell, I wanted to do more than just kiss him. Flashes of our previous night together flooded my memories, and hunger settled in my core.

"You need rest," he said, biting his lower lip. My barrier was down, and I knew he could sense my arousal.

"Then don't do that," I said playfully, motioning to his bottom lip, which I longed to taste again. Gods help me ... I wanted him in every way possible.

"What will help you sleep, Spitfire?"

"Stay with me?"

"As you wish," he replied, leaning back against the chaise, allowing my head to fall onto his chest.

He rubbed my back and hummed a quiet tune I immediately recognized. It was the song he somehow sent me while I was in the hunter's keep—the melody that wrapped me in a blanket of his strength and allowed me to overcome the darkest depths of my fears and possibly even death.

"Sleep," he whispered. "I've got you, Spitfire."

Chapter Seventeen

The training grounds of the Silver Meadows warriors would be my new home for the next two months. It reminded me of my pack lands in Solace, pulling at a longing to see the shoreline of my home once again.

Scattered patches of trees lined our dirt pathway from the Summit, opening into a massive clearing encircled by waist-high stone walls at each corner of the grass area. Inside, there was a long target range for archers, sparring rings for hand-to-hand combat, and racks of different swords, spears, and countless other weapons for battle practice. This was hands down two, perhaps even five times larger than our training field outside the alpha's home. Beyond the stone walls, secluded in the nearby towering trees, were multi-level barracks for soldiers with outdoor bathing areas near the small creek that flowed from the main river. A narrow, covered structure lay in the center of the living quarters with numerous tables and scattered benches for a mess hall.

Countless High Fae warriors scattered the thick pine-wooded area, practicing various combat skills and weaponry. Some were in stone-gray training clothes, and a large grouping of others wore black lined with silver.

There was a clear divide between the two, and I couldn't help but notice I was labeled as a trainee or cadet with my stone-gray shirt and pants.

Males and females in black training attire with silver-threaded designs earned the title of Silver Meadows warriors. One peak on their shoulder meant they had conquered the Ice Gauntlet and could march into battle within the ranks. The second peak was received in victory, and the third was earned when you defended your people, bringing honor to Silver Meadows and those they had sworn to protect.

Off toward the edge of the training grounds, the Ice Gauntlet towered over us—the assessment tool used to determine if a cadet or anyone brave enough was worthy of marching into battle with the banner of a Silver Meadows warrior. The daunting obstacle course was carved into the mountainside with sheer rock cliffs leading to different levels higher and higher up. I didn't know why, but the challenge of the Ice Gauntlet was tempting.

Oh, so gods-damned tempting. I couldn't keep my eyes off it while Daxton led me to our sparring area that morning. I didn't know if the challenge itself was driving me and my animal's competitive spirit or if it was a secret desire to prove to myself that I might just be worthy of enough for … well, for a lot of things.

Stupid idea? Quite possibly. But then again, it could also be brilliant.

"There's a rotation between two outposts that guard my realm," Daxton said as we made our way through the training grounds. "One is here at the western side of the mountains in Silver Meadows, and the other two are further north. The northernmost outpost is adjacent to the Aelius territory, and the other borders the wilt on the western side of the Inner Kingdom. The warriors rotate every two weeks."

"So, for a month, they're away from Silver Meadows?"

Daxton nodded as we approached a clearing. "The two weeks here are less rigorous for those on distant patrol. I manage a smaller section that always guards the Summit and the city borders. My warriors on patrol are ordered to rest, recuperate, and spend time with their families if they decide to have them when they return."

"That is generous," I stated.

"I ask them to leave everything behind for a month and risk their lives. It is only fair that I grant them half that time back in return for their service. When war becomes a way of life, and you don't know anything different, you make the best of what you have."

"Do warriors volunteer for these rotating outposts? Or is it preferred that they remain here in your personal guard?"

"On the contrary," Daxton snickered, "it's hard to keep them away from the northern patrols. Those who desire to become Silver Meadows warriors are dedicated to a cause greater than themselves. In their eyes, it is an honor to fight, defend, and die in battle protecting their home if the Gods deem it necessary."

"And this has been the protocol for …"

"For the past five hundred years. Ever since the wilt appeared, and every day, we are thankful to see the next."

"Five hundred years," I muttered to myself, unable to comprehend how much time that was to be living in a constant state of dread and fear. Always on guard. Always willing and ready to fight. "So, what keeps the wilt from progressing? From it reaching Silver Meadows?"

"When it began, Minaeve placed magical wards at our outpost along the wilt border that I must replenish with my magic, or else the decay spreads along with the hordes of harpies, hounds, and unnamed dark creatures that would keep any sane person awake at night." He stilled for a moment, glancing sideways at me. "We must keep the occasional fallen at bay too. We have to be cautious. If too many were to gather, they could overpower the ward and destroy it."

"You all have been fighting for so long." I looked out into the forest surrounding the training area beneath the Ice Gauntlet. The vertical obstacle course built into the mountainside itself seemed impossible. "How do all of you do this? For five hundred years, you've not given up fighting a plague that threatens to swallow you whole."

The look on Daxton's face hid a dark truth, one that damn near broke my heart to see written in the hidden tells on his face. Daxton quickly recovered, turning toward me with an odd stillness, and gave me a half-smile to try and comfort me but also himself. "We've experienced downfalls and difficulties, but there is no other choice. We keep fighting, or we die."

"Surprised you're admitting to a lack of perfection," I teased, trying to lighten his mood.

He chuckled, softening his gaze and hardened exterior, allowing me to see beyond the Silver Shadow stigma. "I've built a strong circle of friends that I have been able to lean on in my darkest times."

I saw the pain and regret flash for the briefest second in his eyes. A dark truth about his hardships, one that I recognized in Shaw when he said he would take my place in the trials.

Gods above ...

"But in the last handful of years, especially the past few months, we've been given a reason to hope for something better. And that, Skylar, has been the most powerful breath of life we could ask for." Our eyes locked, and I swear if we didn't need to keep our distance, I would have leaped into his arms without a second thought.

"Did I just hear my high prince give a compliment without blood or flesh being scraped off the battlefield or training ring?" A playful-sounding voice echoed as a tall, striking High Fae male warrior in black training leathers stepped into view with three mountain peaks on his shoulder. "I think pigs have begun to fly."

Daxton rolled his eyes. "Are you saying you'd like to go flying today, Gunnar? Because that can be arranged after I chase your ass up the Ice Gauntlet and throw you from the top."

Gunnar clicked his tongue, crossing his thick muscular arms at his chest as a large, cunning smile spanned his clean-shaven face. "If you think you can still beat me. I believe your years are catching up to you, Dax, and you're becoming *slow*." His dark brown eyes squinted, giving him a playful facade that contrasted with the hard tattoo markings around the side of his half-shaved head, continuing just below the base of his throat. The silver mountains on his uniform mirrored the tattoos on the right side of his head, and a circle of gilded thorns rested in the center of his chest, sporting an arrow and sword crossed over each other in black ink. The top half of his head revealed silver-trimmed hair streaking through long dark brown locks braided into a tight bun.

Daxton narrowed his gaze as his jaw muscles ticked. "I believe I've been gone too long if you think you can beat me up the Gauntlet. Is no one around here up to the task of challenging you properly? And here I thought you were succeeding in your role as my weapons master and general of my armies."

"Hard to curb perfection," Gunnar snickered.

"Indeed," Daxton said in a low, calm voice that had even his trusted general taking a step back.

"Gunnar?" I asked, tilting my head around Daxton to get a better look at the High Fae warrior I'd heard about on the *Opal*.

"In the flesh," he said, uncrossing his arms and giving me a beaming smile.

"About to be beaten out of his flesh is more like it," Daxton growled, "if he keeps this attitude up."

"You mean the high ego ... and the air of arrogance?" I asked, lifting my brow at Dax. "Sounds oddly familiar. I wonder where he gets it from?"

Gunnar burst out laughing. "Oh, you are my new favorite person, little shifter."

I recalled that Gunnar was orphaned as a child, rising in the military ranks, and holding the title of the youngest to enter the Ice Gauntlet and succeed. Earning Castor and Daxton's trust through his service and battle, he became third in command of Silver Meadows. He was also general of Daxton's armies, and he had stepped in to oversee their realm for the past months while they were away.

"I don't recall ever being nicknamed *little* after my growth spurt at thirteen and becoming one of the tallest females in my pack," I countered.

"Well, standing next to Daxton, everyone is *little*," Gunnar said, stepping forward to give me a once-over. "I guess little is an understatement. You're just about as tall as me—I'll give you that. Odd though ... I thought shifters were smaller."

"And exactly how many shifters have you met before?"

"Quick on the wit. Beauty and brains," Gunnar purred with a wink. "I bet you keep Daxton here on his toes … as well as on his—"

"That's more than enough," Daxton growled. "Skylar, this is Gunnar. My general, and believe it or not, a trusted friend. His smart remarks might have cost him that pretty head of his years ago if he had not rightfully earned his station."

"Another compliment!" Gunnar beamed, widening his grin. "Pigs are soaring above our heads … I knew today would be a good one." Daxton didn't seem amused, but he also didn't lash out. "All right, in all seriousness now …"

"Can you manage that?" Daxton rebutted in a low tone with his eyebrows arched. His grimace held a twinge of amusement, but I wondered if many others could detect it.

"Believe it or not, I can," Gunnar answered without missing a step. "That's why you keep me around. I remind the warriors to loosen up when we can."

"And surprise them when your skills as my top-seated warrior are put to action. Yes, I'm aware. I taught you how to balance it all."

"But I perfected it." Gunnar grinned as Daxton shook his head, hiding a glimmer of pride in his expression.

Daxton turned to me, placing a hand discreetly on the small of my back. Any onlookers would easily write off the soft touch, but it sent goosebumps racing across my skin like lightning. "Don't let Gunnar's entertaining personality fool you. He's one of the most skilled warriors in the Inner Kingdom and experienced instructors. He'll assess and begin your training while I attend to our recruits and other meetings with the Dryads outside the city today. I'll see you after your assessment is done."

"You won't be training me yourself?" I asked in disappointment.

"I want Gunnar to assess your skills and offer additional insight into where we focus your training against the creature in the next trial. Once this is done, then yes, of course, I will assist in your training exercises."

"All right. Until tonight, then. Will I see you later in the library?"

"Wouldn't miss it." Daxton gave me a soft smile as he stepped back to teleport away. His absence left me in limbo momentarily before shaking my head and pivoting back toward Gunnar.

"All right, little shifter. Let's see what you can do and where your training needs to start," Gunnar said, guiding me toward an array of weapons.

His black training clothes were loose-fitting around his broad chest, highlighting a warmer skin tone that paired nicely with his dark brown, silver-streaked hair. "What experience do you have in killing a creature of death, in combat?"

"Quick to the point. How refreshing," I answered. "I was an archer and scout in my pack, but I learned self-defense early in my youth. My uncle thought it was essential that we learn how to defend ourselves and fight in our human forms and animals … once we shifted."

"Smart, I like the male already. What weapons are you comfortable with?"

"I prefer a bow and arrow, along with shorter swords and daggers. I'm not as comfortable wielding weapons like Daxton's sword."

"Valencia is a beast in its own right."

"Valencia?"

"The sword of Silver Meadows. Valencia is an enchanted weapon that only Daxton or those of his house can call to wield. It never dulls, is sharp as fuck, and is an extremely lethal weapon with its own power for whoever wields it," Gunnar said. "Seamus has eyed it for years, but the mind-fucker will never be able to wield it."

"Why would Seamus think he could use it if it is enchanted for only Daxton's house?"

"Their mother was—"

"Of Aelius," I finished for him. "Dax told me about his parents."

Gunnar gave me an impressed nod before continuing, "She was a descendant of Seamus's family line. Not direct, more like a third cousin. So naturally, Seamus thought it could extend to him. But that's not how the sword works; it requires a direct descendant or connection." Gunnar casually stretched out his arms, rolling his thick shoulders as we walked. "For all his shortfalls, however, the High Prince of Aelius would be one fucking hell of a fight if I had to face him; I'll give him that."

"How does the sword work then? Could Castor summon it?" We strode to the target range on the far side of the training field near the waist-height stone wall.

"Castor could, but it wouldn't work as well." Gunnar stepped toward the weapons rack and retrieved a bow and arrows in a quiver for me. "Daxton holds the title and power of a high prince. The sword recognizes the power he commands, and even though Queen

309

Minaeve siphons most of it away and he refuels our wards along with Adohan's on occasion—"

"Wait, what?"

Gunnar's eyes widened, and he turned his lips inward, biting them with a scowl. "Shit, you didn't know that bit, did you? Dammit. It's hard to keep these secrets when Daxton told us about ..."

"About what?" I asked, strapping a quiver to my back and holding the bow steady in my left hand.

"About ..." Gunnar looked like he was on the verge of exploding. He was definitely not the best at keeping secrets. "About *things* I can't share." I glared at him but surprisingly kept my questions to myself and didn't push him for answers ... for now. "All right, enough about Valencia and all these other side topics ... let's see what skills you have with this."

I nocked an arrow and aimed at the target approximately eighty yards away across the field. Concentrating on my breathing, I steadied my hand and pulled back on the fletching, anchoring my right hand beneath my jaw adjacent to a nock in my ear—the same place I always drew. I stilled, exhaled, and released the fletching, watching the arrow soar and hiss through the air, landing with a thud as it sank in the middle, just where I aimed it.

"Impressive," Gunnar said.

I nocked another two arrows, sending them flying to the target, landing above and below the first. "I could split the shaft in two at this range, but I've lost far too many good arrows performing that trick."

"Really?" Gunnar's brows rose with a sheepish grin. "Cocky much?"

"Confident," I answered, releasing a fourth arrow to create a diamond-shaped grouping.

"But … can you still make that shot with enemies on all sides and running through battle?"

"And how do you intend to simulate that?"

He grinned all too eagerly as if the assessment and the topic of wargames were playthings to him. "Oh, I have my ways, but that's for later. Today, we begin with the basics. Luck is completing a task once, but true skill is being able to repeat a successful task more than once."

"Even if I tried this at night, I would still hit my target without faltering."

"Aren't we challenging Castor's level of arrogance now?"

"No," I countered, drawing the fifth arrow and firing it in the center of the other four, completing my design. "I'm just confident."

Thanks to countless hours of practice with Magnus and working through training courses to perfect my skillset, I had *earned* my weapon and my place as a scout within my pack. Rhea might have the upper hand with daggers, while Shaw, Gilen, and Talon all surpassed in sparring and the use of other larger weaponry, but I always excelled with my bow.

"I shot Daxton and almost killed him the first time I met him," I added.

"He did mention that," Gunnar said, holding his hand out for my bow, his expression morphing into a serious scowl laced with a warning. "Despite my humor, I'm fond of and fiercely loyal to my high prince. Hearing that he was almost killed …"

"Noted." I nodded, dipping my head.

Gunnar's hard smile stretched across his clean face. "Good—let's move on. Now that we know what you are good with … let's put your skills with the other weapons to the test."

For the rest of the morning and the better part of the day, Gunnar assessed my abilities with daggers, a long sword, and other smaller blades utilized in battle. As I predicted, my skill with the long sword was far from perfect, but at least I wasn't a complete novice.

Gunnar said he was confident that if I was in a tight spot, he could rely on me to put the pointed end through an enemy. I glared at him at first but ultimately laughed at his remark. He had a unique way of making me feel at ease even though I was struggling through portions of his evaluation. I had to remind myself that even though I felt like I was failing … the trials were not war. I wasn't training to be a warrior on the front lines.

I doubted I would ever physically outmatch fighters such as Daxton, Gunnar, or even Castor without shifting into my animal form. Well, as long as my animal wasn't a songbird or a small house cat. They had centuries of training under their belts compared to my twenty-two years. I had to be realistic. Even if I secretly wanted to prove myself in the Ice Gauntlet, it might not be the best idea.

The evening was approaching, and my gray training clothes were thoroughly soaked through with sweat and a few spots of blood from the split lip Gunnar gave me on the mat. It was 100 percent my fault for not reacting to his counter in time, and my lip, along with other bruises, would be a good reminder to stay one step ahead of my opponent when it mattered.

"How's the lip and chin feeling?" Gunnar asked as he sank next to me on the grass, handing me a canteen filled with ice-cold water from the nearby river runoff.

"I've had worse … and I imagine there's still more to come." I took a long swig from the canteen, practically draining the contents. "This is helpful, though. Thanks."

"No problem. I imagine the life of a shifter or champion, in your case, is not an easy path to follow."

"No, it definitely hasn't been," I replied, glancing down at the three eight-pointed stars on my left arm. Ever since I'd made the choice to become the champion, my life had been anything but easy. "Capture, torture, death, recovery, adventure, attacked again, and … the trial of the mind. I could go on, but I'm sure you've heard all this by now."

Gunnar leaned back onto his hands and extended his legs out in front of him in a relaxed position. "Yesterday, Daxton informed us briefly of what you've gone through, yes." He paused for a moment, catching my attention. "But I always prefer firsthand encounters. It isn't the same secondhand. And it isn't healthy to bottle up what you are feeling and let it explode. Talking about it helps the healing."

"Personal experience?"

"Absolutely." Gunnar grinned.

"Daxton has been … He's been there for me each step of the way since that night in the meadow. I've been able to confide in him more than anyone." Gunnar's smile grew wider as the corners of his brown eyes softened—something lurking behind that cheerful grin.

"What? What is it?" This was a different male from the general who had thrown me around and taken me to the dirt a few moments earlier.

"Nope." Gunnar gestured with his palms facing me. "Not my place. No way am I stepping into that."

"Not your place for what? There's something you're not telling me."

"Damn right, there is. But understand this," he added, leaning toward me and lowering his voice, "I may play the lighthearted, humorous role, but I also know when to keep my mouth shut. *This* is one of those moments."

I rolled my eyes. "Fantastic. You're going to be zero help."

"With regards to *that*? Abso-fucking-lutely. But regarding your training assessment, I believe I do have some news that will lift your spirits."

"Really?"

He glanced backward toward the base of the mountain, where the Ice Gauntlet lay in wait. "I think *that*," he said, gesturing behind us, "is exactly what you need to prepare for the trial."

"Really?" I questioned with eager, wide eyes. "Seriously?"

"I've noticed you eyeballing and practically drooling over it since you stepped foot into the training grounds." I practically squealed with glee. "You're not afraid of a challenge—good. Having the Ice Gauntlet as your training goal will help you defeat whatever creature you're up against. You'll need stamina, to be quick, agile, balanced, and strong enough to defeat this beast. The Ice Gauntlet will challenge all this and more."

I turned and glanced up at the obstacle course built into the mountain. "Fuck, yes. I want to run the Ice Gauntlet." I couldn't help it … I loved this idea. This course was the best way to test my physical limitations and prepare me for the battle with the beast.

"Um … care to repeat that decision, Gunnar?" Castor's tone was unmistakable. "You want a half-shifter whose animal hasn't emerged yet to take on the most difficult assessment in the Inner Kingdom? Come on,

Daxton, tell me you agree with me and not Gunnar on this."

I turned and glanced near the tree line to find Daxton shirtless and downright delectable, likely fresh from his training session with the other cadets he had told me about earlier.

"What do you want to do, Spitfire?" he asked, knowing my answer, a half-smirk growing at the corner of his mouth.

"Spitfire?" Gunnar muttered to himself. "That's endearing."

Ignoring Gunnar, I smiled at Daxton, recognizing the tempting defiance in his silver-gray eyes. He wanted me to do this. He also believed that the challenge of the Gauntlet would be the perfect tool to push my training. "I want to run the Ice Gauntlet."

"But this is an *unnecessary* risk! Magic does not work on the course. If she falls, you cannot teleport in to save her!" Castor pleaded. "Trainees die running it."

"She won't die in the Gauntlet," Daxton answered. His smoldering gaze bore into mine, heat flaring in his eyes as his excitement for me rose. "Skylar is too stubborn for an obstacle course to kill her. She's defeated the trial of the mind. I do not doubt her ability to figure out the course and complete it in a faster time than yours, brother." Castor scowled.

My grin grew even wider, ignoring the pain of the split on my lip and jumping to my feet. "Let's get started then!" I shouted, tracing my gaze toward the looming challenge I desperately wanted to conquer.

"Tomorrow," Gunnar said.

"You've got to be kidding me." I turned to him with a confused look.

Gunnar rose to stand next to me. "Believe it or not, there is a balance to life—even when you're a champion of the trials—and I've been kicking your shifter ass all over the ring today." He leaned in and sniffed the air around me. "You also need a bath."

"You mean in everything besides … *archery*," I countered, pushing him away. "Sorry, this is what hard work smells like. Must be new to you?"

Gunnar laughed. "Yes, well, I admit … that was surprising. I understand now why you were able to catch this one off guard and drill him with an arrow through the chest. I would decorate that mark and wear it as a symbol of luck if it were me, and then …" Daxton looked at Gunnar without saying a word, and the general stopped mid-sentence. "Like I said—balance. You need to recover if you plan on training for the Ice Gauntlet."

I glanced between them, trying to decipher Daxton's silent command, but I couldn't figure it out.

"To the library then," I announced. "We still need to figure out what I'm facing in the next trial."

"Finally, there's a hint of the common sense I have been accustomed to." Castor sighed. "You know, you could have come out of the shadows and helped end this matter."

I glanced toward the shade along the tree line, and the outline of a female figure stepped forward. The dark brown skin with wisps of black markings and ebony eyes were unmistakable.

"Zola! I didn't even know you were here!"

True to her shadow-jumper-spying nature, Zola held no emotion in her expression, but she gave me a small nod, which I took to be the same as a giant hug or greeting from Idris. I would take it. "Glad to see you alive, Champion."

"Really, you didn't know?" Gunnar asked me. "Who did you think I was conspiring with for my assessments?"

My eyes widened. I had no idea she was watching us the entire day. But then again, I wasn't looking for her or anyone else lurking in the shadows trying to spy on us. I turned my lips inward, mulling over the fact that I had let my guard down in one of the most dangerous places I had ever been. Even though I was comfortable here, danger lurked around every corner, and I needed to be on my guard at all times.

"Don't be too hard on yourself, Skylar. It's my job to be unseen," Zola said.

Castor cleared his throat. "I thought you were with …"

"Nyssa," Zola said, cutting Castor's question short. She said the name like it was some kind of code, "is comfortable with the scribes in the archives tower."

I glanced at Castor to try and assess his mood, but I knew whatever he was truly feeling was likely tucked away in the corner of his calculating mind. He was never one to show his hand early if he had the choice.

"Nyssa," Castor repeated the name slowly, his expression turning somber as he looked down at his feet for a moment, deep in thought.

"She asks about you." Castor's eyes widened, but Zola averted her gaze away from him and straight to me.

"Me?" I asked, pointing a finger at my chest. "I don't believe I know any Nyssa …"

Zola flashed me a look that read, *Are you fucking kidding me, shifter? Get your head out of the sand and figure it out.*

In utter embarrassment, I suddenly realized that she was talking about the fallen fae I'd healed. "Oh, Nyssa!" I exclaimed. "Sorry, names and places get jumbled when you are put through a labyrinth of literal mental torture," I shot back, and Zola flashed me a half-smirk of approval once more as she shifted in her black leathers, meticulously counting the daggers sheathed along her chest like it was second nature.

"You've spoken with her then?" Castor asked.

"I've taught her to sign with the help of the scribes. Those bookworms are caring in a way I can never understand. And the female attendants have officially taken her under their wing, shooing me out before one of my knives tore through another of their precious ancient scrolls." Zola sighed. "That, in my opinion, had nothing of worth on them anyway. It's not my fault that one time three hundred years ago, I was using some for much-needed target practice while being cooped up in their tower."

"I barely saved you from their wrath … Not my easiest years pleading with the scribes to grant you sanctuary and getting you back into their good graces," Daxton added. "You do remember why we hid you in there, right?"

"That prickly cunt … Anjani. Yes, I remember. The archives are warded, so no magic works inside," Zola said, turning to me. "I can't shadow-jump. You can't teleport or use your ice magic. Castor can't see, and Anjani can't manipulate anything. It was a good plan."

"Don't sound too surprised," Dax said, but Zola only glared at him.

"My warriors were on patrol day and night until we finally chased her out of Silver Meadows. Her desire for your head for the trick you pulled on her was …"

"She deserved it," Zola snarled.

"Never said she didn't. Anjani is unnerving and slightly twisted, if not insane." Gunnar shivered and shook his shoulders, his hand tracing over a scar along his arm. "She can make it seem like you're living your worst nightmare … and then laughs as your soul is torn apart with grief."

"She sounds like a real peach," I added.

"I brought Idris and Adohan to the door of the archives, and they allowed Adohan entrance … with his mate carried in his arms, of course. Adohan wanted me to make sure you knew they were taking your recommendation seriously," Zola said.

"That's good," I answered with relief as my stomach grumbled.

Daxton's smirk curled at the side of his delectable mouth, which I desperately wanted to taste again. Hell, I was on the verge of forgoing food if it meant I could be alone with him inside the Summit and have his lips crashing into mine with his tongue devouring me with savage, unrelenting strokes. His kisses from the library last night were light and comforting, but I craved more from him.

"We haven't shown you the kitchens yet, have we, Spitfire?" Daxton grinned. "I should've shown that to you first."

"No, and that's a shame because I want to help earn my keep while I'm here. I can bake or help with meals." Dax gave me a look that said, *really?*

"We have cooks and attendants that work inside the Summit, Skylar. That won't be necessary," Castor replied.

"What my brother means to say," Daxton interjected, "is that you don't have to earn your keep while you're here. Remember, you are the champion of the trials, and it is *us* who are tasked with looking after you. But whatever you would like to do, we'll do our best to accommodate your needs."

"I can take care of myself," I stated.

"I recall," Daxton said in a low voice, his eyes shimmering with a dark intention, recalling our night on the *Opal*.

I raised my brow and slightly bit my bottom lip, remembering how his magic danced over my skin. How even with a barrier between us, he was able to have that kind of effect on me.

"All this finery and whatnot are lost on me, and I'm happy to help pull my own weight around here."

"Hmm." Gunnar glided out from behind me. "Refreshing that she has the mindset of a warrior, Dax."

"I'm aware," Daxton answered. "Let's get you cleaned up and then venture off to the library with some food. Once we decide where to begin our research, we can discuss how you can pull your own weight. With your training sessions being the primary focus, our time is limited."

"I'll take that compromise." I gave him a knowing look that said even though I agreed, I wasn't going to back down and cave to his request so easily. Alas, much to my displeasure, Daxton was right.

Over the next three weeks, I didn't have time to help in the kitchens, let alone think or do anything but prepare for the second trial. In the mornings, after falling asleep over a folded book in the library or in the corner chaise with one on my chest, I ate breakfast and then raced out to meet Gunnar. Half the time, Daxton teleported me to the training fields, encouraging me to eat a more robust meal before I was thrown off one obstacle or the next.

My body ached, and my muscles were strained from the rigorous high-intensity interval training Gunnar had designed especially for me. It was his own specialized kind of torture that was "good for me." After the first two weeks, he was so pleased with my increased stamina and endurance that he insisted Daxton add this to the workouts for their new recruits. With all my training, however, I hadn't even touched the Ice Gauntlet yet.

I was promised, *soon*. Whatever the heck that meant. All I knew was that despite all our research, the answer to the riddle of the beast was still a mystery.

Idris and Adohan worked meticulously in the ancient archives, with the scribes carefully pulling different scrolls for them to read. It was a painstakingly slow process but a task that thankfully kept them both busy.

We each took a piece of the riddle and searched through folklore and history books to try and identify what beast I was going to face. I took the lead in researching the line: *To look upon my white crest is to know true death* White crest. I knew it had to be a physical trait of the creature, but the line about death was a mystery.

Daxton identified the cliffs near the sea where the monster likely lived, and soon, someone would have to venture out there with the key to see if there was any sign of the entrance. I had only five more weeks to complete training for this trial.

Chapter Eighteen

"If you're going to enter the Gauntlet, you'll need to see the course run properly first," Daxton said as we exited the library to find Gunnar.

Walking through the Summit, I admired the tasteful elegance crafted into the stronghold. Amazed at how the architectural designs utilized the surrounding mountains, the forest, and the meadows that the city itself was built upon. The vaulted high ceilings were framed by towering white columns along the hallways and an open grand staircase that connected the various levels. My favorite design of the Summit was the skylight and ceiling-to-floor arched windows that held a breathtaking northern view of the three towering peaks.

Nox was the second tallest to the left, Dagur was the widest to the right, and Meja was at the center, the tallest peak with a hanging valley just below its top.

As we rounded the grand staircase, I traced my hands over the stone-carved railing, admiring the intricate swirling wind designs with various flowers, vines, and trees carved in as well. I could easily lose myself in the details that I managed to find more of each time I looked at them. The artists who helped build this palace had a unique way of combining the strength of the mountains with the beautiful nature surrounding them.

"Today, a group of cadets are trying their hand at the course, and before they enter, I'll run the Gauntlet and show *all* of you how it's properly done." Daxton's hair was tied back, giving me a glimpse of his pointed ears and the strikingly handsome contours of his face.

"Did you have humble tea with breakfast today?" I asked, catching a glimmer of amusement in Daxton's expression.

Castor and the others helped us research the second clue, and although I appreciated their aid, Daxton and I hadn't had a second alone together. With the threat of Anjani lurking in Silver Meadows, we were forced to be discreet.

But honestly, I was too exhausted to even think of doing anything other than sleeping, with Daxton always nearby. Here, in this hallway, however, was the first time we had been alone together, not surrounded by others or the threat of wandering eyes.

"If you want something done right, more often than not, you must do it yourself. I don't want you learning any improper techniques before you enter the course," Daxton insisted, marching us down the marble-stoned hallway off to the side of the staircase.

"You do know … our elders say that we can learn from failure just as much, if not more, than when we succeed."

"Failure in the Ice Gauntlet is a death sentence." Daxton stopped and turned, giving me a firm look that held my steps in place. "I'll never try to hold you back, Skylar. It's not my place to do so, and I respect you too much to attempt to force your hand. But I do ask that you take caution with this task," he said in an even tone. "I ask that you carefully watch me run the course today and take extra care in preparing for the Gauntlet. I can't step in and save you if you fall. You must rely on yourself to reach the end."

"I understand," I said with blazing certainty shimmering behind my eyes. "I'm not scared of what I might fail at, Daxton ... I'm terrified of what I might never try because I'm afraid to fail. I'm a shifter. We're sturdy and annoyingly stubborn to a fault."

Daxton nodded, with a sincere look of pride beaming in his eyes. "And that ... along with many other qualities you possess, is why I know you'll ultimately win the trials. The strength of your heart in all things defies the very fabric of logic."

He glanced around us before moving over me and pressing my backside against the wall. His arms bracing the bulk of his weight on either side of my head. My core tensed, and my breathing became erratic as his gray eyes shined with an intense desire that I knew mirrored my own. The Gods be damned, I wanted this. I wanted him more than logic or common sense could control.

His fingers grasped my chin. His thumb delicately caressed my bottom lip as he shifted his weight, leaning his chest against mine. He was gentle with his touch, but I knew beneath the surface he was just as wild and unhinged as I felt. I watched his eyes scan my face, darkening with a hunger for something more than a stolen embrace in the hallway.

"Well," I barely managed to breathe, "are you going to kiss me?"

A toe-curling grin pulled at his lip. "There's only one problem with that, Spitfire." I raised my brows, tilting my chin so our mouths were just breaths from touching. "If I kissed you here and now, I wouldn't be able to stop."

"I don't see a problem with that."

This time, I took what I wanted. I wasn't going to wait for him to make the move. Gripping Daxton's hips, I aggressively coveted his delicious mouth with my own.

Daxton's lips were warm and soft, more decadent than a rich dessert or the finest wine. Drawing me into a lustful haze that I never wanted to leave. I sucked on his bottom lip, encouraging him to open his mouth so I could kiss him harder, deeper. Exactly how I knew he wanted it. How I knew we both *needed* it. This kiss felt like I was being swallowed and devoured by the raging sea, with Dax as my lifeline. The one thing anchoring me, preventing me from floating away. Nothing else outside this moment existed. Nothing.

His moan was a delicious sound that I could listen to again and again. I would forever strive to entice that sound from his lips for the rest of my mortal life if I could. It turned me on, knowing that he wanted me just as much as I wanted him. Daxton shifted to move against me, his hard, growing length seductively rubbing against the apex between my thighs. I reached my hand down between us and curled my fingers around him, stroking his erection through the fabric of his pants.

"Gods. Fuck, Skylar," Daxton swore against my lips, feverishly kissing me as I opened my mouth to allow his tongue to enter. He grabbed my backside, hoisting me up so I could wrap my legs around his waist. "I have countless ill-mannered things I want to do with this," he growled, gripping my ass tighter.

Our kiss turned wild and unhinged in less than a heartbeat, tasting like sweet insanity, mirroring the danger of what we were kindling in this hallway.

Once my lips parted and his tongue licked inside my mouth, I couldn't resist releasing my own sigh of blissful pleasure. With my thighs spread around him, I could feel him hardening even more through the thin layers of fabric separating us. His kiss held a burning, ravishing need that left me hungry for more. More of him.

"I need you, Spitfire ..." Daxton rasped. "I don't know if I can wait any longer before I get to taste you again. You have no idea how unhinged I am when I'm around you. It's utterly maddening."

"No one's stopping you," I said breathlessly, pausing our kiss to cup his face between my hands before running my fingers through his hair, forcing his eyes to find mine. "Your move, Princey."

The blazing storm of desire burned inside his hooded, lightning-gray eyes. He leaned forward, pressing my back harder into the wall to help hold me while his palms explored the curves of my body. Daxton kissed me with the passion and heat of a thousand blazing suns. Time stopped, becoming nothing more than a mere notion. One second, my lips belonged to me, and the next, they were his.

"Look at me," he commanded, pulling back as I snapped my eyes open. His control was beginning to slip away, but I still, for the life of me, didn't understand *why* he was even trying to hold back.

His grip on me tightened as his cock ground against my throbbing center, sending waves of pleasure through my entire body. He was winding me up like a top. The teasing feel of him was almost unbearable.

Daxton's breath was heavy and ragged, matching my own maddening rhythm as we continued to stare at one another in complete silence. Daring the other to push past that invisible thread between us and lose all control.

Footsteps padded down the hallway to our right.

"Fucking timing," Daxton cursed as he quickly bent to kiss the sensitive spot on my neck, my center aching with a need to be filled. "This is not over yet."

"I'll hold you to that," I said, arching my back to press my breasts and hardened nipples into his chest. The faint sound of his sensual moan echoed once more as he reached up to fondle one of them, his lips still on the base of my neck. Again, I sank into the bliss of his touch, making me forget anything but him. Fuck ... this was a dangerous game to play, but I was done being careful and cautious.

Daxton slowly released me and stepped away, physically bracing himself and trying to regain his composure. I reached up to smooth my hair as best I could, quickly tying a braid across my brow before pulling it into a long ponytail that draped over my shoulder. Daxton watched me with liquid fire burning in his penetrating stare, never once taking his gaze off me.

"You're so fucking beautiful," Dax whispered as he tucked a stray hair behind my ear, his hand cupping the back of my head. I smiled, my cheeks flushing. "Just one word from you ... and I won't be able to hold back. I'll ruin you, Spitfire."

"That's exactly what I want," I said with absolute clarity. "I need you to lose control with me. I want you to be wild." I could feel my animal's power surge to the surface, making my amber eyes glow like fire, challenging him. "Ruin me, so no other could dare try."

His throat bobbed as he closed his eyes, the final threads of his self-control threatening to come undone. "Understood," he said in a dark, rough tone, rushing in for one final kiss before leading us out the door of the Summit.

"Those of you who wish to advance into the ranks of Silver Meadows warriors must first successfully run the Ice Gauntlet," Daxton announced as he stood at the base of the towering mountain that housed the obstacle. "The course is warded against magic, so you will only have your strength, stamina, and sheer willpower to progress you through. If you do not complete this course within the allotted time, you fail. If you fall from an obstacle, you fail. If you slip and grab onto one of the ropes at the higher tiers—"

"You fail?" a mocking cadet asked.

Daxton shook his head. "No, you have two minutes added to your time. But two minutes added is better than falling to your death."

Silence broke out amongst the crowd, but the look of determination on their faces did not change.

"How long did it take you to finish?" I whispered to Gunnar.

"Twenty-seven minutes. Fucking close, but luckily, I didn't grab onto a rope."

"And you were how old?"

"Fifteen."

My eyes widened. "Wow."

"Not the fastest time … That record belongs to none other than the high prince himself, who accomplished that feat at only seventeen," Gunnar replied, lowering his voice so he didn't draw attention away from Daxton's instructions. "And it only took him fifteen minutes. Half the time allotted for him to complete it."

"I ran it when I was twenty-one," Castor added, stepping to my other side. "I did have to grab one rope, but lucky for me, I was still fast enough to make it under your set time, Gunnar." I didn't miss the taunting look the silver prince gave his general.

Gunnar audibly rolled his eyes but managed to keep his comments to himself. Castor was still a prince, and he knew when and where he could push the boundaries. Here, in front of potential new warriors in their armies, was not one of them.

I took the opportunity to look around at the eager faces of those gathered as Daxton and the others called them forward, waiting for a chance to test themselves in the Ice Gauntlet. I envied them. I wanted to be standing with them to try my hand at the daunting obstacle course.

The Gauntlet held five different platforms of staggered obstacles, leading to the top of a cliff that overlooked the entrance and training fields below.

Daxton met each cadet's gaze and gave them all a silent nod of luck before turning around and preparing for the course before him.

"Once I reach the top, the rest of you are expected to follow. General Gunnar will send you in waves of three at a time, and you will have thirty minutes to complete the task. Once the thirty minutes are up … or the three of you in the wave fall, give up, or miraculously achieve your goal," he announced with a slight drop in his tone, "then the next three will enter. Questions?" Silence followed, and Daxton didn't hesitate as he sprinted into the course. "Start the time."

A small hourglass appeared in Castor's hand and he turned it over and placed it on a natural shelf made of boulders from the surrounding mountains.

Daxton glided across quintuple steps using explosive lateral movements before leaping through the air and grasping a long horizontal bar. He clutched the bar in his hands and pressed his feet against the angled wall below, traversing sideways until the end of the wall. He pulled his knees close to his body and jumped 180 degrees in the air to the other side. He climbed until he came to a ledge that held stone steps leading up and onto the next obstacle.

"Not bad timing on that first one," Castor complimented. "It's not as easy as it looks."

"The spinning logs are next," Gunnar added. "Those get about half of 'em."

Daxton emerged from the hidden stone staircase, at least fifty feet higher than when he had begun the course. From this height, I could see why this obstacle took out so many of them. Dangling ropes hung along the mountain rocks to his left, should he or anyone else slip and fall. Like he said earlier, adding time was better than dying.

Thick iced-over logs were lined up perpendicular to the mountain cliff face, and this obstacle required him to maintain balance while sprinting fifty feet across to reach the other side safely. There was a standing platform about halfway through to use as an aid, but I had little doubt Daxton would utilize it. Taking off at a steady run, Daxton's feet barely touched the icy logs as he ran across.

"The trick is not to stop moving your feet. If you can manage that, then you're safe," Gunnar instructed. "Don't worry, we'll practice this."

I wasn't worried. This portion of the test seemed simple enough, and this obstacle had the ropes if needed. What worried me more was the inverted ladder and plank walk on the next level.

The narrow walkway was barely visible from this distance, but contenders had to meander across three twenty-five-foot peaked beams to reach the inverted staggered bars that they must climb to reach the next platform of stone steps. Daxton extended his arms to his sides as a gust of wind whipped upward, surrounding him. To my amazement, he didn't even flinch. Daxton simply fixed his stare forward and walked across the beam with nothing below him. The drop was well over two hundred feet by now, and it would certainly kill anyone who wobbled and fell over. At the end of the beam, Daxton jumped to grasp the bars and effortlessly climbed the ladder to the stone steps that carried him higher up and to the second-last obstacle.

A metal ring dangled over … nothing but empty cold air above jagged rocks of death below. The task was simple, in theory: take a running leap, grab the large ring, and using his momentum, swing himself over onto the stable platform and scale the next fifty feet to the final obstacle of the Gauntlet. Daxton completed this without hesitation, executing it with astonishing perfection. I might have been in awe of his abilities before, but now, he was officially on an entirely different level.

The final obstacle, which the high prince was able to accomplish without missing a step, was a vertical wall. He needed to run up and jump to propel himself skyward to grab the top ledge before pulling himself to victory.

I glanced over at the sands on the hourglass. The remaining grains indicated that Daxton finished the entire course in only half the time. He had tied the record he set when he first ran this course over five hundred years ago. And this … This was just a demonstration.

"That was unbelievable," I stated with my jaw practically scraping the ground.

"Think you can beat him?" Gunnar countered with a teasing tone. "I would pay good coin to see that."

"I believe not falling to your death would be a more appropriate wager … and focus," Castor said with a furrowed brow. "I'm still not in favor of you doing this."

"As you have said numerous times before," I said with a stern glare. "I want to do this."

"Glad to see you were able to tear yourself away from whomever you were with last night, Cas. You left the tavern before it started getting interesting," Gunnar said, but Castor ignored him.

"It's sad to see that logic has fallen on deaf ears. This is an unnecessary risk for you Sky."

"Come on, Castor," I sighed. "Where's your faith?"

Lines creased between Castor's brows, but he quickly morphed them back into the neutral expression I had seen him wear countless times in disagreements with Daxton and Gunnar over this very subject. "At least I won't be around for your turn at the death wheel. Daxton is sending me to the Southern Sea Cliffs to investigate the potential lair we believe holds the beast and the entrance to the second trial."

"And you need the key," I said, untucking the golden trinket from the chain around my neck. I had fashioned the key into a necklace and worn it at all times since arriving in Silver Meadows.

"Obviously … and the sooner, the better. I can't teleport, so I'll be venturing south on horseback and then on foot. The pegasi are beautiful, but they attract too much attention."

"Wise." I sighed.

"Please don't insult me by suggesting otherwise." Castor reached out and accepted the key, tucking it around his neck and into the high collar of his shirt. "And with this, I'll take my leave. Oh, and by the way," he said with a pause, flashing me a cunning grin, "don't die, Skylar." I grinned at him with a firm nod.

"Stopping by the archives before you leave?" Gunnar asked in a taunting tone with an all too knowing smirk spreading wild across his face.

Without so much as a reply, Castor grunted and waved away Gunnar's remark and turning on his heels to leave.

"Touchy," Gunnar muttered under his breath. "All right," he said, turning to the gathered cadets. "Ready?" He raised his hand. "And ... go!"

My attention on Castor lasted only a second before cheers and echoes across the group of budding warriors drew me away.

Gunnar and I watched wave after wave of High Fae enter the course with only about half reaching the top under the allotted time. Those who were successful were granted the patch of a single mountain on their shoulders from Daxton. Wearing brightly beaming smiles as they descended the rocky pathway winding down the backside of the course. Thankfully, none had fallen to their deaths, but the looks on the faces of those who did not meet the time constraint indicated they almost wished they had.

"Are they able to try again?" I asked.

"In due time, they may train with us again and re-enter," Gunnar answered, "but many don't."

"Why not?"

"Shame and embarrassment cling to us longer than they do to your kind, I'm afraid. Call it one of the downfalls of our immortality ... but some refuse to give up and try again even though they fail. Daxton keeps a close watch over them and tries to help in any way he can. The strength of their will and determination is worth watching."

"What if—" My question was cut short when a deafening scream tore through the sky. "Oh no!" I gasped in horror as a silver-and-brown-haired male High Fae cadet dangled from the narrow beam walkway toward death waiting below.

Gunnar tensed and grasped my arm as he yelled out, "No! Fuck, Reece!"

Reece, my memory connected with the name, and I remembered where I had seen him before. This was the male who helped carry Daxton to Castor's room at the Court of Aelius.

Daxton looked over the edge of the warped wall, unable to step in and help the dangling cadet. "Grab the ropes!" he screamed.

"No!" Reece yelled in reply, his dark eyes wide and full of terror. "If I do, then I fail. I said this was the last time. I reach the top or I die trying."

"Grab the rope!" Daxton commanded this time.

Reece shook his head and tried to swing his leg up onto the beam, but he slipped. The ice on the wood made his grip give way, and he fell.

"Reece!" Gunnar yelled as he sprinted toward the bottom of the Gauntlet with me close on his heels. A fall from that height would surely kill him. If the jagged rocks hadn't already torn through his flesh and caused him to bleed out from catastrophic injuries that even his High Fae healing couldn't combat.

Reaching the bottom of the course outside the wards, I gasped at what I saw. Reece's body was twisted and broken with his back arched at an unnatural angle, so his head lay next to his feet. Blood pooled underneath him from cuts and scrapes from the jagged rocks ... No one could survive that. Then slowly, as if the Mother and Father themselves reached out their hands, his chest rose and fell.

"Move!" I yelled at Gunnar, shoving him aside and calling upon my healing magic the next second. I couldn't believe his luck. The male was still somehow, by the grace of the Gods themselves, alive.

"You're one lucky bastard," Gunnar cursed.

"Keep him still or else he won't be alive much longer despite my healing magic," I grunted, not once allowing my gaze to leave the frail body.

I let my powers flow through me, mending what had been broken and trying to feel where the body experienced the most pain. "Slowly unbend his spine," I instructed Gunnar. "Very slowly."

My magic glowed, golden in my palms, as I felt it flow into the mangled body of Reece. The bones bent and snapped back into place with the guidance of Gunnar pulling his body straight. I moved to mend the open wounds next, closing the gaping holes in his flesh and stopping the bleeding before there was nothing left to bleed out. The color returned to his tanned face, and the ends of his hair once again shimmered with the vibrant silver color that matched the metal threading in the ground around him. His chest fully expanded, and his eyes flashed open once more to see the world anew.

"What ... What?" he stammered, looking around to assess his surroundings before finding me. "I fell."

"You fell," I replied in a low tone, trying not to startle him, "and I healed you."

"You saved me," he answered with darkened, sorrowful eyes pooling with tears of gratitude.

"I'm still in shock that you were able to heal him like that!" Gunnar said from up ahead on the spine of the Nox mountain trail.

The thick pines of the surrounding forest and green grass of the meadows gave way to the rocky path leading up the spine of the second-tallest peak of Silver Meadows. Large boulders and slick gravel terrain guided our way, with an increasingly thick fog. My sweat-slickened hair at the nape of my neck began to freeze as we climbed higher and higher toward the peak.

"You and everyone else, apparently," I mumbled. "I'm thankful Daxton suggested we take this training route to get away from everyone. It was beginning to be a bit much."

"I'd heard about your healing magic," Gunnar added as he gracefully leaped across a crevice, "but seeing it is entirely different. You worked a miracle today, Skylar!"

Reece was a high-ranking citizen of Silver Meadows, admired for utilizing his unique skills to influence trade and management of the local shops and ports. Despite his status within the city, he always envisioned himself on the front lines, serving his people from the battlefield. I admired his dedication, but we were not all born to be warriors. Some had to utilize different strengths to achieve their goals.

Everyone in my pack had become accustomed to my healing gifts, but apparently, it was an extremely rare talent in the Inner Kingdom. There were healers by trade and minor healing abilities like Daxton, but not magic like mine. I just hoped this news wouldn't draw any extra unwanted attention our way.

"You sure you don't need a cloak?" Gunnar asked me for possibly the tenth time since we began our trek up the mountain. "I have a spare in my bag in case you change your mind. The winter hits harder and faster on the mountain trails up here."

I slouched my shoulders with a loud sigh. My face turned downward. Annoyance could not properly express the frustration I was feeling. "Shifter ..." I repeated slowly, emphasizing each letter. "We run warmer than all other species. The cold does not bother us like it does you."

"Fine then." Gunnar huffed, shouldering his bag. "Sorry for caring."

"If you cared, you would've listened the ten other times you asked me."

"If I *didn't* care," Gunnar countered with an annoying grin, "then I would cut through your rope and make you walk this trail without a safety line."

"All right, you two," Daxton said from behind, "don't start this again."

Through the three weeks spent training together, Gunnar quickly caught onto the fact that I had a strong stubborn streak and thrived on the thrill of tackling a challenge head-on instead of slowly working my way through it. He noted on several occasions how odd it was for someone who took the time to read as much as I did and asked every question under the sun to find herself in the middle of so much chaos.

Some might think you're smarter than that.

The first time Gunnar told me this, I promptly flipped him off and stuck out my tongue. He rolled on the grass laughing, apparently proving his point exactly.

I glared up ahead of him. "I'm not happy about this either." I tugged at the rope attached to my waist, glancing behind my shoulder at the other half of the line that was attached to Daxton. "It feels like a leash," I grumbled.

"You do tend to wander." Daxton chuckled.

"High prince's orders," Gunnar said with a wide grin, laughing alongside his friend.

"The fog is expected to drift in from the north, making it easy to fall from these cliffs. We guide all our cadets through this pathway linked in this exact formation, and I'm not taking any chances on *either of you* getting lost," Daxton said, probably for the fifth time.

This was the final piece of the training I needed to master before being allowed to enter the Ice Gauntlet. Even though Castor didn't agree with me taking this risk, I refused to budge on this decision. I knew it was one of the reasons why Daxton had sent him on his mission to the Southern Sea Cliffs with the key.

"Hurry up," Daxton said ahead to Gunnar. "It'll be dark by the time we reach the top if you keep this slow pace."

"Just being cautious for Skylar's sake." Gunnar scoffed in response.

"If you think babying her will help ensure her success, perhaps I should be rethinking your rank and station as my general."

"You can always lead the way yourself," Gunnar said, swinging his arms around with his brows arching.

Daxton huffed a laugh paired with a mischievous smirk as he reached my side. "I'm fine here." He then bent to whisper in my ear so only I could hear him, "I wouldn't dream of giving up this view."

I blushed red and playfully smacked his arm while biting my lower lip. His smile curled around his chiseled jawline, revealing the dimple on his cheek that softened his cold exterior in a unique way that always seemed to melt my heart.

Gods, I could look at him all day, and somehow, I knew it would never be enough.

Gunnar grunted and mumbled something to himself, looking unimpressed, but did not say anything about Daxton's comment or our obvious flirtations.

"Come on then," the general announced, quickening his pace and leading up along the rocky spine to the top of Mount Nox.

After beginning this grueling trek, all the obstacles in the Ice Gauntlet made perfect sense. We scaled boulders, leaped from jagged cliffs, and then ran along beaten trails to reach the endpoint. Silver Meadows was surrounded by mountains on all sides but one. Warriors not only had to meander over these routes to reach their outposts, but they were also expected to fight on this terrain if needed.

My legs ached, and my feet had blisters that housed more blisters, but I didn't complain or ask for Gunnar to slow his pace. This was my chance to prove myself. If I was going to defeat the trial of the body, I damn sure better be ready for it.

The beast I had to defeat would not stop or give me grace if I was tired or injured. So, I didn't expect it here either. The Ice Gauntlet had become my own personal scale of self-worth, and conquering it would give me the boost of confidence I needed in order to bravely enter the second trial.

The clouds became thick, and visibility dropped to only a few feet in front or behind where you stood. I had to admit, the ropes were a good idea.

"Last jump is up ahead!" Gunnar shouted from behind a veil of clouds. "That's the summit."

Daxton quickened his strides to meet me at my side. "It replicates the final obstacle atop the Ice Gauntlet."

"That giant twenty-foot inverted wall?" He nodded, and my stomach churned a little. "I'll need a running start, I imagine."

"It helps." He chuckled.

The rope on my waist slackened, indicating Gunnar had cut through his own end and began his assent up the face of the massive wall of stone and rock. "Your turn," he called out.

"Fantastic." I scoffed. "The added layer of fog makes this so much more fun ..."

"It wouldn't be *fun* if it were easy, Spitfire. Easy is for simple people. You and I are far from simple." Daxton leaned against a nearby rock face, giving me a taunting look. "Are you saying you're unable to do this? Are you admitting to failure before even attempting to try your hand?"

"Well played, Princey."

A victorious grin spanned across his face. He knew exactly what to say to get me sprinting along the rocks and up the wall.

Ignoring his gloating, I untied my rope and pushed it firmly into his chest with a harder-than-necessary shove. The fog lifted just enough to see the edges of the boulders stacked on top of each other, with the final rock stretching out into a smooth, flat surface that I had to jump and reach in order to pull myself up. Gunnar stood at the top, waving hello, helping seal in the taunting, enough to encourage me to stop thinking and just ... run.

I propelled my aching feet forward, keeping my balance centered as I ran across the rock faces to the base of the stone cliff. Pumping my arms, I willed myself to sprint faster, turning my horizontal momentum into a vertical leap and reaching my arm out for the ledge at the very top. My hand found the stone corner, and I latched on. My other hand joined the first, and using my legs, I was able to climb up to the top of the wall.

Daxton ran the same route and joined us at the top.

"I did it!" I said with a bright, beaming smile, catching my breath.

"Why was that even a question?" Daxton asked, pride swelling in his eyes. "You're ready for—"

Daxton's entire body tensed and his sword, Valencia, materialized in his hand. Gunnar unsheathed his blade strapped to his waist, with a dagger in his other hand. Not good ... Something was very, very wrong.

The two males silently scanned our surroundings, searching for any sign of danger they both could feel but not yet see. Daxton's jaw flexed with unease as he signed for Gunnar to stay with me while he investigated the rocks below.

"Take this," Gunnar whispered, slipping a long dagger into my hand.

I didn't know what was out there, but if Dax and Gunnar were this worried, I knew I should be, too. The whole area surrounding us seemed to settle into an unnatural silence. A loud thump was followed by rocks tumbling along the opposite side, where Daxton jumped down to investigate.

"Wait here," Gunnar commanded in a low voice. His humor and carefree personality had flipped, and I was now with the commanding general of the Silver Meadows armies.

I nodded, moving to place a section of rocks at my backside.

He crept silently toward the mountain's edge, peering off into the fog but failing to find anything below. My heart thundered rapidly in my chest, and my animal's awareness fueled my body with her power and heightened abilities. I was in fight or flight mode, all my senses kicking into high gear.

A faint scraping caught my attention, followed by a slither that reminded me of a long snake hiding in the tall grass. Gunnar didn't seem to notice anything, so I turned away and decided to investigate it myself. Leaning over the edge, I crept forward, trying to pinpoint the odd sounds coming from the array of tangled boulders just off the trail. I needed to get closer to figure it out.

Sheathing my dagger at my hip, I rose to my feet and scouted a pathway down from the top. A stable, solid platform just ten feet below me looked like the perfect place to land, so I squatted down and jumped, but the platform *vanished*.

I screamed as I plummeted through the fog, helplessly falling and colliding into the jagged mountain rocks. My vision blurred. My body bounced off the cliffs like a child's ball dribbling across the ground. My right arm bent sideways as it smacked into a sharp rock, slicing it open to the bone as I continued to fall. I desperately tried to stop my momentum, but I couldn't manage to grab onto the cliffs.

I fought to keep my consciousness, but I somersaulted once more and hit my head hard against the mountainside. My world turning black.

Chapter Nineteen

Groaning, I tried to move my body, but shooting pain along my arm and the back of my head forced me to stop. *At least I'm still alive*, I thought. Pain meant I wasn't dead, which was a fucking miracle.

"Spitfire?" The concern in Daxton's voice was enough to make my heart shatter into a million little pieces. Without even opening my eyes, I knew who it was. I knew … he would be waiting at my bedside.

"Alive … Somehow," I grunted, slowly shifting toward Daxton's voice. "And thankfully mending. Even though it feels like my body's seen better days."

"Thank the Mother and Father above."

"I know, I know. I'm impressive." I kept my eyes shut as another wave of pain rolled through my body.

I heard Daxton's half-hearted chuckle of amusement and knew he was shaking his head. "How fortunate that the Gods made shifters as tough as nails. I doubt many High Fae, and definitely far fewer humans, would've survived tumbling halfway down the mountainside as you did."

"Thanks, Dad," I murmured, followed by Daxton's chuckle that teetered on the side of laughter.

"High Fae might have the upper hand with magic and good looks, but shifters are built for strength and durability." I forced myself to smile, adjusting my shoulders and gritting through the pain, remembering I had been through much worse than this.

My eyes fluttered open to see Daxton leaning over me in a spacious room that I had spent little to no time in at all while I was here. The open window to my left looked across the wild mountain pines that separated the Summit from the training grounds. The sweet fragrance of the forest mingled with the crisp air of the fast-approaching winter season.

"I knew you would eventually appreciate a room with one of the better views," Dax said softly, resting his hand on my knee atop the blanket. He knew the essence of nature had a calming, healing effect on me that settled the aches in my bones.

I couldn't help smiling. Daxton remembered how, in the healing quarters in Solace, I wanted—no, needed—to feel connected to nature within the confines of the walls.

My bed was remarkably soft, with silk sheets paired with a down-feathered blanket that made me feel like I was floating on a cloud. The room's walls were accented with darker gray colors along the window side and lighter shades on the others. Silver swirls mimicking the cold mountain winds whirled along the high vaulted ceilings. Directly ahead of me, near the door leading to the washroom, was a painting of Mount Meja with the hanging valley below its summit highlighted in the orange and yellow rays of the sunrise.

"Glad you found me," I said with a half-cracked smile as I looked at Daxton, trying to ease the worry pinched between his brows.

Despite his calm demeanor, Daxton's posture was tense. Dark circles of exhaustion formed under his hardened eyes. His lips pressed into a thin line. He was barely holding himself together.

"I will always find you, Spitfire," he answered, sensing my need for his touch or perhaps fulfilling his own. He reached for my uninjured hand, cradling it before threading my fingers with his. "We will always find each other."

A familiar sense of tranquility settled into my chest. I could feel my animal stirring and flooding me with magic that united me and Dax through an invisible tether. The connection I had with him was frighteningly beautiful and all-consuming at the same time. Gods, Mother, and Father help me. I had fallen so hard for him it was a wonder how I hadn't recognized it sooner.

His lips brushed the back of my hand, sending a pulse of heat along my flesh and melting my core. Hooded eyes blinked upward to meet mine before he stood and walked to the large double doors, opening them to speak out into the hall.

Maybe, just *maybe*, he was falling for me, too?

"She's awake," Daxton said into the hallway.

Without waiting for a further invitation, Gunnar came rushing in with Idris, Adohan, and Zola following suit.

"What were you thinking, Skylar?" Gunnar practically shouted at me as he came barreling toward the right side of my bed. "H-have you gone insane? Did the trial of the mind really fuck with you that much, and it's only now catching up?"

Idris promptly marched up behind Gunnar and gave him a firm smack on the back of the head. "Sometimes it's best for you to *not* speak, Gunnar."

"You shouldn't be walking around," I cautioned Idris, "or I guess waddling is perhaps a more accurate description of what you're doing."

She waved me off. "Don't try to change the subject, Skylar. Besides, do you really think Adohan would let me *walk* anywhere? Overprotective males," she groaned. "He was holding me in his arms outside the door like a frail female or infant! I had to threaten to burn his hair off in his sleep if he didn't let me walk across the room. And don't even think I'm done with you yet, either."

"Smart," I stated, catching Adohan's eyes. He gave me a half-smirk in reply because while Idris continued scolding me for another minute, he caught the intent of my compliment.

Daxton moved to sit in the chair to my left, his back toward the open window. He carefully watched the room and patiently waited for the others to have their moment.

"I'm guessing I was unconscious for at least a day or so?"

Daxton nodded.

"Yes! That's another fucking trick I didn't know about you shifters," Gunnar cursed, looking around the room. "After Dax caught you in mid-fall and teleported you to the Summit, I ran as fast as I could to make sure you were not dead. When you still weren't awake that evening … or the next morning, I was a mess." Gunnar slumped onto the bed, folding to lay at my feet. "I had no clue how he," Gunnar said, gesturing at Daxton, "was so gods-damned calm!"

"The injuries she sustained would not have been enough to kill her. I've sensed her near death's door once before, and she was far from that state. She was sleeping off her injuries so her body could quickly heal them," Daxton answered.

The stiffness in his jaw suggested that Daxton might have known I would survive, but he was not as calm about it as he appeared to everyone else. "Also … panicking does not help a situation."

"I was *not* panicking," Gunnar rebutted in a flat tone, sitting up and crossing his arms with a scowl. "I'm the general of the Silver Meadows armies. I do not … panic."

"Once you understood she was just healing … yes, I agree. You were not panicking then, but before that …" Zola said, stepping out from the shadows. Her black leathers molded to her strong, petite frame, exposing the midnight shadow marks along the dark brown skin of her exposed arms and throat. "Well, that's a different story."

"How long?" Time was a plague on my life. I had to know how much was wasted on this mishap.

"One full day has passed since your *incident*," Zola answered. Her dark eyes narrowed on the word incident, and I got a strange feeling that something else was beginning to brew.

I nodded. "Then we have only four more weeks until I enter the second trial. How's the research coming?"

Adohan stood at the foot of my bed, his long red and brown braided hair falling over his shoulder as he leaned forward. He flashed me a confident, beaming smile that contrasted against his dark skin. "Impressive that you've only just awakened from a fall to your death, and your focus has not faltered."

"Is that a compliment?"

"It can be, but I realize, coming from me, it usually isn't intended as such. I don't hand out praise as easily as most." He gave me a wink, his hazel eyes shining with humorous glee as he walked to his mate's side and kissed her braided hair. "You, my love, are still the most impressive being in this world."

I heard—actually *heard*—Gunnar roll his eyes this time. "So, I have to ask … Why did you jump off the top of the mountain, Skylar?"

Daxton had moved to hand me a glass of water, which I managed to finish just as Gunnar asked me his question. "I didn't *jump* off the mountain," I said, handing Daxton the empty glass for a refill.

"Yes … Yes, you did." Gunnar's brows furrowed together. "I turned at the last second and watched you jump onto nothing."

"There was a ledge beneath me," I countered, leaning forward and sitting upright, determined to make my point.

"What do you mean?" Daxton asked, handing me another full glass of water.

"I heard something below us along the rocks," I answered, taking a sip. "My animal heightened my senses, and I could tell by Gunnar's position he hadn't heard anything, so I went to investigate. I intended to jump onto the lower ledge, but when I did it …" I stopped, not wanting to sound crazy, but there was no other way to really say it. "It just disappeared."

"Disappeared," Zola repeated slowly, glancing at Daxton with hatred burning in her dark, ominous eyes. "My high prince … I …"

"Anjani." Daxton clenched his jaw and gritted his teeth, gripping the back of the chair near the window so tight the leather snapped under his fingers as ice flowed along the legs and onto the floor.

"The female has a death wish." Daxton abruptly turned and faced Zola. "I sent *you* to track and find her." His tone was low and deathly firm.

Adohan placed himself between Daxton and Idris while Gunnar immediately stood at attention on my other side.

"I tracked her outside the border lines leading to Aelius. She crossed along the river three days ago."

"And obviously, she has retraced her route and returned." This time, his voice carried the rage hidden beneath the facade of the Silver Shadow now standing in the room. "It's disappointing that Anjani has outwitted my spymaster."

Zola clenched her hands into fists as her head tilted downward in shame. Shadowed hints of rage and guilt curled around her narrowed eyes and pinched brow. "It will not happen again."

"No, it will not," Daxton answered, stepping forward and staring her down with ice in his storm-gray eyes. "Because I am going with you. Prepare yourself … *We* are going hunting."

Within minutes, Daxton and Zola gathered various weapons and donned black and silver armor, looking like they were heading onto the front lines of a battlefield. I sat on the bed silently, watching the wrath in Daxton's expression consume his every thought and movement. The Silver Shadow was amongst us now, and I knew Anjani had no hope of outrunning him.

"Leave us for a moment," Daxton commanded.

Zola held a cold, expressionless stare, readying herself for what lay ahead. She silently gave me a curt nod before departing in her shadows and jumping out of the room.

"We'll see you in the library tonight, Skylar." Idris hugged me once more before Adohan scooped her up in his arms. "Adohan and I have a list of theories, and we want to run them by you if you're up for it."

"We'll have enough to keep you busy while you finish healing," Adohan added.

"I'll be strong enough to make it down there tonight," I said. "I can already feel my wounds mending—healing perks of being a shifter. If I had full access to my animal, I would already be out of this bed."

Adohan paused on his way to the hallway. "Anjani will have her spies with her. She never travels alone, Daxton. You won't have a simple fight on your hands. Shall I come with you?"

"I'm aware of Anjani's strengths, Adohan, but I would never ask you to come with your mate and child in this condition. Zola and I are more than capable of handling Anjani. Her powers are no match for mine while we are in *my* kingdom."

"Glad to see your ego is still in check, my friend." Adohan gave Daxton a long, hard stare, eventually nodding his head, accepting Dax's decision, and taking his leave with Idris secured in his arms.

"Gunnar," Daxton called.

"Yes, High Prince."

"I'm placing you in charge of overseeing Skylar's safety while I'm away. Don't leave the Summit until we return, and above all else, protect her and guard her as if she were me."

Gunnar raised his brows in surprise, glancing at me before returning to Daxton. "Understood, High Prince." He turned in my direction. "Let me know when you wish to go to the library or anything else you need, Skylar. I'll be outside until Daxton leaves."

"Thank you, Gunnar." I watched him depart, giving Daxton a shallow bow before closing the door behind him.

"I don't know when I'll be able to return," Daxton whispered, standing by the door in his black and silver battle armor, perfectly molded to his broad, muscular frame. Even in his armor, I could see the perfect dips and valleys of his strong arms as they flexed in angst.

Valencia, his magical silver blade, was strapped across his back with daggers sheathed at his hips and a small sword attached to his right side. When he turned his shoulders to face me, my eyes traced over every inch of him, leaving nothing to chance and memorizing every feature of the male standing before me that carried my heart wherever he ventured. The three silver peaks on his shoulder shone in the dimming sunlight from the window across the way, perfectly matching the silver that streaked across his midnight hair.

To anyone else in the world, he looked fucking terrifying, but the menacing warrior standing before me ignited a spark in my very soul. Blasting me with rolling waves of desire that flushed through every inch of my body. He was a challenge that I very much wanted to master.

"Don't look at me like that, Spitfire."

"Like what?" I asked, swallowing heavily.

"Like I should be removing my armor, instead of putting it on." He marched over toward my bedside, sitting next to me, careful not to brush against the healing wounds on my arm. "I cannot let this threat to your life go unchallenged, Skylar. It's not in me to forgive this kind of attack on my house and in my lands. I just can't …"

"I'm not asking you to," I said with unwavering clarity. His half-smile gave me a rush of encouragement. "Do what you must, and then hurry back home. Back to … me." I silently cursed at my own cowardice. Failing to tell him that he needed to return because … because *I was in love with him*. And the thought of continuing without him terrified me more than the trials themselves.

His hard eyes softened momentarily as he reached to cup my cheek, leaning in to gently steal a soft kiss before pressing his lips to my brow and whispering, "I will always find you, Spitfire. Always."

He released me, and then, in my next breath, he teleported away.

Five days came and went without a word from Daxton or Zola.

Worry couldn't begin to describe the falling pit of despair in my stomach. I tried focusing on identifying the creature in the second trial, but my mind wandered to Daxton. Needing to know if he was safe and when he would return. His absence was necessary, but it also made me miss him in ways that I had only read about in my stories.

Cursing myself for the words I should have said … *I love you, Daxton Aegaeon.*

The reality of it had hit me like a ton of bricks in the trial of the mind, even though I knew I had been falling for him long before that. The moment I first saw Daxton in the meadow, I was drawn to him in a way I had never experienced before. And through our time together, through the darkest, most terrifying moments of my life, he was my light. He was my constant strength, encouraging me never to give up and reminding me that I was never alone. The depth of our connection was so strong that I found myself questioning if I had ever truly loved anyone before him.

And now, he was in danger. Risking his life and his kingdom to avenge a threat made against me, and I couldn't even muster the courage to tell him how I felt before he left. I was a fucking idiot ... a coward.

Each day, Idris and Adohan ventured between the Summit and the ancient archives that were in the center of Silver Meadows. The lead scribe pulled ancient scrolls for them to read, but they wouldn't allow the scrolls to leave their tower. Meticulously caring for the parchment was a task they didn't take lightly.

Do you want Daxton to skin me alive when he returns home? Gunnar said when I asked about going to the archives tower myself. Much to my surprise and his, I didn't push the matter further. His well-being wasn't the only thing keeping me outside the archives tower.

"Nyssa is doing well," Idris informed me when she and Adohan returned one evening. She knew I was curious about how the fallen High Fae was faring in her new role amongst the scribes.

Castor, before leaving for the Southern Sea Cliffs, told me that she was petrified when I healed her in the wilt, with no memory of who or what she was. In her dreams, however, flashes of her life as a fallen plagued her thoughts, tearing her from sleep with silent screams of terror and regret.

Before leaving, Castor suggested I give her time and space to find herself before seeing me again. How could I not oblige her simple request? I couldn't imagine what she had been through. No one really could. My heart went out to her, and the least I could do was respect her wishes. I might have saved her from the magic of the wilt, but she was somewhat lost in this life as well.

The scribes in the archives had taken her under their wing, and she was able to find work that steadied her shaking nerves while aiding her broken memories. I was happy to hear Nyssa was adjusting to a new life here in Silver Meadows and finding her place when she had been lost for the Gods only knew how many years.

"The lead scribes are teaching her how to shelf and care for the oldest scrolls in their collection, and when she is not working," Idris added, "Nyssa is searching through different arcs of history, trying to find a link or spark of a memory."

"I'm glad she seems to be finding her niche." I smiled, moving from the couch and onto the loveseat so Idris and Adohan could take my place.

Hours seemed to pass in the blink of an eye, just like every night since Daxton and Zola's departure. The four of us spent our days burying our heads into different folklore, mythical creatures, and countless journals, trying to identify the creature of the second trial.

"I know … It's a dragon!" Idris declared from a reclined position on the couch. Her feet were atop the armrest while her head was cradled in Adohan's lap, a book flayed open across her ever-growing belly.

Our group had moved our research sessions to the open sitting area outside the library that held large soft couches, a roaring fireplace, and direct access to the glorious kitchens in the Summit. I claimed I needed a change of scenery, and Gunnar, who watched over me like I was a newborn baby, agreed, stating the library was boring on more than one occasion. I resisted the urge to throw a book at his head for such an insult … just barely.

"Dragons prefer open skies, not sea cliffs and narrow caves." Gunnar laughed as he bent backward to glance at Idris. "That was not your best guess. I assume you're planning to chalk that one up to the pregnancy brain females get once they are in this stage?"

Idris gave Gunnar a death glare, while Adohan smirked. The high prince threw a small fireball at the back of Gunnar's head, making him jump and practically yelp while slapping the flames into submission.

"You deserved that one," I said, my smile hidden behind an open textbook about the history of fae folklore.

"Okay, sure … but maybe not the two before that crisped my favorite shirt." Gunnar frowned at his burned clothing.

"If that was your favorite shirt, I need to enlighten you about your fashion sense and the basic finery you desperately need to try," Idris said mockingly. "Your station alone should be able to afford you something nicer than that charred shirt."

"It wasn't charred before tonight," Gunnar murmured. "And why am I the only one being lectured about fashion? Skylar is wearing a baggy shirt and stretchy pants. No comments to her attire?"

"I choose comfort. That's my fashion." I didn't bother to look up from my book at his remark. After all, the new pants were mine. I had found them in the drawers of my room that I still didn't really sleep in. But the shirt. Now, that didn't technically belong to me.

I was aware the others could smell who it belonged to, but they politely didn't say anything about it. I had found it in my room, actually, in the corner of the washroom, tucked behind the door. Daxton must have forgotten it when he stayed with me after my fall. I had been sleeping in it every night since he went hunting for Anjani.

"Never question a female's attire after hours, Gunnar," Adohan said with a half-smirk as he stroked his bearded chin. "You foolishly thought teasing my mate would go unnoticed or have no consequence? Think again."

"Clearly," Gunnar huffed, slouching against an array of pillows near the crackling fire in the mantle as Idris and I tried to muffle our laughter.

"Have we discussed a chimera yet?" Adohan asked, changing the topic back to our research. "The fire breathing, paired with a venomous tail and a lion's head, fit many pieces of the riddle."

"But not the crest or the fact that it is supposed to be a king, meaning the creature is likely a male … The chimera is female," I answered, flipping the pages of my book that described the different fae creatures that were labeled deceased or mythical.

"Does it have to be male? What if …" Gunnar asked, quickly gaining our attention. "When you look at it, do you see your death, like in a third-person situation?" Our expressions turned to surprise as Gunnar's shoulders dropped. "Don't look at me like you're shocked that I asked a decent question. It's insulting. I'm more than just a handsome face and a strong sword."

"But we are," Idris mumbled, biting her lip to avoid snickering.

"Idris," I began in a scolding tone. "He has a good idea. Let him run with it. Don't let it die before it takes hold. Go on, Gunnar …"

"What about a banshee? Her scream is an omen of death, and she has white hair, so a crown?"

I leaned over my book and framed my chin with my finger to think on his suggestion. "Close and a good idea. But I still believe in my gut that this creature is a male. The king part of the riddle stands out."

"Then I'm out." Gunnar groaned in defeat and sprawled out backward with a book open on his face. "I can't read anymore. A battle brief is one thing, but this, all this is …" He gestured widely to the massive collection 'of books we had spread around us. "Maddening!"

Idris and I rolled our eyes in unison, trying to hide our amusement at Gunnar's outburst behind the open books in our hands.

"Can you recite the riddle from the beginning once more, Skylar?" Adohan asked, purposely cutting off Gunnar's groans.

"To find the key that you seek, you must first defeat the beast." I had written and thought about it so much I didn't even have to look at the parchment I copied it down on anymore. "To look upon my white crest is to know true death. I'm the king of my world, and only my equal can dethrone me. In the waters, I hunt, and in the darkness, I wander … now released from my silver cage of slumber. Between the slickened rocks, I creep, feeding on the weak and the meek. The first key will show the way to anyone who dares to come and play. My bars are gone, and now I'm free, but only the champion can take the second key. Two cycles of the Father shall pass, and then I will forever be free at last."

"All right … so what do we know?" Gunnar mumbled beneath the pages of the unfolded book still resting on his face.

It was moments like this that I missed Castor's logic. He would have been extremely useful in this task.

"A lot, actually, considering we began with knowing absolutely nothing," Idris said in a motherly yet scolding tone. It was enough to make Gunnar sit up and rejoin the group.

"First," I said, holding one finger up. "The Southern Cliffs with silver veins running along the ocean edge is the lair of this beast that Castor is currently investigating. If he can enter, then that means, unlike the labyrinth … I could potentially have someone with me." Although I had not shared with them that I was not in favor of that happening. "Second," I pulled up another digit, "I have three weeks remaining before I enter. The clue about two cycles of the Father is two full phases of the moon."

"It feeds, likely meaning a predator," Adohan added.

"That's the third," I said with a triumphant grin. "The key opens the trial gates, and Castor is pinpointing exactly where this is."

"All right," Gunnar groaned. "The layout of the lair of the beast will help narrow it down further, but we are stuck on—"

"We're stuck on the white crest, king, and death stare." I had been researching spitting venom, venom bites, and all other ways something could kill you, but the only fable I read was about a stone-killing gaze from a woman with a head of snakes … And that didn't fit the king clue. "Maybe this thing is so ugly that when you look at it, you die because it's so hideous?"

The others looked at me and burst out laughing. I couldn't help but follow. Our mental exhaustion was finally reaching a limit.

"What a trial," Gunnar said through gasps of breath. "Could you bring a mirror, or have it look into a pool of water, and its reflection would kill itself?"

Silence followed.

"What?" Gunnar stammered. "What did I say?"

"You're a genius!" I lunged over and tackled him to the ground with a giant hug. "Fucking brilliant!"

"Again, what did I say? And please tell Daxton it was *you* who jumped into *my* lap. Not the other way around."

"I could kiss you right now, Gunnar! It's so simple I can't believe we missed it. Your plan might just work!"

"Remember that you jumped onto me. Be very clear about that one, Skylar," Gunnar repeated, inclining his head to the doorway.

I stilled, releasing Gunnar, sensing Daxton before he even entered the room. The scent of pine and cold mountain air tantalized my senses, bringing me a serene feeling of comfort and home. Every time he was near, it was like a piece of my soul returned that I didn't know was missing.

"Daxton!" I practically shrieked with relief and joy.

Springing up from the floor, I leaped across Gunnar, who was still splayed out on the pillows, no longer caring about hiding my feelings, and blindly flew into Daxton's open embrace. Immediately, his arms wrapped around my waist, lifting me off my feet with ease and holding on to me with every ounce of strength he had.

"You're back." I exhaled, nuzzling into the nape of his neck.

"Why do you smell like Gunnar?" he grumbled.

"I was lying in his lap just before you arrived."

"What?" Daxton tensed, but I kept my hold firm around him.

"Calm down. You're lucky I didn't kiss him."

"I'm not—"

"He figured out a defense against the beast I have to slay, Dax. A mirror! A mirror to reflect this creature's stare of death. We may not know exactly what it is, but we have an idea for how to counter it."

His sigh was heavy as his lips brushed against the brow of my head. "I missed you, Spitfire," he whispered before squeezing me tightly once more, returning my feet to the ground. "I'll warn you, prepare yourself."

I pulled back, settling my feet against the carpet and creasing my brows together in confusion. "For?"

"What the *fuck* were you thinking, Daxton?" Zola yelled as she stormed into the sitting room from the shadows in the far corner.

Gods above. Her gifts were amazing but also terrifying. An important reminder of what she could wield.

"You are my high prince, and I will follow you to *my* death … but I will not remain idle and silent as you seal your own demise!" Zola's face was pale, and her eyes wide with worry.

"I don't regret my actions," Daxton replied with a calm, collected stare, pulling me to his side. "She's lucky to still be breathing."

"You acted alone!" Zola roared, her hands splayed to the sides as she removed her daggers along her hips, slamming them onto the side table near Idris and Adohan. "There is no blood on *my blades*."

"You were too slow."

Zola's dark eyes burned like cold embers of death and silent rage. "This …" Her voice dropped lower. "This should have been done by my hand. Not. *Yours!*"

"Again … You were too slow," Daxton said, not wavering under his spymaster's glare.

Zola's eyes narrowed as she marched across the room toward where Daxton stood with me at his side. "I jump in the shadows," she growled. "Not the fucking sunlight, you stubborn male!" Daxton didn't even flinch against Zola's rage. He only tightened his grip on my hip as I placed my hand on the small of his back, silently supporting him as best I could.

"Careful how you address our high prince, Zola," Gunnar warned, standing at attention now with his hand on the hilt of a long dagger, unafraid and ready to intervene if needed. I doubted many, if any really, had ever seen Zola in this state.

"What did you do, Daxton?" Adohan asked, rising from his seat. His eyes burned with the fires at his command, challenging the Silver Meadows high prince from across the room.

"I spared her life," Daxton answered calmly.

"What did you ... do?"

Without uttering another word, Daxton strode forward, leaving my side, and threw the black bag from his other hip onto the dark wood sitting table in the middle of the room. The top untied, and out rolled a severed delicate, fair-skinned hand with a golden ring holding an elegant emerald in the center. The cut was clean, performed in one smooth stroke that could not have been done by any other blade aside from Valencia. The still oozing blood staining the table meant it was severed from a living host. The crimson liquid shimmered against the crackling fire in the hearth.

"Fuck," Gunnar cursed under his breath.

"This ... This is Anjani's hand," Adohan said with a wide, gaping mouth. Fear threaded its way through his darkened expression.

My gaze shot toward Idris, who held her composure, but I could see the alarm widening in her eyes as she clutched her unborn baby. "Daxton, this is a direct act against Aelius. Seamus will see this as an attack."

"Crimson City cannot afford a war with Aelius right now, Daxton," Adohan said. "You know this ... or do you not remember what we discussed only a handful of days ago?"

"Silver Meadows is not asking you to march to war against Aelius." Daxton strode to the center of the room, with all eyes narrowing on him. "This was my decision. My mercy."

"*Mercy?*" Adohan stammered. "Do you understand the gravity of this? What Seamus will do to you with Minaeve's backing?"

"I'm aware. And unlike Crimson City, Silver Meadows does not fear war. And unlike your sire, Adohan, we will no longer bow to tyranny and suffrage at the hands of self-proclaimed royals who treat us like puppets in a play. I'm done kneeling before a false queen. Silver Meadows will prepare for war when it comes to that. And we will be ready."

"Ready and more than willing," Gunnar added, bucking his chin and moving to stand by Daxton's side. "Simply waiting for our high prince's command."

"And you choose now," Adohan said, shaking his head. "Now ... to do this?" Adohan yelled with fire curling across his skin, mimicking his internal rage. "Daxton, after everything, my friend, this ... This could be your death sentence."

"We will not allow our high prince to—" Daxton placed a silencing hand on his general's shoulder.

"My hand was forced. I don't regret my decision."

Adohan fell silent for a moment, his mate reaching up through his blistering fires to grasp his shaking hand. "Let's hope your decision does not condemn us all. You understand the consequences of your act then?"

"What consequences?" I asked, stepping into the circle of the High Fae. My heart thundered in my ears with concern for what this all meant for Daxton and Silver Meadows.

Idris spoke quietly. "Daxton has cut the hand of Seamus's second, potentially hindering her ability to wield her particular magic of the mind." Her voice was trembling at first, but then it steadied. "It is a direct attack against Aelius carried out by the High Prince of Silver Meadows."

"Silver Meadows warriors are ready to answer their call," Gunnar said.

"You may be bred to kill and fight," Adohan sneered at Gunnar, "but even Daxton understands that there is more to war than wielding a sword."

"Anjani's unwelcomed presence here in *my* kingdom caused this," Daxton growled. "She performed the first act of aggression. I was fair in my price. Allowing her to return home alive sent a warning to their kingdom."

"And what warning might that be?" Adohan asked, crossing his arms. The band of gold adorned with rubies along his bicep glimmered as it caught the fading light from the fire in the mantle.

"That death is a quick mercy I shall not be granting them … if they endanger me or my people ever again."

Daxton turned his gaze to me, and I could see the raging storm inside his eyes churn with an unyielding turbulence. For the first time since knowing him, he seemed unsure.

"The punishment, whatever Minaeve decides, shall be mine alone to carry. And no one else."

"Daxton," I pleaded, desperately wanting to comfort him and ease this burden in any way I could.

He shook his head. "No."

In the next second, silver flashed in the room, and he was gone.

"Where did he go?" I stammered, looking around the room for someone to answer me. "We have to go after him."

"Up for a stroll through the mountains?" Zola asked, and I nodded my head. "Good, because none of us are foolish enough to follow him in the mood he's in right now."

Chapter Twenty

Thankfully, Idris called a pegasus for me to mount, and I was able to fly to the hanging valley beneath Meja, the tallest mountain, watching over Silver Meadows. The hike alone would have taken me all night, but it wouldn't have mattered. All that mattered was finding Daxton. The winged horse neighed as we gracefully landed on the outskirts of the hanging valley with a serene meadow clearing just up ahead. I dismounted quickly, affectionately patting the mare's neck before sending her off.

Zola told me where she believed I could find Daxton, but I didn't need her direction. I could feel the essence of his magic by simply following my instincts. It was the same draw I had felt with him since we met. Bravely, I swallowed my nerves, allowing the pull of his magic to lead me to him.

I hardly noticed the beautiful landscape around me as my eyes fell on the lone male sitting atop a large stone boulder. His shoulders were hunched over, with his silver sword, Valencia, twirling in his hands. The tip of the majestic weapon pressed against the earth, swirling in his palms like the waters in the nearby babbling brook that flowed through the clearing. He … He seemed almost lost, like the hope that burned so brightly inside him was flickering, threatening to fade away.

"Daxton." He didn't turn to face me. "Daxton," I said again, stepping into the clearing.

"Why are you here?" he grumbled, closing his eyes and tensing the muscles along his shoulders. "It's dangerous for you outside the Summit, Skylar … and clearly, I've failed in my duty to look after you properly."

"It's apparently dangerous no matter where I am," I answered, halting my approach. "But this. This isn't about me right now. I didn't come here for—"

"I came here to have some space and to clear my head. Is it too much to ask to be granted that peace?"

"And I'm not trying to stop you from—"

"*Yes*, you are," Daxton interjected, the ice in his voice trickling onto the flowing waters at his feet, creating a barrier between us. When he looked back at me, his eyes mimicked the cold, hard stone he sat upon.

"We're worried about you, Daxton. What's the reason for this distance? Why did you leave like that?"

Daxton scoffed and turned his back to me again, gazing off into the meadow with his sword spinning in his grasp.

"If this is about Anjani, you can talk to me, you know. I'm here for you." I didn't know the price he would pay, but I did understand that Daxton would be forced to atone for his actions against Anjani and Aelius.

"I didn't take the most tactical approach in addressing the threat today."

"All right, that's a start," I said, cautiously stepping forward.

His hands clenched around the hilt of his sword, freezing in place, as the rest of his body strained like he was in pain. Gods, I didn't want to be the reason for him to feel any kind of distress. No matter how much I wanted to be here for him—to help him. If he needed me to leave, I would.

"Do you want me to go?" He remained silent, but to my surprise, his posture seemed to relax as a breeze of wind swept past me in his direction. "You didn't say no, so I'll take that as a maybe or even a stretch of a yes. And I'll stay," I said crossing the frozen blockade created by his magic. I was only an arm's span away from him, but even that minuscule distance seemed like miles. "Dax. Dax … Look at me, please," I whispered, praying he would answer.

He shook his head, refusing to meet my gaze. "I crossed a line today. I knew better. And still, I crossed it." A heavy weight seemed to press on his shoulders, and I couldn't help but wonder what it all entailed. His disposition didn't solely stem from what he did to Anjani.

I lowered myself to the earth, kneeling before him as I timidly reached for his clenched fist. "I didn't want you to endanger yourself or your people because of what she did to me."

"That's the problem," Daxton roared, tearing his hand away from mine and standing with his back toward me. His sword vanished from sight as he faced the never-ending looming night. I had never seen him like this, and I would be lying if I said I wasn't beginning to worry. "When it comes to you, Skylar," Daxton lowered his voice to a hushed whisper, yet I heard every word. "There's no line, simply because none *exist when—*"

My throat bobbed with a heavy swallow, still kneeling on the cold stone earth, barely allowing myself to breathe with heightened anticipation.

"What are you not telling me, Daxton?" Rising to my feet, I squared my shoulders, finally ready and willing to shatter every wall that separated us.

"For you ..." his voice trembled with emotion as he turned. "For you, I would watch the world burn if it meant keeping you safe. All reason—all sense of logic and responsibility I carry—is thrown to the side when it concerns you."

My heart started racing as my hands began to shake. "Daxton, I ..."

Dax shook his head, glancing down at his feet. "I need *you* to know that if I were given the chance again, I would make the same decision. You don't carry any burden or guilt. I will gladly suffer the consequences of my actions—*alone.*" He slumped back into a seated position on the boulder, the glimmer in his eyes fading behind his mask of stone.

I gripped my chest, swallowing a heavy breath, barely hearing, let alone understanding, what he was telling me. Did he think I would let him do this alone? Did he believe I would not stand beside him in a hurricane and refuse to leave? *Does he truly not know?*

"You're not *alone* in this, Daxton," I said in a hushed tone, carefully enunciating every word.

"I'll—"

"No!" I shouted, staring him down and forcing him to lock his gaze on only me. "No. You're not alone. You'll never be *alone.*" Standing, I leaned forward, taking his hand in mine while my other cupped his cheek, meeting his hardened stare. My magic flared, linking with his in a silent melody that intertwined our beating hearts—the same serene music I had heard in the depths of the hunter's lair, that had kept me alive. That kept me breathing and hoping for a light to follow out of the darkness.

Silver Shadow's stare bore into me, and just like the first time I saw him in the meadow, I remained unafraid. There was no part of Daxton I feared. I loved every broken and shattered piece of his heart and soul. I would never abandon him. I would stand by his side through his darkest times, just like he had for me.

"You say this, but—"

"Daxton," I said in a firm tone that silenced his tongue. "You're never alone because you will *always* have me." I moved closer, stealing his undivided attention. "You've had me since that first night in the meadow," I said with a sincere smile, trying desperately to reach him. "And every moment since then."

His gaze softened. The muscles in his jaw relaxed as his lips briefly parted to inhale a sharp breath. I could see the depths of his true soul come forth. His mask falling to the side to reveal the Dax I had grown to love.

My voice quivered with anticipation. "Meeting you was no coincidence. These trials were a gift from the Gods themselves." My chest heaved as I swallowed a heavy breath. "Even if I fail and never reach the end, all of this, every step or twist of fate in my life was worth it because it has led me to you." I encircled my arms around his neck, trying to steady myself against his immovable strength. "Of all the people in this world, you're the one I was meant to find."

His arms tightened around my middle, but I shut my eyes, pressing my brow to his to summon my courage. My animal's presence pushed on my subconscious, encouraging me with a flood of strength to bare my soul to the male who held my heart.

"With you, I feel at peace. No longer searching because I've found where I belong."

Daxton's voice was barely a whisper against my cheek. "What are you saying, Skylar?"

"I love you, Daxton Aegaeon, High Prince of Silver Meadows … *my* Dax. I will always find you because it was *you,* I've always been searching for."

Without hesitating, Daxton pulled me into his lap as my legs wrapped around his waist, consuming my mouth with his and leaving me utterly breathless with a soul-binding kiss.

My hands threaded through his hair, pulling it free as his calloused palms traced over the curves of my hips before migrating under my shirt. Electricity sparked between us as our magic combined, enhancing the feel of him that vibrated over every inch of my scolding flesh. I felt like I was on fire. His touch. His kiss. I would never have enough of him—of this. Even if my mortal life somehow lingered for eternity, it would never be enough.

Gasping for breath, Daxton pulled his lips from mine. "Ask me," he rasped, teetering on the edge of his self-control.

"W-what?" I stammered, barely able to think, let alone ask a question at a time like this. "Wait, *what*?" I fought to regain my senses for the moment. "I tell you that I love you … and you reply with, *Ask me*?" I released my hold on him. "What the actual fuck, Daxton?"

His smug smirk, paired with his dark, humorous laugh, was unequivocally infuriating.

"Ask me," he repeated with a devilish grin, revealing the dimple along his ebony bearded cheek. "Ask me what I couldn't answer our first night together in Crimson City."

My mind was a whirlwind of confusion, finding my way back to our first intimate night together after he saved me from the nightmares brought forth by Seamus's mind-reading magic. I looked up and met those mesmerizing eyes that flowed like liquid silver in the moonlight. And then, I knew.

"What were you discussing with Adohan and the others in Crimson City?"

Daxton reached out to caress my cheek, looking at me like I was the only fucking person that mattered in this entire world. The intensity of his stare was enough to send me over the edge right then and there.

"Skylar," he said my name softly, leaning forward to kiss my lips before trailing a line of kisses across my chin and down my neck. "I'll never forget that first time I laid my eyes on you. How you took my breath away with your fierce beauty and even more with your cunning bravery, my Spitfire." He stilled and closed his eyes before a bright, beaming smile unfolded across the span of his mouth. "That night, my *soul* found its other half. What it's been aching for—for centuries. You're the reason *why* I believe and hope for a future because you are my future."

My entire body trembled. Everything he was telling me was leading to an answer I never thought could be possible.

"Can't you see that you're my *everything*, Skylar Cathal? My hope. My salvation." He pressed his brow against mine, taking a full breath and holding it captive before releasing it into the night. "My heart ..." He paused, and the world outside us ceased to exist. "You, my Spitfire. You are my *mate*, and I'm hopelessly and eternally in love with you."

Mate.

A bond more powerful than any spell or magic cast in this world—a union that transcended all logic and reason. A connection that spanned through time itself, forever linking two souls together in this life and the next.

"I-I don't understand," I stammered, unable to move or even think. "Why can't I—"

371

"I believe it's because you haven't shifted yet," Daxton answered plainly, like it was a simple response one would give a small child. "I know you feel at least a whisper of our connection, but our mate bond will not be sealed until you can shift. Your other half can't recognize it until your animal form emerges."

"That's why you didn't tell me? You didn't want to—"

"Yes, but I also couldn't place this additional weight on your shoulders, not to mention the danger of it. Not with *everything* you were facing and striving to overcome. But now…" His voice trailed off.

The trials, Minaeve … Gods above, even Gilen.

"How long?" I asked, grasping his hands but forcing myself to take a step back. I needed answers, and I couldn't think straight with his arms wrapped around me. "When did you feel the mate bond between us? How long did you keep this to yourself and think it was okay *not* to tell me?"

Regret flashed across his somber face, making me rue my harsh tone, but I had to know. I had to know how long he'd hidden this from me. And why he had kept this secret. I *deserved* to know.

"The night we first arrived in Solace." Despite my frustration, Daxton couldn't help smiling as his eyes shone in that special way that made my core melt. "When a spitfire shifter demanded I stay alive after trying to kill me." His scoff of a laugh was endearing despite my mood. *Asshole.* "Since that first moment, a part of me knew."

"How? When?" I narrowed my eyes and crossed my arms, trying my best not to let his charming humor soften me. "*How* did you know?"

"Looking back on it, I knew before I ever met you. It was the sole reason I wandered into the meadow that night. I was drawn to you." Dax became quiet, lost in his thoughts and memories, which I knew spanned beyond my comprehension. "When I bit you on the arm," he motioned to the scar above my wrist, "and tasted your blood, my mind became a haze. Thoughts of you consumed every waking moment, even my dreams." Dax stilled, his eyes never leaving me. "Before you arrived to heal me later that first night, I knew … but I still questioned it." His brow furrowed as he tried to pull me closer, but I shuffled back to keep my distance, silently demanding for him to continue.

"Since meeting you, my soul has been tethered to yours, a bond forged beyond my control. As much as I tried to resist getting to know you, or forming any type of relationship in fear of what Minaeve or any other may do … Alas, my heart inevitably became yours. The bond drew me to you, but I fell in love with you because of who you are—my intelligent, stubborn, brave, and indescribably beautiful *Spitfire*."

I glanced at my right wrist, where his bite mark scarred my flesh. "Not even the mage could heal this scar," I mumbled, "because it was the mark of a mate bond. High Fae stake claims on their mates like shifters?"

"Rarely," Daxton replied quickly, shifting uneasily, and rubbing the nape of his neck. "But that's not exactly what I did to you." He was quiet, letting this information settle before continuing. "Please don't think I staked a claim on you that night; I honestly didn't mean to bite you. It isn't the *true* mating mark of the High Fae. That act is performed with willing partners during more intimate moments together," Daxton countered with a shadow of unease pooling in his eyes. "I researched your culture as best I could regarding this. Determined to understand your mating bonds and how they align with ours. I was desperate to find explanations for why I was feeling the influence of our bond, and why you might not," he added, his eyes cast downward.

"It's because I haven't—"

"Shifted," Daxton finished for me. "That's what I concluded."

"Why did you do this?" I asked, holding my arm out between us.

"Instinct." He almost sounded ashamed as he swallowed. "I was dying, and ... there's no real excuse. Just an explanation of why."

"Instinct?" I repeated, shaking my head. "Wait." I paused. "This? This was how you found me in the hunter's lair. The mate bond led you to me?"

"Yes." He nodded his head slowly. "There's nowhere you could go that I wouldn't find you. Even if our bond is not sealed ... death itself would not keep me from your side. The bond would lead me to you. Once a High Fae recognizes their mate, even if the other rejects it, they will always have a vague sense of each other."

Silence passed between us as I paced along the babbling brook, holding myself tightly and staring blankly at the ground.

"Skylar, please understand that I would never force this. I could *never* do that to you. When you were chosen as the champion, it only complicated things more. I couldn't burden you with another twist of fate that you didn't ask for." Daxton spoke with a sense of urgency laced with a dash of fear in his voice. "That's why I didn't say anything. Why I tried to keep my distance, and even when—" He froze, his voice becoming nothing more than a whisper. I turned to see every muscle of his body tensing. "Even when I forced myself to step aside and allow you the chance to find happiness in a life that didn't include me. A chance to renounce your role as champion and mate another male. To keep you safe, I would force myself to step aside."

Gods above. He was talking about Gilen and the loophole that allowed another shifter to take my place.

I recalled the night he left me his first letter. He'd picked up Gilen's painted stone and placed it back into my hand. And then the morning after I refused Gilen's claim, Daxton was a raging lunatic in the training field with Castor. The reason why he was so pleased to hear I had slept alone in the forest that night was now so clear. The violent interactions with Gilen during my last night in Solace.

It all made sense now.

Even if the mate bond was not sealed, the strength and willpower required to allow your mate to be claimed freely by another was *unthinkable*. Yet he was willing to do that for *me*. To keep me safe. To find happiness if I should choose a life without him. I didn't know what to say. His actions went beyond what words could articulate.

"But I couldn't bring myself to stay away." Daxton's hand tentatively reached out to brush against my arm. "Our night together in Crimson City, I submitted to the feelings I had been trying to hide, but in the end ... I could never stay away. The night before the first trial, I knew I would forever be at your mercy. I belonged to you."

Everything he was saying ... was true.

"And now," Dax said, "hearing you confess those three words shattered every barrier I've fought to build, and I could no longer keep this secret. I'm yours, Skylar."

I turned away and continued to march along the smooth stones that framed the gently flowing waters.

Trying to wrap my head around the fact that Daxton was my mate.

My mate.

A half-human shifter mated to one of the most powerful High Fae in history. What the fuck kind of twist of fate was this?

"Skylar, say something … Anything," Daxton pleaded, his hands splayed at his side with his stare bearing into me. "Yell at me. Ask all the questions I know you have spinning in that cunning mind of yours." I marched along the meadow's edge, wordlessly working through all this. "Fuck … please, just say something!"

"I love you, you idiot!"

Daxton's expression softened as hope gleamed in his bright eyes.

"I meant what I said earlier, Dax. I'm not a fickle female who breaks down or runs away when things are … *complicated.*" I paused, and I swear the air itself froze between us, heavy like morning fog over the vast seas. "I love you," I said, seeing his panic vanish. His chest heaved, as he finally allowed himself to take a full breath.

"I'm just trying to get a grip and understand all of this." I glanced around the meadow and took in the beauty of the surrounding mountains, which sparked a faint memory or perhaps even a dream. "Wait. Where are we exactly?" I asked. "I … I've been here before."

Daxton cautiously approached, placing his hands on my shoulders as he stood behind me. The warmth and comfort of his touch was exhilarating, and I couldn't help leaning into him. My love for him was never in question, but the gravity of a mate bond was monumental. Practically unheard of outside of a species, but then again, I had always questioned if my existence stemmed from just that.

Had my father, a shifter, experienced a mate bond with my mother, a human? If the veil had not separated us, would more mate bonds appear between our species?

"This hanging valley is my sanctuary, comparable to the green sand beach for you," Daxton said as his arms encompassed me in a fortitude of strength and support that made me confident enough to take on the world. "Remember me telling you about my work with plants and creating different types that would grow and bloom in the moonlight?"

"Yes."

"The moondance flower. Your favorite, as I recall?"

"Yes."

"I created it."

The next second, if almost by magic, the clouds parted overhead, and the moonlight danced across the meadow, bringing to life the ebony-stemmed flower from my dreams. They fanned open, revealing the vibrant orange and silver pedals that stretched out to the sky. I gasped, clutching onto Daxton's arm with one hand while the other flew to my gaping mouth. I couldn't hold back my tears if I wanted to. This was the meadow from my dreams. My place of solace in times of turmoil and defeat, and this place was all created by *him*.

"I've been dreaming about you my whole life, Daxton." I turned and looked into his storm-gray eyes that shone with a depth of love and devotion that made dreams a reality.

"You *are* my mate." Tears fell to my cheeks as Daxton pulled me closer to him, cradling me in his arms as the rest of the world faded around us. "I love you," I murmured, turning my head to kiss his cheek. "I love you," I breathed again, trailing a light caress across his bearded chin. "I love you," I repeated once more, the words falling short of how deeply I felt.

Grasping my chin between his thumb and finger, Daxton guided my lips to his and kissed me. The world beneath my feet gave way, and I could have sworn I was flying. I parted his lips with my tongue, tasting his sweetness that intoxicated my senses, leaving me numb to anything but him.

A strong surge of desire overtook me as his hands crept up from the bottom of my shirt. His rough palms fondled my hardened nipples, teasing them between his fingertips. Slowly, I trailed my hand along his growing shaft, needing to feel him, touch him, taste him in every way possible. My arousal lit up like a candle as our kiss deepened. Consumed by the feeling of him, I moaned into his mouth.

"Do you want this?" Daxton rasped as he forced himself to pull away, his hooded eyes blazing with desire that was solely centered on me. "You have a choice," he said, his deep voice trembling. "I'm in love with you, Skylar Cathal. My heart will always belong to only you, but if you don't want this bond …" He paused to steady himself. "If you don't want the mate bond, we can stop." His tone shifted with a hardened edge. "I need to know because, once I take you, once I taste you and devour you fully, I will *never* allow another to *ever* take my place." Gods, the intensity of his stare, the way he held me, the pure essence of this male was mind-altering.

"You belong to me," I answered with a low growl in my throat, my power rising within me alongside my animal's acceptance. "You're *mine*, Daxton Aegaeon."

I wouldn't allow any other to ever claim me— nor would my animal. Daxton was the only one who ever could. "And I willingly accept our bond … Even if it's not sealed. I can't deny feeling the threads of it connecting us. But, regardless of a bond, I've already decided that there's no one else for me. I love you. I'm yours."

The smile spread widely across Daxton's decadent lips. He looked at me with nothing other than pure ecstasy and bliss. "I love you," he declared once more, his heated gaze traveling down my torso. "Are you wearing my shirt?" he asked playfully.

"Guilty."

A deep growl of approval echoed in his throat. "You have no idea how fucking hard that makes me. To know that even when I'm away, you wrap yourself in my scent and keep me tucked around your perfect body."

"Show me," I said.

"See for yourself." He chuckled, taking my wrist and guiding my touch toward his pulsing length.

"Cocky, are we?" I teased, as I pressed my palm against him. "Would you like me wearing *nothing* but your shirt?" I whispered into his ear.

"I'd prefer nothing."

Daxton bent to lift the bottom of his tunic I was wearing, devouring my already taut nipple in his mouth. He meticulously swirled his tongue around the pink-skinned bud and sucked on it until it hardened like the silver peaks surrounding us. I moaned loudly, lacing my fingers through his free-flowing hair, leaning my head back and soaking in the haze of pleasure. He migrated to my other breast, coveting the previous one with his hand as I whimpered in delight. The ever so fucking delicious pleasure of his mouth on my skin, of me in his arms, of our love for each other … was downright sinful.

Quivering beneath his touch, I rasped, "I'm calling on your promise." His mouth made a popping sound as he released my nipple from his lips. "I believe you promised to make me come with your mouth, fingers, and then finally, that delicious cock of yours the first time you had me—"

"Making that beautiful voice of yours hoarse from screaming my name over and over again." His hooded eyes closed as he raised to kiss me hard and fast. "I remember," he purred. "And I believe I told you the first time I fucked you, you wouldn't be able to leave my bed."

"Yes," I said with a heavy breath, my chest rising and falling rapidly against his. "Something like that."

"Then I know exactly where we should be then."

In a silver flash, Daxton teleported us from the earthy meadow onto a soft, luxurious surface clouded in shadow and darkness. My back lay on plush bedding, with Daxton looming over me. My thighs opened to take the weight of his body while his forearms rested on either side of my head.

"These need to be on." He waved his hand, illuminating the fae lights in what I soon realized must be his room. "I need to be able to see all of this gorgeous body I've been dreaming about taking for months."

I didn't bother to notice the details of his room. The only thing that drew my attention was the gorgeous male with far too many clothes on.

Daxton remained deathly still as I moved to sit up. His intense stare bore into me, waiting for me to take the lead. My fingers danced along the opening of his tunic, feeling the hard muscles of his chest rise and fall with each heated breath. Looping my arms around his neck, I pulled his lips to mine. Daxton followed my guided touch without hesitation, eagerly coveting my mouth with his.

This kiss was different from before. It was soft, gentle, and above all else, it conveyed the depth of his love and devotion to me. Whatever I needed, I knew Daxton would do everything in his power to see it done.

My hands wandered to the bottom of his shirt, and I hurriedly pulled it over his head and tossed it onto the floor. Gods, this male was absolute perfection.

Kissing him once more, I pressed a palm to his chest, taking my time to admire his sculpted physique carved from hundreds of years of battle training. My fingers danced along the tops of his shoulders and the marks adorning his skin before I threaded my fingers into his hair along the nape of his neck.

As I shifted to lean forward onto my knees, Daxton froze, granting me full control. My lips moved to find the scar I'd made the night we first met. I kissed across the swirling tattoo designs that danced along his skin, the only place on his body that was inked.

"What is it?" he asked as I stilled.

"I can't believe I didn't know," I spoke softly. "When you tattooed this on your skin, I should've guessed it was more than just highlighting a scar." His eyes softened at my remark, but he didn't move to take me just yet.

My hands moved along the bumps and bulges of his rigid abdomen muscles, leading to the cut-in lines of his hips. He adjusted one leg, moving off the edge of the bed while another remained bent on the mattress. I reached for the fastening of his pants, unleashing the tension that held them up along his hips.

I bit my bottom lip in anticipation, watching him like a predator ready to strike as he stepped back to strip them away. His hard erection sprang outward, coming to life in front of me, causing my mouth to water with the desperate need to taste him again.

I eased forward, eagerly taking the base of his shaft in my hand while sucking on the tip with my swollen lips. His moan encouraged me, urging me to take him deeper into my throat and swallow him whole, just like I had the night before the first trial. Slowly, I sucked, teasing him by remaining on the head of his magnificent cock before quickly swallowing his length until it collided with the back of my throat. I gradually backed out, returning a moment later. His girth choking me in the best way possible.

My arousal was beginning to build. My apex ached for his attention, but I hadn't had my fill of him just yet.

Daxton fisted my hair as his hips thrust forward, his shaft disappearing in my mouth, making it impossible to breathe let alone think about anything besides the taste of his delicious cock.

"Fuck … yes," he growled. "Take all of me, Spitfire." Daxton cursed as he released his grip, allowing me the chance to breathe. The slight twinge of pain and sliver of danger heightened the intensity of pleasure. Once I caught my breath, I dove back down his shaft, fondling his balls with my free hand while the other wrapped around the base.

"Yes, Gods. That feels so fucking good."

He tensed, his balls contracting in my hand as I worked him with my mouth. Gods above, having control over him like this was invigorating. This huge powerful male was completely at my mercy, and I fucking loved every second of it.

Suddenly, Daxton pulled himself back. His cock popped out of my mouth as he reached down to grab my shoulders and push me backward onto the bed.

"Sorry, my *mate*." His predatory growl sent trickles of lightning up my spine, the wetness between my legs pooling in response to him calling me "mate." "But I believe I have a promise to live up to."

Hooking his fingers into the waistband of my pants, he managed to grasp my soaked underwear as well, pulling them free and adding them to the pile of discarded clothing on the floor.

"And I believe I may have misspoken before." The hunger in his eyes glowed as he looked me over. "Having you in nothing but my shirt is a fucking masterpiece. Anytime you want me to shut up and kneel before you like the queen you are, all you have to do is walk into a room with nothing on you but this, and I'm at your mercy."

"Noted," I answered, my chest heavily rising and falling with heated anticipation as I removed the tunic.

"But naked," Daxton rasped. "You naked is— *Fuck*. It's indescribable." His cock pulsed in response as his eyes devoured me.

Rough hands splayed over my thighs, spreading them as Daxton lowered himself onto his knees at the edge of the bed. His calloused palms rubbed against the smooth skin on my ass, admiring every inch of my body. His touch migrated across my feminine curves before gripping my hips and pulling me down toward him.

"I *need* to taste you, Skylar." I bit my lower lip as his intense stare bore into me. Gods above. I was already dripping wet, and he had barely even touched me yet. "I love it when I can smell your arousal, especially when I know I'm the one causing it."

"You're *always* the cause of it," I said with a raspy voice paired with a playful wink.

"Good," he answered as he lowered his lips, hovering just over my sex. "No one else will ever be allowed to taste or touch you like this. Not while I'm still breathing." He flicked his tongue over the bundle of nerves at my apex, then applied the perfect amount of pressure with his lips, sending me soaring through the stars.

"Daxton!" I moaned, almost shattering.

"Yes?" he sinfully whispered against me. "Say my name again," he commanded as he feverishly sucked the sensitive point between the apex of my throbbing center. His tongue vibrated against me, sending waves of intense pleasure rocketing through my core.

"Gods above … Fuck! Yes, Daxton, don't … don't stop."

Daxton raised his head slightly, before he slowly licked downward toward my opening. He was eating me like a decadent dessert, and I loved every second. Pressure built between my thighs, everything tightening. I was craving a release, yet still drowning in the pure ecstasy of his mouth.

I reached for my breast, but before I could touch myself, Daxton's hand was already there. "Allow me," he said before burying himself back between my thighs.

My hard nipple rolled between his fingers as he licked my throbbing center. I almost blacked out from the waves of ecstasy he was giving me with just his mouth alone. My hips bucked and rolled, grinding into his mouth, chasing an orgasm that was building higher and higher on the verge of splitting me apart. And when I thought I couldn't take anymore, Daxton gave me just what I needed to push me over the edge. With his mouth still on me, he slipped one finger and then two inside my dripping-wet entrance, sensing exactly what I wanted. What I *needed*. The sensation of him lit my world on fire.

"Oh, Daxton!" I screamed as my climax tore through me.

I groaned as he remained between my thighs, my inner walls contracting around his digits with each wave of my orgasm. His continued attention elongated the pleasure, making it last longer than I thought possible.

"Dax," I whimpered, head still foggy.

"Keep riding it," he rasped, only releasing his kiss on me for the briefest second.

"It's too much."

"Relax," he breathed against me, gently releasing the pressure but still giving me his undivided attention. "Let it build. I want you to come for me again, Spitfire."

I threw my head back, squirming against the soft bedding beneath me, and ground my hips harder into his willing mouth. Doing just as he said, I let go, relaxing and allowing the pressure to build again. My breathing quickened as his fingers began moving in and out of my soaked pussy, thrusting deeper and deeper with each agonizingly slow movement that brought me into a new level of heightened bliss.

"You're so fucking wet," he growled in a low, husky voice. "You have no idea how gods-damned stunning you are. How delectable you taste, and how hard you make me." My entire body trembled, climbing higher and higher toward the edge again.

"Come for me, Skylar," Daxton commanded. "I want to taste your climax," he growled against me.

My body collapsed on the bed as my second orgasm rolled over me like a thundering hurricane out in the high seas.

"Good," Daxton purred as he kissed the inside of my thighs, his fingers helping me ride the waves of my orgasm. "I could feel you come on my tongue. Fuck," he cursed, eyes dark and heavy, "it's by far one of the most arousing things in this world."

My chest heaved as I fought to catch my breath. My limp body was useless at this point, having experienced two of the most mind-blowing releases of my life. I opened my eyes to see Daxton towering over me with one hand wrapped around the base of his pulsing cock. He stroked himself, using my release as his lubricant, never once taking his eyes from mine. "You're ready for me now, Spitfire."

I licked my lips, salivating over the drop-dead gorgeous male kneeling naked before me.

"The Mother herself is envious of your breathtaking beauty, Skylar," Daxton said as he moved his body on top of me. "And you're all *mine*. How the fuck am I this fortunate?"

I smiled, moving so our hips were aligned. "Everything … happens for a reason." His gruff chuckle sent goosebumps across my skin. "I want you, Daxton," I said with heavy breath. "I want you to be my first. My last. My *only* …"

"As you command, *my mate*."

Mate. The title was still so new, but it also felt so fucking right.

Daxton settled between my open thighs, his hard length brushing against my slickened folds, testing my reaction before entering me for the first time. I thought I would be nervous, perhaps even scared, but I was far from either.

I leaned up and kissed him, our mouths opening as the kiss deepened, setting the tone for what we shared together.

This was more than a burning hunger or mere attraction. It was a consummation of our love. Whether our bond was sealed or not, we both knew it was there.

"You have my heart," Daxton whispered, "my soul."

"And you have mine," I answered, trusting that we both meant it.

His hips rolled back, the head of his cock lining up perfectly. He bent to kiss me, and all my senses blurred until no one else in the world existed outside this moment together. I fell into our kiss, devouring his mouth with my own, showing him that I wasn't afraid. I tilted my hips up to meet Daxton's as his tip glided into my center that was pulsing with need.

At first, the pressure was intense. The thickness of his cock stretched against my inner walls as a sharp bite of pain ripped through me with only half his length buried inside. I tensed, fingers digging into his shoulders, biting back the sting of losing my maidenhead.

"Are you all right?" he whispered. "Skylar?" Genuine concern laced his voice.

"Don't move for a second," I breathed, trying to adjust to his girth.

Slowly, the pain subsided, and the need to move against him grew stronger with each passing second.

I moved my hips as a soft moan purred in my ear. "You're mine," Daxton said, the final strands of his control disappearing. "Are you ready for *all* of me, Spitfire?" he asked.

"Yes," I cried out, my pain a distant memory. "Yes, Daxton—"

Releasing the threads of his restraint, Daxton gripped my hips and thrust his entire length inside me, euphorically filling me until he slammed into his hilt.

"Daxton!" I moaned, my voice becoming harsh with the repeated screams of pleasure that were erupting from my throat. Fuck. He was huge. I didn't know how I was able to hold his girth inside me, let alone his length.

"Move with me," he instructed, grabbing onto my ass and guiding me in rhythm with his thrusts.

"Oh, fuck!" I cried out, reaching up and grabbing onto his shoulders for support.

I wrapped my legs around his waist, giving him the reigns to guide us through this together. The friction on my apex from his hips thrusting into me heightened my rising pleasure. His glorious cock filled me, hitting every angle and space inside just right like he was made specifically to please me. His thrusts quickened as I wrapped my arms around him. Dax leaned his head to the side and kissed my neck at the base of my collarbone, driving me wild with an entirely new rush of pleasure.

"Yes!" I roared as he moved to press me flat on the bed, forcefully pinning my wrists above my head with one of his hands.

This dominating hold he had on me heightened my shifter side, fueling me with a rush of heat against my skin that trickled along my spine. He looked me over, taking in the sight of my breasts bouncing to his thrusts before they ventured further down. Desire turned my blood to magma as I watched Daxton's eyes lock onto the sight of his enormous cock sliding in and out of my soaked sex.

"You … are … mine," he roared again, his free hand grabbing my hip as he continued to bury himself inside me over and over again.

I rolled in sync with his thrusts, causing him to release a gruff moan as his head tipped back and his eyes closed to sink into the pleasure we were giving to each other. "You feel so fucking unbelievable, Skylar."

His grip loosened on my wrists, and I managed to snake out of his grasp, clutching the back of his head, my amber eyes blazing with power from my animal.

"And?" I growled.

"I'm yours," he answered with a devilish smirk. "I belong to you, my Spitfire. My *mate*." He snarled the last word, thrusting hard into me and forcing a loud gasp from my throat with the mind-blowing sensation that followed.

Daxton's hand moved between our thriving bodies, his thumb rubbing against my sensitive bundle of nerves as his cock plunged deeper inside me.

"Oh, Gods!" I yelled as his thumb circled my clit while he buried himself to the hilt.

"Come for me, Spitfire," he commanded. "I need to feel you come around my cock."

My eyes rolled to the back of my head while his lips crashed into mine. Daxton's kiss devoured my screams of pleasure with each thrust of his hips and flick of his thumb. "Come," he commanded against my lips, and instantly, I shattered.

Daxton rose, grabbing my hips in his hands and thrusting hard once more, roaring as he came. His magic blasted out across the room, shaking the walls and coating every surface in a thin layer of ice. His body became limp as he folded over the top of mine. He turned his head to the side and kissed me, savoring our climaxes as he remained inside me.

Then, I felt the phantom strings of our bond begin to intertwine and smelled the merging of our scents until I was his, and he was mine.

Until there was only us.

Chapter Twenty-One

Somehow, I managed to uncoil from Daxton's arms, locate my discarded clothing, and creep silently out of his room without waking him.

The most difficult part was not cautiously placing my steps, silently getting dressed, or opening the door. No, the hardest part was leaving him. There was a pang in my chest that grew with each step I took down the hall. Gods above ... The Mother and Father themselves blessed me with Daxton as my *mate*.

Last night, after Daxton fulfilled his promise, he cradled me in his arms while helping me wash away any remnants from losing my maidenhead. I was surprised at the stain, but then again ... I didn't just climb a small hill my first time. I took on the fucking Meja mountain herself.

When I told Daxton this, he chuckled and kissed me softly before joining me for a quick wash himself. The ease of our kisses and comfort in each other's company was so natural you'd think we had been doing it for years.

After helping me clean up, Daxton, staying true to his word, promptly carried me back to his bed. We curled up together, silently closing our eyes and drifting into a calming sleep. Our limbs were so intertwined while we slept that I didn't know where he began, and I ended. We naturally tossed and turned in the night, but we never once lost contact with one another.

Last night was everything, and I do mean *everything* he had promised me the night before the first trial. It was more than I could have ever hoped for … *He* was more than anything I hoped for.

I awoke in the morning with Dax's head tucked under my chin, his face cradled against my chest, sleeping so soundly that someone might think he was dead. I couldn't help curling around him, enjoying how the passing minutes ticked by slowly, basking in our combined scents, which now blended like burning cedar on top of an ice-capped mountaintop—frigid like ice yet blazing like fire.

When I turned to kiss his dark brow, stroking his thick, hair away from his face, I made an effort to memorize this blissful moment.

The only reason why I was leaving his bed was, of course, my stomach. I was starving … And I wanted to make a special meal for my mate.

Peeking through the slit of the drapes on the windows of Daxton's room, I saw that the day was well underway. The arching windows on either side of the large balcony were draped with heavy curtains, shielding the room in darkness despite the daylight outside. My footsteps were thankfully muffled by the plush rugs leading to the doorway, aiding in my departure.

I didn't bother leaving a note. I knew he would find me.

I couldn't help the girlish smile from crossing my face as I walked down the vacant halls of the Summit in my bare feet.

My mate, I repeated almost a dozen times, unable to hide my glee. *Daxton Aegaeon, High Prince of Silver*

Meadows, is my mate, I said to myself, still in disbelief that last night had actually happened.

I blissfully passed the large arched windows decorated with elegant silver and white trim leading to the grand staircase. I gazed upward at the unique skylight framing this section of the palace that highlighted the beautiful sky above. My hand glided over the railing, admiring the detailed carvings with a new set of eyes and a feeling of tranquility settling in my center.

When I reached the kitchens and pushed the swinging door open, all sets of eyes snapped up to me; their busy hands froze as they stilled. I hesitated uncomfortably in the doorway, not sure of what to do.

Lydia, the lead kitchen staff member, was the first to speak. "Skylar." She stood up straight, matching my height with her shoulders back and head held high. I could see her nostrils slightly flare as a look of surprise flashed over her expression before quickly fading away.

"Good morning," I said softly, trying to smile. "Or maybe afternoon?"

Lydia glanced at the other kitchen staff as they began whispering to each other with quick nods.

"That's enough," Lydia snapped. Her hazel eyes as sharp as the knives she wielded. I would have probably mistaken her for a Silver Meadows warrior if she didn't have flour constantly splattered on her face and apron.

"My lady," she said, turning toward me with a bow of her head.

My lady? Okay, what was going on? I stared blankly at her with an arched brow, unsure of what to do or say in reply.

"Would you like us to cook you something or to clear the kitchens?" Lydia asked, her head still bent low.

"Y-you don't have to leave your workstations," I stammered, not wanting to put anyone out of place. "Please don't feel obligated to do something just for me. I was coming in to prepare a meal like I've done every day this past week. You don't have to leave on my account."

Lydia straightened and whipped her head around. "Clear out. Lady Skylar wishes to utilize the kitchen." She returned to me, giving me a kind smile and another bow as the others filed out behind her. "We're just cleaning up from breakfast, my lady. It's no trouble at all. If you or High Prince Daxton need anything, alert us, and we'll happily oblige your request." With that final comment, she gave me a nod and swiftly exited through the kitchen's back doors with the rest of the staff.

That was strange.

Right on cue, my stomach rumbled. I quickly brushed off their odd behavior and started creating one of my favorite breakfast dishes. It was pirozhki time.

I snacked on apple slices while my hands kneaded the dough before placing it near the heat of the burning stovetop to rise. I would have killed to have this kitchen back home. It was an absolute dream. Once the dough began proving, I got to work dicing onions and garlic, combining them with the browning meat, needing one hour for the dough to rise before I began filling the pastries. The spices were added next, allowing the flavors to soak into the meat and fill the space with a delicious chili scent that made me think of Julia and Solace.

My back was turned to the swinging door, but I knew who was standing in the opening before I even turned around. The scent of pine with a touch of burning wildfire and open sky drifted across the spice-filled air of the kitchen. My heart raced as goosebumps danced across my arms with anticipation.

"I seem to have not fulfilled my promise to you," Daxton purred. His voice was heavy, dark, and full of sultry promises. My toes curled in response.

I pivoted to face him, accidentally dropping the spatula. My eyes widened as I swallowed a heavy wave of need that pulsed through me like a thundering storm, making me forget all my reasons for leaving his bed.

Shirtless, Daxton casually leaned against the doorway with his large arms crossed in front of his chiseled chest. My eyes scanned his perfect body, lingering on the loose, low-hanging pants that rested just below his hips, intersecting the deep V in his lower abdomen that my eyes could not waver from. The ache between my thighs pulsed with a demand to have him inside me.

"*Ahhh-hem,*" he announced, clearing his voice. "My *eyes* are up here, Spitfire." I blushed and quickly tilted my gaze, biting my lower lip to keep myself steady. Dammit, I could feel the wetness building between my thighs already. "Fuck, Skylar," Daxton cursed in a low voice that made the hairs on my neck stand straight. His muscles flexed as he inhaled a full breath, closing his eyes as he tilted his head back.

"What?" I playfully asked, bending down to pick up the spatula I dropped on the floor.

"You're enjoying this. Aren't you?" He groaned, opening his slitted eyes with a devilish smile. "You know … I should be scolding you for leaving the bed without me releasing you. Yet here I find you barefoot in my kitchen," he paused, looking me over, "and still wearing my shirt?" He arched his brow. "Unfair."

"There weren't many options for me to change into. Or would you prefer I was naked in your kitchen? Is that the better choice?" I asked him with a mischievous smirk.

"Shifty little shifter," Daxton snickered with a spirited heat dancing in his eyes. "I'm already arranging for your things to be brought to *our* room if you don't have any objections to the idea."

"Our room?" I stilled, turning off the flames to allow the meat to cool before stuffing it into the dough. "*Our*?" A serene smile spanned my face.

Daxton uncrossed his arms, pushed away from the doorway, and sat himself on the other side of the kitchen island. Leaning forward onto his elbows, he rested his chin on his knuckles, giving me a swaggering half-grin that told me more than it should.

"Didn't miss that one, did you?" I shook my head, giggling at how casual this all seemed when, in reality, it was the exact opposite. "Regardless of our bond not being sealed or the trials, you are my mate, Skylar. I won't hide my feelings for you any longer. In fact, I refuse to do it."

"Good," I answered. "It's about damn time. Minaeve can go kick rocks barefoot for all I care." His chuckle put me at ease. "We'll overcome anything together," I added in a more serious tone.

He flashed me a full, unencumbered smile and, in a silver flash of light, reappeared next to me. He wrapped one arm around my waist while the other tilted my chin upward between his finger and thumb. His ever-watchful gray eyes scanned over the features of my face before bending to kiss my brow, then each cheek, before finally finding my lips.

I sighed, sinking into the feel of him and wrapping my arms around his neck to pull him closer. As our kiss deepened, our breathing became heavy as I lost myself in the sweet taste of his lips. The ache in my center pulsed harder, longing and begging to be fed his magnificent cock once more.

"How are you feeling?" Daxton asked me, his own scent of arousal fueling my already blazing fire.

"Ravenous." I sighed with a slight whimper.

"I knew I'd find you in the kitchen, and I didn't need the threads of our bond to tell me that." His lips ventured down to my collarbone, seductively nipping at the nape of my neck with his teeth. I threaded my fingers in his hair, clutching onto his shoulder with my other hand while my whole body trembled with pleasure.

Gods. He was intentionally toying with me, and I loved it.

"Still ravenous?" he asked, backing me up to the kitchen island so I was sitting atop the slab.

"Yes," I answered, reaching for the hem of the shirt and ripping it off and over my head. "For you."

Without hesitating, Daxton's mouth immediately went to my breasts, devouring one of my nipples and making it harden before moving on to the next. My head fell backward, with my legs spreading wider to hold him close.

I shifted to the edge of the slab, his erection seductively grinding against my sex. He felt so fucking good I might shatter to pieces right there on the edge of the island. I was on the verge of coming from the friction of him alone. I wanted more, though. My yearning for him was almost indescribable, and I couldn't wait another second before having him inside me.

"Gods above," Dax snarled possessively. "I could fuck and come on your beautiful breasts alone, Skylar." His hands caressed my curves as he continued to worship my body with his lips and glorious tongue. Heat flared in my blood, my apex throbbing with a desperate aching need to be filled.

"But that's for another time. I need to be inside you. I'm afraid I'll go mad if I don't … Are you—"

I leaned forward, lifting my backside off the countertop to quickly slide my pants down, answering Daxton's question before he could finish forming it.

His fingers quickly unfastened the tie of his pants as they dropped to the floor, freeing his long hard cock from its tethered cage. We were both naked in seconds, and it still didn't seem fast enough. My mate pulled my hips to the edge of the counter, his mouth eagerly finding mine. Our kiss became hungry, hot, and heavy, mimicking our heightened desperation.

This time … we would fuck without restraints, acting purely on desire and drive.

I wrapped my legs around his hips, interlocked my ankles together, and clutched onto his shoulders. Lowering himself to the edge of the counter, Dax grasped the base of his shaft, guiding the head of his moistened tip through my aching sex. He brushed his tip across my clit, teasing us both with the promise of sweet release soon to come. Lining himself up just right, he brought his hips back and then, in one powerful movement, sheathed himself inside me.

"Oh, Yes!" I moaned as my head fell back, my inner walls aching with the feel of his length filling every inch.

My mate thrust into me again, and again. Each movement stretching and satisfying me with more mind-numbing pleasure than the last. "Daxton, yes! I need you to …" I moaned.

"Tell me what you want."

"Dominate me."

Daxton stilled for a moment, a deep predatory growl of satisfaction erupting from his chest, sending waves of excitement and anticipation. "You're sure?"

J.E. Larson

"Yes," I breathed heavily, my magic rolling through me and combining with his. The words effortlessly spilled out of my mouth, forming without a second thought.

There was a sharp flicker of amusement paired with desire deep in Daxton's stare that told me he was happy to oblige.

One of his hands raised to my throat, as he pushed me flat onto my back, looming over me with his shaft buried to its hilt. His eyes devoured the sight of me splayed across the slab, while his cock slowly slid from of my entrance.

"As you command, my *queen*."

Daxton's strong thighs banged against the edge of the island as he thrust into me with his dominating hold. I moaned, moving to meet his hard thrust, clenching my legs around his waist, and devouring the luxurious friction between our two thriving bodies. Daxton's grip on my throat was just enough to push my animal to the surface to fight for control, the dance of dominance heightening the building tension. His show of power, with his hold on my throat paired with his pounding cock, sent me soaring higher toward a sweet release.

He held the power this time. Fulfilling the part of me that was driven to find a mate worthy enough, strong enough to claim the title.

"Fuck, you're so wet, Skylar," Daxton growled, finding a slower, deeper rhythm with his long, powerful thrusts. "Look at me," he commanded.

My eyes snapped open, feeling the swell of power from my animal in response to his magic, the dominating hold on me, and the sultry, rough tone of his voice.

"Good." He leaned himself forward, his length fully seated inside me, causing me to gasp loud enough for the entire Summit to hear. "I want to see that fire in your eyes while you come. I want to feel you tremble with pleasure as you find that sweet release." He kissed me, our tongues intertwining and desperate to taste each other.

Backing away, Dax's stare bore into me, the intensity of it spinning my arousal even higher. Releasing my throat, he cupped the back of my neck, ensuring I couldn't look anywhere but those heated silver-gray eyes. His pace quickened, and I clung to him with every ounce of strength I could muster.

The pressure was rising, and I could feel my climax building. With a free hand, Daxton reached down to stroke my clit while he continued fucking me, and I came undone. My inner walls contracted around him as I screamed in pure ecstasy.

Daxton continued to fuck me, refusing to move his thumb, extending the length of my orgasm until he was ready with his own. With one final thrust and a roar of pleasure, Daxton found his release.

My mate remained buried deep within me as he rose up, pulling me with him to rest against his chest. I turned to kiss his neck, my lips trailing a line of kisses toward the scar I made in the center of his tattoo. His fingers interlaced with mine as he brought them to his lips, delicately kissing their backs as his other arm draped over me.

"Now, the kitchen has become appetizing for an entirely different reason," Daxton whispered. "But . . . we do need to find you some actual clothes."

"Why?" I teased. "When the result of me not wearing any has this sweet of a reward?"

"You're clever for someone so young." He chuckled, threading his fingers in my golden-brown hair.

"I planned on making you some breakfast and carrying it back to bed for you."

"How sweet of my mate."

My … mate. I sighed, hearing him say it again, giving his all too perfect ass a tight squeeze. "Well, if I need clothes, then so do you. It's not fair showing up in the kitchen topless, flaunting," I leaned back slightly, waving my hand over his chest, "all of *this.*"

"Fair enough," he answered with a sheepish grin and kissed me before moving himself backward, pulling up his pants, and donning my— well, his—shirt. "Now for you." He waved his hand, magically conjuring a black and silver slip dress that appeared over my bare skin. He then frowned.

"What?" I asked.

"I was wrong. It doesn't help much."

I leaned back, giving him a heated look with lust still burning in my amber gaze. "Nope. Same. Clothes don't help when you know exactly what's hidden underneath."

He moved closer and possessively pulled my mouth to his as I looped my arms around his middle and sank into his embrace.

Like fucking clockwork, however, my stomach began to rumble in protest.

"Gods above!" I cursed, and Daxton laughed against my lips.

"Finish making your meal, Spitfire."

"Care to help?" I asked as he lifted me with ease from the island.

"I'd be honored."

"Good answer," I said with a playful wink.

I instructed Dax on how to separate the dough, fold the meat over, and prime the edges so they baked properly with the delicious mixings inside. We harmoniously worked side by side, making the pirozhki and talking about anything and everything simultaneously. I told Daxton how Julia had taught me this recipe when Neera was just a baby. It was Magnus's favorite breakfast with the odd but important jelly dipping sauce that he never left evidence of on the plate.

Daxton, in turn, shared fond memories from his childhood. His mother's influence helped lead to his passion for gardening and books, while his father's lessons on tactics and the sword helped prepare him for his role as high prince.

"Would you like some fresh raspberries for your jelly?" Daxton asked me.

"Yes, that would be amazing. Do you know where we could get some?"

Daxton smiled. "I have a full row of raspberries along the outer wall in my gardens. The bastard plant began as one bush, but before I knew it, they dominated the whole area. That and the blackberries on the other side constantly battle for the best growing patches of earth." I loved hearing about his gardens. I didn't have a green thumb or any skill with plants, but it didn't stop me from admiring those who did. Plus, cooking with the fresh ingredients they provided was always the best.

"I'll return before the pastries are out of the oven," he said sweetly, squeezing my hand and brushing his lips against my cheek. "Be right back."

Silver flashed, and he was gone. I rummaged for the sugar on the higher shelves, and before I was done measuring out the amount I needed, Daxton was back with fresh handfuls of ripe red raspberries.

"Perfect," I said with glee.

When the breakfast was done baking, I served Daxton the first pirozhki and waited eagerly to hear his review, but he didn't need to really *say* anything. Once one was devoured, he immediately went for another, encouraging me to join him. We sat in the kitchen enjoying our meal together, loving the simplicity of the time spent in each other's company. Living in the beauty of the moment.

Sadly, we knew this would all too swiftly come to an end.

"I'm going to run the Ice Gauntlet today," I said as I finished my plate.

Daxton nodded, swiping the last bit of jelly from his. "I assumed so."

"Really?" I asked, inclining my head toward him. "You *assumed*? Am I that easy for you to read, Princey?"

"Hardly," he huffed. "Fate did not pair my soul with a meek and narrow-minded female. I knew you would enter the Ice Gauntlet as soon as you were physically able. And judging by our physical exertions last night, and then again, this morning…" He grinned widely, his gaze sweeping over the counter. "I knew you were ready to enter. And today, you'll earn a silver mountain peak on your shoulder."

"That … and so many other reasons," I said with confidence and excitement shining in my amber-glowing eyes, "is why I love you."

Chapter Twenty-Two

As we walked along the stone-lined pathway to the entrance of the Ice Gauntlet, my heart raced with excitement or nerves—I honestly couldn't tell them apart anymore.

Today, I wore black training clothes. I was informed that my gray-silver ones would no longer be necessary. Daxton ordered them made for me the first day I began training with Gunnar, and they were magically already waiting for me when we ventured back upstairs to his—no, excuse me, *our* room.

There were more questions than answers regarding my future, and now, adding Daxton to the mix multiplied them tenfold. But right now, they would all have to wait. Thankfully, when Daxton and I saw the others before leaving for the Gauntlet, they didn't seem surprised at seeing us together.

Idris was giddily grinning, of course. Adohan gave Daxton a serene smile while Zola nodded with a half-grin at the secret finally being revealed, and Gunnar ... Well, he sighed loudly, adding a very sarcastic, "*Finally* ..."

They all had known about the mate bond and were pleased to see us together.

"Ready?" Gunnar asked as he followed close behind Daxton and me.

"Clearly, or else she wouldn't be here," Zola said to him with a scoff. She was still in a sour mood since she and Daxton had returned, not keen on hiding it. "I still have a gold coin on her besting your time, and Idris wanted me to remind you of hers …"

Gunnar scowled and rolled his eyes. "I know. Regardless of what Skylar accomplishes up there, I'll still hold the record for youngest to complete it." His cocky, smug smile was almost too much.

"There is a wager, huh?" I asked, casually throwing him a glance over my shoulder.

Gunnar grinned, scratching the back of his head. "Possibly."

"Good to know," I said before turning toward Daxton. "I go in alone, and I finish this on my own," I said.

He raised his brows with a pleased, almost proud look. "Giving commands already, I see … How fitting."

Zola and Gunnar continued bickering about the different wagers they had placed on me. I couldn't help but overhear that Castor and Adohan had also joined in on this.

Adohan and Idris remained in the Summit. The baby was giving her some trouble this morning and she needed to take precautions and rest.

"I mean it, Dax. I need to do this on my own," I said as we reached the start of the course.

"Wouldn't dream otherwise, Spitfire. My mate is strong enough to conquer anything … All you need is the opportunity." He stepped back, allowing me to face the massive vertical obstacle course on my own. "Get ready," his deep voice boomed over the rocks along the entrance.

"Ready." I crouched down, prepared to take off at a sprint and attack the first obstacle.

"Go!"

The hourglass turned, and I sprinted into the course.

I hadn't noticed the massive gathering that had followed us to the Ice Gauntlet, but the roaring cheers blasted through my focus as I leaped onto the first obstacle of the course, encouraging me to complete it.

Using the balance techniques Daxton had taught me, I glided across quintuple steps before leaping through the air and grasping a long horizontal bar. The metal was ice cold, but I ignored the bite of it against my skin as I traversed the wall. Reaching the end, I crouched down and leaped through the air to the other side, successfully finding my footing and landing on the platform leading to the stone steps that would take me to the next level.

I heard Gunnar cheering below, with other cadets and warriors dressed in black and silver joining him. Zola held a stern look that I would guess to be amusement, and I knew that somehow, even from this distance, Idris and Adohan were cheering as well. Daxton simply gazed at me with pride swelling in his eyes. Gods, that look alone from him was enough to make me scale a thousand gauntlets.

Climbing the massive steps that were obstacles themselves, I prepared myself for the next task. Iced-over logs rolled before me, and I knew that I had to leap across them like a stone skipping over a lake to make it to the other side. From watching Daxton and the other cadets, the trick was not to stop moving your feet. If I stopped my momentum on a log, I would lose my balance and plummet down the side, or I would be forced to grab onto a rope and add time. Neither were options for me.

At the top of the stairs, I lined up with the logs, counted to three in my head, and sprinted as fast as I could to the other side. This obstacle reminded me of the games I used to play along the falls of the river with Rhea and Shaw. Stay too long in one place, and the current would sweep out your feet and take you downstream. I smiled as I took a running leap, gently tapping the top of the logs and scurrying across until landing safely on the other side … exactly like the river rocks.

"Two down, three to go." I knew my time on these first two would be quick. It was the remaining three that had me nervous.

My legs remained strong and steady despite the dull ache in my quads, but I knew my upper body strength would be tested on the ladder following the balance beam next. The traverse up the stone steps between the different levels challenged my body as much as the obstacles themselves, with large, staggering stairs that pulled at the much-needed strength in my legs.

The climb to the third obstacle was steeper than the last, adding in a falling factor that the previous two hadn't. I approached the narrow beam that looked far more treacherous from this vantage point than it did on the ground. The slick wood was coated in patches of ice, adding a layer of difficulty I hadn't anticipated but, in reality, should have expected. Stepping out onto the beam, I outstretched my arms to gain balance, carefully placing one foot in front of the other. The winds swirled with a life of their own at this height, spinning around my arms, but not strong enough to topple me over, thanks to my increased balance and strength training these past months.

Reaching the first inclined bend of the beam, I crouched down to hold onto the ice-cold tip before swinging my feet around and over to the other side. I scoffed, remembering how easy Daxton had made this look. I safely traversed the beam, not in the time I was hoping for, but I figured not falling to my death was a bonus. Passing smoothly over the second, I approached the third bend in the beam, looking ahead at the ladders I would have to climb.

That was where I made my gravest error yet.

My balance wavered for less than a second, but that was all it took for the strength of the winds to slam into me with a forceful jolt. My foot slipped from underneath me, my hip colliding hard with the ice, and I slid over the edge. I reached out and clutched onto the pointed top, one hand on either side while I dangled helplessly over the deathly drop.

"Skylar!" Daxton roared below in sheer panic.

"I've got it," I bellowed back toward the ground. "Don't you dare come up here!"

"Then pull your ass back up and get on the course. And … don't fucking fall," he commanded, his stern voice echoing off the rocks along the cliffs.

You will not fall. You will not die today, I told myself.

Bending my arms, I swung my legs in place, gaining momentum to hook my foot and then my knee around the beam, interlocking my ankles to get a firm hold. Releasing one side of the bent peak, I wrapped my hands loosely on the other side, carefully sliding down the rest of the walkway toward the safety of the platform beneath the ladder.

Not wanting to waste the adrenaline rush, I jumped up to grab the bars, steadily climbing the angled ladder. My hands were freezing against the bite of the cold metal, but my grip refused to loosen. The muscles in my arms ached as I swung myself forward to the next bar and then the next. I refused to acknowledge my aching fatigue as I passed the halfway mark. I was so close to the end ... Approximately another twenty feet and I would be safe. The winds howled as the cheers from below encouraged me to push forward. With one final surge of my remaining strength, I grabbed the last bar with both hands and swung myself through the open air down onto the stone. I landed on my feet, rolling forward into a somersault before springing up and climbing to the fourth obstacle.

I dared a glance down at my hands to see openings at the base of my fingers from the friction of the obstacle on my skin. The bleeding wounds would sting, but the pain would be well worth the reward. I clenched my fists tightly, willing the bleeding to stop. I knew if I wrapped my hands, I would lose my grip on the metal rings in the next task.

Foolishly, I looked down the sheer drop that separated the opposing sides as I approached the edge of the stairs. Fear caused cadets to fall here but not me. Without overthinking my plan, I stepped back, bracing myself with one deep breath, and jumped out over the drop. I gritted my teeth against the sting of the ring on my hands. Kicking my feet forward, I swung my legs back and forth until I had enough momentum to let go. After flying through the air, I landed on the other side and, most importantly, safely.

One more left, I told myself with a cunning grin.

I was now hundreds of feet off the ground, almost at the tallest point of the Ice Gauntlet with one final obstacle to conquer—the vertical wall. I gave myself as much room as I could, placing my back to the stone cliff face and crouching low. I had already passed this test along the spine of the Nox Mountain … I could do this.

I used the mountain to my advantage, giving me an extra push forward and pumping my arms as fast as possible to turn my horizontal momentum into vertical. Every muscle in my body burned with fatigue. The speed required to complete each task tested my endurance and pushed me to new limits.

Don't stop. Keep your feet moving until you can feel the edge with your fingers. Whatever you do, just don't stop moving your feet until you have your grip. Daxton's advice proved to be exactly right.

My feet kept moving, and even when I didn't think I could move anymore, I forced myself not to stop. Stretching out my hand, my fingers danced along the edge of the wall and immediately latched on, with my other hand following suit. With my grip firm, I pulled myself half up, swinging my legs up to help me the rest of the way. I groaned as I rolled over the top, bending onto my knees, trying to catch my breath.

"I thought shifters were supposed to be faster than that," Daxton's voice caught me by surprise.

"I thought the Ice Gauntlet was warded so that no magic could be wielded inside the course," I fired back over my shoulder.

"The outer steps and the surrounding area are not warded," he said, his eyes shining with pride—the same look from when I first volunteered to be champion of the trials.

"I did it." I breathed heavily with a wide grin as I stood up and ran into Daxton's outstretched arms. He brushed his hand over my shoulder, and when I looked down, I saw the outline of a silver mountain peak appear on my black training clothes. "If I can do this," I panted, "then …"

"There never was a doubt," Daxton answered, knowing exactly what I meant.

I was ready for the second trial.

Chapter Twenty-Three

Earning this silver mountain peak on my left shoulder might seem pointless to the outside world, but in my realm, it meant everything. This was my personal test to determine if I could defeat the second trial.

Idris and Adohan admitted they were exhausted from researching, and Idris threatened that if they didn't get a break from the library and study duty just for one evening, we would all regret it. The look on Adohan's face when Idris made her threat was priceless.

"Don't you dare utter a sound," Idris threatened. "This is … happening. I'll sit on you if I must and not in the way that led us to this treasure growing in my belly."

Sheer terror shone on her mate's face as his fiery, very pregnant mate glowered at him with a dark, menacing stare.

Gunnar was happy to oblige Idris's demands, with Zola surprisingly following his lead. I swear the Shadow Jumper never did anything I expected her to do, only adding to her shrouded facade of mystery. Castor was due back any day from his scouting mission on the Southern Sea Cliffs, and without his intel to help, all we could do was wait.

I wandered down the hallway to the sitting area that now doubled as the research station for our group. I managed to carry two bottles of wine in one hand, with a third tucked under my other arm. A corkscrew was stashed away in my pocket, and, of course, a snack of cheese and bread.

We were celebrating. And yes, I was ultimately forced into it by Gunnar's persistence, but in the end, it didn't take much.

"Come on. We have to celebrate! A *shifter* passed the Gauntlet!" Gunnar exclaimed. "I still can't believe a shifter was able to do it, but yet, it happened." I smacked him in the back of the head for that remark.

Daxton, on the other hand, was harder to persuade, but they wore him down in the end. I admired the closeness they all shared, realizing they were a family. And somehow, aside from my relationship with Daxton, I had become a part of it too. I now had something more to fight for than my pack across the sea. I was fighting for my family here as well.

Walking into the arched opening, I smiled, seeing everyone scattered and relaxed on various cushions, warming themselves around a roaring fire in the stone hearth. While the Summit was open with cooling colors and decor, this enclosed space was warm with deep red walls and tapestries depicting the oranges and yellows of the fall season.

"There she is!" Gunnar beamed brightly. "And there *they* are!" he announced, leaping up to take one of the bottles from my hand.

"Haven't you already finished one yourself," Zola scoffed from her reclined position on the velvet sofa. Her frown turning upright as I slipped the second bottle onto the pillows next to her. She gave me a nod of thanks before Gunnar caught her attention again.

"Don't be so jealous, Z. I intend to share this one," Gunnar said. "But you have to be nice about it." His grin, paired with the sultry raise of his brows, vaguely suggested something more than just Zola's prickly attitude.

Zola, true to her character, kept her composure. Only a hint of a sly smile grew at the corner of her mouth as she stalked toward Gunnar's chair. Her dark ebony braid swayed with her narrowed hips as her tawny brown skin shone with a golden glow from the roaring fire. She was a predator in this scenario. Her midnight eyes focused with an intense stare that made the hair on my neck stand upright.

"Come on, Z." To my surprise, Gunnar simply laid back in his chair as Zola strode across the room to where he sat. His legs were spread wide as he looked up at her with a smug, overconfident expression only an arrogant male could achieve.

Bending over, Zola rested her hands on either side of the armrests. She looked him over, almost like she was sizing him up. "Do you *really* think you can handle what I have to offer? Did you not learn your lesson last time?" Zola purred the question in a low, seductive voice.

My jaw practically fell open. I gawked at the two of them, utterly dumbfounded.

"Remind me." The flash of Gunnar's white teeth was visible in his wide smile as he set the bottle of wine between his legs and laced his hands behind his head. "I've come a long way since then, Zola. Care to find out just how much?"

Shadows crawled up the legs of Gunnar's recliner. I don't know how or where they came from, but I knew Zola's unique magic was somehow manipulating them.

"Props this time?" Gunnar chuckled, his eyes darkening. "How fun."

Without warning, Zola moved the bottle and straddled Gunnar's lap, pulling back on his top knot and forcing his head to fall backward as she snarled against his exposed throat. "Don't bite off more than you can chew, *General*."

"Biting, huh? Don't tempt me with a good time."

"Keep dreaming, brute," Zola scoffed. "I told you it would *never* happen again." She growled before slowly backing away and retaking her seat across the room, cast in shadows.

Gunnar didn't look afraid. He almost seemed intrigued, perhaps even more enticed than he had been a moment ago.

"Miss me?" Daxton whispered in my ear.

Startled by his sudden appearance, I pivoted and smacked his shoulder. "I warned you about sneaking up on me like that."

Daxton's deep laughter rolled over me as his arms possessively looped around my waist.

"What's so funny?" I asked as he pulled me against his chest.

"I'm imagining all the different ways I can surprise you," he said with his lips nibbling the base of my ear as his fingers danced along the seam of my pants.

I swallowed heavily.

"Interested?"

"Do you honestly have to ask?" I turned and softly kissed his lips, grinding my backside against his hardening shaft.

"You catch on quick." he answered as he tugged me closer to his frame.

"I'm a fast learner."

"*Ha ha*… Indeed, you are." His laugh was low, the vibrations in his chest snaking their way through my own. "Tonight, can't come soon enough."

I nodded; my eyes shining with longing and a promise to feed our ravenous desires.

"Oh, and by the way, *that* …" I inclined my head as Daxton reached for the bottle under my arm to set it on a side table. "I would've never guessed that Zola and Gunnar …"

"The history between those two would take all night to explain," Daxton said as he pulled me back toward him. "Care to slip away early, Spitfire?"

"Oh no you don't!" Idris scolded from across the room. "You have a minimum of one more hour with us. Then, and *only* then, can you whisk her away."

"And I would ask that you wait to—" Adohan stopped as Idris stroked his chest with her fingertips. Her serene smile was unmistakable, reeling in the fact that she could stop Adohan from finishing his sentence with the mere power of her touch. "Well, then again, I do remember what it's like to be in the frenzy of a new bond."

"Frenzy?" I murmured to Daxton.

His lips curled in as his hand rested on the curve of my hip. "Some couples don't leave their room for days or weeks on end when they first consummate their bond. The need," he whispered in my ear, as my core tightened, "the desire … is all-consuming."

His mouth moved to taste the nape of my neck as my eyes fluttered shut. I sighed as his tongue seductively caressed the skin where his mating mark would soon be.

"Exhibit A," Gunnar teased, chuckling to himself.

Daxton pulled away and I sighed in protest to the loss of his attention. Gods, I didn't know if I could wait the whole hour.

"It's how Astro and Finn were made," Idris said mockingly. "Careful, you two."

My mind suddenly sobered as I grasped Daxton's arm, the heart-stilling question written all over my face.

"I take the monthly aid, Spitfire, and this topic," his silver-gray eyes slanted toward where Idris and Adohan were seated, "should be left for another time and place where outside ears are not listening in." I nodded in agreement, placing the idea of children on a shelf to discuss at a different time.

Idris pouted and audibly scoffed. "Don't blame me for wanting a playmate for our baby."

"Just one?" Adohan mocked with raised brows. Idris shooed him playfully as he laughed.

"Hey!" Gunnar suddenly roared, drawing our attention. "Not fucking cool, Zola! I picked that one out for a reason."

Zola smiled in victory, pouring her glass of wine to the brim with a triumphant look. "I win." Gunnar strode over to where Z lounged like a queen on a throne, stretching out his empty glass for her to fill. "And why should I fill yours?" she asked with an arched brow.

"It's for Sky. Mine is sitting empty and alone on the side table."

"How fitting."

Gunnar scowled, but Zola filled his glass, and he brought it over to Dax and me. "Here, Sky, but be careful, our wine is a bit stronger than the ones from your mainland."

"I'm aware," I answered, recalling the one glass I had on the *Opal.*

Gunnar glanced up toward Daxton and gave him a curt nod before slowly backing up and returning to his chair. I took a sip and leaned into Daxton's chest, feeling a release of his magic dance across my skin, tantalizing my senses and sending a delicious chill over every inch of my body. My animal seemed to roll within me, flooding me with a surge of power that complemented Daxton's perfectly. The effect made me move closer, my attention centering on only him.

"Nice trick," I murmured so only he could hear.

"Whatever do you mean?" Daxton asked, pulling his arm around me and holding me tightly.

"All right. Tone down the pheromones, you two," Adohan bellowed. "We all know she's your mate regardless of the bond not being fully sealed. You don't have to keep throwing your scent and magic around and claiming her like that, Dax."

I tilted my head to the side, giving Daxton a questioning look. "Claiming me, huh? Is that what that is?"

"In a way."

"Have you been doing this the whole time, and I just haven't noticed?"

"Not exactly."

"It's instinct," Adohan said. "He did it once in Crimson City when Astro and Finn first met you and then again during one of your training sessions. The Silver Meadows warriors were abuzz with whispers. Now though … I fear it will be constant bombardment on Daxton's part until the bond is sealed."

Daxton gave Adohan a look and cleared his throat in a low gruff of annoyance.

"Dax," I said sweetly, drawing his immediate attention. "I don't mind. I want the world to know you're mine, and I'm yours." He bent to softly kiss me, heat and desire lingering in his quieted movements. "I just wish—"

He tenderly cupped my face in his hand, looking into my eyes with such unquestionable love that I cursed myself for not sensing our bond sooner. "I'm yours, Spitfire. Forever."

To hear him say those words to me in front of those he trusted most meant everything. I understood the depth of meaning and importance of his declaration. I leaned my brow toward him, inhaling our combined scents and sinking into his touch.

"I'm not starting the hour until you both sit with us around the hearth," Idris warned.

"How quickly she seems to have forgotten the hold the mate bond had on her and Adohan," Daxton mumbled, making me chuckle.

He took my hand as we joined the others, sitting on the floor near the roaring fire. We reclined against the base of the couch, with large pillows softening the hard floor beneath us. I sat between Daxton's legs, leaning back against his chest and settling in comfortably with his arms wrapped around me. I leaned my head against his collarbone, nuzzling my forehead against the soft scruff of his trimmed beard. Even though I was wrapped in his arms, it still didn't feel like I was close enough.

"I love you," I whispered so only he could hear.

He tenderly kissed my forehead. "I love you, too."

"All right, enough of *this* ..." Gunnar said as he gestured toward us. "Some of us like the idea of venturing out and finding new partners to indulge in various ... excursions with no commitments." His eyes scanned over to Zola. "Know of any willing participants this evening?"

She burst out laughing, bending over and trying not to spill her wine. "That was one night. And one night only," Zola said in a low, unamused tone. "I have centuries of experience you could never dream of mastering."

"I'm a good student. And I've learned plenty since that night. I wager I could even manage to make those shadows of yours curl."

"Far from it." Zola sneered, sipping from her glass. "My fingers work just fine compared to what you may have ... *learned*."

"Oh, Zola!" Idris chided. "Okay. Enough! Gunnar, that one time with Zola is all you'll get, so stop praying to the Gods for more. How much have you had to drink anyway? Have you lost your mind already tonight?"

"Not yet." Gunnar laughed. "Sorry. Impossible things are happening as of late, so I thought I would try my hand," he replied, raising his brows in unison.

"A hand is all you'll get tonight," Zola said.

"Is that an offer?" Gunnar leaned forward, his dark brown eyes contrasting against the silver streaks of hair shimmering in the fire light.

Zola narrowed her eyes into a piercing glare, and I fought back the laughter bubbling up in my throat, feeling Daxton's deep chuckle rumble through his chest.

"Don't encourage him," Dax warned, "or this will continue for days. Gunnar likes to tease Zola, but sometimes, he pushes too far and ends up in the healers' quarters for his efforts."

"But they—"

"One night, centuries ago."

"So, they could ..."

"Never, according to Zola," Dax continued, "Gunnar likes a challenge, so he keeps pursuing her.

And apparently, from his account, it was one of the best nights he's ever had."

"Right." I nodded, glancing between the two of them. "They could make a good pairing."

Daxton shook his head, bending his knees and sitting up to grab a glass of wine. "Don't start trying to play matchmaker now, Skylar. We've spent hundreds of years together, and nothing has changed. They love each other like family and would kill for the other without hesitation, but a pairing? A relationship beyond what they have now would be a nightmare for all of us."

"And for those involved," Zola added, tilting her glass skyward before draining the contents.

"You just lack imagination," Gunnar said.

"Or you lack taste and the sense to treasure a fine wine rather than a cheap mug of mead at the local tavern," Adohan added with Idris giving him a loving look of approval.

"Whatever gets the job done." Gunnar grinned and emptied his glass, looking for the other bottle I brought.

"Where's Castor when we need him?" Daxton murmured, sipping his wine.

I watched the red liquid drip on his delicious lips, biting my own in response, unable to help imagining licking the remnants remaining in his mouth before tasting it on his tongue.

Daxton's eyes dipped to meet mine. "Careful, Spitfire."

I flashed him a smug grin, sucking in my bottom lip. "I don't always play by the rules." His throat bobbed and his throbbing length hardened against my backside. I moved my hips, letting him know I could feel his growing arousal.

"As soon as Idris is distracted, we're out of here," I said.

Daxton huffed a muffled laugh in reply.

"Castor would only add to this madness," Zola growled with an unamused scoff to the group, drawing our attention away from each other. "When he and Gunnar start going, there's no stopping them."

"True," Daxton answered before lowering his voice to whisper in my ear, "but then we would have a larger distraction that would allow us to slip away outside of Idris's time frame."

"I *heard* that," Idris snapped.

"I meant you to." Daxton laughed as he placed his hand on my thigh.

"All right let's play a little game," Gunnar said to the group. "Each person takes a turn and tells us two truths and a lie. The others around the circle must decipher and agree which ones are which, and if your lie is caught, you drink."

"Shit, I always lose at this," Idris cursed. "Glad I only have water in my cup tonight."

"I'm clearly at a disadvantage here," I told Daxton.

"You'll catch on quick. Don't worry."

"I'll start," Gunnar announced, "then Zola, Daxton, Skylar, and—"

"We know," Idris said. "Now on with it, Gunnar. This is your game, so you start."

"Very well … Hmm." He stroked his chin, contemplating which truths to tell and what lies to spin.

"But," Zola said with a hint of mischief in her tone, "it can't be one you've used before in this favorite little game of yours. If it is, you drink."

"Fuck. Really?"

"I second," Adohan announced. "And it's even more entertaining that Gunnar is going first."

"Gods above," Gunnar cursed, "this game just got more complicated."

"Third," I answered, surprising everyone in the room. "What?" I shrugged. "Gunnar has been royally kicking my ass for a solid month now. I'm loving this turn of events and seeing him grimace for once."

"And just when I thought we were becoming friends, little shifter."

"It's settled," Daxton said to the group. "New rules are set ... Gunnar, let your games begin." Dax hugged me, stroking my arm lightly with his fingers. "Very amusing, love. We shall see if you or I actually earn a turn at this before the hour is up."

"All right," Gunnar said. "One night along the docks, I managed to have my way with a—"

"A water nymph on the shoreline," everyone but me finished for him.

"Drink up." Daxton chuckled lowly with an amused grin.

"*Shit*," Gunnar swore before taking a sip.

"Will I ever have a turn?" I whispered to Daxton.

"Perhaps not. I'm doubtful I'll even have a turn with how many times Gunnar's played this over the years and spun various tactful lies."

"He and Castor must always play this," I added.

"Hmm, it appears I've arrived just in time." The familiar sing-song voice broke the commotion of the group. All eyes turned toward the silver-haired figure in the hallway.

"Castor!" Gunnar sprang to his feet, welcoming his friend and prince with open arms.

Zola gave him a nod from the shadows, which was friendly by her standards. Castor then entered the room, bent to kiss Idris's hand, and clasped Adohan's forearm with an affectionate pat on the shoulder. Daxton remained relaxed, his hold on me unchanged, almost like he was waiting for something the rest of us were not seeing.

"Cas," Daxton's voice was low, "I'm glad you have safely returned. Were you able to find the entrance to the second trial?"

"That and fucking more." Castor's eyes scanned the room, finding a bottle of wine and eagerly pouring himself a glass. "I went in ..." he added before draining the contents the next second. "Damn. You got the good stuff out, brother. And without me? I'm slightly offended."

"Castor," Daxton pushed, my anxiety beginning to rise.

"I see things have become a bit cozier here since my departure." Castor raised his brows, looking at the two of us. "Smelled it once I entered the godsdamn Summit, Dax. You're not hiding much anymore, are you?" His eyes shot back and forth between us. "Does this mean I'm out of a job pretending to be in love with your mate then?"

"Gods. Please, yes," I answered for Daxton, who gave me a soft half-smile before his gaze traveled back to his brother.

"Ouch," Castor answered. "You could've hesitated just a little bit to save my pride."

"What did you discover, Castor?" Daxton asked. "Did you encounter the creature?"

Daxton's fingers found mine, and I squeezed them tightly. I wouldn't allow my fears to break through—not here, not in front of the others.

"Thank the Gods, no … I didn't encounter the creature with death's stare, hence why I'm still breathing and able to grace you with my glorious presence. I know you've missed me." Castor waved his arm in a dramatic display. "But," he said, his tone shifting, "I did bring other means to help us answer the question of what Skylar will be facing."

Daxton's attention snapped to the hallway. "She's here?"

"Who?" I asked him.

Daxton's lips pressed into a thin line. "Nyssa."

My stomach jumped into my throat as I stood. Daxton moved in time with me as I rushed to the hall's opening.

Since healing the fallen fae, I had dreamed of seeing her again, talking with her, and learning anything about her I could. She was a Gods above blessing that I somehow had healed. Questions swirled in my mind, ranging from her own experiences to what she felt now.

"Hi," I said softly, seeing her standing in the center of the hall just outside the doorway.

Castor walked past Daxton and me while the others remained inside. I had a feeling that if we all jumped up and ambushed her, it would not go well. Castor stood beside Nyssa, offering a warm, kind smile and gently placing a hand on her shoulder, inclining his head to encourage her forward.

"Nyssa signs to communicate," Castor said, "but she can understand the spoken word. When I returned, I went to the archives first, and to my surprise, she was waiting there for me." Castor's eyes were fixated on Nyssa, his attention unwavering. "She asked to come see you."

"I can interpret for you, Spitfire," Daxton told me, and I nodded in agreement.

"Do you have something for me? Is there something you wanted to tell me?" I asked aloud, searching Nyssa's face for any indication of what this sudden meeting was about.

Her golden-undertone peach skin looked soft and utterly flawless, even beneath the plain tan robes of the scribes. Her beauty was breathtaking. Dark, slanted eyes were framed by a delicate oval face, paired with midnight-black hair that cascaded down the length of her back.

She looked at me after handing a scroll to Castor with her hands raised to her chest. Daxton spoke the words as she began signing.

"I've been working with Idris and Adohan to try to help decipher your second trial, and I believe I have found the answer," she signed, her dark eyes soft, yet her expression remained focused.

My eyes widened with surprise. I could not speak … My mouth was suddenly dry, and my throat cracked. Nyssa stepped forward, extending her hand toward me, causing Daxton to tense at my side.

"Let her touch you," Castor pleaded. "I promise Skylar is safe, Daxton. Nyssa would never hurt the one who saved her."

"It's all right," I told Dax. My animal was giving me a comforting feeling, indicating that I was safe. "I trust her." I knew his curt nod was all I was going to get.

Nyssa reached out her hand to touch my cheek, and as soon as she did, I was whisked away in a vision.

Cold, wet stone surrounded me, and I was no longer standing beside Daxton in the Summit. Darkness enveloped the area with the feeling of death itself curling into the air I breathed.

I blinked as talons clinked against the stone, echoing through the narrowed passageway. "*Clink, Clink … Hiss.*" My head turned abruptly, and I saw the long tail of a serpent-like creature escape down the cavern.

The next thing I heard was a muffled scream of death … and then it was silent once more. The hissing sound crept into my senses, making my insides tighten, followed by a large gulping noise. My body moved forward, gliding around the corner to inspect the disturbance, and that is when I saw it.

The creature was slender with dark green, almost black scales along its back and a lighter shade of green on its underbelly. It was massive, stretching approximately fifty feet in length with four small legs supporting its body that held long black talons of death. It reminded me of a land-bound dragon. The massive head, which had a white crest in the middle, tilted backward as it swallowed its prey whole.

The creature finished its meal and moved toward the tunnel. Its eyes were tilted downward as its body slithered like a snake yet still crawled resembling a lizard over the stone. When it opened its mouth, I saw rows upon rows of razor-sharp teeth half my size, curved inward. Perfect for gripping and killing before devouring its meal.

Suddenly, its head snapped in my direction. Massive yellow eyes glowed in the dark cave with magic swirling within them. Haunting and utterly terrifying.

The power of its stare hit me like a brick wall. The air around me was heavy, but I wasn't breathing. I didn't *feel* anything.

Gods above. I was seeing Nyssa's memory as a fallen.

The creature's long tongue slithered out of its jagged rows of teeth, smelling—no, tasting—the air around me. It recoiled immediately, rolling its head and hissing violently in my face. Yet it didn't attack. It simply slithered away into a different tunnel.

The connection severed, and I gasped aloud, trembling as my legs gave way in fear. Daxton caught me before I hit the ground—his hold on me was steady against my quivering limbs. His touch was gentle, but that was where his kindness ended.

Ice exploded around us in a protective barrier, forcing Nyssa back on the ground with sharpened points hovering against her exposed throat. "Move, and I'll kill you."

"Daxton, stop!" Castor shouted, blasting out his own magic to combat his brother's. Castor couldn't summon ice, but he could manipulate it. He protectively threw himself over Nyssa, pushing back against Daxton's ice daggers as best he could.

"I mean it!" Blackness engulfed Castor's eyes, and my heart dropped.

"I'm all right. I'm all right," I told my mate.

"Bullshit," Daxton cursed.

"Dax." I scowled at him and forced myself to stand on my feet. "She showed me a vision. That's all, I swear."

"Try again," Castor sneered, baring his teeth. "It was a fucking memory. *Her* memory." The brothers stared each other down, neither one giving an inch. "Stand down, Daxton. Don't push me on this." The look on Castor's face matched Daxton's. Two brothers at a standoff, ready to clash in the center of chaos.

Fire erupted in the halls, melting the ice directed at Castor and Nyssa. "Enough!" Adohan boomed. "Must I be the voice of reason with you two? Gods above, you never make a visit uneventful."

"I'm all right," I told Daxton again, but his eyes were stone. I reached out to cup his cheek to try and bring him back to me.

Thankfully, he dropped his stare and tucked me into his side, his arms folding me into his frame as his hands gripped me with as much strength as he could muster. "What did you see?"

"I saw …" I could barely form the words. "I saw the creature I have to defeat for the second trial." My grip on my mate tightened, trying to extract every ounce of courage I could. Absorbing it like a dry sponge. "It's … It's—"

"It's a basilisk," Castor finished for me, with Nyssa tucked protectively behind his back. "Dax, she has to slay a basilisk."

Chapter Twenty-Four

"You're ready for tomorrow," Daxton whispered against my ear. "I'm confident we'll share endless nights together, just like this one, for many years to come." His arms encircled me as his kisses traveled along the nook of my neck, down to my shoulder.

We had just finished making love, and still, I wanted him again. The feel of his touch was invigorating. Our love bridging our connection despite the missing threads of the unsealed bond. A powerful yet deadly weapon of the heart that could heal or destroy the world.

"You should be resting," I said in a whispered hush.

"It's *you* who should be resting," he countered, his fingers seductively caressing the curves of my hips, leaving goosebumps in their wake. "Yet I find our bed empty with you standing naked in the moonlight. I'm entering the second trial with you, but I'm not the one tasked with slaying the basilisk."

Two weeks had passed since the night Nyssa showed me her memory, revealing the identity of the beast I had to defeat in the second trial.

It turned out the wilt had granted Nyssa a magical gift after all. Zola could jump through shadows, and Nyssa could share her thoughts and memories through her touch.

Nyssa encountered this creature while still a nalusa falaya, so she was already, in a sense, deceased. The basilisk's stare could not kill what was already dead.

"I'm still not sold on the idea of you going in there with me," I said. "Dax, it's not safe."

"I believe I've already won this argument two weeks ago."

"That doesn't mean I'm happy about it."

"I'm shocked."

"Prick," I muttered under my breath.

"I heard that."

"I meant you to." I couldn't help biting my lip as Daxton nuzzled into me with a deep chuckle in his throat.

After Adohan helped simmer the tension between the two brothers, Dax and I went to our room to discuss our options and begin formulating a plan. Castor's ability to enter the lair gave way to new ideas that Daxton was keen on fulfilling, which, to my dismay, involved him entering the second trial with me.

To say I was upset would not do my disposition justice. It was one of our biggest disagreements yet, and judging by how stubborn we both were, it wouldn't be our last. I was against it from the moment he suggested the idea, refusing to allow him to put himself in that kind of danger. But Daxton remained calm, his patience winning me over and helping settle my raging fury.

He ended up using logic and our mate bond against me, saying, "If the roles were reversed, would you idly stand by as I faced this threat alone?"

"Of course I wouldn't!" I told him. He knew I would charge in with him regardless of the threat against my own life. *Bastard.*

"Where you go, I go." Daxton said as he wrapped his arms around me. So sure, like there was no other option. "The key showed Castor the doorway just like we thought, and he passed through the entrance unharmed. The riddle for the second trial didn't limit it to only the champion being allowed to enter like the first."

"Or else you would've entered the labyrinth with me?" I challenged.

"You know I would," Daxton answered firmly. "Do you really want to waste our time together asking me ridiculous questions you already know the answers to?"

His hands lightly cupped my exposed breasts, causing me to moan, before curling down my front and resting comfortably on my waist. Chills ran through me. My arousal built once again despite being fully sated only an hour ago.

"I can think of more useful things to do if you refuse to sleep."

"We could always put in a few more hours of training," I teased. "Should I call for Gunnar to meet us at the training fields?"

"Tonight, you selfishly belong only to me," Daxton said. "I will not be sharing you." The gravelly sound in his voice crept over me like an erotic caress. "Besides, our fighting techniques have synced like we've been training together for years. We move like one being, Spitfire."

Daxton and I had spent countless hours training together over the last weeks. Since we no longer needed to research the identity of the creature, we focused on how to defend and fight against it as one.

It took a lot of missteps, of course. I lost count of how many times my bow was knocked out of my hands, I stepped on his foot, or I nearly stabbed him. Thank the Gods above that he was fast. On the third day, things started to click into place. And then, by the next week, we were no longer clumsily colliding and fighting like two separate entities. Instead, we flowed together like a deadly current in the ocean.

Castor crafted maps of the area and instructed us on narrow caves and passageways along the cliffside where the basilisk lived.

With Daxton joining me, we had to learn each other's fighting styles and how to work flawlessly together in small quarters. I was in awe of Daxton's exceptional fighting skills, realizing that his magic effortlessly supported his brute strength and speed, hiding in plain sight. His power flowed through him in each attack, blending into these movements like a perfectly choreographed dance.

Although my Silver Shadow had little to no weakness in his technique, understanding each other's vulnerabilities helped formulate a solid front to combat any foe—even a mythical serpent king with a death stare.

Moving closer behind me, I felt Daxton's length hardening against my backside.

"Ready again, are we?" My heart began thundering with anticipation.

"It never seems to stop when you're near." His chuckle of amusement vibrated low in his throat. "This *need* to have you is all-consuming." He kissed my neck, nibbling at my heated flesh. "You're not complaining, are you?"

"Wouldn't dare," I rasped, reaching up and behind me to pull his delicious mouth to mine.

I savored the way he tasted, opening my lips to allow him to slide his tongue inside with ease. I moved my hips back, threading his erection into the line of my ass and stroking his inner thigh with my other hand. He moaned into my mouth, making my center throb with need.

"In that case …"

Daxton moved so fast that I barely had time to react. His grip tightened around my waist as a blast of cold air rushed in, the doors to the balcony swinging open as he carried me out toward the railing.

"Bend over," he growled, "and don't muffle your moans. I want all of Silver Meadows to know who you belong to." The dark edge to his voice sent a thrilling rush through my center.

"Yes, *Princey*." I moaned as he spread my legs and pushed my palms onto the stone railing, gripping both in one of his massive hands.

"Hold tight," he instructed as I wrapped my fingers around the stone, preparing myself for whatever he had planned next. "Very good, my *queen*," he said as he moved to kneel behind me, running his fingers through my slickened folds. "You're ready for me. Fucking perfect as always."

The anticipation was killing me. At the very least, I needed to feel his lips finish what his fingers had started. Damn—correction, I needed all of him.

His tongue ran through me as I gasped aloud, my body trembling in response.

Daxton paused and leaned to whisper in my ear, "Since I've held my title, I've never *willingly* submitted myself or kneeled before another aside from you." I stilled at his confession, the world itself ceasing to move.

"*You* are my true queen, Skylar Cathal. I'll shatter the world on your command alone."

I turned to look at the male who held my heart—who tethered my very soul to this life and the next. Words could not accurately express the love and devotion shining in his eyes, and I knew … I knew he would take on the world for me.

I kissed him, laying my soul bare, giving him every piece of me. "I need you—now."

Daxton grabbed my hips between his strong hands, and in one thrust, he buried his perfect cock deep inside me.

"Gods! Yes, Daxton!" I screamed over the balcony into the chilling night air, meeting his thrusts in rolling waves of pleasure that made the strength in my limbs disappear as he filled me from behind.

He remained buried inside me, wrapping my hair around his wrist and pulling me upright. "We were made for each other, Skylar. I'll never stop wanting to have you like this."

He slowly pulled out before powerfully thrusting back in once more. His balls were slick from my arousal, and our combined releases from earlier that night. They brushed against my clit each time his hilt slammed into me, giving me a welcomed friction that enhanced the pleasure building in my core.

My inner walls tightened as another blissful orgasm threatened to break free, and I wanted … No, I needed to feel him come with me. I reached down between my legs, fondling his balls with my fingers and giving them a slight tug as he jerked his hips forward.

"Fuck," he moaned.

"You like it when I touch them?"

"Yes," he breathed, quickening his pace.

I continued holding them, happily stroking my sex in tune with his hard thrusts with waves of heat coursing through us both. I could feel his sack tighten as he continued to fuck me within an inch of my release.

"I'm close," I rasped.

"I know." He pushed me forward, bending over to grab my breasts as he pounded harder into my dripping-wet center.

"Gods! Yes, just like that … Yes!" I screamed. He shifted forward to slide his mouth down to the base of my neck, thrusting deep inside me. "Daxton!" I wailed as my orgasm spiraled through me.

Daxton moaned in response, his legs trembling as he emptied himself for the second time tonight. Thank the Gods he was taking the monthly aid.

"I don't want to move, or more accurately, I don't know if I can." I leaned over the railing, my face flushed from my climax and my skin warm from his touch.

Daxton hadn't yet marked my neck with his bite. He had asked me if I wanted him to claim me, following our shifter customs, but I didn't want him to until I was able to reciprocate. Until the trials were over and our bond was sealed.

"Come with me," he said, his breath still labored. "I want to show you something."

"All right," I answered, immediately intrigued as we strode from the balcony.

"And I need to find some clothes. My blood isn't as thick as yours. Without your gorgeous body keeping me warm, the winter chill will likely freeze my balls off."

"I wasn't the one who carried us out here onto the open balcony," I teased, unaffected by the cold sting of night air thanks to my shifter half. "Don't you command ice magic?"

"I don't routinely freeze myself." He smirked, his mouth spreading into a wide smile. "Well, actually, there was one occasion."

"When?" I asked, crossing the threshold of the doorway to pull a night slip over my head.

"That morning in the bathhouse."

"In Solace?"

Daxton reached for his pants, pulling them up and over his muscular thighs before securing them loosely around his waist. "How else do you think I managed to stay on the other side of that hut while you were very naked … and very wet in the bath across from me? I froze my ass to the bench so I wouldn't take you right then and there."

"Maybe you should've," I said with a dangerous look.

"Careful, Spitfire." His gray eyes darkened like storm clouds, ready to unleash themselves in a raging downpour.

"What about no peeking?" I scolded him, arms crossed in front of me. "You peeked, didn't you?"

His saccharine smile grew wide, the dimple on his right cheek visible even in the dim light. "Never."

"Daxton!"

"All right, all right …" His laughter was deep and pure, one of the most beautiful sounds I would hear in this lifetime. "I might've stolen a glance of that perfect ass sliding underneath the surface of the water," he said as he pulled me in close, placing his hands firmly on my backside.

"Might?" I challenged him.

He squeezed harder, attempting to make his point. "All right, I did."

I scoffed and rolled my eyes, my arms crossed under my chest, purposely pushing my breasts upward just to tease him. "And here I thought you had such high moral standards. That my mate was a true gentleman." His smile practically reached his ears, and I knew it was in response to me calling him *my mate*. I would be lying if I didn't feel the same every time he said it as well.

"You and I both know you'd never settle for a vanilla mate who always stuck to the rules and never challenged what they thought was right. That is mundane, my love. You and I were never meant to live meek and uneventful lives."

I was about to argue, but then again, we both knew he was right. "Fine, point taken, *High Prince of Silver Meadows.*"

"Forgive me for peeking yet?"

"No." He frowned slightly. "But …" I paused. "I do have some ideas on how you can make it up to me."

His smile returned as he bent closer to my lips. "Gladly."

He stopped with our lips breaths apart, but neither of us moved forward. "Weren't you about to kiss me?"

"Weren't you about to forgive me?"

I cocked an eyebrow at him. "Are you withholding your kisses until I do?"

"Maybe."

"You won't last long."

"Is that a challenge, Spitfire?"

"Yes," I said with a smirk.

Daxton released his hold and silently stepped backward. His expression was unreadable, and his demeanor mimicked one I had seen on the sparring fields and in the midst of battle.

"Challenge accepted," Silver Shadow replied. "We'll see who caves first." He looked at me with cold, calculating eyes that mimicked raging mountain storms.

Fuck. I gulped, barely able to keep myself from spreading my thighs and begging for him to take me again. His smoldering stare of menace only managed to turn me on all over again. He would never intimidate or frighten me. I knew him. I loved every part of who he was and apparently was even aroused by the deathly terrifying Silver Shadow facade dictated in the history books of Solace.

"Fine," I groaned with a glare, knowing he could sense my arousal. "Wasn't there something you wanted to show me?" I asked with my own blast of power fueled by my animal, my eyes glowing like amber fire.

I watched his eyes flare, knowing he could feel my magic skittering across his taut flesh, feeling the same exhilarating and arousing caress I experienced when his power reached out to find me. It put us in a sort of fight or flight. Well, no, more accurately, a fuck mood. The adrenaline rush was overwhelming, followed by intense, lustful waves of pure desire.

"Don't look at me with those eyes, Spitfire."

"What eyes?"

He narrowed his gaze at me, his muscles flexing across his chest and arms as he fought to keep them pinned at his sides. "Like you're hungry and already waiting for me to fill you for a third time tonight."

"Maybe I am." He went utterly still, every ounce of self-control teetering on the edge. "But alas, you're withholding your kisses until I forgive you for peeking. And I have ideas in mind for you to earn your way back from that." I licked my bottom lip, sucking on it for a moment, never letting my eyes wander from his. "Your move, Princey."

"You're a cunningly wicked female ... who most certainly does not play by the rules."

"We both knew that."

He chuckled a dark laugh, reaching up to untie his hair and adjusting his pants lower on his hips.

"Who's being unfair now?" I scoffed, taking in his fucking delicious body for everything it was worth. My arousal sparked as I drank in the sight of him. The Gods themselves could not have made a more perfect male body. He was so handsome it was a crime.

"Over here." He inclined his head, leading me to the far corner. "This is what I wanted to show you."

Waving his hand, the illusion of the wall melted away, revealing a hidden cubby with a pure white stone the size of a small pebble nestled in the middle of a jet-black velvet pillow. I stepped closer, mesmerized by the beautiful swirls of silver etched along the edges, with glittering specks dancing along the surface. It was small, able to fit in the palm of my hand, yet I could feel the strong magic swirling around it.

"What is it, Dax?"

"A very rare trinket, a memory stone. This was my mother's most prized possession, aside from the silver bow that you now carry."

I remember when he first gifted me the silver bow and *then* told me its significance to him and his family. At first, I tried to refuse the gift, but it kept appearing in our training sessions. And I had to admit, no other bows could compare. Its strength, flexibility, and weight were perfect.

"I can't believe you let me use it when we first arrived in the Inner Kingdom without telling me it belonged to your mother," I said. "Castor's surprised look makes so much more sense now."

"He understood the reason why I gave it to you."

"*He* did. And apparently, everyone else in your inner circle besides me."

I learned that Daxton confessed the mate bond to Castor the first night after I snuck into the alpha's house to heal him. Later, when we arrived in Crimson City, he told Adohan, Idris, and finally Zola.

Gunnar admitted he didn't need to be told. "The way he looked at you without you ever noticing told me everything," Gunnar said. "It was obvious that Daxton had fallen in love with you before ever bringing you to Silver Meadows."

I was shocked at the depth of Gunnar's confession, and when I told him just that, he scoffed at me despite my apology and grudgingly sulked for a few days.

"We used to have four memory stones," Dax continued. "But when my parents died, and through the war, three of them disappeared."

"I'm so sorry to hear that, Dax." He shrugged nonchalantly, accepting my sympathy but not dwelling on it. "What do they do exactly?"

"They're magical stones that hold memories. If you offer one worthy enough to the stone, it will grant you access to the memories stored within. Ironically, the smaller the stone, the more powerful it is and the more memories it can hold."

"Interesting," I said, tilting my head to inspect it further. "Have you offered a memory to this stone?"

"A small handful through the centuries, yes. One more recently," Daxton admitted, standing behind me and watching me admire the stone.

"Which one?" I asked, my curiosity spinning, desperate to know which memory he would offer to this precious stone to be kept for all eternity. "The bathhouse?" I teased.

He merely chuckled in response.

"When I emerged victorious from the first trial? The first night we met when I almost killed you?" I asked.

"Those are excellent guesses, but no." His outstretched hand gently cradled the stone. "I believe you'll have to offer one to see it," he answered with a cunning smile.

Grasping the stone, I knew which one I would choose. I willed myself to sink back into one of the darkest times of my mortal life to a moment when I was sure it was over.

"May I see it with you?" Daxton asked.

I nodded. "You're the only one I would ever dare to share this with."

I allowed my mind to wander into darkness— into the place I swore I would never return.

I was in Blade's torture chamber after he struck me with his iron-tipped whip. Diving into this memory was almost harder than living it. I remembered how alone I felt. The pain muffled to a dull ache that covered every inch of my body. I was in so much agony I almost didn't register the feeling anymore.

But the worst was realizing that the fight to stay alive was fading. That was the most terrifying piece of all. At that moment, I no longer wanted to breathe. I no longer wanted to live. I had given up, and death's door was opening.

And then, I heard a call.

A familiar melody that sang to my soul, forcing my primal instinct to emerge and willing me to fight against death's pull, convincing me to come back to the world of the living. It was him. His magic, his essence, raced through the abyss of darkness to find me. Daxton was my salvation, calling me back from death's crossing.

"I should have known then," I said as we returned, holding back my tears. "I should've recognized the bond right then and there. *You* found me. You brought me back. I couldn't turn away when it was *you* calling me home."

Daxton's brow pressed against mine, his arms scooping me into his embrace that chased away my fears. "The power you mustered to come back was not mine alone. That beautiful strength came from within you, Skylar." He stilled, holding me tight. "I'm the luckiest fucking male in existence that you're my mate, and deeply honored that I'm yours."

We held each other in silence, simply basking in the presence of each other's company and treasuring the time we had.

"I believe you'll now be able to access my memory."

"How?"

"How else do you get something you want?" Dax teased. "Simply ask. And it does help to say *please*." I chuckled, following his directions, asking the stone to reveal Daxton's most recent memory.

In a rush of magic, I was jetted through time, standing outside the outskirts of the meadow in my home of Solace ... but in a body that was not mine. I was in Daxton's. The meadow seemed so peaceful, yet inside, my heart was racing. My anxiety was spinning so high that I thought I would snap in two.

My sharpened eyes scanned the moonlit meadow. Shifters were changing into their animal forms left and right, but my focus was on ... well, me.

As Dax, I watched myself fall forward into the tall grass, and it looked like my skin was crawling with sparks of fire shooting beneath my flesh. Panic and dread coursed through Daxton—a desperate need to help alleviate the pain he was witnessing overwhelmed all sense of logic. Something had to be done ...

Yet I sensed him hesitate, thinking. Stopping the shift meant I would be among the few who could be chosen for the trials.

As Dax, I heard my scream, and the sound of it vibrated across every bone of my body. The pain morphed into my own. The bond, although muffled, was guiding Daxton to help me. Instinct drove him to release his magic to help counter the pull of the shift that was tearing his mate apart.

Castor's frightened stare bore into his brother. "Dax," he warned.

"I have to," Daxton growled, watching my glowing skin dim as a deep sigh of relief washed through him.

"That was not wise, brother. She'll know."

"It's unsealed. Minaeve will never suspect anything until I allow her to."

Then the presence of Gilen's roc stole the crowd's attention, and as Daxton, I watched as Minaeve made her way through the meadow, eventually stopping at Neera and declaring her the champion. Dread coated Daxton's beating heart. Even he knew this young, gentle shifter would not survive the trials.

"What the actual fuck is she thinking?" I growled as Daxton.

"You presume she actually thinks before she acts. Cute," Castor snickered.

Then, an all too familiar voice rang out from the crowd, making the world stop. "Take me! I will compete in the trials. I will travel to the Inner Kingdom and unlock the Heart of Valdor."

"Has your female lost her mind?" Castor mumbled.

Daxton's eyes never left me as a warm sensation coursed through his chest. A sense of awe and amazement shocked him to his core. Hope. There was a reason to hope again. "She's the one. She will defeat the trials."

"Has your muffled mate bond made you mad?"

"No, it has made me hope." His voice, my voice, was deathly calm. "She's the spark of something greater ... a belief that a different life is possible. She's the key."

The memory suddenly faded, bringing us both back into the present.

"It was the first time I knew I was falling in love with you," Daxton said with admiration and passion shining deep within his eyes. "You held my heart long before I believe you even knew it existed," he teased.

I looped my arms around his neck. "I knew it was there—just guarded in a gilded cage. Forced to harden into stone. Do you remember my ramblings about geodes in my letters?"

"Fondly."

"*You're* my geode." I sighed, running my hand through his silver and ebony strands. "Hard and bitter on the outside but breathtakingly beautiful on the inside. It just took time and patience to break you open."

His grin stretched across his face as he held me close. "I love you, my Spitfire."

"I love you, Dax."

"Forgive me yet?" he asked with a raised brow.

I smile sweetly. "How could I not when you share *that* memory with me? You've tied my hands."

"Well, I didn't intend to tonight, but in the future, if you'd like to try it … I'm all in."

"Dax!" I thumped him in the back of his head. "Seriously?"

"You're the one who brought it up."

"I'm beginning to regret forgiving you so easily."

"Then allow me to remind you why you did."

His mouth crashed into mine, feverishly devouring me with the sweet taste of his lips and his well-skilled tongue. I moaned into his kiss, pleasure rolling through me in delicious waves of ecstasy that made my body come alive again.

Dammit, he was right. I was glad I forgave him because this was worth it. He was worth *everything*.

Chapter Twenty-Five

When we rematerialized atop the Southern Cliff face, the chill of the ocean breeze against my skin was refreshing yet terrifying. We were finally here. The outcome of the second trial would be decided today.

Daxton stood beside me, his silver-lined black armor gleaming in the early rays of dawn, with three mountain peaks visible on his broad shoulder. His hair was pulled back as his gray eyes hardened, determination setting in for our task ahead. He looked just as formidable as the fables depicted him, and I was thankful, if not slightly infuriated, to have him at my side.

"Didn't forget the key, did you?" His half-hearted attempt at a joke was oddly comforting.

"I've got it," I said, pulling at the chain around my neck. The sun-moon key rested against my chest.

He nodded, magically summoning his sword, Valencia, to his back. I tucked the key safely under my armor, my own single mountain patch stitched into my clothing underneath. Again, I wore the armor of Aegis to help protect me in the trial. I only wished it could protect Daxton, too.

This trial could kill him just as easily as it could me. But if the roles were reversed, I knew I would be standing here with him if I could. I squared my shoulders, inhaling the familiar sea air as I readied myself.

"You lead, Spitfire. I'll follow." He looked at me with an unwavering swell of confidence embedded into each line of his face. "You've got this. Remember I'm simply along for the ride to witness history in the making."

I nervously reached up to push my long braid over my shoulder and unstrapped my silver wooden bow, nocking an arrow along the tight string. The feel of the bow in my hands fed me a calming sense of strength and security, steadying my racing heart to an even rhythm that matched my breathing. This was it. Our months of training had led to this. I would come out alive and victorious or dead.

"You ready?" I asked.

"If you are."

I nodded. "Let's go." I climbed steadily down the black volcanic rocks along the top of the cliff, with Daxton in step behind me.

According to Castor, the arched formation of lighter stone glowed brighter the closer the key was to its entrance. "Like calling to like," he said. "The key to the first trial recognizes its counterpart."

It made sense.

Traversing down the cliff face was simple enough—a mindless task after training on top of mountain ridgelines and preparing for the Gauntlet. The rock face cascaded in a simple pattern, creating steps that we easily scaled down.

Ocean waves crashed against the rocks below, the spray slowing our descent as the slickened stone held little to no grip. The colorful orange and yellow rays of the morning sunlight bounced against the smooth surface of the volcanic rocks, shielding the entrance of the trial in shadow.

"High tide must cover half if not the entire entrance," I said.

"That's what Castor's intel suggested. I imagine that's how the serpent king can devour his ocean prey. They venture unknowingly into the caves and are trapped."

As we reached what we believed to be the final ledge, I pulled out a small handheld mirror from my pocket. Holding out the front of my bow, I moved it to the top wooden arch, waiting for Daxton to seal it in place with his ice magic.

"How does the balance feel?" he asked.

I straightened my left arm and lightly pulled back on my bow string, carefully bringing it back to rest. "Perfect. Just like we practiced."

My archery skills were put to the test during our final bouts of training. We practiced with a mirror attached to the tip of my bow, allowing me to scan the area in the reflection behind me to find my target before spinning around with my eyes closed. The first few attempts were a joke, but I wasn't allowed to quit—nor would I.

Eventually, I figured out how to execute my blind shot. Daxton ended up crafting a small shard of mirrored glass molded into the horizontal hilt of a dagger strapped to his hip.

The archway of rocks was striking, contrasting beautifully with the surrounding Southern Sea Cliffs and framing a fifteen-foot-wide opening hidden from the viewpoint atop the cliffs. As we approached the entrance, the key on my chest seemed to hum with power, and a dark veil lifted, allowing me to gaze inside the cavern.

"Can you see inside?" Daxton asked.

"Of course," I countered. "You can't?"

He laughed despite himself. "High Fae cannot see in the dark, my love."

I almost forgot he couldn't. After having the ability to see in the dark since I was a child, it was practically second nature.

"Well, that means you can keep your eyes closed. That increases your odds of getting out of here alive."

During our training, Daxton had been working on relying on his other senses while fighting, often sparring with Castor and Gunnar with a blindfold covering his face.

"Our odds," he corrected. "Remember, where you go, I go."

"I remember." I smiled, reaching for the small rope at my hip and tying it around our waists. "Don't wander."

"Never," he answered, but the look in his eyes was not as convincing.

As we stepped inside the entrance, Daxton paused. "What is it?" I whispered.

"The entrance is warded with ancient, powerful magic. I can't teleport us out, only within."

"Good to know," I replied, understanding we had no immediate escape route. "Let's keep moving. Castor said he only lingered in the entrance and down the first turn. Through my research on snakes, I know they have a den in the middle of their tunnel system, which should be larger than the passageways."

"Ever the clever student, Spitfire," he said with pride. "Keep your shield up and guard your scent. We might have the element of surprise if we can enter the den undetected."

I nodded as we crept through the tunnel, the hairs on my neck standing straight as we lost the final rays of sunlight from the mouth of the arched entrance. My animal was on high alert, and instinct drove me to utilize all my senses to try and safely navigate us through. I couldn't quite place the looming threat that felt like a shadow following us, but I knew it was there. Lurking and waiting for the perfect time to strike.

Silently, we walked through the underground maze. Daxton's footsteps were soft, following in perfect sync with mine only a few paces behind. The echoes of dripping water from the various crevasses and overhangs combined with the ocean's crashing waves were the only sounds in the cave. It created a disturbing melody, paired with the growing stench of decay and death the further we crept into the caves. Everything about this place screamed to turn around and run away, but still, we continued.

Rocks to our left buckled and broke away from the surrounding wall, causing us to halt and draw our weapons toward the invisible threat. *Silence.* Nothing.

"The saltwater must weaken the structure of the cave," I whispered. "I don't think anything is there. I don't smell or see anything."

Daxton remained utterly still. Not even his chest rose and fell with his silent breathing. His eyes were useless this far into the creature's lair, relying solely on my touch and his keen hearing.

"Or something was there and is no longer."

"That area isn't large enough to house the basilisk," I countered.

"You sure?"

No, I wasn't, but that didn't mean I had to say it aloud. "The air seems warmer than before. Doesn't it?"

"It does," Daxton said, feeling his hand along the basalt rock wall before leaning his back against it. "Does that help us navigate this tunnel of death?"

"In a sense," I answered, reaching for my canteen before handing it to him. "The basilisk is a *serpent* king. So, I imagine he has similar physical needs or traits as any other normal reptile."

"Meaning?" he asked, taking a sip.

"They are cold-blooded creatures."

"Don't let him hear you say that. We don't know if he will take that as an insult or compliment." I rolled my eyes at Daxton, giving him a stern look. "I can't see you, but I know exactly what face you're making right now."

"This isn't the time for a joke," I said.

"If you stop to think about how insane we must be to be in here … it's appropriate."

"I should've brought Castor with me," I said.

I watched his expression drop as he handed me back the canteen. "All right, continue."

"Cold-blooded animals can't generate their own body heat needed to survive," I said.

"So we're following the warming draft of hot air to find its nesting area."

"Yes, exactly."

He paused for a moment, and I could see his mind feverishly working through different scenarios. "The Inner Kingdom once had an active volcano erupting in this area, but that was thousands of years ago."

I smiled widely. "Is there still an active volcano here on the landmass?" He nodded. "Then there may be an ancient magma lake or chamber buried underground helping keep the basilisk alive."

"So literally," Dax sighed, "this creature's den is likely dangling over a fiery pit of molten rock."

"Yep."

"We truly are in hell." Daxton shook his head slightly, laughing to himself. "Only for you, Spitfire, would I willingly drag myself through the fires of death."

"Good thing we're in this together then," I added with a smile he couldn't see, but I knew he could hear. I grasped his hand tightly. "Let's just make sure we don't stay here."

"Agreed," he answered, squeezing my hand in return.

Deeper into the passageways, the evidence of a basilisk dwelling in this place became more and more evident. There were sheds of molted skin, piles of bones from devoured prey, and deep claw marks along the stone. He was here all right. It just worried me that we didn't know where. Daxton and I had been walking for hours and still hadn't heard or seen anything.

There you are, a slithering snake-like voice echoed in my ears.

My heart froze as my hands immediately had my bow at the ready. My eyes locked onto the small mirror secured at the front.

"Did you hear that?" I asked.

"I heard a low hissing sound. What did you hear?"

The other is not a ssshhifter. He cannot hear my wordsss asss you can. But he doesss sssmell delightful. He even carriesss a twist of your sssscent assss well.

"It found us." I decided not to relay the exact words. Daxton was immediately at my back, Valencia drawn and ready to strike with his dagger in his other hand.

"You can understand it, can't you?"

"Sadly, yes …"

It isss a gift to hear my radiant voice.

"It's not shy," I whispered, "nor lacking in vanity."

I've been watching you both sssince you entered my lair. The sssecond trial hassss officially commenced.

"Why not show yourself?" I yelled into the abyss of the cave.

I wassss never taught table mannersss, having devoured my siblings and then my mother when I wassss large enough to do so. Besssidesss, I enjoy playing with my food.

"Fan-fucking-tastic," I murmured.

"Do I even want to know what it's saying?" Daxton asked.

"No. Let's keep moving."

We stepped forward, following the increasing temperature in the air and the feel of the rock walls as our guide. Every few feet, something slithered with the all too familiar tapping sound of talons on rocks. The memory from Nyssa made me shudder, along with the all too recent encounter with the beasts from the labyrinth. A feeling of helplessness washed over me, and I couldn't help the sting of panic that crept up my spine despite my animal's power surging through me.

Daxton's hand gripped my shoulder. "You all right?"

His touch helped bring me back. "Yeah, I'm good."

I was angry at myself for allowing a memory to have such a hold on me like that. I was never going to stop fighting. Too many people relied on me. Not only was my mate's fate now tied to my victory today, but the fate of his home. All the people I had grown to care for in Silver Meadows treated me like I was one of their own, just like my family in Solace. I couldn't allow another one hundred years of fear and tyranny to rule over their lives. That wasn't living.

"I'm fine," I repeated, a little sharper than I intended. "Let's keep going."

Dax nodded in understanding, following my lead until I stopped, hearing the serpent king speak again.

You ... You ssssmell sssssstrangely familiar.

There was a loud crack, followed by the ceiling above our heads buckling and crumbling.

"Run!" Daxton shouted, pushing me forward.

The tunnel began collapsing all around us. The faint sound of laughter echoed in my ears while the blackened stone crumbled, the ceiling disappearing before our eyes. My feet couldn't move fast enough, so Daxton grabbed my arm and readied his magic to teleport us out of the collapsing passageway.

Fuck. This is dangerous.

Daxton couldn't see. He had no idea where he was sending us, needing a destination for his teleporting powers. We could end up inside a gods-damned wall! But it was either die under the falling rocks or try to escape.

When we reappeared in a different tunnel, my entire body trembled, but I still managed to remain standing.

"Lucky break?" I wheezed.

"It was either die under the falling stones or ..."

"I know." I sighed, leaning against him. I could feel his heart beating just as fast as mine. "I would've done the same."

His arms wrapped around me, and I inhaled the fresh scent of cold mountain pine combined with my burning fire. His hold on me was brief but desperately needed.

"Where'd you take us?" I asked, assessing our surroundings. The new tunnel we teleported to was much wider and taller than the first.

"Up," he answered. "The sound of the basilisk seemed to be coming from above our heads, and since we scaled down the cliffside as far as we did, I assessed that it was the safest place to take us."

"Again, lucky break?"

"I wouldn't say that just yet," Dax replied.

Looking around, I could see why. This was an enclosed chamber, possibly an old magma pimple or bubble with slits in the rocks just large enough to slip through, leading to other tunnels that seemed to have no end in sight.

"At least it's brighter in here," Daxton said. "Or my eyes are somehow adjusting?"

"We must be approaching the magma chamber. The intense heat can create a glowing effect." I ran my hand along the curve of the opening, the ceiling of it just out of my reach. "What do you think this place is?" I asked.

"You want my honest opinion?"

"Maybe." I cringed.

"A cage."

Shit. He was right.

"These rocks over here are warmer to the touch, Spitfire. This opening may lead to the den we have been looking for."

"Good place to start," I said, hearing the distinct sound of a very large body moving behind us.

I readied my bow, placing an arrow along the string and angling the mirror over my shoulder, meticulously watching the opposing side of the opening through slits in the outer walls. My stomach leaped into my throat as the black rocks behind us moved. The basilisk was on the other side of the very thin, slitted rock wall.

"He's here," I whispered.

"I can hear him," Daxton said, cautiously moving a few paces from me so I had enough room to turn and fire an arrow—just like we'd practiced.

A massive jaw with elongated sharp teeth gleamed through one of the openings in the mirror's reflection. Saliva dripped from the rows of ivory fangs, and the putrid smell of death flooded the small space between us.

Clever trick, its tongue hissed.

After cutting the rope, I remained still, watching and waiting for an opening.

The basilisk's body slithered as a large yellow eye filled the opening, directly aimed at me.

"Ahhhhh!" I screamed. Not out of fear but sheer blinding agony.

Every inch of my skin exploded with fire. I could have sworn a thousand blades were cutting through my flesh. My bones ached, and my blood felt like it was boiling. I tried to look away, but I was paralyzed. The golden-yellow eye with the black eight-pointed starred pupil stared at me in the reflection of the mirror. Its magical gaze didn't kill me but made me wish for death if it meant this pain would stop.

"Skylar!" Daxton roared with panic and fury swirling in his voice.

"The mirror …" I could barely hear myself speak. The internal torment of my body swallowed my voice. My vision blurred, but I couldn't move my arms nor look away from the basilisk's stare.

Thank the Gods above, Daxton heard my whimper. He lunged forward, feeling his way through the dark, and smashed the mirror on the end of my bow.

My animal roared inside my head, splitting it in two with a rush of power exploding through me. If I didn't have the champion's mark, I guarantee I would have shifted right then and there.

"Skylar!" Daxton gripped my shoulders, cradling my limp body in his arms. "We need to move. Now." My body was in shock. I was disoriented, my vision a blur of white stars. "I guess it's my turn to lead the way, then."

He looped one of my arms over his shoulder, grabbing my waist with the other and leading us forward, trying to encourage me to move my legs and regain feeling in my limbs.

Niccceee idea. But poor exxecccution. Luckily, your sssnack was able to dessssstroy that mirror. The reflection of my sssstare may not be powerful enough to kill you, but it will make you wisssh for death.

"No shit." I gritted my teeth, trying to push through each agonizing step.

"Is the basilisk speaking to you again?" Daxton asked. I nodded. "I can't hear anything besides a low hissing sound."

"Trust me. I wish I could too. How are you managing to navigate this place, Dax?"

"My eyes are slowly adjusting, and there seems to be a light from up ahead. I followed the opening with the warmer rocks as a guide."

I managed to crack open my eyes, and my vision slowly returned. "The magma chamber."

"Seems we've found its den."

As we reached the end of the tunnel, a large open area the basilisk undoubtedly called home came into view. The nest housed bubbling pools of molten magma along the edges, heating the space to an almost intolerable temperature. The light from the free-flowing molten rock illuminated the underground fortress, with jagged spikes along the floor and ceiling, stalagmites and stalactites meeting at the corners.

Molted black and green skin lay on the far side, along with a worn, smooth patch of heated stones in a circle formation. This was the nest—the den of the serpent king.

"Well, at least you can see now. But I'm not so sure that's a good thing."

"Are you hurt?" Daxton set me down on a nearby boulder, meticulously looking me over for any sign of injury.

"No, I'm just recovering." I grimaced. "By the way, don't use your mirror."

"Clearly," he replied, taking my face in his hands. His gray stare was unbreakable and full of concern. "You're not allowed to die on me, Spitfire. Besides … Castor will be a terrible ruler just to spite our deaths."

I huffed a half-laugh. "No pressure, then."

A rumbling sound echoed along another opening leading to the den.

"I don't think you have much time left to recover." My mate reached into his pocket and withdrew two black handkerchiefs, wrapping one around my head before securing his own.

"Stay alive," he whispered, kissing my brow before turning around to combat the approaching threat.

"Dax! Don't!" I couldn't get the words out fast enough as silver flashed from the bottom of my blindfold, followed by hissing sounds from the basilisk and the clang of Daxton's sword. The handkerchief he tied allowed me to see only portions of shadow along the ground but nothing higher than our ankles.

"That fucking stubborn male!" I cursed, hearing him engaging with the basilisk without me. I slung my bow over my shoulder and withdrew my long twin daggers in both hands. The commotion of their fight was only a few lengths ahead of me. I swallowed the aches in my bones and pushed myself to stand, racing into the fight.

Gods. I didn't know where one part of the basilisk's form ended and where the other began. From the vision Nyssa shared with me, I knew the main body resembled a ground-bound dragon, but it held a longer whip-like tail and a stretched neck that could turn around on itself and devour you in one savage gulp. I used my keen sense of smell and reached out through the mate bond to try and search for Daxton's magic, feeling the chill of his ice to my left.

"Daxton!" I called out to him.

Immediately, his back was flush against mine as we readied ourselves to fight as one.

How sswweeet. I will have two tasssty treatssss.

We refused to answer as the serpent king slowly coiled around us, a predator stalking its prey. This prey, however, would not go down without a fight. The sound of its body slithering across the rocks gave me a good sense of this creature's size and where best to strike.

"You hear the clicks?" Daxton whispered.

"Yes." I knew those were the sounds of its talons clanking against the volcanic stone.

"Strike there first."

I nodded, tilting my head back so he could feel my response. I sheathed one of my daggers in my belt and withdrew a slender short sword. Perfect for slicing flesh and bone.

"When it starts speaking again," I told Daxton under my breath, "that's when we attack."

"How do you know it will?"

I smiled. "It's a king all alone with no one to boast to about its greatness. He'll start talking again before he strikes."

Can you feel death looming? Can you hear the echo of riverssss from the great crosssssing where the Mother and Father are waiting? I'll gladly help you reach them.

I moved first, with Daxton following my lead. We leaped away from the sound of its voice, attacking the beast's hind legs, intending to slice them from the serpent king's body.

Daxton teleported over the torso, and I could hear his sword, Valencia, slice through flesh and bone. The basilisk's roar of pain shook the ground. I stumbled forward, managing to keep my balance with my sword drawn and ready to do my part. Black talons as long as my arm crunched into the jagged stone, and its body shifted, its attention drawn to Daxton's side. I raised my sword and brought it down with as much force as I could muster, but my blade was not magical like Daxton's.

Shit.

I managed to sever the tendons and muscles of the creature, black blood spraying all around me, but I couldn't detach the limb completely.

Before the basilisk could turn its attention to me, it roared with pain once more, and I knew Daxton was on the attack, intentionally drawing its focus. Its body pivoted, and being blindfolded, I didn't see the strike coming, but I sure as hell felt it.

Whack. The tail of the serpent king slammed into me, sending me flying across the den and colliding with the far wall on the other side. My armor took the brunt of the hit.

"Skylar!" Daxton yelled.

I lost one of my daggers along with the short sword, rolling down the jagged wall and collapsing onto my front. I tried pushing myself up and even contemplated crawling on my hands and knees to rejoin Daxton in our fight. Thankfully, one dagger was still strapped to me with my bow and quiver remaining in one piece.

I was disorientated. Having the wind knocked out of me after flying fifty feet across a cavern would easily do that to a person. *Fuck, that hurt.* The all too familiar taste of blood trickled from my mouth. I cringed as I moved my right leg, realizing I had a large gash slicing through my thigh. Thankfully, the wound was not from the basilisk. It was a gash from the jagged volcanic rock it threw me against.

The clang of Daxton's sword echoed from across the way, and my heart dropped when I heard him scream. *"Gahhh!"*

Without thinking, I jumped to my feet and raced across the distance between us. The pain in my leg fell to a distant memory at my mate's bellow of distress.

"Daxton!" I roared, charging ahead. I could make out the shadows of Daxton facing off against the head of the basilisk. "Watch out for its—" I tried to warn him, but I was too late.

Like me, the basilisk's tail struck him on his side, flinging him across the nest. Turning and lifting the corner of my blindfold, I gaped in horror.

"Dax!" He was soaring over an open hole in the den leading to the magma chamber below. "No!" I screamed, unable to do anything from this side of the den.

Before tumbling into the opening, he called upon his ice magic and slid safely over, only to violently crash into the wall. His head collided with the rocks, and his body fell limp.

Thank the Gods he didn't fall in. I sighed in a moment of relief, only to have it turn into dread. He didn't have the armor of Aegis protecting him like I did.

The basilisk didn't hesitate and turned on him again. I unslung my bow and aimed, angling my head upward and peeking out further than I knew I should.

Gods be damned, I still couldn't see enough.

Cursing, I reached up and peeled off my blindfold. This very well might be the last thing I ever saw in my mortal life, but that didn't matter. What mattered was saving my mate from becoming a basilisk's meal. If I died here today saving Daxton, I would accept that fate. To die while saving those you love, would be a worthy end.

I watched the serpent king coil around Daxton's fallen body, its mouth opened wide, seconds away from devouring him whole. I released my arrow, watching it fly straight and true with a steady, unmovable mountain of confidence.

It found its target ... The glowing left eye staring directly at my mate.

The creature roared, the cave walls trembling against its cries of agony.

Silver flashed, and Daxton appeared beside me, pulling me into his arms and tucking us around the corner of a boulder.

"Now ... it only has one." I breathed heavily.

He clutched onto me with everything he had. "Thanks for that," he said.

We didn't have time to say anything else. The basilisk came crashing into our hideaway, forcing us to jump in two different directions to face off against its wrath.

Daxton grunted as a loud slam boomed in the den.

With my blindfold discarded, I was forced to shut my eyes, no longer having a window below our ankles to see what was happening. A powerful weight struck me, knocking me down and pinning me against the ground. I roared, the breath in my chest involuntarily pressed from my lungs, making it impossible to breathe.

You ssstolle my eye! the basilisk hissed.

Its hot breath burned against my skin as its saliva dripped from the sharp fangs that were only inches from my face. *Shit, not good.* I was pinned under one of its remaining forelimbs with only one dagger sheathed along my thigh remaining to defend myself. My bow and quiver were gone—dropped when the basilisk ambushed us.

The pressure on my chest intensified with a pinpointed sensation narrowing on my breastbone. "*Ahhh!*" I screamed.

Daxton, I pleaded through the threads of our bond. Desperately searching for him.

Why do my talonsss not ssskewer—

The clang of Daxton's sword silenced the basilisk's hiss. I couldn't tell what was happening. I had to keep my eyes closed to avoid the death stare from the creature still looming over me. Even with one eye, I knew it could still kill me. I'd only seen one eye in the reflection of my mirror.

I remained trapped under the weight of the creature's talon, but thankfully, I was still alive. The armor of Aegis had saved my life for the second time today.

There was a sharp hiss, and drops of blood splattered across my skin. The grip of the basilisk loosened, and I made a move to reach for my blade. I wrapped my hand around the hilt, but before I could bring it up, the pressure shifted back, taking away my freedom to move.

"Ahh, dammit!" Daxton cursed as the serpent king released a very low, sinister chuckle. "*Skylar* ..." Daxton's pained voice made my heart stop. He was wounded.

I know who he issss now. The taste of his flessshh unlocked a guarded memory long thought repressed. The prince who was promised, the serpent king taunted. *The one born to unite and rule usss all. How graciousss of you to join ussss, Your Majesssty.*

"Spitfire, I can't reach you. I've been ... Skylar ..." The fear in his voice was not for his safety. It was for me.

"Daxton!" I tried to yell out for him, but the weight on my chest made my cry nothing more than a whisper.

My venom worksss quickly.

"No!" I roared. My animal's power rose to the surface of my skin, fueling me with liquid fire rushing through my veins.

And you ... The basilisk now turned his attention back to me. *You ssseem so familiar. Isss that you in there? Has it truly been five hundred yearsss?*

I wasn't listening to a fucking thing this snake was saying to me. I no longer cared if I lived through this or died. All I cared about was getting to Daxton and saving him. The trials would ultimately choose another, but the Inner Kingdom ... Silver Meadows would not survive Daxton's death. Valdor would find a way to continue combating the wilt. *They could last another hundred years*, I told myself, *but they wouldn't survive losing him.*

I knew my magic could heal Daxton's wound. All I needed to do was reach him; the power swirling inside me would be enough. My mate would not die today.

Open your eyes, my instincts roared at me, an unknown voice echoing inside my mind. *Release your power!*

Maybe one eye of death wouldn't be enough to kill me after all?

The well of power inside me burst open, overflowing like water spilling across a river dam. It was wild and beautiful. Terrifying yet comforting.

This was a creature of Valdor. And in my bones, I knew my alpha command would grant me control over the serpent king.

I opened my eyes that I knew were blazing like wildfire. One large golden yellow eye with a black eight-pointed star pupil in the center stared back at me.

No! the serpent hissed, its one eye widening as its pupil contracted wildly. I could feel the kiss of death's magic brushing against my skin, but it did not affect me.

"You'll be the one who dies today," I said in a low tone laced with power and untapped fury. "Release me," I commanded, my magic intertwined with each word I spoke.

It hissed wildly, fighting my alpha command with every ounce of magic it could muster. I watched it cringe and coil within its pained expression as it released its grip on me. The head of the serpent king bent down, its jaws unhinging to try and swallow me whole.

I remained calm. This was the opening I was waiting for.

As it lowered its jaws around me, I thrust my dagger up and inside its skull. The basilisk screamed and roared with the sound of death's gasp. The creature's flailing body squirmed around me as I drove my dagger in again. And again. Drenched in its blackened blood, I still didn't stop. With one final thrust, I pushed my blade up into its brain.

"Die," I commanded.

The pressure of its talons slackened, unshackling me from its hold. I scrambled outside the gaping mouth of ivory fangs, standing next to the head of the fallen serpent king. The yellow eye was open, fixated on me, but I didn't flinch or turn away. I met its stare, my power wildly flowing through me, combating its lingering death magic until it dissipated into nothing.

The basilisk hissed one final time. *You have dethroned me, but know thissss, Champion. In the end … the Heart of Valdor will assssk you for what wassss given before. When your kind firssst ssssealed it away. Be ready … Be willing.*

With those last words, the basilisk released its final breath.

Chapter Twenty-Six

"Skylar?" Daxton's voice was barely a whisper.

"Dax!" I screamed as I rushed to his side. His coloring was devoid of its natural glow, his hands cold as ice, and his breathing staggered and shallow. "Hold on, don't move."

My healing magic worked immediately when I touched the bleeding wound on his arm. I could feel the wisps of death in the poison rushing through his veins. Another thirty seconds and this would have taken him into the crossing of the afterlife.

My hands shook at that realization. The thought of losing him made me practically hysterical. My animal inside me was racing with unease, panicking at the thought. I couldn't lose him. Not when we had just found each other, but then again, I knew there would never be enough time with him.

"That's good enough." Daxton tried to influence me to stop using my magic for some stupid reason I couldn't fathom.

"No, it's not," I said, my voice unwavering, refusing to stop until I knew all the venom was out of his system. "And," I rasped, attempting to calm myself and regain my composure, "stop telling me how *my* magic works. Let me heal your gods-damned wound and erase the poison that was *seconds* away from killing you!"

"I would say it was closer to a minute."

"Daxton!" I yelled. "Gahh! You're unbelievable."

"There she is," he said as he flashed me that stupid half-grin and removed the remaining tie holding his blindfold.

"And," I said with an edge, "don't you dare fucking die on me."

"*Ha ha* ... I was waiting for that," he teased as he grasped my hands.

"Where you go, I go," I answered, meeting his silver-gray stare with my blazing fury. There was a shift in the air, a silent exchange and understanding passing between us that reached the unsealed threads of our mate bond.

We hadn't dared discuss it yet. The fact was that Daxton was immortal ... and I wasn't. My mate's immortal lifespan meant he could live for centuries, while shifters only had a fraction of that time. We eventually had to confront this reality, but for right now, we had both agreed it was best left alone.

"Well played." Dax nodded, releasing my hands so I could concentrate on healing the basilisk's bite. Reaching up to remove the rest of his blindfold.

"Why was your covering partially lifted? You could've died with just one look Dax!" I scolded, my limbs shaking as the adrenaline rush from the battle subsided.

He took a long breath before answering. "I could feel the poison from the basilisk's bite tearing through me. I didn't believe I would survive long enough for you to reach me in time." I went as still as death. "I thought ... dammit. I didn't really know what I was thinking, but I knew—" He reached to cup my cheek. "I knew the last thing I needed to see in this life was you." His eyes never strayed from mine. "And to my delight, not really a surprise, when I peeked through the blindfold, I witnessed you slaying and dethroning the serpent king."

I bit my lip, breaking his gaze as I turned my head away and moved my magic along the wound of his arm, searching for any traces of poison. "I-I don't have an explanation for the power I was wielding. I don't know how I did it."

"I do," Daxton answered plainly, leaning forward to inspect the gash on my thigh I had long forgotten about. "You're an alpha, Skylar Cathal. A gods-damned queen in your own right." He moved forward, sitting up on his own, his eyes finding the wound on my leg. "Why do you think I never referred to you as a mere princess or lady." His smile grew wide as he reached out, allowing his magic to coat my skin, closing the wound on my thigh. "I always knew." He chuckled. "I was just waiting for the day you realized it too. Your father's alpha bloodline and your ancestor's power have all re-emerged within you, my stunning mate."

"I guess it would've been foolish for the Gods to match you with anything less."

"True." Dax laughed without humor. "But I believe it's the other way around." He reached to gently brush his thumb over my lip before allowing his fingers to migrate along the curve of my chin, memorizing every arc and feature of my face. "Even covered in the blood of our enemy, I still find you the most utterly breathtaking creature to have ever walked this earth."

"You aren't too bad yourself," I said, leaning into his hold and kissing him.

"Don't twist it," Daxton whispered against my lips. "We both know that I was the one who gained status with our pairing. I landed myself an alpha queen who mastered the labyrinth and slayed the basilisk. A champion who's fated to save us all."

"All right ..." I said, exhaling a curt laugh. "Prince who was *promised*."

"Promised." He paused, giving me a look that stilled the breath in my lungs—the kind of look that said so much more than words could ever articulate. "Promised to become a deadly weapon for a worthy queen to wield at her side."

"Dammit," I cursed. "How are you so much better at this than me?"

"Centuries of practice and waiting. You could say my patience is a gift from the Gods to match my fiery mate's fighting spirit."

"Good thinking on their part," I answered, moving closer to him. I reached up to trace my hand along his bearded chin, reassuring myself that he was safe. "I heard you scream, Dax," I said, dropping my voice, "and I've never been so scared in my entire life. I thought I would lose you."

"You can't ever lose me, Spitfire."

"True." I grinned recalling the words we've said to one another time and time again. "Let's get the second key, get out of here, and go home."

"Home." He smiled as I helped him to his feet.

Daxton's body was healed, but it was pushed to its physical limits with the venom. Miraculously, he still managed to give me a saccharine smile full of hope and joy. "Glad you're starting to come around to that idea." He grunted, pushing up against the rock, struggling to stand on his own.

"Not so fast there." I snaked under his arm to help steady him. "I might have extracted the poison and healed the wound, but it seems to still have some lingering effects."

"Yes, I'd love to know whose brilliant idea it was to create a monster with a stare of death and lethal venom in its bite. Did it not already have the advantage?"

"I think even Zola would agree," I replied. "Heck, whoever had the idea to create this thing might be her best friend—or possibly her mate." That made him laugh, and I could see that even though it strained him, he didn't dare hold back his release. "Sorry." I winced, seeing him stiffen. "I shouldn't …"

"Don't be." He reached his other arm around me, our bodies molding together like puzzle pieces. "Broken ribs will heal, but I'll never recover from missing moments with you. Don't apologize for making me laugh, Skylar." And I knew I wouldn't—I would cherish the sound of his laughter for all eternity.

"Okay, now where could this key be?" Dax asked, but I already knew the answer.

"It's the eye."

"You're sure?"

I nodded. "It holds the same eight-pointed star in its pupil as the markings on my arm. It must be it."

"I trust your instincts on this, love." He kissed my brow, hugging me tightly just because he could. Because we were alive.

I was one step closer to unlocking the Heart of Valdor and healing our world. One step closer to our hope of a better life becoming a reality.

"So, how are you going to retrieve this eye? Doesn't it still have the magic of a death stare?"

"I don't think so," I replied, stepping closer to the carcass of the once proud serpent king. "When the basilisk died, its magic dwindled and eventually disappeared. But I think the first key," I said, extracting the sun-moon key from the labyrinth underneath my armor, "is supposed to help."

I could feel the familiar thrumming of magic from the entrance pulsate against my palm as I clutched the sun-moon key in my hand. I knelt next to the massive head of the fallen king, unable to subdue the swell of sorrow and heartache in my chest.

This magnificent being was locked in this isolated cave system its entire life, waiting for this battle to decide its fate. It almost seemed cruel that this majestic creature was meant only for this end. I felt sorry for the basilisk and sent a silent prayer to our Mother and Father for their compassion. Were we not all creatures of their creation?

"Spitfire?" Daxton asked with concern, stepping behind me. I hadn't even noticed the tear trailing down my cheek. He knelt beside me and took my hand in his. "Only you, my alpha queen, could feel compassion for a creature whose sole purpose in this life was death itself. Your mortal heart is a gift, my love, and one I hope you never lose."

"I wish I didn't have to kill him," I whispered. "As stupid as I know that sounds. But, before he died, he spoke to me ... Maybe even warned me?"

"What did the basilisk tell you?"
I tried my best to recite the serpent king's final words. "You have dethroned me, but know this, Champion. In the end ... the Heart of Valdor will ask you for what was given before. When your kind first sealed it away. Be ready." Leaving out the final warning, *Be willing.*

Willing for what? I wasn't sure. But I had one final trial to conquer before that came to pass.

Daxton pursed his lips, the lines in his brows and along his forehead creasing in concentration as he tried to understand what the basilisk told me in his final breaths.

"What was given before," Daxton repeated to himself. "I don't understand. I don't remember anything about the Heart being sealed. I was there. Why don't I remember?"

Again, that strange look of bewilderment clouded my mate's expression. He had the same frustrated blank stare on the deck of the *Opal* when we traveled to the Inner Kingdom, when he'd forgotten details of Queen Minaeve's rise to power.

"Why can I not remember?" he cursed, his magic flaring out around him as he ground his knuckles into the rocks at our feet. His frustration turned to anger as he tried to remember but failed to catch the fleeting memory.

"Dax." I quickly reached out and took his hand, trying to calm him. "Look, you were just seconds away from dying. The venom is gone, but there are still lingering effects. You need time to recover. Don't push yourself too much, my love. Once we retrieve the key and bring it to the scroll, another riddle or clue about the final trial will be revealed." I knew he was listening, but it didn't eliminate his disappointment. "We're so close."

There wasn't anything I could do to temper his emotions. It wasn't my place to try to do so. I needed to allow him space to work through this and trust that he would ask when he was ready to let me in and help.

"All right," he answered. I gave him a nod in return.

I lowered the key toward the closed eye of the dethroned serpent king and watched in awe as it magically began to glow in my hand. The key sparkled like living sunlight, casting shimmering rays of gold and red that hovered in the air and swirled around the basilisk's body.

The light created from the magic of the first key collected at the tip of its tail, swallowing the blackened scales until they disappeared and added to the magical sparkles of sunlight. The shimmering magic wound up the scaled back, stomach, chest, and neck until finally it reached its massive head, and the body that was once there no longer was. A flash of blinding light forced us to shield our eyes and turn away. When we lowered our arms to see, only a single remnant of the creature remained. A small yellow orb with a black eight-pointed star pupil.

The eye. The second key.

I reached out for the orb and grasped it in my left palm. The warming glow of the magic hummed against my skin as the second star on my arm transformed from an outline to a painted black star.

The second trial was complete. I had defeated the beast and obtained the second key.

"Your prayers might have been answered by the Gods, Spitfire."

I glanced at him, so grateful that he was here and thankful he was everything I wanted and needed. "It seems so."

"Shall we go home? The magical ward has been lifted. I think I can still manage to teleport us to the entrance of the Summit." I didn't miss the flicker of hope and happiness that shone in the depth of his mesmerizing gray eyes when he said the word home. And to be honest, Silver Meadows was beginning to feel just like that to me.

"You sure?" I asked in hesitation.

"Not doubting your mate, are you?"

"Never." I smiled, tucking myself into his arms. "Let's go."

In a flash of silver, the cave disappeared.

We arrived on the stone steps outside the large, marble-framed, tempered glass double door entrance of the Summit. Before leaving for the trial, Daxton placed extra wards around the Summit. Even he couldn't teleport us inside.

As I opened my eyes, Silver Meadows reappeared around us, except … it was not in the state we had left it.

"Oh … My, Gods," I gasped in absolute horror. I flung a hand over my mouth, feeling Daxton's grasp on my arms tense as his entire body went utterly still.

I wordlessly screamed inside my head, my voice disappearing in a horrid roar. Silver Meadows was *burning*.

Witnessing the sight of this beautiful paradise sweltering with its people screaming in pain and fear was like a knife had plunged straight through the center of my heart. The kingdom was under attack, ambushed from within its center, where the flames roared as tall as the sky. High Fae were frantically running and screaming, trying to escape. The pine tree forests separating the different sections of the city were smoldering, with citizens racing to help douse the flames.

Cries from the Dryads within the city could be heard wailing through the meadow and the surrounding mountains. Their trees were burning—dying … And them with it.

I knew the bulk of Daxton's armies were stationed north of Silver Meadows, doubling his defenses from the wilt in anticipation of Minaeve and Seamus's arrival.

The city itself was not defenseless, but somehow, the bulk of the destruction seemed to erupt from within. Silver Meadows warriors were valiantly fighting against soldiers adorned with deep forest-green armor, belonging to only one other faction of the Inner Kingdom—Aelius.

Oh no. Seamus and Minaeve were already here. She must have used her newly acquired magic to create a portal straight into the heart of the city and aid in Seamus's attack.

Valencia materialized along my mate's back. Pure rage, agonizing hatred, and wrath for his people bursting from every inch of him. I could feel the intensity of his grief and fury through our bond like it was my own.

"Skylar! Daxton!" Castor's voice erupted across the way. "Watch out!"

"Anjani, blind them," a voice commanded, "before they can escape inside the Summit!"

My world went black.

Before I had a chance to do anything, strong hands gripped me, throwing me toward the humming magic of the Summit wards. I landed with a firm thud, sliding across the smooth marble floor entrance of the palace, crashing against outstretched hands. My vision immediately returned, but by the grace of the Gods, I almost wished it hadn't.

"Keep her in there!" Daxton bellowed just before his words morphed into a terrifying roar of pain.

"Daxton!" I screamed, my voice cracking with panic. "No! Daxton!"

Out of nowhere, iron chains encircled my mate, and a cloud of iron power engulfed the space surrounding him, infiltrating his lungs and slicing him from the inside out with each breath he dared to take.

Blood pooled on his lips as he collapsed onto the ground, unable to withstand the weight of the chains.

It was too much. Daxton was the most powerful High Fae born of the Inner Kingdom, but the iron powder, paired with the damaging effects of the basilisk's venom, created a mountain too steep for even him to climb. He couldn't fight back. He wouldn't be able to free himself.

"Daxton!" I roared again in desperation from inside the safety of the wards.

Gunnar hoisted me to my feet, his arms clutching me so tightly I could barely breathe, stopping me from running back outside the protection of the Summit. Forbidding me from running straight into danger. Preventing me from reaching my mate.

"Stay in there ... all of you!" Dax commanded through gritted teeth.

Every muscle of his massive body strained. He was fighting through blows of sheer agony with each breath he struggled to take. The iron chains made it impossible for him to move or free himself.

With my focus solely on my mate, I hadn't noticed the others around me until now. Adohan stood closest to the door, his red-hilted blade drawn and at the ready. Fire skittered along his arms and weapon, with Idris safely tucked at his back. Zola's cold stare searched the invisible threat with piercing black eyes as deadly as the wilt itself. Castor stood across from Adohan, staring helplessly at his brother, hatred burning in every shadow and line on his face. Gunnar's shaking limbs still held me tight despite the overflowing rage coursing through his own veins. Even Nyssa was here with us, tucked away in the corner across from the entrance. She held a dagger, ready to charge out into the fold with us if called to action.

"Let me go!" I screamed, squirming in the High Fae general's grip. "Fucking let me go, Gunnar!"

"I can't," Gunnar grunted, tightening his hold on me. "Stop. Skylar … we can't." The pain in his voice cut through me like the chains that were burning through Daxton's skin. "Daxton commanded us to stay in here. He threw you inside the ward so we could keep you safe. Don't let that be for nothing."

"Gunnar, he's—"

"My high prince gave me an order." His dark brown eyes, which always showed me such kindness, now bore pure lethal violence. He wouldn't break Daxton's command. I knew in my gut that none of them would.

Even Adohan, who was a high prince in his own realm, wouldn't betray Daxton's orders. He couldn't dishonor or challenge his friend's rule or leave his pregnant mate unguarded. Dread settled over me as the reality of this situation sank in like a anchor falling into the sea. We were ambushed. And we were outmatched.

"Bastard!" I swore, fighting back tears.

I was angry. No, I was furious. My animal roared inside my head, pulsing what remained of my power through my limbs … but it was not enough. I had used so much of my magic against the basilisk that I couldn't break free from Gunnar if I tried.

"I know." Gunnar sighed. I could hear his regret and dread buried in his voice. In the strained lines etched in his expression. "It all happened without warning. I blinked, and they were here. I sent our remaining warriors to guard the city center and then rushed to secure the Summit. Castor pulled me inside the ward, and then you two arrived."

"They've been waiting," I said slowly. "This whole time."

Chapter Twenty-Seven

Whips of black shadow surrounded Daxton. A loud crack echoed with a twist of his shoulder, making my stomach plummet and twist into knots. My animal raged inside me, urging me to break free of Gunnar's hold and run toward him.

Like an unearthly creature of the wilt, Queen Minaeve magically stepped into view, standing above Daxton with a venomous look of satisfaction spreading across her glowing grin. Her skin shined with a golden hue against the silk of her black gown, with shimmering green and purple dust in her wake. The gilded crown of the Inner Kingdom rested comfortably atop her cascading raven hair, with the three sparkling stones shining like starlight against the burning city behind her.

Her mask of elegance and beauty hid her black cruel-natured heart. How many lives was she sacrificing today? How many innocents were dying all because she desired power above all else? How many more would feel the wrath of her magic in search of absolute control?

"Well, what do we have here?" Minaeve's bitter voice echoed across the distance as she bent toward Daxton. "Apparently, the creature didn't kill you," she sneered, turning her eyes to glare at me within the Summit. "Well, that's disappointing."

478

"Don't you fucking touch him!" I roared, almost managing to free myself from Gunnar's grasp. The instinct to reach my mate fueled me with a rush of adrenaline. "I'll kill you myself if you do!"

Minaeve's haunting turquoise eyes, painted with a faint purple trail, followed the Summit doors' archway. "Why don't you come on out, Champion? We know you hold the second key. We've been patiently watching the scroll in our keep, waiting for the perfect moment to strike." Her elegant midnight-black silk dress flowed behind her in delicate waves of finery as she circled Daxton.

"We?" Castor breathed.

"No!" Daxton grunted, but the queen cast her shadows to silence him.

"Shit," Gunnar cursed, struggling to hold me. "Sky!"

"Release my brother, and you'll have the key," Castor announced, stepping closer to the ward's boundary. "It's as simple as that. There's no need for war when we are on the brink of salvation. The shifter has only one more trial to defeat."

"Hold your silver tongue," Seamus spat, appearing from thin air at his queen's side, the veil of magic hiding him slipping to the side. "This has nothing to do with the trials. *His* crimes against Aelius will be answered." Seamus was dressed in tailored dark green, almost black, fitted battle armor with a golden cloak draped over one shoulder. A smaller crown of gold encircled his brow, pulling his hair back and exposing the sharp lines of his high cheekbones. His eyes gleamed with pride as he approached Minaeve's side—like he had won a prize.

Minaeve tenderly stroked Seamus's arm, gaining his full attention. "My love, my king … Don't allow your anger to jeopardize all we have worked for."

"Did she just say *king*?" Idris whispered from behind Adohan.

"She did," the Crimson City high prince answered, his fire blazing wildly across his arms. "Gods be damned, he finally did it."

"May I introduce you to your high king consort, my husband, Seamus." Minaeve's words struck everyone like a bolt of lightning from the sky. "I'm sorry you missed the ceremony. We were wed … and sealed in a blood oath shortly after your departure. Which means, High *Prince* Daxton," Minaeve's fingers traced over my mate's shoulder until his chin was firmly in her grasp, "*you've* not only attacked Aelius but the crown of the Inner Kingdom by dismembering my husband's cousin, Anjani." The coldness in Minaeve's eyes sent a death chill up my spine. "I believe my king seeks retribution from Silver Meadows for this crime."

"As do I." Anjani emerged, allowing her illusion to disappear.

Her dark green eyes matched her cousin's with sublime perfection. Her short brown hair was braided to the side, falling behind her shoulder as she strode to Seamus. She was dressed in dark green leathers to match her realm's colors. Their likeness was uncanny, but Anjani's features held a feminine air, with round lips and darker hair.

Behind Anjani, at least fifty guards stood, armed to the teeth and ready for battle.

Rhett, the scroll keeper, materialized to the far-right side of the stone steps leading to the Summit entrance. His piercing blue eyes widened for a second as he took in the scene unfolding around him, the ancient scroll of the trial clutched tightly in his hands. He held a scowl of disapproval, and I could have sworn I saw a flash of pity in his eyes when he looked down to see Daxton lying in chains with Silver Meadows burning around him.

"War with Silver Meadows will only result in your deaths," Castor warned. "If you take our high prince, you'll spark a flame that will engulf our entire world. Our people will not stand for this."

"Nor will Crimson City," Adohan bravely added, with Idris nodding in agreement.

"And what of *my* mistreatment!" Anjani roared, holding up her severed arm as evidence. "He cut off my hand!"

"You tried to kill me!" I countered, the remnants of my power rising to the surface. "Daxton spared your life only because you didn't manage to take mine."

"He's taking the role as your protector too far," Anjani hissed. "Regardless of whether you're whoring yourself out to the lot of them ... you're still just a half-breed shifter piece of trash." She spit on the ground. "Even if you somehow managed to win two of the trials, there is still one more. The Heart of Valdor will never see you as worthy. Your blood is tainted."

I blinked, almost dumbfounded at her unjustified resentment. Did she not want the wilt lifted?

"They still can't sense your bond," Castor cursed under his breath. "Gods-damned fool. That fact could help."

They didn't know Daxton and I were mates. Even now, he was hiding the threads of our bond from them—protecting me in every way he could. Well, now, it was time for me to start doing the same.

"Enough of this pettiness," Minaeve said, almost sounding bored. Seamus stiffened, his eyes narrowing as his lips pressed into a thin line. "You'll have your pound of flesh when I deem it fit to serve, Anjani."

Glancing at her king, I could see that Seamus was not pleased with her response. Welcome to the fucking team.

"Remember why we are all here. The trials of the Heart of Valdor. Our champion has successfully passed the second trial, and now we must ensure she moves on to the third." Minaeve said.

"If you don't release Skylar Cathal to us, the high prince and people of Silver Meadows will pay for their ruler's actions here and now—with blood," Seamus added. "Release her to us, and together, we can unlock the riddle to the third trial."

"No …" Even with the gag of shadows, Daxton managed to fight through its hold. "Skylar, no!"

Minaeve almost looked shocked. "Silence," the queen commanded her magic, extracting my mate's silent scream of heart-wrenching agony. The sounds of his bones cracking shattered the threads of my sanity. "The victory of the trials will not belong to Silver Meadows."

I couldn't take this anymore. The city was burning. People were dying, and my mate's life was in danger … all because of me. *Screw this.* I was not hiding from a fight. I wouldn't stand for this. Not when I could do something to change it all.

"No!" I screamed as I reached for my dagger and sliced through Gunnar's arm to the bone, forcing him to release me.

I couldn't allow this to happen. I sprinted around Castor, whose eyes had turned black. A vision overtook him, allowing me to escape past the safety of the wards.

"Release him," I commanded, angling my bloodied weapon at the high queen.

My animal rose within me, fueling me with power. The warriors surrounding her drew their weapons at my threat, but I did not back down. I simply stared at her, my eyes glowing with pure fire and a promise to drive the weapon through her blackened heart if she didn't follow my command.

"Release the people of Silver Meadows. Call off your warriors or—"

"Or what?" Minaeve answered. Her eyes narrowed, meeting my challenge, and she waved a hand at her guard to wait. In this state, with her siphoned magic from all three high princes, I knew I wouldn't be strong enough to stop her. Not right now.

I raised my dagger to my throat. "You'll no longer have a champion to compete in your trials." Blood dripped from my neck as I pressed the blade into my flesh. "You think I won't do it?" I challenged. "Well, think again." I stared her down, noticing her eyes flicker behind me to Castor, realizing the cause of his blackened vision. "That is my *mate* you have chained and bloodied on the ground. There isn't anything I wouldn't do to protect him and the people of this land."

"She'll do it!" Castor screamed, his eyes returning to their normal state.

I dropped my barrier and allowed my scent to fill the space. Anjani's magic blinded Daxton to his surroundings, but he managed to pivot his head on the stone and still find me.

"No, Skylar." He was broken and chained, but still he tried to crawl toward me.

"We all know the Inner Kingdom won't last another hundred years against the wilt." A piece of me believed they might survive despite the odds, but not if Daxton wasn't in the picture. I had to be careful and play their games to win this. "I'm the only hope you have for a future. If I die, so do you." I stared down at the queen with a savagery that rivaled the fires threatening to burn Silver Meadows to the ground.

"What are your terms?" Minaeve asked, spewing hatred in every syllable.

"What?" Seamus started, but Minaeve's stare silenced his questions.

"Call off your warriors. Release the people of Silver Meadows." I knew Daxton would have wanted to ensure their safety first.

"Done." She waved her hands, and her black smoke flew out in all directions, dousing the flames and signaling a retreat for their troops through the portals she created. "Now, show me the key." I reached into my pocket and withdrew the basilisk's yellow eye, the eight-pointed ebony star gleaming in the pupil. The queen's smile twisted like the black tendrils of mist at her command.

"Rhett," Minaeve commanded, and he slowly stalked forward with the scroll in his oddly steady hands.

"Do you recall what you need to do?" Rhett asked me as he unrolled the ancient scroll. His eyes turned downward, cast away from mine, almost like he was ashamed to even look at me.

I nodded and silently brushed the orb over the second star of the scroll, leading to the third and final trial of the Heart of Valdor. The ink instantly formed on the page, but there were only two lines of text, followed by an illustration of what I needed to achieve next.

"What does it say?" Seamus asked.

Rhett finally looked at me with more than a mere question lingering amongst the abyss of his deep-set blue eyes. I re-read the two inked lines and gave him a shallow nod to read them aloud to the others. His midnight-black hair fell below his brow as he turned his chin down to read aloud. I knew exactly what I needed to do.

The trial of the soul ... Gods above. This would be the most challenging task yet.

"*Retrieve the blade guarded by the alphas of old. Once the cut is made and the trials are complete, the heart will be unleashed,*" Rhett read aloud.

"What does that mean?" Seamus asked. "Show us!"

Rhett obeyed and held up the magical parchment. Without glancing at the scroll, Queen Minaeve's gaze turned to me. She knew. She knew the identity of the blade without even looking at it, and she also understood that I knew it, too.

How could a shifter *not* know the blade guarded by the alphas of old? The ancient dagger carried by each alpha of the Solace pack. The blade that never dulled and could cut through anything in its path.

"I've never seen this weapon," Seamus began.

"It's the dagger carried by the alpha of the Solace pack," Minaeve told Seamus. "It seems our champion must cross the sea and return with the blade to complete the third trial."

"I've done my part ..." I said slowly. "Now, release my mate," I commanded in a low, even tone. "We'll leave immediately to—"

"I think not." I couldn't help the twinge of fear curling up my spine at the wicked smile stretching across not only Minaeve's face but Seamus's and Anjani's as well. "Daxton will remain our prisoner."

"*What?*" I roared wildly. Rhett quickly disarmed me of the dagger, ensuring I couldn't follow through with my threat from earlier. I glared at him, shaking with rage at him and for letting my guard down.

"Like hell we'll let you keep him as your prisoner!" Castor echoed from behind me.

"Who's to say you won't retrieve the key with your mate in tow, and then leave us all to die? A life at home on the mainland with your mate at your side seems like a dream come true," Minaeve taunted. "I wouldn't put that past you."

"I would never leave countless people suffering at the expense of my happiness like you do," I growled.

She didn't know I had already turned down that offer from inside the labyrinth. That I could never … Daxton could never recklessly abandon the people for our desires. We were not like the self-proclaimed queen.

"Right, because you're *selfless*." Minaeve rolled her eyes as Seamus walked to her side near where Daxton was lying on the ground. He had barely moved, but I saw his chest rising and falling with each labored breath he fought to take.

"I remember," Minaeve sneered. "You're the first, the only shifter to volunteer for the trials. Taking the place of your gentle cousin. How noble." Minaeve mocked as she bent toward Daxton. I stiffened with dread building with the beat of my racing heart.

"Touch him, and I swear I'll—"

"You'll what?" Minaeve challenged as she leaned in, taking Daxton's chin between her fingers and tilting his head toward her. "He is *my* subject, and I will take the same offering of submission I have demanded for the past five centuries as I see fit. Someone must keep the prince who was promised in line …" Daxton tried to fight against the hold of the chains and magic even though it was useless. "The retribution I will take from him will be rewarding, as it has always been."

With that, she feverishly devoured Daxton's mouth with hers, stealing a kiss while siphoning what remained of his magic.

Rage exploded inside me—pure, maddening, white-hot fury that burned like the sun itself. I reacted purely on instinct, retrieving my dagger from Rhett, who was preoccupied with the scroll, and sprinted toward them. My arm raised to strike, but as I brought my blade down with as much force as I could muster, however, it met the steel of another's blade.

"Ah-ahh," Seamus snickered. He moved to push me back. I was too distracted to counter his strike properly. My dagger flew out of my hand as his blade turned to slice the flesh of my arm. Moving quickly and showing his skill as a warrior, which I had gravely underestimated, Seamus maneuvered me toward his chest, his sword at my throat.

"Let's see if this mate's claim is true," he whispered as his palm stroked my brow.

His touch was like a hot iron rod as he dove into my mind, painfully rummaging through my most cherished memories with Daxton. Seeing them all.

He saw the meadow in Solace the first night we met, the letters, the bathhouse, the green sand beach. Our first kiss on the *Opal*, our night together in Crimson City, the kiss on my wrist at the ball, and our intimate evening before the first trial. He watched our private moments with a feverish passion, seeking out more and more with each agonizing second. Then, he finally found the memory of the hanging valley. The significance of the moondance flowers when I told Daxton I was in love with him, and he confessed knowing the existence of our mate bond.

"There ... it is." Seamus's voice dropped. He seemed surprised as he slowly pulled away from my mind. "It's *true*," he breathed, looking at his queen, who stood with a heightened glow on her skin from her new swell of magic. "They have a mate bond. It's not sealed, but it's there." Seamus trailed his nose across my neck, inhaling my scent. "She smells of him." His hold on me did not slacken, but I could have sworn his stare softened. "Release his sight, Anjani." His cousin looked at him, dumbfounded. "Obey, or you'll lose your other hand and become entirely worthless to the Inner Kingdom," he threatened.

With a wave of her functioning arm, Daxton's eyes changed from white to his gray stare, locked onto me.

"Skylar!" Daxton groaned as he tried to crawl toward me. Even with his magic siphoned, iron scraping his lungs, and bound in chains, he still fought to reach me.

To my surprise, Seamus let me go.

I raced to Daxton and fell to the floor at his side, tears in my eyes as I tried to loosen the chains holding him, cupping his face in my hands as I lowered my brow to his, soaking in his touch.

"One minute," Seamus told us before stepping back.

"You can't be—" Anjani began protesting, but Seamus silenced her with a glare as he reached his queen's side.

"You attacked his *mate*." His voice had an eerie calmness that would even cause the serpent king to cower in fear. "Tricked her into almost falling to her death … In my opinion, his mercy was not warranted, cousin. If you had attempted to kill my mate, I would have killed you without a second thought." He held his arm for Minaeve to take. "I saw everything. Their bond is true but not yet sealed."

"Because the shifter has not—"

"Precisely," Seamus finished as Minaeve's lips thinned and pressed into a hard line. "I know you enjoy your variety in companions, as do I, my queen, but it seems you may need to find a new one for the time being. The bond is not something we dare manipulate once consummated. It's protected."

"You're fortunate you already wear your crown," Minaeve growled. "What else do you have in mind?"

"You did choose me for my wicked nature." He snickered, making me want to vomit. "Anjani can have her revenge in other ways. Her creativity will blossom while Daxton is in our keep."

"Ahh. There … There's the cunning, twisted mind I seek to devour," Minaeve purred, pulling Seamus in for a kiss.

I pushed them aside, turning my attention to my mate. I reached for my healing magic, desperately wanting to help him.

"It's no use, Spitfire," Daxton whispered, somehow managing to rise onto his knees despite his injured shoulder and his arms remaining bound to his sides.

"Gods, above," I cursed aloud. "Daxton, I can't leave without you." I sobbed, carefully wrapping my arms around his neck.

He took a deep breath, nuzzling into the base of my neck, entangling himself in my hair. Our combined scents surrounded us, leaving no room for doubt that we were bound to each other.

"You won't," he whispered as I pulled back, seeing the depths of his love shine even through his pain. "Remember, where you go, I go. You're never alone, Spitfire, because you carry my heart with you. Always."

"I will return, Dax. I'll return with the dagger, unlock the heart, and free you ... all of you. I swear it." I clutched onto him tightly. "I love you."

"I love you," he answered as I touched his lips, sinking into his kiss until the world around us no longer existed, utilizing these precious seconds together to try and memorize all that he was.

Gods, Mother and Father, I prayed. *Watch over my mate. If fate guides me to unlock the heart, understand that any sacrifice you ask of me is not worth it if he is no longer in this world. Daxton is the heart and soul of his people. He is a true leader who will bring them out of the darkness cast by the wilt and the self-proclaimed queen. He is your warrior. He will fight to protect your children and save us all.*

"Bring him to the portal."

Hands seized Daxton, but still, he fought against their hold to remain at my side, the separation forging a chasm in my heart. Castor and Gunnar exited the safety of the ward to grab me and try to pull me back. In the end, Queen Minaeve had to threaten to take them as well if we didn't cooperate.

Our hands were tied. Our fates decided. Daxton would be held prisoner until I returned with the alpha's dagger. The blade my father and my alpha ancestors carried. The blade that Alistar, or perhaps now Gilen, held as our pack's leader.

I had to challenge the current alpha ... And I had to win.

Seamus grabbed Daxton's chains as a portal appeared, shoving him toward the magical circle of swirling lights. I never took my eyes off my mate, catching one final look before being forced through the portal.

"You're my light," I said, fighting to hold back my tears. "You're my *hope*, Daxton Aegaeon!" I roared, my voice loud enough for all of Silver Meadows to hear. "Each beat of my heart echoes your name. Every breath I take is filled with your essence. My love for you has no bounds of time or distance. I will fight through the great crossing itself to have you in my arms again. I will find you!" My declaration forced even Seamus to pause.

"We will always find each other, Spitfire. Every day … until there are none left." And with those final words, Daxton was forced through the portal.

He was gone.

"No … No … No!" I roared so loudly that there wasn't a single soul in Silver Meadows who didn't hear my cry.

My power shot out from me, rippling across the landscape and causing a powerful force to shake the ground from under my feet. I collapsed onto the marble, the chasm in my chest opening and flooding me with wave after wave of unbearable sorrow.

Castor and Gunnar hung their heads and stepped back. There was nothing they could do to comfort me. They were just as afraid as I was. Daxton, their high prince, was gone, taken prisoner—again. Their high prince, whom they had sworn to protect, was once again held in the queen's dungeons.

Light footsteps echoed on the floor beside me as a long crimson and gold cape draped across my shoulders. Warm arms encircled me with the gentlest of touches. Only the love of a mother's embrace could reach me now.

"Skylar," Idris whispered.

I fell into her open arms, allowing myself to weep without fear of judgment. She knew. She understood exactly what it was like to have her mate controlled and stolen from her.

Another pair of black boots entered my line of sight and I looked up through tearful eyes. Zola stood behind us, staring me down with fury burning in her darkened eyes.

"Now get up," the Shadow Jumper demanded.

I controlled my breathing and wiped the final tear aside, facing her.

"You're the mate of the High Prince of Silver Meadows. The slayer of the basilisk. Victor of the labyrinth. You *do not* give up. You *never* back down." She bucked up her chin, staring up at me without a hint of fear or hesitation. "Call upon the *Opal* to take you to Solace. Reclaim the alpha's dagger and return where the Heart of Valdor waits to serve *you*."

Her calmness … Her certainty was odd, even for her. Then it clicked. I didn't know why it took so long to realize what had happened. I cursed my foolishness for not noticing it earlier. But then again, my reactions helped make this all so real.

"What's the plan?" I asked, turning toward Castor.

He tilted his head in confusion at first, looking at me like he was seeing another person altogether, and in all honesty, maybe he was. I was a half-human shifter torn from her home, separated from her mate, and tasked with achieving the impossible to save our world. These things changed a person. It made them harder, stronger. Transformed them into a survivor, a skillful warrior to call upon in times of need … and right now, we were neck deep in this mess of an existence.

"I know there's a plan in place, Castor. There has to be. You, above all others, are not only one but ten steps ahead in your schemes. Gunnar and Zola could never be this calm while Daxton was captured or remain in the wards, let alone Adohan. Whether he commanded them to do so or not …"

Castor's expression remained the same, but Zola's grin only grew. Gunnar nudged Adohan, bucking his chin up in a smug manner that said, *I told you so.*

"You're a sharp little arrow, aren't you?" Idris added, patting my shoulder as she gently wrapped a cloth around my bleeding arm.

"This was not a definite plan but a precaution. He knew … Daxton knew the queen might do this, didn't he?" I asked.

"You may be savvy enough to survive here, after all, Skylar Cathal," Castor said, casually crossing his arms.

"There's no way you would be this fucking calm otherwise, Castor," I shot back, not needing him to confirm my suspicions. "Trust me, I will throttle Daxton myself once I return, and I know he's safe for keeping this secret from me. But now. Now … you need to tell me the plan."

"As you command, Alpha."

Chapter Twenty-Eight

Daxton Aegaeon

I kept my eyes shut as the portal's magic closed, and I was once again in the prison cells beneath the city of Aelius. The putrid stench of rotting flesh and cold isolation in this pit of despair hadn't changed, so I imagined everything else was likely the same. There was no light from the outside world here. Nothing and no one was meant to survive in a place like this. Here, dreams of a better life—of hope itself—came to suffocate and drown.

I should know. I was a prisoner here for years. Most only lasted months before taking their own lives or breaking, losing their minds under the queen's hand.

"Move it," Seamus ordered, shoving me forward, purposely hitting my broken shoulder to seal in the sting of pain now radiating through my torso.

The powder they'd dosed me with upon their ambush was thankfully fading. With each breath I forced myself to take, it worked out of my system quicker. Still, I didn't need to open my eyes to know where I was going. I kept them sealed shut, holding onto the last thread of hope for as long as possible … to the image of *her*.

"And here I thought kings had better manners," I chided with a half-cocked grin, knowing exactly how to push Seamus's buttons and get under his skin. "You know, *please* goes a long way."

I anticipated the strike long before the words escaped my lips. My left knee buckled, colliding with stone. This was followed by a swift strike to my face, cutting my cheek just below my eye socket. *At least he learned how to throw a decent punch … Five hundred years of practice managed to do some good.*

"Stop lying to yourself, thinking you're playing the role of some kind of tortured hero. Or have you forgotten what happens when you oppose our queen?"

"I'm not," I answered, spitting blood onto the ground.

I remembered. I remembered the ten years in these cells, followed by the century of chained servitude in Aelius until the first shifter failed in the trials. Only after that did she allow me to return home to Silver Meadows, but I was never truly free from her hold. That was … until I found my mate. Until hope once again became more than just a distant dream.

"The real heroes are the ones who tolerate you on a daily basis and somehow don't kill themselves because of it." Another strike to my already busted lip was well worth the insult. Seamus always enjoyed inflicting pain on those who couldn't fight back, and right now, I couldn't. For so many reasons, I couldn't.

It took every ounce of my willpower to simply take his beating and act like I couldn't break free of these chains and crush his pathetic excuse of a life with my bare hands.

Minaeve didn't know, but over the centuries, I had been poisoning myself with her iron powder to build an immunity against it. That and working on sealing away my magic during her frequent siphoning sessions. I was her favorite, so thankfully, I had more practice than most. The night before the trials began, I didn't hold back just to throw her off ... But this time around, I did.

No one outside my brother and Zola knew what I was attempting. If Minaeve ever found out, she would severely punish me and simply find another way to try and weaken my power and reign.

"Can you manage to walk yourself to your cell, or do I need to drag your sorry ass there?"

I rolled onto my knees with my arms bound to my sides and stood on my feet. "I remember the way," I muttered with disdain.

My eyes were still shut tight. I didn't want to lose her just yet. I needed to remember every fearsome, beautiful detail for as long as I could. Those entrancing, powerful amber eyes that glowed with fire would be my light in this place. I would hold onto that final sight of my awe-inspiring mate as long as I could.

Hearing her swear to find me and retrieve that dagger without an ounce of fear in her declaration, beaming with defiance and power, warmed my darkened soul. I was honored and *beyond proud* of her fire.

"Then walk," Seamus said in a low, gruff voice as he shoved me forward.

Fucking prick. He believes that because he can simply fuck a false queen, he's then entitled to a crown of his own. I couldn't wait to see the look on his face when he realized all this was a carefully calculated trick to undermine *everything* he had worked for these past five centuries.

I heard the iron bars open, and I stepped inside the all too familiar prison I dwelled in once before.

"Thought it was fitting to have you in the same one."
Seamus's smugness was sickening.

"How generous of you and *your* queen." I did not
say *my* queen, and judging by his pause, he noticed.

"Have some gods-damned sense for once,
Aegaeon," Seamus hissed, and I almost dared open my
eyes to turn and glare at him. Almost. "Show some
respect for the powers that kept you alive ... That
continue to keep you and your kingdom safe from the
wilt. The way you behave toward Queen Minaeve is a
disgrace."

The chains loosened and dropped to the floor,
but I held my ground and didn't lash out, the remaining
threads of my self-control keeping me still.

"Besides. Your *whore* of a mate will—"

That last remark about *her* shattered my restraint.

I shifted my stance, easily discarding the
remaining chains despite my injured shoulder, and
turned on Seamus with the force of a thousand storms.

It was his mistake, forgetting the timeline of the
iron powder's potency. Careful not to touch him, I
gripped his throat with my ice magic, freezing his hands
and holding his life within seconds of meeting the
crossing to the afterlife.

"Watch what you say about my *mate*, Seamus," I
said slowly, ensuring he heard every word. "Call *me*
whatever you like ..." My lips pulled back as I snarled.
"Degrade my throne and my kingdom for all I care.
Your words fall on deaf ears when it comes to me, *but*,"
I growled, "speak ill of my mate again ... and I will no
longer be able to restrain myself from finally killing you."
His eyes widened a fraction, and I knew he could sense
this was no threat. "I'll make good on my promise and
end your feeble excuse of a life. High prince or king
consort, I don't give two shits what your title is. War in

the Inner Kingdom will begin with your death at my hands, and I will smile as I march over your corpse onto the battlefield of blood."

My brother's clever voice echoed in my mind, warning me. *Idiot, brilliant job hiding the fact that you weren't as weak and wounded as they thought.*

Fuck it. I didn't care. I would worry about that later; I'd have the time.

"You so soon forget," I whispered in a dark voice, "I earned the name of Silver Shadow before entering these cells, but Shadow ... was truly born from within these walls." Seamus's grave expression turned into fear. He remembered.

The guards' footsteps were already barreling down the hallway toward my cell, but I squeezed harder around Seamus's throat with my magic, just for an added bit of fun.

I didn't so much as flinch as guards began slamming their weapons across my back, breaking my ribs and tearing at my flesh. I refused to break my stare from Seamus. The same look of death that bore into countless others before ending their existence with my blade in service of the self-proclaimed queen. Our eyes were locked until a clubbed weapon struck me on the back of the head, knocking me unconscious.

It was surprisingly pleasant being unconscious in this shit hole. In my daze, I reached out for the threads of my mate bond, tying me to Skylar. To the other half of my soul that I knew would be drifting farther and farther away. Soon, she would travel beyond the veil, and as much as I tried to prepare myself for our separation, I knew my heart would ... Gods. My very soul would feel like it was breaking in two.

I groaned as I turned on the cold stone floor of my cell. Moving onto my back, I looked up at the blackened ceiling above, reminding myself that this was all a part of our plan.

Our rebellion, as I liked to call it, had been in the works for centuries. Ever since I was able to return home.

When Adohan's father died and passed the crown to him, we became allies, working to undermine Minaeve's rule in any way we could. It was small at first—trade routes falling, disgruntled citizens. But eventually, we made a play to question Minaeve's seat of power within her court. Asking dangerous questions.

Why does she deserve to be our high queen? Where is she from? Where did she gain her powers?

Zola led the charge of gaining intel from within Aelius itself, working to relocate anyone who sought refuge in Silver Meadows or Crimson City. Her shadow-jumping ability allowed her to sneak citizens to safety right under the nose of Seamus and Minaeve. They were too self-absorbed in their riches and power to notice their population slowly dwindling. But still, we couldn't manage to break the inner circle of the Aelius court.

Then, everything changed when my stunningly beautiful, selfless mate volunteered for the trials. After her success in the first trial and the deepening of our bond, I knew I could end up here as leverage or a bargaining tool to force her hand. However, instead of allowing this to be a burden, we plotted this possible outcome to our advantage.

What better way to gain intelligence than from inside the palace itself?

I was the only one who could do this. I had survived here, made it out alive, and knew I could do it again. I would suffer the beatings and endure the torture

Anjani would force me to witness, bearing the agonizing absence of my mate and my home once again. I would do this all in the hope of our victory. I would do this knowing that Gunnar was already assembling our armies to march north. Knowing that when my Spitfire returned with the final key and unlocked the Heart of Valdor, there would be an army waiting for her. An army ready to fight to free the Inner Kingdom from a tyrannical ruler.

It would all be worth it.

By now, I imagined the *Opal* was preparing to set sail toward Solace and that Castor had informed Skylar of our plan. I instructed him to give her a letter when she left our shores. It was the least I could do.

Gods, I knew I would never hear the end of her rantings and carefully selected four-letter words for what I had done, for the secret I kept from her. But it also meant I would hear her voice again, and that was well worth the price.

End of Book Two

Book Three:
"A Trial of Two Worlds"

"Two worlds tied together by one fate."

Acknowledgments

First, I will always thank my husband. There is not enough whiskey in the world to say thank you, and I know I can hear you scoff at my mention of this … even though it is 100 percent true. Thank you for being there through this wild ride of anxious nerves and encouraging me to be brave. Also, being a caring father to our beautiful daughters who bring all types of laughter chaos and love to our lives.

Second, I must thank my beta readers. KD, you were there from the start … giving me essential feedback to buff up Skylar's story and making it relatable and authentic. My mom and aunts for reading and always being willing to answer my next question or just give me the encouragement I needed. And to my friend Sarah, who found the time to read between running a business and being a bad-A mama herself. You all have my immense gratitude for giving me your valuable time to help me on this journey.

Third, I have an amazingly strong team of ladies with me that helped make this story sparkle and shine. Jen, my copy editor, gave me endless feedback and went above and beyond with her guidance and support. Cherie, my cover artist who brought tears to my eyes by bringing my cover and characters to life. And my proofreader Eleanor, thank you for helping finish this project and making sure it was ready for the next step.

And finally, *I thank you, the reader*. For without you, this story wouldn't have breath, or come to life. I hope you enjoy this journey. There is more to come in Valdor.

ABOUT THE AUTHOR

J.E. Larson is an Alaska-grown author with a passion for being active and outdoors while daydreaming in her own worlds. Wife to an ever-patient husband and mother to two beautiful girls. J.E. Larson has been writing and creating stories since she was young. And now, she finds the time to write in the quiet five a.m. mornings and secluded hours after bedtime.

Social Media

TikTok: j.e.larson

Instagram: j.e.larson8

Made in the USA
Columbia, SC
13 December 2024

47858854R00305